from Shetland, with love at Christmas

Erin Green was born and raised in Warwickshire. An avid reader since childhood, her imagination was instinctively drawn to creative writing as she grew older. Erin has two Hons degrees: a BA in English Literature and a BSc in Psychology; her previous careers have ranged from part-time waitress, the retail industry, fitness industry and education.

She has an obsession about time, owns several tortoises and an infectious laugh! Erin writes contemporary novels focusing on love, life and laughter. She is an active member of the Romantic Novelists' Association and was delighted to be awarded the Katie Fforde Bursary in 2017. An ideal day for Erin involves writing, people-watching and drinking copious amounts of tea.

For more information about Erin, visit her website: **www.ErinGreenAuthor.co.uk,** find her on Facebook **www. facebook.com/ErinGreenAuthor** or follow her on Twitter **@ErinGreenAuthor.**

Praise for Erin Green:

'Thoroughly entertaining. The characters are warm and well drawn. I thoroughly recommend this book if you are looking for a light-hearted read. 5 stars'   Sue Roberts

'I loved spending time on Shetland with this story!'
Christina Courtenay

'Uplifting'   *Woman & Home*

'Full of humour, poignancy and ultimately uplifting this is an absolutely gorgeous read. We loved it! Highly recommended!'   *Hot Brands Cool Places*

'Like a scrummy bowl of Devon cream and strawberries, this is a tasty, rich and delicious summer read laced with the warmth of friendships and the possibilities of new beginnings ... The author has the knack of making her characters spring off the pages so real that you'll care about them'   *Peterborough Telegraph*

'A pleasure to read ... A summer breezes treat'
Devon Life

By Erin Green

A Christmas Wish
The Single Girl's Calendar
The Magic of Christmas Tree Farm
New Beginnings at Rose Cottage
Taking a Chance on Love
From Shetland, With Love
From Shetland, With Love at Christmas

from Shetland, with love at Christmas

ERIN GREEN

H

REVIEW

First published in 2021
by HEADLINE REVIEW
An imprint of HEADLINE PUBLISHING GROUP

1

Cataloguing in Publication Data is available from the British Library

ISBN 978 1 4722 8152 4

Typeset in Sabon by CC Book Production

Printed and bound in Great Britain by
Clays Ltd, Elcograf S.p.A.

HEADLINE PUBLISHING GROUP
An Hachette UK Company
Carmelite House
50 Victoria Embankment
London EC4Y 0DZ

www.headline.co.uk
www.hachette.co.uk

To the art of the blacksmith –
where true beauty is forged through fire and force

People are like stain-glass windows. They sparkle and shine when the sun is out, but when darkness sets in, their true beauty is revealed only if there's a light from within.

ELISABETH KÜBLER-ROSS (1926–2004)

Shetland Glossary

Peerie – small/little

Daa – grandfather

Crabbit – bad-tempered

Yamse – greedy

Chapter One

Friday 1 October

Entry: 09.10.1965
Bake: a wedding cake (replica)
Event: 25th anniversary cake
Serving size: 50 small slices
Decoration: royal icing with pink roses

Notes: I spent all day making my parents an anniversary wedding cake. A replica of their original cake, which was made at short notice because my dad, Duncan, had signed up for active service back in 1940. I've rationed the amount of sugar and fruit to mimic what they had during wartime. Family donated their rationed goods, apparently. Mum promised to pay them back, plus a little extra as interest, which she did over time. I'll skimp by using marmalade instead of apricot jam to seal the two tiers. They didn't have almond marzipan beneath the royal icing, so a smooth finish was difficult to achieve. It's my present to them, as I have very little money to buy them a nice gift to celebrate their silver anniversary.

Verity

'That's fifty-four pounds exactly,' says the taxi driver, turning around in his seat, my ear adjusting to his Scottish twang. 'I can't drive any nearer, as there's very little space at the top of this narrow driveway.'

I peer at the red digits displayed on his dashboard. A yellow pine-tree air freshener is swinging from his rear-view mirror.

That's easily the most I've paid for an airport transfer; hardly surprising, given that my last flight was over two decades ago. I ferret in my handbag, grab the bundle of crisp notes from my purse and hand them over. It might seem ungenerous of me, but still, I'm expecting my change. Watching my pennies has become a way of life for me.

'Thanks. Is anyone meeting you here?' he asks, flicking on the interior light before digging into a fabric bag – I assume in search of a pound coin.

I'm in two minds to lie, but I don't. Having spent the entire day travelling by train and plane from the Midlands, I haven't the initiative or energy.

He seems a friendly chap, mid-thirties, blond hair poking out from beneath a woollen beanie, and sporting matching stubble on his chin. His rugby sweatshirt looks fresh on today, though his jeans could do with a freshen-up in an economy wash, if nothing else.

'No. I have instructions to get into the cottage, so I'll be fine.' I was relieved when the email arrived yesterday, providing a door code and instructions on where to locate an information folder. I assume that'll contain everything: from cooker instructions, to emergency numbers and bin collection details. The website states that a complimentary basket of essentials will be awaiting my arrival. I'm hoping for fresh milk, but UHT will be welcomed. All I need at this late hour is the door code, a hot brew and a clean bed.

Tomorrow, I'll begin afresh.

I accept the offered coin before peering out of the window. I can't see a single thing: it's pitch black. Worse still, I can't see Harmony Cottage, which I assume is in close proximity since we're supposedly parked in the driveway. Peering briefly into the rear-view mirror, I can see my bedraggled appearance. My pale blue eyes look bloodshot and my light brown hair could do with being introduced to a brush despite its fashionably tousled style.

'I'll stay till you're inside, if that's OK with you?' he says, eyeing me cautiously under the yellowish glow of the interior light.

I act blasé but I'm grateful. The headlights illuminate a section of the driveway, after which I'll be on my own.

The driver pops the release on the car boot, leaves the vehicle and collects my single large suitcase from the rear. I follow, ensuring I have retrieved all my belongings from the rear seat, and find myself standing in the darkest darkness I have ever experienced. The night air is warmer than I was expecting. In the distance – I'm assuming it's the direction from which we've driven – I can see a smattering of orange and white lights but very little illumination close by.

In approximately five minutes' time, I will be surrounded by a nothingness unlike any I have ever encountered. I will be alone for the very first time in my entire life. Not the alone that I'm used to – where people are in an adjoining room, living next door, or sharing a womb – but totally alone.

And I can't wait.

It might seem abnormal to most, slightly freaky or unhinged to others, but I'm about to be granted the one wish I have craved for a lifetime: solitude.

'Your case is fairly heavy,' says the driver, lifting it from the boot.

'I'll manage,' I retort. Having lugged it for most of the day, I don't need reminding. I should invest in a modern lightweight one, with rotatable rubber wheels and a comfy handle, but this battered old case is a faithful friend from my teenage days. I can't justify expensive luggage, given my home-bird nature.

'I'll carry your case to the door,' he suggests. 'It's not too far,' he says, heaving my suitcase on to his shoulder and leading the way.

Once we've left the beam of the headlights, I grab my mobile, flicking the screen to illuminate our path. The terrain underfoot is rugged, compacted mud, with large boulders jutting up, which would wreak havoc on the underneath of a low-slung chassis. And he's right, it is very narrow in places; I wouldn't wish to reverse a vehicle the length of this driveway in the dark.

'I do appreciate your help, but I could have managed, honestly,' I insist, keeping my eyes on the bulky outline some steps ahead of me.

'No problem. I'll at least know that you got inside safely,' he answers, before adding, 'and are not wandering the coastal path by mistake.'

I can hear him puffing within minutes.

'Are you staying for a week or two?' he asks, after a lengthy silence.

'A year,' I reply. 'I should have brought more luggage but the flight allowance curbed that idea.'

'Wow! That's unusual, most folks . . .' His words fade.

I assume he presumes I'm not *most folks*. And he's right, I'm not. I'm Verity Kendal, mother of three, daughter of two, twin of one, aunty to another. But for my forty-third year of life, I'm choosing a gap year. I feel incredibly guilty for wanting or even needing such an indulgence but I'm putting myself first for once. I'll miss an entire year of family events, Christmases and birthdays, but I've been dreaming of this since my three sons were munching on Farley's rusks. And tonight, I've arrived on the eve of three hundred and sixty-five days of pleasing myself.

Harmony Cottage is my ideal getaway. Proudly sitting in a solitary position high upon a cliff top overlooking the North Sea, within the aptly named Bay of Sound. There's a different vista from each window denoting a 360° picture-postcard setting. I'll be surrounded by paddocks, coastal pathways and grazing sheep amidst a backdrop of autumn bracken. The nearest house is a short distance along the lane, so what more could I ask for? I'd been slightly embarrassed asking for a house tour via a flickering iPad screen, but the lady was obliging in every way. 'It'll be roomy for a solo occupant,' she'd said. 'The usual bookings are families, given the two-bedroom and two-bathroom layout.' It's tastefully decorated and partially furnished, which suits my needs. For me, it was simply love at first sight, so I signed the contract as soon as she emailed the paperwork.

We trek for a few minutes, taking the gentle climb at a steady pace, before the whitewashed walls of a cottage loom out of the darkness, complete with drystone walls on either side. It's quaint, peaceful and promises complete solitude.

'Here we are. The main door into the porchway should be unlocked,' says the driver, adding, 'you'll need the code for the inner door—'

'Yes, I know.' I interrupt, having memorised the details from yesterday's email. I silently repeat the digit sequence: three, four, six, five followed by hash.

'Just punch in three, four, six, five, then the hash symbol before turning the latch,' says the driver, dropping my suitcase beside the porch door.

My mouth drops wide as I stare in disbelief.

'Get away with ye. You'll be fine. Folk around these parts are old-school, not like these mainland folks who trust nothing and no one,' he says, waving aside my shocked expression. 'We leave our doors unlocked around here. Our motto is, "If it isn't yours, don't touch it," which works a treat in most situations – unless you've an allotment plot, but you needn't worry there.'

A sudden neighing from beside us makes me jump out of my skin.

'What's that?' I ask, lifting my mobile to illuminate a five-bar gate set in the adjoining drystone wall. A pair of reflective eyes appear eerily out of the darkness. 'A pony?'

'That there's a Shetland pony – you'll find one or two about these parts,' he says, giving a deep-throated chuckle. 'That's peerie Jutt, he'll not harm you.'

'We'll make friends tomorrow, peerie Jutt,' I say, stepping into the unlocked porch and finding the inner doorway. I press the number sequence, as memorised, turn the locking device and the door springs wide.

The driver lugs my battered suitcase into the porchway, before stepping back outside. 'You'll be OK, now?'

'Fine, thank you,' I say, feeling along the interior wall for a light switch and illuminating the hallway.

'No worries, you're safely inside,' he says, striding off into the darkness. 'See you around.'

I stand for a moment on the porch step staring out. I can hear the pony snuffling at the gate, the heavy tread of boots descending the driveway, but I can barely see my hand before my face.

'Excuse me . . . and your name is?' I call into the darkness.

'Me? I'm Levi Gordans . . . everyone around here knows me.'

'Thank you, Levi – I do appreciate your help,' I reply, before continuing, 'I'm Verity, by the way.'

'Pleased to meet you, Verity. Welcome to Shetland.'

Chapter Two

Saturday 2 October

Verity

I'm woken by my mobile ringing. It's only half six, I'm in a strange bed but I know who this will be: Avril.

'What's your bloody game?' screeches my twin sister.

'Morning, Avril, how are you?' I answer, knowing full well that I'm in for a telling-off.

'Cut the crap, Verity. You've upped and offed leaving a damned note! Where are you?'

'I'm fine. I'm taking time out for myself, that's all. There's no need to make a major fuss. The lads will be fine, I've left provisions . . .'

'So I've heard. According to your Tom there's a chest freezer full of sodding lasagnes, apparently.'

'Home-made food, not shitty microwave meals which some people live on,' I say, knowing such a reference to her culinary cop-out will hit a nerve.

'Oi, some of us are busy.' And now she's twanged my nerve, as always.

'Avril, we're all bloody busy at something. No one in our family has got it cushy.'

'Where are you?'

I take a deep breath; I sense what's about to follow.

'Shetland.'

'Where?'

'The Shetland Islands.'

'Above bloody Scotland?'

'Yep, the place with the little ponies and beautiful knitting,' I declare proudly, knowing she'll have rolled her eyes at the mention of knitting.

'It's hardly visible on the weather map, let alone being a holiday hotspot.'

'Exactly, which is why it'll suit me.'

'That didn't happen overnight, so how long have you been planning this for?'

'Kind of for ever, or at least since the boys were little. I wanted to say, but you know what our family are like. The minute I mention anything others don't approve of, you all clan together and quickly talk me out of doing it. So I thought, bugger the lot of you, I'll do it my way.'

'Verity!'

'I know, I know. It's not what you all want to hear, but there are times when I'm smothered by the lot of you.'

'Thanks a bunch!'

'Sorry, but it's true. Every day of my life, I've got people pulling at me; demanding my time and attention. If it isn't the three lads, then it's you, or Mum and Dad. There are times I would simply like to be me. And have no one asking what time I'll be clocking back in to my "being Mum" role as chef, maid or bottle-washer.'

'Don't you think we all feel like that?'

'Perhaps, but you have Francis to share the load with; I don't have anyone. I've been doing it single-handed for nearly eighteen years, and enough is enough.'

'We've always supported you and yours the best we can.' I can hear the hurt in her voice.

'And I'm very grateful. But now, I'd quite like some alone time.'

'How long?'

'See what I mean? "Verity, what time are you clocking back in to home life?" That's precisely what I'm on about, Avril.'

'This is ridiculous!' says my twin, her patience clearly wearing thin. 'I'm simply trying to establish how long I'll need to . . .'

'You don't need to do anything. At twenty-three, Jack is more than capable of running the show. I've made arrangements for everything: the utility bills, the mortgage and, as soon as I'm ready and settled, regular contact via the iPad. Give me some credit, I didn't just up and off, you know.'

'How long have you booked a room for?'

'A cottage actually, and I've paid for the year.'

'A year!'

'Yes . . . but I could be home next week if I choose to be, so don't worry.'

'Believe me, I'm not worrying. You're obviously out of your tiny mind, being utterly selfish and self-centred. I can't believe you've actually done this, Verity.'

There's a long pause.

I get that Avril doesn't get it. We may be twins, but we are very different in personality, outlook and how we navigate this world. She's the yin to my yang. She'd never slope off without her beloved Francis and their young daughter, Amelia, in tow. But then she gets weekly 'me' time via her yoga, her mid-monthly book clubs and her weekly gardening group.

I don't; my life isn't like that.

'Avril, do you remember when we were children and you always talked about running away, finding a new family or living in a different country?'

'Kind of.'

'All because Dad wouldn't let you have your ears pierced or let you stay out till after dark. You were planning a runaway escape once a week, twice in some weeks.'

'Yeah, so what's your point?'

'I've thought about running away more as an adult than I ever did as a child.'

I let my words sink in. I hear her sigh.

'Is that it? You feel the need to run off and find yourself?' Her voice is calmer; she's finally listening.

'Not find myself; I already know myself. I simply need some time to do the things I want to do, without anyone calling on me as their mum, sister, aunty or daughter.'

'Have you quit your job at the solicitors?'

'Yep, that too. A receptionist only needs to give four weeks' notice.'

'And George. Have you told him?'

'Have I heck! If you can find George Kendal, then be my guest. In fact, remind him that he has three sons who've grown up since he last saw them. He might like to step up to the plate during my absence. And, before you ask, I have the means to support myself. I've rented space within a local gallery and started a small business selling knitted and crocheted garments. You know how much I love my knitting, so I've turned it from a hobby into a business.'

'I see.'

'Do you? Because if you do ... would you kindly relay the details to the others?'

'You aren't going to speak to them?' Shock returns to Avril's tone. 'You realise it's Amelia's birthday in a few days.'

'Amelia's six years old – she won't notice if I'm there or not. I'll pop a card into the post and send a birthday gift. As I said before, I've made extensive plans and left an explanation for the lads. I want this time to myself. To do as I please and –' I inhale deeply before proceeding – 'I'm not about to explain myself ten times over to each concerned relative. If they're angry with me, then so be it. I'm sorry, but it's frustrating when you know what you want and yet your current life doesn't permit it.'

'Verity, please, Mum's nerves won't take kindly to this.'

'Avril, give them all my love, tell them I am quite safe. Can you ensure Jack organises the food money? Otherwise Harvey and Tom will blow it on a Domino's Pizza street party. Tell Amelia that I'll send a gift. I'll leave my mobile on charge, but I have no intention of using it purely to hear complaints, OK?'

'I think you're being incredibly selfish, Verity.'

I'm silent for a moment. That sounds like such a negative judgement, yet she's absolutely right. 'Why thank you, I intend to be! I'm putting myself first for once. Love to you all. Bye.' I swiftly tap the screen, ending her call. I throw my mobile on to my duvet for fear of feeling her wrath burning through the phone casing.

She'll be annoyed that she wasn't able to talk me round; that's Avril's superhero power up the Swanee.

I'm proud of myself and it's only 6.45 a.m.

I scramble from the double bed, my feet padding on the stained wooden boards, and head for the kitchen to make a fresh brew. As sole occupant, I don't need to navigate three young men seeing their mother nipping about in her scanties. It feels oddly liberating to walk about half naked in my underwear.

Last night I'd been grateful to find fresh milk and decent tea bags awaiting my arrival, so I'd forfeited any exploration of the cottage before succumbing to the comfort of the first double duvet I found. I hadn't drawn all the curtains, ignited the wood burner or even bothered to unpack my battered suitcase, apart from rummaging for my toothbrush and toothpaste.

I sip my tea now as I explore each room: there's a bedroom and bathroom on each floor, a huge open kitchen and a beautiful lounge with picturesque views. I return to my bedroom and sweep the heavy lined curtains aside. And there, less than a metre from my ground-floor bedroom window is a middle-aged man with a mop of unruly brown curls, in a split leather apron, with the Shetland pony's hoof thrust between his thighs, staring back at me in all my semi-naked Marks and Sparks glory. His metal rasp is suspended in mid-air and the expression on his face suggests that he doesn't need his eyesight testing. I do the only feasible thing: I grab the curtain, wrap its heavy folds around me and cover my voluptuous figure, before giving a hearty wave and mouthing 'hello' as if butter wouldn't melt.

I stand there for a moment, attempting to convey an air of confidence, whilst dying inside. The pony is jet black; there's no wonder I couldn't make him out when I arrived last night. His back dips deeply from shoulder to rump and his stubby legs are squarely set, supporting a low-slung belly.

Enough pretending; I can't sustain such a level of self-confidence whilst wrapped in a curtain. I drop the fabric and swiftly close the bedroom curtains. Thank God he doesn't realise that he's the first to witness such a sight in eighteen years – since my youngest, Tom, was born. I vow to keep my bedroom curtains closed for the duration of my stay.

After replaying my interaction with the local farrier numerous times whilst showering, I grab some comfy yet casual clothing: black leggings and a long tunic.

I need to begin my day, which means getting to grips with my new business premises. The gallery's grand opening is tomorrow. And that, I imagine, will take up the majority of my day.

But first, I grab my tiny make-up bag and dash into the down-stairs bathroom. Using my one and only decent kohl eyeliner pencil, I write on the vanity mirror: Do as I wish and please myself!!!

I stand back to admire my handiwork. The lettering is wonky – but who cares? I'm the only one to see it. And that thought alone fills me with a renewed glee. Wow! I can officially do as I please, when I please, and for however long I please!

I slam the cottage's inner door firmly behind me, knowing I

don't need a key. I pull the porch door to, leaving it as I found it last night. Even this small act provides a renewed sense of freedom that I haven't known since my teenage years, when Avril and I were deemed 'sensible' enough to be given a house key.

The weather is overcast and slightly windy. I'm unperturbed by the threat of rain but pray that the door code works on my return. Modern technology has a knack of malfunctioning for me. Vending machines frequently flex their powers by denying my request, despite the simple instructions. After a full day at the gallery, I'll feel utterly ridiculous if I have to nip to the nearest cottage to seek help breaking into my new home. One embarrassing incident a day will be quite enough. I scour the lengthy driveway, ensuring it's empty, for fear of bumping into the visiting farrier.

The driveway has a paddock on either side. To my left is a large grassy field with a simple wooden fence, homing a rust-coated Shetland pony and a bay horse; both are eating but quit to stare at me as I pass by. To the right is a smaller paddock edged with wire fencing and filled with a formation of sheep busily engaged in synchronised grazing. Their tiny front teeth protrude energetically, revealing pink tongues as their jaws robotically chomp. I shiver slightly as I notice their weird rectangular-shaped pupils stare in my direction. I quickly stride past, causing the sheep formation to slowly turn in unison. My haste is a combination of my short legs and the steepness of the incline. I imagine the sheep can probably empathise. Somehow I never associate beautiful knitting yarn with these animals; their clumpy fleece splattered with droppings and mud looks undesirable in its natural state.

On reaching the road, I'm greeted by a view that is to die for: an open stretch of furling sea crashing upon the black rocks edging the coastal road. Choppy waters stretch into the distance to be greeted on the far side of the bay by a vast array of purple mountains. A sliver of golden sand curves along a nearby coastline, and at the far end of the headland stands a proud lighthouse painted with broad bands of red and white, its glass fascia sparkling in the morning light.

I make tracks along the coastal road, heading towards the centre of Lerwick, whilst admiring the landscape. My destination is Lerwick Manor's gallery, which lies a short distance from the busy town centre.

Chapter Three

Nessie

I never thought this day would arrive. For so long, I've dreamt of having my own forge with the freedom to sustain an income from my talent.

It takes time for my coal pit to burn properly. I begin building the kindling into a neat pile, tucking a layer of coals around it and building my pyre in the centre of the blackened hearth, with a tiny char cloth poking out ready to light. Then I fiddle. I always fiddle, can't help myself, making sure there is maximum contact with each combustible. It still amazes me that with fire and force I can create such beautiful items that will last a lifetime. It's like waking a dragon each morning after a long sleep. Within an hour, the coals are glowing. The flaking ash provides a grey frosting on each blackened edge; a comforting sight from the fire pit.

I've previously had observers laugh at the precision with which I approach this morning ritual. If they knew the importance, they wouldn't take the mick. I know from experience that if I rush my morning fire, I'll spend the rest of the day regretting it, making for a tiring day; the heat levels won't reach their maximum if there is an inefficient burn between oxygen and energy source. The heat affects my metals, my creativity and, ultimately, my products.

I've undertaken a major career switch to study, qualify and follow my dream, reigniting the passion for fire within my family. Today is simply day one of the rest of my life.

My coals are the primary task of any morning, so I don't rush.

'Morning . . . Wednesday, isn't it?' says the male voice behind me.

I turn about to view my recently acquired stablemate at the forge: Isaac Jameson.

'Hi, that'll be me!' I say, extending my palm to receive a warm handshake.

His eyes take in my appearance in one fluid glance; he's certainly not shy. I can guess his opinion, based on first impressions: my pixie-cut hair is dyed a vivid pink, and I'm wearing my standard wardrobe of denim dungarees and vest top beneath my leather apron, with my bulky steel-toecapped boots. I'm not your average woman, but then I don't have a regular job!

'Isaac Jameson, engineer in glassware,' he says, flashing a white-toothed smile, highlighting his Scandinavian colouring, typical of many Shetlanders: blond hair with piercing blue eyes.

'I like it,' I say, chuckling; a sense of humour will certainly make life easier in sharing our work space. It's one thing to benefit from a decrease in rent; quite another if the set-up doesn't work on a day-to-day basis. I want a positive vibe, not a toxic environment that could drain me – physically, mentally, emotionally or creatively – and affect my output. 'Wednesday Smith, engineer in metal, thanks to force and flames – though friends call me Nessie,' I say, correcting his original address.

'Nice to meet you, Nessie. I'm ready to face the day – and you?'

'I will be, once I get my coals going . . . there's nothing worse, is there, than a bad day of coals?'

'A tough day with little reward,' confirms Isaac, removing his flying jacket to reveal a tartan lumberjack shirt. 'I've wasted entire days trying to temper molten glass over a poor heat, only to smash the lot after it cooled. I can't stand poor-quality work.'

'I'm exactly the same. Shoddy workmanship – there's nothing worse, is there? I mean to hit the cobbles running, given the short run-up to Christmas.'

'Same here, though I have a stash of items in storage. I can bring them in for my displays if customers clear me out – not that I'll complain, if that happens.'

'No, nor me.' He's nice, easy to talk to, and on the same wavelength regarding a passion for his craft. 'I'd best nurture this fire, otherwise today will be a non-starter for me.'

'Sure. I'm glad that my furnace is somewhat easier to light.'

'What are using?' I say, nodding to the bulky equipment dominating his workspace.

'Oxygen and propane for the furnace – enabling me to control the temperature. Then a sand and limestone mix for my glassware. The set-up works pretty well, to be fair; coal or charcoal wouldn't give me the extreme temperatures I need. And you?'

'Bituminous coal – it gives me the heat I need, with very few impurities to contaminate the metal. Though I tend to call it my coal pit, rather than my forge or a hearth.'

I reluctantly return to my coal pit, which ordinarily should be well under way by now. Funny how easily distracted I suddenly became – I'll need to have a stern talk with myself, if that becomes a regular occurrence.

'Did you go to Bell's Brae primary school as a child?' asks Isaac, as he unpacks his belongings on to his shelving unit. 'Your name sounds familiar.'

'I did, though only for a few years – my parents took me out by year six,' I say, reverting to the shy kid on the front row.

'Did you move house?'

'Oh no – I've always been a bit . . .' I gesture towards my pink hair. 'A bit way out or alternative, as some might say, but that doesn't always fit in well at school, does it?'

'Nope, not always. Kids can be pretty cruel,' adds Isaac, stopping his actions to focus on me. 'Sad, really. Especially when you mature and realise that the most interesting folk are those who don't follow the pack.'

'I agree, but then I would, wouldn't I?' I jest, knowing that a childhood filled with insecurities has resulted in that flippant answer.

'Did you finish school and get your qualifications?'

'Yeah. I was home schooled by private tutors – my parents did all they could, once they realised that I really wasn't happy at school. I followed a typical path after taking my Highers and then started working as an admin assistant in Lerwick, but it didn't suit me. I was always a hands-on creative type, more practical than any desk job allowed. If you get what I mean.'

'Sure. I'm pretty much the same. I went into insurance when my heart really wasn't in it. I developed my skills for glass blowing as a hobby until, eventually, I made a switch by jacking in the day job.'

'Strange, isn't it? How, deep down, we understand ourselves, yet fall into careers that are totally unsuitable,' I say, grabbing my small tinder box. I strike the flint hard against the carbon steel; a tiny spark lands on the exposed cloth poking out from my constructed kindle and coal tepee. I could use matches and a splint, but choose not to. I gently blow, encouraging it to take hold. I love how the tiny flame licks the pale kindling and leaves a black scorch mark in a twisted wave before taking hold. I could watch a naked flame all day; only ever stepping away once an efficient burn is under way. Sometimes additional kindling is necessary, but not this morning; the forge's fire is looking pretty perfect. I only hope that is a good omen for future business here at the Lerwick Manor gallery.

'We'll need to decide where the boundary rope is best placed,' says Isaac, gesturing towards the pile of moveable metal posts and accompanying bundles of red rope complete with silver hooks. 'It'll make an adequate divide between the visiting public and our working space, as long as they respect it.'

'They'd best respect it – otherwise we'll be dealing with nasty burns and all sorts, given our tools of the trade,' I say, praying we don't encounter such fools here in the forge.

I lay out my bench with my vast array of tools, my protective goggles and mitts whilst keeping one eye on the progress of my reddening coals, preparing to make my first item: a coal shovel, not for sale but for my own daily use here in the new forge.

Isla

I tenderly finger the oxblood leather cover of my dear granny's recipe book. How many years did she own it? Was it hers when she left school, or traditionally as a young bride starting out on her married life?

I flick open the cover to view her neat handwriting; as recognisable as my own, it brings me comfort much like a hug or a kiss used to. As long as I have her recipe book, she'll never be far from me. In time, I'll pass this heirloom on to another young woman, be it a daughter, a niece or a daughter-in-law who I hope will treasure it as much as I do.

This page is titled 'tattie soup'. She's listed the ingredients, not aligned to the left margin but filling the entire line to save space. Economical, even at such a tender age. Several amendments have been made to each page, a simple crossing out with additional notes made above the original quantities. I love her quirky little notes, each one dated. I've started a similar book of my own recipes, but I rarely use it in preference to my granny's.

Today I've spent hours flicking through and creating numerous desserts, ready for tonight's gallery party. I'm desperate to make a good impression; I know my bosses have invited anyone remotely connected to their new venture.

Having cleaned my working surface, I turn in a circle, eyeing the gleaming stainless-steel surfaces surrounding me. Oh my

God! My dear granny would have given her back teeth, right arm and Granddad's gold pocket watch to be working in a kitchen such as this. Brand new, state of the art, including all mod cons, chrome accessories, a perfect tiled floor and more sinks than I'm used to.

I'm not used to wearing a sensible shift dress, pinned hairnet and flat shoes, either – all of which adds to the strangeness of today.

I want to cry with pride, but don't because my dear granny would never have been so soft in her kitchen, let alone in the work place. *My* work place: The Orangery within The Gallery, Lerwick Manor. I don't know why I reel off the full address; maybe I simply like how it sounds.

I move from the catering area, basically the behind-the-scenes kitchen, and enter the front of house, where another beautifully tiled countertop sweeps the length of the serving area, creating a barrier between staff and customer. And boy, what a customer area! I raise my chin, taking in the full view of the wrought-iron-and-glass architecture spanning gracefully overhead. I didn't notice how magnificent it was during my interview; I was probably too nervous. Worried that I was actually up against two experienced women – and even more so, as one was the cook from my primary school days, though she didn't recognise me. I suppose I've grown, but my features haven't actually changed that much.

The artisan café is dominated by an arrangement of plush couches, upright armchairs and hard-backed chairs arranged around numerous dining tables and low-lying coffee tables in a fusion of designs, woods and paint finishes. My mum turned her nose up when I described it after my interview, but even she said it looked pretty swish when we nipped in for a quick view last week. She called it 'bric-a-brac' but I don't reckon that's a true style, more like one of her made-up things. My mum does that; she makes up stuff as she goes along in life. Not like me and my granny – we were two peas in a pod. Is that actually a saying, or did I just make it up? It doesn't sound quite right. Anyway, I know what I mean. Granny always knew what I meant too. That's the beauty of being two peas from the same pod – heck, that phrase still doesn't sound quite right.

I walk around the seating area; there's plenty of free space for pushchairs, walking frames and even those mobility scooters that some folk have nowadays. My granny would have loved one; it would have given her the chance to remain independent and sociable around town, or at least chatting and busy, until her battery ran flat.

I tweak the angle of various armchairs as I pass; I have every intention of the café remaining as pristine and delightful as it looks right now. If that means a daily walk-about and inspection during and after opening hours, then so be it. I might be young, according to my mum's thinking, but I know what I want to achieve. I wish to be as proud of The Orangery as if I were the true owner, and not Ned and Jemima. I recognise how successful he is but I think she's the brains behind the gallery project, or so someone was telling my mum at the post office. Anyway, this is my little domain; I'll be treating it like my own. Who knows? One day, way in my future, when I'm my mum's age perhaps – maybe sooner if I work really hard and save even harder, both of which my granny always told me to do in life – I may be able to buy a café that is truly mine.

I reach the rear wall of the seating area and scan the view towards the counter. It looks so different standing here, but I suppose some customers will only ever enjoy this view whilst sipping their coffee. My scrutinising gaze traces the outline of the front serving counter, the electric till (which scares me when it buzzes), but most importantly the arrangement of glass cloches awaiting the five delicious cakes I'll make later today, now that tonight's party food is prepared.

Part of me can't wait for customers to arrive, bringing a bustle of clinking crockery and lively chatter, but my stomach flips each time I think of the sole responsibility. I only left catering college in the summer. I wonder what my college tutor would say if she could see me now? Most of my course mates accepted jobs in hotel kitchens, planning to work their way up. Me, I chanced my hand by applying for this role. Thankfully, my granny's recipes never let me down during my interview. Perhaps I'll make a batch of bannocks as a celebratory offering so my dear granny is present on tomorrow's opening day.

The heavy glass door from the stable yard swings open, making me jump out of my skin, as a blonde woman carrying a huge cardboard box enters. She heads for the counter area first, before spying me standing at the rear of the room.

'Hi, I'm Melissa, one of the artists who will be displaying goods in the glass cabinets.' She points to the row of display shelving which dominates one section of The Orangery. 'Is there any chance I can have my key so I can start filling the shelves?'

'Sure. I'm Isla, by the way. Jemima gave me a load of keys this morning. She said she's assigned each artist a specific cabinet and has placed the shelves at various heights depending on the size of your craft goods. Does that make sense to you?' I say, hotfooting it to the till area to retrieve the box of labelled cabinet keys.

'Yeah, I get that, Isla.' Melissa places her box on the tiled floor. 'I'm assuming my shelving will have extra depth between each shelf, as my ceramics and textile pieces can be quite large.'

'Oh, right, I suppose the jewellery person has more shelves because their items are tiny.'

'They'd be lost if the shelf spacing is too big, though some artists are sharing cabinets, I think. Jemima's worked out a deal that makes sense for everyone.'

I rummage through the keys to find ones labelled for 'Melissa – Cabinet 1'.

'Jemima thinks of everything, doesn't she?' I say, handing over the key ring.

'Thanks. She certainly does. She's quite savvy.'

'There's a spare set kept in the back room here; I believe Ned said he had another set in his office, just in case.'

'Excellent. I'm not great with keys, as Jemima knows full well. I'd suggest giving a copy to our old mate, Mungo, purely for safe keeping.'

I haven't met Mungo, so I don't comment.

She grimaces before adding, 'Sorry, that's a private joke between me and Jemima from our allotment days.'

'Jemima had an allotment?'

'She's still got it – it belonged to her Granddad Tommy. Obviously, she's not there much these days, but yeah, she's still got her girls … her chickens, I mean. Which is where we know Mungo from.'

'There's a Mungo here too.'

'Bloody hell, no way! He's kept that quiet.'

'He's an older gent. Ned's employed him as the handy-man-cum-caretaker for the gallery. I haven't met him yet.'

Melissa smiles, leans across the tiled countertop and whispers, 'A word of warning, never ask him about keys unless you want an hour and a half's lecture about his dedication to security. Should you be bored one day, it's worth a laugh, but otherwise don't bother.'

I like how she pulls a comical expression whilst talking. Melissa, I'll remember that name. She's my kind of person.

Chapter Four

Verity

Walking along the gravel drive towards Lerwick Manor, I feel like the new girl at school who's arrived on the second week of term. I'm sure everyone else has settled in nicely and is prepared for the opening tomorrow. Nerves are dancing in my stomach and I'm praying fervently that I can locate a woman named Jemima on my arrival. Given the enormity of the task ahead of me today, I'm not sure I'll be leaving here until after dark. I know what to expect; I had a virtual tour of the gallery before signing the contract, much like the cottage rental. The thought of decorating The Yarn Barn in just one day will be a tall order, but I'll give it my best shot. The promise of a hot bubble bath and a chilled glass of wine will be my reward later tonight – if I manage to nip to Tesco, an unexpected find whilst admiring the coastal landscape. Otherwise, I'll consume the remainder of my complimentary hamper.

It has taken thirty minutes to walk the distance from Harmony Cottage to Lerwick Manor; not an issue in dry weather, but I doubt it'll remain so with winter fast approaching. I don't intend to purchase a car just for the year; it seems like an unnecessary expense. Plus the prospect of clocking up the mileage on Shanks's pony might have unexpected benefits for my hips and waistline. The last time I walked on a daily basis was back and forth to school – with a double buggy, and an older child tagging along from the side frame.

A grand manor house stands ahead. Set within the red sandstone masonry, numerous rows of windows watch as I stealthily approach. The enormity of my recent decisions suddenly feels weighty, threatening to overwhelm me, but I have no other choice. I can hardly turn back, so I continue to plod along the sweeping driveway that leads to a stone archway denoting a stable yard and signposted: The Gallery.

Standing beneath the archway, a hive of activity is laid out before me. I stand mesmerised by the view; a pretty horseshoe of stable doors, each pinned wide, is set around the cobbled courtyard. At the far end, a large conservatory of painted wrought iron supports plate glass which sparkles in the morning sunshine. There's a constant stream of people busily criss-crossing from doorway to doorway, indulging in happy chatter and frantic gesturing without time to stop, delivery vans are manoeuvring to unload, and the rhythmical sound of a blacksmith's hammer rings out across the scene. It's like a magical world of theatre, as if I've stumbled on to the stage partway through Act One, needing to catch up with the script.

The rhythmical hammering ceases and a woman wearing a long leather apron appears in the doorway of the nearest stable on my right, wiping her brow with a red cloth. Her T-shirt reveals bare shoulders which glisten despite the autumn breeze.

'Hi,' I venture. 'Can you point me in the direction of Jemima, please?'

'Are you Verity?'

I'm sure I'll become attuned to the local accent in no time.

'Yes, I am.' I'm startled that a stranger would know my name.

'Are you after your keys?' asks the woman, stuffing the cloth inside her dungarees pocket and wiping her hands down her aproned thighs. 'I'm Wednesday Smith, the blacksmith here at the gallery.' Wednesday's warm palm firmly shakes mine.

'Nice to meet you. I'm Verity Kendal,' I reply, retrieving my hand from her grasp.

'Jemima's had to nip out but she's left your keys with Isla in The Orangery.' She gestures towards the elegant conservatory. 'Go straight through – she's expecting you, as Jemima said you'd be arriving today.' Her short pink hair is tousled and cute – and practical, I imagine, given the heat in which she must work.

'Thank you, everyone seems so busy,' I say, glancing at others toing and froing across the cobbles. I now notice that just one stable door remains closed and secure; it must be mine.

'Yeah, most artists arrived yesterday. They're unpacking their goods and creating displays ready for tomorrow's grand opening. I'm trying to get ahead with a few small items I can display and possibly take orders for. Drop by once you've settled in.'

'That's lovely of you, Wednesday.'

'Most people call me Nessie ... it's easier. I believe you've had numerous deliveries. Jemima has stacked them all inside your pitch.'

'Thank you, Nessie. Fingers crossed the wholesalers have supplied everything I asked for – I'll head on over and see you in a short while.'

After another round of thank yous, I head across the courtyard towards The Orangery, passing a rusty horse trough in which a speckled brown duck glides up and down, rippling the surface of the brimming water – not a sight I see every day. Once inside, I'm taken aback by the level of comfort and luxury afforded by the arrangements of soft couches, armchairs and hard-backed chairs scattered around an array of tables. Obviously, the coordinated mismatched style has been carefully thought through, as the overall impression is designer chic rather than cluttered cast-offs.

'Hello there!' calls the smiling woman behind the serving counter, efficiently unpacking serviettes into a wooden dispenser.

'Can I help?' Her auburn hair is neatly pinned beneath a netted cap and her freckles dance as she speaks.

'Hi, I'm Verity, I believe you're expecting me.'

'Oh yes. Jemima said you'd be arriving soon, though she'll be miffed because she wanted to be back in time to welcome you. I'm Isla, the catering manager for The Orangery.' Her hand sweeps in an arc, encompassing the beautiful surroundings.

'Nice to meet you. I'm told you might have my keys.'

'I have. Right here, labelled "The Yarn Barn" – nice name,' says Isla, pushing aside her task and reaching underneath the counter to produce a bunch of keys.

'Thank you, I've had long enough to think of an apt one,' I say, knowing simplicity is key in the name game.

'Sounds great. Now, don't ask me which key is which; I'm still fathoming my own out. On here there's a key for your stable plus a spare, which Jemima wants you to remove and keep safe. There's a key for the toilet block, which you'll find in the end two stables on this side, directly opposite the forge.' Isla nips from behind the counter to stand before the large plate-glass window looking out across the cobblestones, pointing to the far side. 'There's Nessie the blacksmith and Isaac the glass blower together in the forge, though I think she's got the majority of the space. Next is the upcycling man, who literally takes bric-a-brac and transforms it, the handmade cards lady after that, then the weaving ladies, who I haven't met yet. There's candle making in the next stable; it's quite unbelievable how he carves and twists patterns into the wax. Then me here in the artisan café in The Orangery, then in the corner next to me is the soapery where they use local goat's milk and add other ingredients—'

I grimace at the thought.

'I know. I'd never heard of that before, either. Apparently, it's full of vitamins and protects the skin's moisture levels.'

'It's actually good for you?'

'So she says. I haven't tried it yet. But didn't Cleopatra bathe in milk? Who knows? Then there's the wood-carving guy; it smells beautiful inside, as he leaves the shavings on the floor. Next to him is the masonry guy and then, finally, the jewellery team are next to the toilets – but they were latecomers so took what was offered. It's so lovely to stand here and see everyone busy preparing. I've only been here a few days and already I can see huge changes as the artists begin to make themselves at home. What is it you're selling?'

'Pretty much everything, from yarn – be it knitting or crocheting – to babywear, adults' clothing, blankets, even toys.'

'Very nice.'

'And you're busy preparing too?'

'Yes, I'm catering for tonight's party but I still have cakes to bake for tomorrow.'

'Oh, right,' I say.

'I think you'll find your invite is inside your premises.'

'That's nice,' I say, taken aback at the owners' gesture.

'Short notice but nice if you can make it.'

'Exactly. I need to get cracking, otherwise I won't be ready for tomorrow.'

'Phuh! Tell me about it . . . but I'll get there.'

'Thank you for these. I'll hopefully see you tonight,' I say, jangling my keys.

'I'll be the one flaked out in the corner having a snooze,' jests Isla, returning to her counter.

I hastily leave The Orangery with more urgency than before. I now need to get ready for tomorrow's opening, plus return home to freshen up and come back to attend their party. Not that I had other plans for tonight. But still, I'll be cutting it fine.

'Hello, hello!'

I straighten up from emptying yet another delivery box to find a petite woman standing in my stable doorway. Her dark hair flows freely about the shoulders of her fawn suede gilet.

'I'm Jemima, we're so glad you made it.' She strides forward and gives me a brief hug before stepping back amongst the packages of brightly coloured Shetland yarn.

At a glance, she's everything I'd imagined: somewhat stylish, yet down to earth in wellingtons; youthful whilst mature in attitude. I instantly like her.

'I'm delighted to be here. Thank you for signing for my stock deliveries too. It would have been a job and a half trying to organise their arrival specifically for today.'

'No worries. That's going to be the beauty of the gallery set-up. Any artist can have a delivery arrive, and somebody will sign and keep it safe in their absence. It's thrilling to see everyone's crafts coming together – and I can see you've wasted no time.'

'There's so much stock to unpack, but I'll get there. I assume I can use these display racks and shelving units?'

'Of course! Ned had those installed for each artist, so just move them about as you wish, it's your space now, not ours. Your wall-mounted heater might smell a bit when it's first switched on, but that burnt dust smell soon disappears. The counter and chair are pretty basic but if there's anything more you need, simply ask. There are mirrors, a few ottomans and a chair or two left over from refurbishing The Orangery, if you'd care for any of them. Just let me know; I realise you couldn't bring much with you, given your relocation.'

'That's lovely – I'll do what I can for today, and see how it goes once the visitors start arriving tomorrow.'

'Perfect. By tomorrow your door sign will have arrived too. Ned's placed two hooks on your outer wall, so customers will know exactly what's what on opening day.'

'Gosh, I didn't expect signage as well.'

'Our pleasure, it helps to unify the signage in the courtyard;

we copied your logo from the attachments you sent with your application. Anyway, I'll leave you in peace. Though hopefully we'll see you tonight for a drink or two?'

'Yes, thank you. I found the invite waiting for me, I'd love to join you.'

'Excellent. It'll give you a chance to meet the other artists, plus some of the locals. Bye for now.'

As quickly as she arrived, Jemima left. There's definitely an energy about her. On the phone, she'd mentioned that it hadn't taken her long to get this venture up and running. I can see how.

Once alone, I stare about the interior with fresh eyes. The newly plastered walls are immaculate; I don't wish to mark or damage those with displays. The chunky rustic beams accentuate the wooden shelving unit. I decide it will be better positioned against the rear wall, enabling customers to browse without feeling watched from the counter. But as for that hard-backed chair . . . I can't see my back lasting longer than a few hours sitting on that when I'm between customers. Jemima's suggestion of a replacement may well be the answer. I can see myself knitting in a cosy armchair before a small heater, serving customers in between casting on stitches and selecting another ball of yarn.

My head is awash with visions for my little venture; I want to pinch myself. For all the moments in which I've dreamt of owning my own business and creating items for sale, I never thought it would feel as good as this. There's a bubble of excitement deep inside which is bouncing about, igniting my passion. A flicker of sadness pokes at me, jabbing my inner excitement. My three lads complained about having to wear my creations throughout their childhood – like a trio of walking mannequins, identical in pattern, only differing in colour – but I know they would have loved to help unpack these boxes of yarn. I exhale, releasing the sudden rush of emotion. Pulling my mobile from my pocket, I check for any missed texts or calls: nothing. Avril's explanation must have satisfied their initial concerns and curiosity.

I'm determined to give this project my best shot and, in a year's time, come hell or high water, I will return home with a proven business model with which to set up my own wool shop back in the Midlands.

'But first there's another eight boxes to unpack,' I mutter, eager to begin dressing my display shelves with beautiful yarns.

Chapter Five

Nessie

I'm determined not to drink too much; a hangover on the opening day whilst wielding a hammer wouldn't be ideal. I'd have preferred a bubble bath and an early night after moving so much gear into the forge over the last few hours. Heavy lifting doesn't begin to describe it.

I sip my red wine as I survey the sea of smiling faces surrounding me, seeking out any of the other artists. I've managed to chat to a few: the candle guy, the two weaving ladies, the masonry guy, Melissa – the ceramics and textiles woman – and, of course, Isaac. Initially, I wasn't sold on the idea of sharing my space. But with a hefty reduction in rent, thanks to his contribution, plus his pleasant personality, I can't see it being an issue for either of us. At least his reaction to my role wasn't 'wow, a female blacksmith!' which is what the wood whittler in the opposite stable block exclaimed. Not that I'm offended; it's hardly the first time I've heard such a remark. If the truth be known, such attitudes only fire me up and push me on to prove a point. It's not all about biceps and strength; iron and steel succumb to the softest touch once heated to white-hot temperatures.

I spy Verity at the buffet and nip across.

'How's tricks?' I ask as she fills her plate with Isla's delicious treats.

'Done and dusted. My main displays are ready and my deliveries are unpacked. Though, to be honest, my day started way before I arrived here.' She begins to giggle, probably one tipple too many on an empty stomach.

I love her accent, so different to us locals.

'Sounds ominous,' I say, instantly wanting to hear more.

Verity quickly tells me about her morning encounter with the local farrier.

'A giant of a guy with brown curls?'

She blushes profusely and nods.

'That'll be our Magnus. Yeah, we're distant cousins in one way or another. In fact, if you trace the family tree of most folk around Shetland you'll find a shared bloodline somewhere. He's a decent sort, you know. He farms sheep just up from you, but he turns his hand to farrier work if folk need him. He'll laugh it off when you speak to him.'

'I'm not speaking to him!' Verity's horrified expression makes me laugh.

'Everyone speaks to Magnus – he's one of life's good guys. Catch you later.' I drift away, allowing her to eat in peace.

The music system is blaring out a strange mix of music to which the retro disco lights respond by switching colour and sequence; it's enough to trigger a migraine, so I head towards the rear of the party. What will I say if Levi asks what I think of his DJing skills? I'll definitely lie. I wouldn't wish to offend a lifelong friend. He always makes sure I'm safely home on those rare occasions when I go out and require a taxi. Though I insist on paying the fare, I wouldn't take advantage of his kindness; a man has to eat.

'Dottie, isn't it?' I say, as a glamorous older woman in a turquoise evening gown that belies her years appears beside me, offering a rosy smile.

'Yes, dear, that's me. You're the blacksmith, aren't you? Such a worthy trade in these parts. I said to Mungo earlier, she's a chip off the old block for sure.'

'Oh, do you know my grandfather?'

'Your daa, and your father too ... but Mungo claims he remembers your great-daa from when he was a little laddie,' she says, patting my forearm gently.

'My great-grandfather? Wow, that's amazing. I'll need to pick his brains one of these days for memories of his old forge.'

'He's got a great memory for yesteryear, though take my advice, lovely – make sure you haven't a busy morning. Love him as I do, he can spin a yarn out for hours when he's reminiscing about his boyhood.'

I giggle at her honesty and her warm manner; she's definitely my tribe.

'I promise to give him all the time he needs. You keep the manor in order, I hear.'

'A bit of light dusting here and there. I arrived as a young girl, straight from school, and Ned's mother made sure I remained on the staff once she married into the family. Poor woman relied on me more than she wanted others to know, but I was grateful for her loyalty. I stay on purely to repay her gratitude; I wouldn't let her down, not where Ned's concerned.'

'And your allotment. I gather you know Jemima through the local allotment plots,' I say, enjoying her company too much to let her go.

'I'll always have my allotment plot; my life depends upon it. Even if I reach the stage of needing a sturdy Zimmer frame with a tray top, and it takes me half a morning to reach my gate, I'll tend my plot in my final days.'

'You love it that much?'

'If I get my way, one day I'll provide worm food for my beautiful blooms for an entire season.'

I'm taken aback, but there's a cheeky smile adorning her dear face. 'Oh, you don't mean that, surely?'

'I do. I couldn't think of a more fitting celebration of my life. Don't worry, lassie – I'm not always this morbid, but it saves a lot of fuss when the time comes if others know your plans.'

I have no idea what to say so I raise my wine glass in her direction. Dottie giggles before moving on.

'Hi, Nessie, fancy a nibble?' asks Isla, offering a large platter filled with fancy finger food.

'No, thanks, but I appreciate the thought,' I quip, raising my glass and showing her all I truly need at the moment.

'Fair enough, there's plenty of booze at the bar,' she says, switching the platter to her other arm.

'Have you made all of these?'

'Yep, it's taken two whole days to prepare all the food for this and the opening day.'

'That is some achievement for ... sorry to ask, but how old are you?'

'Nineteen.'

'You're very talented, you know that?' Isla blushes at my compliment. 'No, you are ... this isn't basic baking, this is on another level.'

'How can you say that when you're ... I don't want to be rude, either, but you're the first female blacksmith I've ever heard of, let alone seen at work. Earlier today, when I nipped in with the loose change you'd forgotten, I couldn't believe you were hammering a red-hot strip of metal, gave it a twist ... and, hey presto, it was a decorative swirl. Surely that's talent.'

'It's in my blood, it's as simple as that,' I say, with a certain amount of pride.

I'm about to ask Isla what she does outside of work when the sound system's microphone buzzes into life, causing everyone to shudder at the ear-piercing noise.

'Sorry to interrupt, folks, but can anyone see Jemima?' comes Ned's deep voice, loud and clear, over the tannoy.

'Here! Here!' shout numerous people in her vicinity, frantically pointing.

'Ah, there you are! Jemima, would you care to join me, please?' instructs Ned.

We all watch as Jemima prepares herself to speak to the crowd.

'Ladies and gentlemen, I'd like to thank each and every one of you for joining us to celebrate the opening of the new gallery tomorrow. A venture brought about thanks to Jemima's savvy thinking and intuition – whilst weeding, I believe,' says Ned, as we in the assembled crowd chuckle at Jemima's surprised expression. Ned nervously gives her a sideways glance before continuing. 'It goes without saying that, despite recently revealing myself to be the bona fide owner of Lerwick Manor, Jemima is the heart and soul behind this new project . . .'

A ripple of applause begins but I don't join in, as I don't quite understand the significance of his comment. Ned waits for the applause to subside before continuing.

'She definitely offered up the solution to a huge issue just in the nick of time. As I can admit now, I was on the cusp of calling in a tourist trust for serious discussions. You all know this young woman, she doesn't accept public praise too kindly – shirks it at every opportunity, actually. So, to save her blushes, I hope you'll join me in a suitable toast, one befitting the new venture, which I . . . *we* hope will bring good fortune to every artist, craftsperson and customer who takes delight in the fabulous wares on display, be it locally or thousands of miles away. Just as each item bears a discrete yet decorative label clearly stating our intent, let's raise our glasses proudly to "From Shetland, With Love".'

'From Shetland, With Love,' chorus the crowd, raising our glasses in their direction.

'Thank you,' mutters Jemima, tipping her glass in our direction.

'Excuse me, one final thing before we return to enjoying what remains of our evening,' says Ned into the mic, his stance softening as he turns towards Jemima.

Jemima politely smiles. It's as if we sense what's about to happen before she does.

'Jemima, it can't have escaped the attention of everyone who knows us that in recent weeks something very special has occurred ... blossomed almost, right before their eyes. I sensed my bachelor days were drawing to an end the very first moment I saw you balancing precariously on top of a skip.' He turns aside to speak to the gathered party. 'I won't go into detail – but I'm sure Dottie will, after a few more sherries.'

There's a ripple of laughter from a small crowd in the centre of the floor.

I notice Ned's fingers curl endearingly around Jemima's hand; such a small act, yet so tender. Melissa mentioned earlier that they hadn't been together as a couple for long, and yet their bond seems so strong. How beautiful. I've forgotten how it feels to relate and connect to another in such a loving manner.

Ned's voice brings me back from my own past, to witness their present moment. He's going to ask her, I'm sure. Well, as sure as I can be about two people I've only recent met. They look good together, him with his mature good looks and salt 'n' pepper colouring, her slightly younger, but not by much, with glossy dark hair and trusting features.

'You and I know that despite ours being a rather short acquaintance and courtship, we fell in love ... undeniably, head over heels, and very quickly. There seems to be a belief in the Campbell family that "when you know, you know" and, Jemima, I definitely know. I know that I couldn't have achieved this ... without you. I know that all my future plans include you by my side. Jemima, I believe you know it too. So, I wish to ask one simple question: will you agree to be my wife and marry me?'

I know her answer without hesitation; you can tell by her expression.

All eyes are upon her. Every breath held a fraction longer than necessary. Each heartbeat a fraction quicker than the previous one.

'Say "yes",' I'm willing her, along with the rest of their guests.

There's silence.

You can hear a pin drop during her pause.

'Yes.'

The answer has barely left her lips when Ned envelops her in a bear hug, complete with a passionate kiss.

We raise our glasses again, with a deafening shout of, '*Congratulations!*'

Chapter Six

Sunday 3 October

Verity

'Good morning, how are you?' asks Nessie, striding across the cobblestones armed with a gooey jam-laden pastry and a steaming mug of coffee.

'Slightly the worse for wear after the red wine and champagne, but nothing a few paracetamol can't correct.'

'Our Magnus might drop by later; I'll introduce him, if you like?'

'You'd better be joking, Nessie. I won't be meeting him eye to eye any day soon,' I jest, struggling with my door lock.

'Let me know if you change your mind,' calls Nessie, heading towards the forge. 'I just spied Ned carrying a comfy armchair, so you might be in for one extra delivery today. Catch you later!'

'That would be lovely, a bit of luxury on my second morning at work,' I say, pinning the door wide. I'm impressed if that's true; I only emailed Jemima an hour ago regarding another chair.

I flick on the lights, illuminating a beautiful world of coloured yarns. My display unit is complete, with Shetland yarns of various ply, prices and brands, some in neat balls, others in twisted skeins. I've made do with a large wicker basket in which to display my knitting needles and crocheting hooks but still, customers will be able to browse without feeling self-conscious. The only job I didn't manage to complete yesterday was to organise the numerous patterns into their folders; it's a fiddly job but one befitting a quiet moment such as this with a morning coffee and a couple of paracetamol.

'Morning, Verity, Jemima mentioned that you were interested in an armchair,' says Ned, bustling through the door with a sturdy Parker Knoll clasped in his arms.

'Yes, please. That's perfect. Congratulations, by the way, you make a smashing couple.'

'Oh, thank you. I hope so, as we've no intention of it being a long engagement,' says Ned, a slight blush colouring his features, before quickly adding, 'Jemima said, and I quote, "There's a footstool too if you want it." So let me know if you'd like that as well.'

I smile; typical male, avoids the sentiment and sticks with the business in hand.

'I'm happy with the armchair, thanks. If you could drop it over there by the end of the counter, I'd appreciate it.' I gesture to a corner space, ideal for a cosy chair in which to knit, between serving customers.

'How's it going for you?' asks Ned, straightening up after positioning the armchair.

'Well, I'm ready for the grand opening – let's put it that way. I need to begin producing a few small items for sale and display purposes, but I can only do that once everything else is in place.'

'Good to hear. We're going to ring a bell calling folk together just before half ten. Shout if there's anything else you need.'

Ned leaves as swiftly as Jemima did yesterday; there's a definite air of efficiency about the pair of them. It's comforting to know that my little business appears to have an additional safety net consisting of hard-working folk other than myself.

I'm all for the old adage 'many hands make light work' – and where the arts and crafts businesses are concerned, if they all have a united attitude towards helping one another, this place should be a busy little venture.

My mobile begins to ring.

My heart rate jumps to panic mode. It's my first call since speaking to Avril. She'd best not be spoiling for round two. I fumble in my pocket, to find Tom is calling.

'Hello, my darling, how are you?' The relief at hearing his voice brings me close to tears.

'Mum? Hi. I thought I'd call and see what you're up to,' comes his tinny voice, as I envisage my baby of six foot two, probably still in bed given the time of day.

'I'm good, did Aunty Avril explain things?'

'Yeah, we all got called to Nan's house. Harvey wasn't happy because he missed his gym session, but Jack insisted he had to attend. Aunty Avril wasn't best pleased, and neither is Nanny but ... Mum, I kind of get it. I've felt like that at times and I reckon you're entitled to enjoy yourself just as much as we three lads do.'

My heart melts. He might only be seventeen, but this is my baby. I might not have had the easiest ride since me and George split, but somehow, I've managed to raise three decent young men.

'Mum? Are you still there?'

'Yes, Tom, I'm here. I was just taking in what you said. It hasn't been easy, has it?'

'Not always, no.'

'But we've always looked after each other. And that's what I need you to do now, look out for your brothers while I'm away.'

'That's what Jack said. He said we need to give you space and peace of mind by sticking together.'

'Jack said that, did he?'

'Yeah, and Granddad agreed with him. Harvey didn't say much, but then he never does, does he?'

'You're not wrong there, Tom.'

I want to cry with joy. I've been beating myself up for so long, wanting to do this one thing for myself, and here's my youngest giving me the green light. It means the absolute world to me. I was half expecting to get an ear-bashing in a teenage-style rant for skipping out as I did, but I couldn't have been more wrong.

'Has Jack explained about the direct debits and the food money?'

'He's drawn up a rota system for cooking, vacuuming and cleaning the bathroom, which he's pinned to the fridge door. I've told him I'm not cleaning the bog!'

'Oh, Tom.' I simply can't believe it; my boys are doing exactly what I need them to do. 'I'm sure you'll play your part when asked.'

'I'd prefer to do double cooking than that!'

'Anyway, what else have you been up to?'

I listen as he explains about football, his closest mates and some never-ending boxset he loves. I drink in his chirpy tones, chattering away ten to the dozen. My behaviour definitely isn't how a middle-aged mum is expected to act, but maybe my lads will have their own adventures over the next twelve months.

'Tom, you know I'll always be here for you, don't you?' I say, interrupting his chatter.

'Oh yeah, of course, Mum. Likewise,' says Tom, continuing his chatter as a bulbous tear trickles down the length of my cheek.

I spend the next few minutes trying not to sniff or hiccup, wary of alerting him to my emotional state before we end the call.

'Give my love to Jack and Harvey . . . tell Nan and Granddad that I'll call them in a day or so.'

Within a second, our phone connection is lost.

I quickly dry my face for fear someone may find me in a dishevelled state. I know I'm worrying unnecessarily – and I still need to shake off this hangover.

I might be six hundred and fifty miles away, but that invisible thread connecting me to my brood is taut and as tightly wound as it ever could be.

And that brings a smile to my face.

Nessie

Just before half ten, I hear a bell clanging in the yard.

'That'll be for us,' says Isaac, laying his blowpipe down on his workbench.

'That or a fire drill,' I joke, knowing full well it's Ned's intention to draw us all together for the official opening.

I ensure my coal pit is safe to leave, that nothing combustible is resting too close, then remove my safety goggles and mitts before grabbing my big cable-knit cardy to cover my bare arms and heading for the exit alongside Isaac.

I'm taken aback to find a crowd has gathered whilst we've been busy working. There must be sixty people of all ages milling alongside the various artists assembled on the cobbles, all facing The Orangery. I recognise many of the faces: Levi, Kaspar and ... oh, shoot me now! My gaze falls upon the strawberry-blond trio of the MacDonald brothers, three strapping blokes known and admired within the community, each as handsome and as rugged as the next. I can't help but stare when, viewed side by side, they resemble the walking equivalent of a winged dressing-table mirror offering a slight variation of the original reflection.

I quickly manoeuvre myself to stand on the other side of Isaac; I can do without the MacDonald trio spotting me, especially Fergus.

'This is a decent turnout,' I whisper to Isaac, who stands head and shoulders above the crowd, surveying those present.

'I didn't notice anyone arriving, did you?' he says, gesturing towards the crowd.

'No, but you were busy blowing several paperweights; and I don't hear a thing once I start hammering.'

'Me neither, lost in the zone once I start.'

The noise and chatter ceases when Ned sounds his bell for a second time; only the faint shuffle of feet upon the cobbles remains. If I stand on tiptoe and crane my neck, I can just about spy a nervous-looking Jemima alongside Ned and his handbell, standing in front of the conservatory. I assume she hadn't predicted she'd be here in the role of fiancée just twenty-four hours ago.

'Good morning, ladies, gentlemen and children, we welcome each and every one of you to The Gallery at Lerwick Manor,' says Ned.

Thankfully, I can hear him clearly, even if I'm denied a clear view due to the size of the crowd.

'Today is our official opening and we're delighted to see so many of you interested in visiting the various artists whose talents and wares are on display. The premise of this new venture is to provide access to a wealth of traditional arts and crafts within our modern era. I'm sure you'll be amazed, as I have been, by the skill and dedication you'll witness as you attend each stable and view each artist. Crafts that have declined in popularity in recent decades are brought back to life before your very eyes. Please interact, the artists have specifically said they want you to ask questions, enquire about goods and simply enjoy watching them whilst they work. They've assured me that you won't be interrupting anyone by asking about their individual journeys, the history of their art, or their accomplishments. Afterwards, we invite you to relax in The Orangery, our refurbished conservatory, where you'll be able to consume the fine artistry on show!'

There's a titter of laughter from the crowd, and Ned gives a knowing smile before continuing.

'So, without further delay, I'd like to introduce Dorothy Nesbit, who many of you know and love, to cut the ribbon declaring our beautiful gallery officially open. Dottie has been with us at Lerwick Manor for many years, and so it's our delight that she has agreed to do the honours.'

I assume they have a piece of satin ribbon and large scissors with which Dottie can perform her duties. My mind's eye imagines her wearing her fine turquoise dress from last night.

'I'd just like to say, it gives me great pleasure to declare this gallery officially open.' Dottie's voice drifts above the heads of the crowd, followed by a hearty round of applause complete with whistles and chants.

I join in, assuming she's cut the ribbon. Bless her, she seems a frail dear. I bet she was so nervous – it's something of a change from her 'bit of light dusting'.

The crowd begins to disperse in all directions, whilst the artists return to their stables to greet new customers.

'Done?' says Isaac. 'Or are you waiting for a glass of bubbles?'

'No bubbles for me. Let's get busy and see what we can do!' I say, as we gratefully return to the warmth of the forge.

Chapter Seven

Isla

'Have you had a good day?' I ask, as Verity returns her mug just before closing.

'I have, thank you. I'm about to lock up but there's been a steady flow of customers wandering in to view the wool, and thankfully many have made purchases. Though I'm surprised by the number of customers who commented, "I can't actually knit." I mean, seriously? I thought, given the cultural heritage of these islands, knitting would be a basic skill.'

I shake my head; I'm not surprised. 'I can't knit, either. I'd love to, but it looks complicated and I wouldn't know where to start.'

'It'll take you less than a few minutes to master the basic garter stitch.'

'Really?'

'Yes. I'll show you, one lunchtime – it's easy.'

We stand chatting for a short while before I ask how she comes to be here in Shetland. When she tells me about her 'gap year', I can imagine my mum wanting to escape on many occasions whilst raising me and my sister.

'I know Harmony Cottage,' I tell her. 'I keep my pony in the adjoining field.'

'Which one? There's a pair kept by the front driveway and a single pony kept in the side paddock.'

'Jutt, the black Shetland. I've had him since I was a child. Mum says I should give him up now, but he's my pet. People wouldn't give up their dog just because they've taken on a new job, would they?'

'Mmmm, some do,' says Verity, grimacing.

'Well, I'm not like that.'

'You don't ride him then?'

'I don't, but he's as gentle as a lamb, so I'm sometimes asked to walk a young rider around the paddock as a first riding lesson. I love days like that. The little kiddies are always so excited.'

'And he doesn't mind?'

'Nah, Jutt loves children. People in general, actually. I bet within a few days he's nosing his face over your wall and staring in at you. His paddock wraps around your cottage from the bedroom to the lounge. Seriously, he'll be watching you as much as you watch him.'

'It is a lovely spot,' mutters Verity, before adding, 'but a fair walk from here each day.'

'My mum gives me a lift in, so shout if you need dropping back any time.'

'Thanks, but I'm thinking of getting a bike. It'll be good for my health if I choose pedal power for a year.'

'Don't buy one, we've got a spare!'

'That's kind of you, but I couldn't,' says Verity, becoming flustered.

'Seriously, my mum would help anyone, but especially anyone staying in Harmony Cottage. I was born there. Not that I remember it, obviously. But one of my mum's relatives owns it, and she was being looked after there. I arrived earlier than expected so, yeah, I was born in the upstairs bedroom.'

Verity smiles.

'What?'

'That is probably the strangest thing I've heard. I've never before met anyone who could say they were born in my upstairs bedroom.'

'Their son owns the cottage now.'

Her brow furrows in confusion. 'I dealt with a lady regarding the contracts and virtual tour of the cottage.'

'Yeah, that'll be my mum. She's at home all day, so she looks after the cottage for him. She'll be the emergency contact if you need anything. We're the next cottage along the coastal lane,' I say, quickly adding, 'in the direction of Tesco, that is.'

'Ah yes, Tesco. I didn't expect to see a superstore when I arrived.'

'Everyone says that!' Now it's my turn to pull a quizzical expression. 'We're no different to you mainland folk – we do a weekly "big shop" too.'

Nessie

It's late in the day and our steady flow of visitors has dwindled. I'm going for it, hammer and tongs, so I don't notice when he walks in. Likewise, I have no idea how long he's been standing there watching me, though Isaac has definitely clocked him when I glance up.

'Hello, Fergus, how are you?' I say, peering through my Perspex goggles, at my ex.

His wavy hair is as thick as ever, falling forward and hiding his sea-green eyes.

'I was about to ask you the same thing, Nessie.' His deep voice fills the forge. 'Long time no see, and all that.'

I carry on working, probably much to his annoyance. Using my tongs, I lift the glowing iron from the anvil and thrust it into my nearest slack tub, causing a plume of steam to rise.

Fergus waits for the hissing sound to cease before continuing. 'I see you're back then.'

'Oh yeah. I'm back.' I can't help the twang of attitude

accompanying that last remark. When I spied him earlier I had every intention of being polite, mature and blasé should he come calling. 'And, as you can see, doing what I love.' I could repeat his quote from that fateful night – 'Smithing is simply your fantasy' – but I don't. I wouldn't lower myself.

Now black and cold, I inspect the iron handle I'm crafting; it's coming along nicely but needs a decorative swirl to complete the toasting fork.

Fergus nods. His eyes are roving everywhere, from anvil, to workbench, to slack tub, and finally resting back upon me. I'm not ready to face the legacy of our break-up; after three years of serious dating and two years apart, I truly didn't expect him to have the nerve to walk in here. Not today, anyway.

'Are you back for good?'

'Yep, made a new home here in the forge, and I intend to give it all I've got,' I say, turning my back on him to push the iron handle into the coal pit, heating the top end and preparing it for the final decoration. He's treading carefully – as well he might, given our last conversation. All I asked for was some time and space to pursue my dream; he refused to contemplate a long-distance relationship, so his leaving present was a heart-to-heart the night before my flight to the mainland. And a broken engagement.

I fuss over my coals, knowing when I turn around he'll still be standing a short distance from my workbench behind the public's boundary rope.

I'm right.

I look up, as if surprised, but I'm clearly not.

'Your parents OK?' he asks.

'Yep. Yours?'

'Yeah, and my brothers.'

I want to interject; he wouldn't be standing here if his brothers weren't OK. Everyone knows that none of the MacDonald trio could survive without the others. They aren't triplets but you'd convince yourself they were.

I acknowledge his comment with a weak smile before retrieving the red-hot metal with my tongs. I select my hammer, rest the toasting fork handle on the anvil and position my sharpened chisel on the glowing end – in a single blow of the hammer, I splice it equally in two. Working quickly, I flatten each before twisting and turning the divided ends into an intricate lattice design where neither strand touches but simply entwines itself around the other. I don't glance up; he's watching intently.

One swift splice is all it took to divide us. We two were strong, tightly bonded, yet there'll be no elaborate finish for me and Fergus, nothing we created that will last a lifetime.

'I heard you got married,' I say, metaphorically kicking myself for mentioning it.

'Yeah, I did.' He shifts uncomfortably, much like I had done on hearing the news, six months into my blacksmith's course. 'Baby's due in three weeks.'

'Congratulations.' I can't be bitter; he and I simply weren't meant to be.

I put down my tools and thrust the decorative end of the toasting fork into my slack tub. The heat hisses furiously before cooling upon submersion, much like my past relationships. I lift the finished article from the water. Wasn't I planning on a decorative swirl – not intricate lattice work – before my one-man audience arrived? Mmmm, it seems plans and designs swiftly change.

'That's lovely,' he says, as I inspect my finished piece.

'Thanks. It's what I've dreamt of doing for a long, long time.'

Fergus nods. I can see the cogs are spinning behind his fixed gaze. 'I'd best be off. Nice seeing you.'

'You too. Good luck with the bairn.' I reach for my rasp to

complete the final stage before polishing. I glance up to witness his retreating figure.

As he passes the other workbench, where Isaac sits tall, they exchange a swift blokeish nod and Fergus leaves.

Isaac returns to his design work. He doesn't look up but simply asks, 'You OK?'

'Fine and dandy,' I lie, as I tighten the toasting fork in the grip of the vice and apply the rasp to the rough edges.

Chapter Eight

Verity

On entering the superstore, I don't know whether to laugh or cry. It might be early Sunday evening but the Tesco store doesn't close until 11 p.m. How's that for service? What's more surprising is that, in an attempt to escape my humdrum life, I've relocated but can still purchase my regular 'big shop', recognise every product in the aisles and maintain my Clubcard points. On arriving in Shetland, I'd imagined sauntering into quirky corner shops to while away the time, chatting about days gone by, watching an elderly dear select my supplies by hand from her aged shelves. I suppose Shetlanders need supermarkets too.

If I squint, fixing my eyes purely on the traffic snaking into the car park, ignoring the stone cottages and backdrop of the North Sea, I can believe I am back home visiting my local store. But hey, I can't complain. Over the years, they've saved my skin during numerous household emergencies: when the Calpol bottle was empty; when a last-minute caterpillar cake was needed; and even, on one desperate occasion, supplying replacement Easter eggs when I inadvertently scoffed the lot after putting the boys to bed.

I can't see its corporate colours from Harmony Cottage, so will pretend it doesn't truly exist until I need groceries.

Traipsing around, pushing a tiny trolley, feels somewhat strange – and definitely cheaper. I'm usually accompanied by the constant nag of a male voice asking, 'Mum, can I have . . .?' or, 'Mum, can we try . . .?' or even, 'Urgh, not that again?'

I'm overwhelmed, browsing every aisle in search of what I'd like to eat. I've forgotten what I like. I've lost sight of me; I've evolved into a living, breathing shell of a woman who fetches, carries and cleans for those she loves, without actually living a life. Thankfully, I haven't lost sight of my promised rewards: bubble bath and vino!

Tonight is definitely one for rewards after the constant stream of customers and sales I've had during our opening day. The sheer thrill of restocking the wool display before leaving for the night was indescribable. The added bonus being that the gallery is closed on Mondays and Tuesdays, so I now have two days free – to spend at home, knitting. The quicker I can create a selection of display items my customers can purchase or knit themselves, the quicker my sales will increase.

Having struggled along the coastal road clutching three heavy grocery bags, I punch the door code into the keypad . . . and open sesame. Much better than rummaging around in the bottom of my handbag for keys. My lads would definitely appreciate such security; they've forgotten their keys on numerous occasions, forcing me out of bed at some ungodly hour. How quickly would my home be burgled, though? Fifteen minutes is my reckoning – unlike Harmony Cottage.

It takes all of ten minutes to unpack my groceries – one advantage of solo living. Another being that my goodies will remain intact until I choose otherwise, and not disappear thanks to one of my lads feeling peckish. My Harvey is a bugger for grazing out of the fridge twenty minutes before I dish up and then complaining he's starving ten minutes after he's finished his meal.

At the moment, the plasma TV is the room's focal point, followed by the wood burner. I'd much prefer the beauty of Mother Nature to dominate. I turn around, surveying each of the three lounge windows and the scenery beyond. I'm unsure which I prefer: the patio window offering a panoramic view of Jutt, the Shetland pony, with a backdrop of the sea crashing in the bay, or the low-level windows opposite, offering a prospect of the driveway and paddocks, or a quaint view of the cottage's rear garden.

This feels like I'm nesting, like I did when I was waiting for Jack to arrive all those years ago. In those days, I'd spend every hour handwashing baby clothes, folding cot sheets and rearranging nursery supplies in an attempt to feel ready for motherhood.

Grabbing the edge of the sofa arm, I drag it from its position along the back wall facing the TV. Inch by inch, with me stumbling backwards and unceremoniously huffing and puffing, I manage to manoeuvre the bulky couch, reposition the coffee table and swivel the two armchairs around. If I'm to be comfy I need to create a home from home. I stand back, surveying my handiwork. I'll try living with this arrangement; if not, I'll change it again.

Within ten minutes, I'm settled on the couch accompanied by a steaming mug of coffee, a fresh ball of Shetland wool and a pair of needles, ready to cast on stitches; there's not a sound inside or outside the cottage. No ticking clock, no endless thump of heavy-metal music or the constant bleep of various mobile phones.

Peace, perfect peace.

I watch the waves crash upon the black rocks of the bay, the white-water spray filling every crevice before draining back into the turbulent sea only to be repeated relentlessly, time and time again. The scene resonates with me on an emotional level. For every moment of every day this scene plays on a loop; never has the pause button been depressed to cease the action. How amazing. The rocks have been battered for millions of years, yet they remain strong, solid and unmoved.

I smile, truly content; there's a deep comfort in that very thought.

Nessie

'How's it gone, lass?' asks my granddad over a late Sunday lunch, as he gestures to my grandma to pass the Pyrex gravy jug along the table. My parents tune in whilst tucking into a roast dinner with all the trimmings; it's our weekly ritual, cooked by my mother at the home of my grandparents – her in-laws. They've delayed the traditional midday Sunday roast waiting for me to return from the gallery.

I can't help but smile, which answers his question.

'I love it, Granddad. I made my coal shovel first, keeping up with our family tradition.'

'That's my girl! Mine's lasted me a lifetime – hanging up in the shed right now, it is, alongside your great-daa's shovel,' says Granddad, beaming with pride.

'You can't make them too strong, though, can you?' Grandma says, adding salt and pepper to her dinner. 'You'll be needing sales from folk around here; last a lifetime and they'll never buy another.'

Granddad's scornful expression appears instantly. 'We Smiths have never made anything that wasn't quality, guaranteed for a lifetime, and it's served us well enough as a standard around these parts.'

'Coal shovels and toasting forks might have put bread on this here table but it won't be doing likewise for our Nessie, not with the modern generation spurning coal fires,' retorts Grandma, shaking her head at her husband's remarks.

'The day a household doesn't need a decent hand shovel is the day my toes curl,' states Granddad, knocking his knife handle on the table to reinforce his motion. Neither of my parents bats an eyelid; Granddad frequently states his views forcefully over our weekly dinners.

'Don't say things like that!' I exclaim, knowing he's all talk. 'I'll be needing your support and advice from here on in.' I fall silent for a second, hoping my father doesn't take that remark to heart; it was his choice to opt out of the family trade.

Granddad gives me a wink before tucking into his mashed spuds, now swimming in a sea of thick gravy.

Between mouthfuls, I chatter on about the toasting forks I've made, the regular flow of customers and my new stablemate, Isaac. I forget to mention Fergus and my lack of sales for fear of curdling the double cream awaiting dessert. There was plenty of browsing, and numerous questions, but the only items leaving the forge were a pair of ornate candle holders – plus my ex. Never mind, it was only day one of the gallery. Word will get around, interest will spike amongst the locals and tourists, then I'll look back and laugh.

Maybe when the goods start flying out the door, I'll share details of my first sales over our Sunday roast.

Chapter Nine

Monday 4 October

Verity

I leave the cottage early in my sturdiest boots. A quick nip through the side gate of Jutt's field, and I find myself strolling along a coastal pathway which skirts the cliff top. A forceful wind brushes my hair backwards, baring my face to the harsh elements, as I follow in the footsteps of previous walkers, treading upon the grassy path worn smooth by generations.

Having been inside for twelve hours, I was beginning to get cabin fever – silence is golden, but it feels like going cold turkey from society when you're used to the constant bustle of three sons.

My heart experiences a pang at the very thought of home. My boys are my life, yet here I am. They'll be fine, I'm sure. Harvey and Tom will cope under Jack's stringent leadership, they won't give him a moment's trouble; probably grow up somewhat, given half a chance. I've no doubts a girlfriend or two will stay overnight, despite my house rules pinned to the fridge. Which I'm sure Tom will squeal about, at the first opportunity.

I scurry up a grassy slope. It's hard work, but worth it to view a turbulent sea from the cliff edge – a swirling delight of aqua green and navy blue, surging and mixing, propelled by a natural force. Such a magical vista simply takes my breath away: sky, sea and ancient rock. The basic elements of nature combine to create a foundation on which is built a landscape that will last for ever.

Had George and I possessed the basic elements to last for ever? How different would life have been if two college kids, besotted with each other, had created a solid foundation. Were we even in love? He was never one for voicing his feelings – good or bad. I was naïve about life, too busy enjoying the freedom that a boyfriend with a driving licence provided; whisking me away from my oh-so-perfect twin. George was the first thing in my life that I wasn't expected to share with Avril – unlike our bedroom, most of my Christmas presents and our doll's house.

As I continue my trek I'm surprised to come upon a herd of sheep littering the hillside, nibbling the short grass and freely depositing their bulbous pellets in pursuit of a multitasking method like no other creature. Their ability to stand on the edge of a coastal path, with a vertical drop just a step away, is also admirable, given their bulky waistline and lack of agility should they stumble.

My relationship with George was forged one crazy night thanks to teenage kicks in a single bed. Only to be confirmed a month later, staring anxiously at a tiny plastic window and awaiting the appearance of a blue line. Again, George had very little to say, whilst I naïvely assumed our happy ever after was guaranteed. We were going to survive the trials and tribulations of daily life, weren't we?

Far from it.

Ironically, we did what we thought was the right thing; which turned out to be the wrong thing in the long run.

Baby number one delivered us into a world of nappies, teething rings and chunky plastic toys. Baby number two arrived in quick succession, creating a mighty blur in my memory book. Five years later, baby number three was our Elastoplast moment, though I didn't realise it at the time. I thought our final child would be the icing on the cake of our little family. Sadly, it was my futile attempt to make everything perfect; I was viewing married life from my rose-tinted viewpoint but not George's. It was all too much, too soon. The building blocks of my life came tumbling down. George was gone. I unknowingly shared him with another woman and I was left holding three tiny boys.

I'm brought back from thoughts of yesteryear by an energetic blue merle dog trotting past me, its black nose held high, its long fringes lolling with each step; it looks like a miniature collie. The dog shows no interest in me, but continues past as if on an important mission. I look back along the path, expecting to see an exasperated owner traipsing up the cliff path, lead in hand, calling for their escapee – especially as there are sheep roaming in the vicinity. Nothing. Obviously, this little fella has run ahead to explore the headland and is enjoying a brief window of freedom, much like myself. I stare after the dog, watching as it briskly climbs the path; it doesn't look back but simply trots on. Where's the owner? Should I call the dog back and hold on to its collar?

I wait a further five minutes but no one appears. When the little dog is a mere speck on the horizon, I move along too, hoping the little fella doesn't come to any harm.

I dawdle along the path, in contrast to the spritely dog, feeling relaxed and content. My cheeks are ruddy, my lips chapped by the wind and my hair a mass of knots. Unbeknownst to me, as I crest the brow of the coastal path I discover that I've circumnavigated a route, much like my life, which delivers me upon the coastal road leading to the driveway of Harmony Cottage. Home sweet home. It's been years since I went for a stroll, but this might develop into a feasible pastime, made even more enjoyable by the wonderful backdrop.

Nessie

'Nessie, come and have a look at this,' calls Isaac, poking his head around the doorjamb, having taken a breather from his work to survey the cobbled yard. 'It's as funny as hell.'

I hadn't bargained on Isaac turning up on an officially closed day, but obviously great minds think alike.

I place my work into the slack tub, creating a cloud of steam, before putting my tongs down and joining him outside. I've no doubt that whatever he's spotted will be cause for a chuckle.

On reaching the door, Isaac gestures towards my display of goods laid out along our outer wall as a practice run, purely to see how much cobbled space they take up. ('Not much' was the official measurement from Isaac.) It's not something I'm keen on doing for fear of folk pinching my wares, but if it boosts customer footfall and browsing, then I'm inclined to pursue it from Wednesday onwards. A pair of candle holders sold on day one won't sustain my livelihood. I'm hoping that Ned or Jemima will comment, either today or tomorrow, if it's not to their liking.

There amongst the wrought-iron hanging baskets and toasting forks I'd crafted this morning is a visitor: Crispy duck, Jemima's much-loved pet, eyes closed, his head lifted, sunning himself in the low autumn sunshine.

'Content or what?' says Isaac, as we watch the creature ruffle his feathers without opening an eyelid.

'He doesn't care, does he?'

'Nope, why should he? Food and accommodation provided for, plenty of attention when the children spied him yesterday, and his own private jacuzzi when he feels like a swim. What a life!'

'If he sits motionless for too long, there's a chance I might be able to sell him as a garden ornament.'

'He won't be staying for much longer, despite what Jemima hopes,' adds Isaac. 'He might have his downy feathers but come spring when he's matured he'll be off.'

'Do you reckon?'

Isaac nods. 'A duck's gotta do what a duck's gotta do, Nessie.'

'Don't let Jemima catch you saying that; she'll be heartbroken if he nips off in search of a mate.'

Isaac raises his eyebrows. 'She'd best get herself ready then.'

He returns to his work while I stand to admire the sleeping duck a little longer. Yesterday, our feathered friend wasn't bothered by the crowds, he simply waddled back and forth all day pecking at the cobbles and cleaning up any dropped crisps, much to the delight of the children.

I glance around the yard before heading back inside; the stables are empty apart from the odd noise resounding from an open door where another artist is trying to get ahead by creating displays and making goods, like me.

My gaze drifts to the stone archway that denotes the entrance to the gallery; its beautiful masonry dates back to the last century. Such a graceful arch, it appears to float in mid-air and . . . I stop, noticing that the very top section is slightly flattened. It doesn't look like much from this angle but I reckon there was once a decorative piece high above the arch, long gone and probably long forgotten.

I wonder what it was? And what happened to it?

A glimmer of an idea starts to form in my mind.

Chapter Ten

Tuesday 5 October

Verity

My thighs are pleasantly aching from yesterday's jaunt along the coastal cliff. I've no intention of traipsing out twice in two days so I'm happily crocheting a white blanket for my niece's birthday. It's in a beautiful baby-soft, fluffy wool which will keep her warm and feel soothing against her skin. I have no idea how I'm going to jazz it up to make it suitable for a six year old, but something will come to mind; it always does.

A day at home, snug and warm, has been most welcome after the upheaval of the last week. I've had a brief chat with both my eldest and middle sons; they both assure me that things are going well at home. Though I can't imagine how much can go wrong on day five in a house full of blokes, when there's enough frozen lasagne to feed the five thousand. In fact, I could do with one myself: heat the oven, slam it in on gas mark 4, and serve within the hour – sounds bloody gorgeous alongside a glass of wine.

It's paradise living here; I haven't seen a soul all day. Instead, I've sat here, in a world of my own, my hands busily crocheting, enjoying the views on either side, watching the ponies and sheep, seeing the waves crash upon the rocks and watching the low cloud drift by.

I glance through the lounge window and spot a figure turning into my driveway.

Who's this pushing a bike?

I jump up, wrap my yarn to save it tangling and hasten to open the front door.

'I'm impressed.' I stand in the cottage's doorway waiting to greet Isla.

Her auburn hair is blowing in the breeze as she slowly wheels a bike, complete with a wicker basket and turquoise-blue frame, up the driveway.

'How drunk was I when we discussed this at the party?'

'I'm glad you remember the party, but you weren't drunk during our discussion yesterday. It's taken me ages to dig it out from the back of my mum's shed. I didn't realise we had so much junk,' pants Isla, leaning heavily upon the handlebars.

'And your mother doesn't mind?'

Isla shakes her head vigorously. 'I can't remember the last time she rode it. This basket has probably never carried a single item home from a shopping trip.'

'There are no guarantees that I'll be changing that little fact, but it'll allow me to get to work quicker – and allow me to explore the local area.'

'Is here OK?' asks Isla, leaning the bike against Jutt's drystone wall.

'Is there a chain or lock?'

Isla pulls a face.

'Sorry. I forgot, no crime wave here.'

'Not in relation to bikes, anyway.'

'You sure your mum doesn't want to charge a hire fee?'

'It's a bike!'

I'm convinced. I can see that my mainland traits are beginning to wear thin.

'Shout if there's anything else you need,' says Isla, turning towards Jutt's paddock.

'You're going so soon?'

'I must, Verity. I can see to Jutt while I'm here, feeding him and mucking out, but then I've got numerous bakes to concoct. I'm desperate to bake some gingerbread for a new idea I've had – there's no rest for the wicked. Anyway, I'm sure you're dying to try out your new toy.' She eyes the bike.

'Dying isn't quite the expression I'd use, but I'll give it a go later.'

Nessie

I barely looked up all morning. And, likewise, now the afternoon has arrived, I've continued to work in the same frantic manner. My back is hunched, my hammering arm is aching from overuse, and the delicate glow which usually glistens upon my forehead is anything but feminine. I haven't stopped to fetch coffee, for comfort breaks or even to enjoy a snippet of conversation with Isaac.

I step back to view my project with fresh eyes. I like it very much. It's turning out better than I'd imagined. I woke this morning having dreamt about it and knew I simply needed to make it, whether it is appreciated or not. I know exactly where the inspiration has been gleaned from; funny how the subconscious mind works. I take a few steps to the right to view it from a different angle, before striding around to the other side to observe the sculpture in all its glory. I can't help but smile, which inadvertently turns into a chuckle, before I turn about to see if I've disturbed Isaac; I'm hoping not, but then a second opinion would be most welcome.

Isaac's watching from his workbench whilst threading coloured glass angels with gold thread.

'What do you think?' I ask, stepping aside and freeing his view.

'Three hours ago, I thought *what the hell?* An hour ago, my opinion changed to a definite *mmmm, maybe*, and now, well, I'm thinking Jemima will love it. I presume it's Crispy duck.'

'Got it in one! I spotted the empty plinth above the stone archway and it struck me that, once upon a time, there was probably a weathervane proudly positioned there. I dreamt about it last night, and this morning I simply couldn't ignore the empty space above the archway as I approached.'

'You couldn't ask for a better advert for your talents,' says Isaac, a coy smile dawning.

'Is that wrong of me?'

'Not at all – I'd suggest encasing it in a glass globe, but combining crafts would surely defeat the purpose of a weathervane.'

'I thought I'd donate it; it's only cost me the raw materials and my time . . . if it becomes a talking point, or brings in commissions, it'll have paid for itself.'

'Makes good business sense to me. When are you planning to unveil it?'

'Probably later on, if Ned and Jemima are both free to come and view. Though Lord knows what I'll do if they refuse it . . . suppose I should have run it past them first.'

'What – and spoil the surprise?'

'You've got a point, Isaac.' Though I'm still not sure I've done the right thing.

'Please don't feel obliged but I wanted to show you a piece I've been working on,' I say, as Jemima and Ned stand staring at the draped linen tablecloth I've hastily nabbed from The Orangery. I promised Isaac that I'd return it tomorrow and apologise to Isla for taking it in her absence without asking permission.

Ned is looking cautious, Jemima eager to know more. Isaac is blatantly earwigging as he cleans down his workbench for the day.

'A weathervane!' I announce, whipping off the cloth and

revealing the metre-high sculpture of a waddling duck, beak held high and both wings slightly outstretched upon a base of rippling waves.

Jemima audibly gasps as her hands fly to her mouth.

'Very nice,' says Ned, walking around the weathervane, inspecting it closely.

'Crispy? How beautiful!' exclaims Jemima, looking as if someone might be about to correct her. 'Nessie, that is awesome!'

'Given that the children seemed delighted to see him waddling about the gallery, I thought it'd be a suitable feature for the stable yard.' I keep talking, hoping to enhance the chances of my weathervane gracing the stone archway. 'I'm sure you'll know someone who will assist with its installation.'

From the corner of my eye, I spy Isaac smirking so I attempt to avoid making eye contact by turning my back towards him. He can see straight through my bravado. If he makes me laugh, my chances of success here are surely blown.

'I'm happy to donate it, there's no charge. If a small plaque is installed at the base of the archway acknowledging my efforts, I need nothing more.'

'For sure, it would be an honour to install it. I'm sure it'll become quite a talking point for visitors, adults and children alike,' says Ned, eyeing Jemima for confirmation.

Jemima discreetly wipes her eyes and gives an assuring nod.

'You are a big softy,' soothes Ned, rubbing her forearm for comfort. 'I think it's a great finishing touch and will enhance the entry to the stable yard. We'll make arrangements to have it in place, just as soon as I've checked the plinth is secure.'

'Thank you, Nessie,' whispers Jemima, audibly clearing her throat. 'I love it, I really do.'

'That's all that matters.' And I truly mean it.

Isaac and I stand in solemn silence, statue-like, watching the pair leave the forge to enjoy their Tuesday night. Not a word, not a glance or a glimmer of humour is exchanged for near on a minute, before Isaac breaks the silence.

'You've got the gift of the gab, you have.'

'Moi?' I say, cheekily gesturing to myself.

'Yes, you, Wednesday Smith . . . and you bloody know it!'

'I need the advertising and commissions created by it,' I say, beginning to sweep my area and tidy away my tools.

'Full marks to you for being so forthright and imaginative. Now, let's put wax on the tracks and slide on out of here.'

'What's with you?' I ask, throwing him a quizzical glance on hearing his humorous phrase.

'Nothing, I'm ready for home and a few pints of Guinness out with the guys. And you?'

'Me? Eat, bath and early to bed – that's about all I can manage after a full day of hammering. I'll ache tomorrow, that's for sure.'

Chapter Eleven

Verity

I can't remember the last time I owned a bike, let alone sat on one. I wait until dusk, there'll be no one to witness me making a fool of myself at that time of night.

I grab the handlebars, which are sparkling clean without a speck of rust pimpling the shiny surface, drag the bike away from the drystone wall and walk in a huge circle to face the downward sweep of the driveway.

I can do this. Easy-peasy.

I stand astride the bike frame and wait, though I'm uncertain why I'm waiting. There's no obstacle in my path; no person, no loose sheep or roaming dog to navigate.

I depress the brake levers once or twice, purely to check they aren't jammed, then ease my bottom on to the wide padded seat.

I don't remember any of my old bikes having such an accommodating seat; it feels spacious, rather like a sofa cushion. My previous ones felt like a padded razor blade: incredibly uncomfortable. I bounce up and down in my seated position, causing the bike's suspension to make an encouraging noise.

This feels comfy, possibly too comfy.

I need to stop bouncing. I need to remove one foot from the driveway and place it on the pedal. I remain astride the bike, with both feet planted firmly on the ground.

I'm not as brave as I first thought; maybe courage deteriorates with age too.

I cajole myself into doing something. I should probably be wearing a helmet – but still, I have brakes.

I remember being quite forceful with my lads when it came to learning to ride a bike. They jumped the stabilisers stage; I shouted encouragement from a distance, telling them to pedal like crazy, kidding them that I was holding on to the seat. I wasn't. I was simply trotting behind, somewhere close by, in case they tumbled. They didn't. The tumbles and injuries came a few years later, with the precarious ramps and wheelie tricks practised on the concrete slopes of our local skate park.

Slowly I raise one trainer into position. I can feel the ridged pedal underfoot.

I spot the shiny bell on the handlebars. My index finger can't resist a ding-a-ling as a distraction before raising my right foot. The air is filled with a tinny warning sound.

I ring the tiny bell a second time.

Third.

Fourth time.

You ridiculous woman – get on with it! If my lads could see me dithering about they'd be laughing their sodding heads off. On second thoughts, how comforting would it be to have someone running alongside, just holding on to the rear of the seat. Mmmm, I doubt it.

No bell ringing. No bouncing. Simply lift your right foot and away you go!

I follow my own instructions and release both brake levers.

Whoosh!

The bike swiftly travels along the bumpy driveway. I wobble from side to side, tugging back and forth on the handlebars and navigating a haphazard path between protruding boulders and potholes in the compacted dirt. My blonde hair sweeps back from my face, my body jiggles up and down as if the bike has no suspension. Gone is the comfy-seat feeling of a few moments ago.

I'm going faster and faster. The wicker basket bounces up and down. I don't feel in control. I feel anything but comfy.

In my mind's eye, I can see myself as an out-of-body experience might appear. A bloody hilarious sight. A fully grown woman with more courage than common sense speeding along the driveway on a contraption which she's forgotten has a fully functional braking system.

I whizz past the paddock. Both ponies lift their heads from grazing to stare at me as I fly past.

I pass the paddock of sheep; they continue to chew, unfazed by my comedy antics.

My knuckles turn white as I cling on to the moulded rubber handle grips; comfortingly, they provide useful ridges for each of my grasping fingers.

The scenery zips past my peripheral vision in a blur of technicolour.

Release your hands from the rubber grips and squeeze the brake levers. The brakes! A brake! Any brake! Hit the brakes!

The end of the driveway looms towards me, after which it joins the coastal road. Beyond lie the rugged black rocks and the crashing sea. I'm preparing myself to hit the icy water and take a dunking.

Brake, woman! Use the sodding brakes!

My mouth opens wide to begin a futile scream—

That's when my body is snatched backwards and I'm lifted from the bike's padded seat. In horror, I watch the bike continue to career towards the driveway entrance, wobbling and weaving yet remaining upright, until it eventually crashes into the bottom of the drystone wall, just left of the entrance.

'That was a near miss, if ever I saw one,' says the man, as he stands me upright. 'Sorry to manhandle you, but needs must.' He steps back from me, as if adding distance supports his apology.

I glance from him to the crashed bike and back again. 'I

thought . . . I didn't . . . I just wanted to . . .' Words fail me. I end up pointing towards the end of the driveway.

'Yeah, I saw. The thing about actually riding a bike is that it doesn't follow the proverbial rules about riding a bike,' he says, raking his hand through his brown curls and chewing the inside of his lip. 'You need to use the brakes – they're not simply for decoration.'

He saved me, repeats my brain. Saved me from a potential broken leg, hip fracture, dislocated arm, fractured skull – the list is endless. The cost to my business would be immense, if I were in a plaster cast for six to eight weeks. I might as well pack up and go back home.

I fold forward to catch my breath, my hands on my thighs, puffing like a steam train and shaking my head, trying to relieve myself of the image of being crumpled at the bottom of the driveway. A long-haired dog, with a striking blue merle coat, patiently sits beside the wire fencing, her eyebrows twitching, giving the game away that she isn't actually a statue.

'Magnus Sinclair, by the way. I was tending to my sheep.'

I turn my head sideways to see him gesturing towards the paddock.

'Your sheep?'

'Yep. Mine.'

'And the dog?'

'Yep, Floss's mine too.'

I stand tall, instantly wishing I hadn't, because that's when I recognise him: the farrier.

'We've met before,' I say, knowing he probably won't need reminding.

'We certainly have. Isla mentioned that you're open for business up at the manor.'

'Open for business? Not like that . . . I'm not . . . I sell wool.'

'I know, Isla said.'

A bell rings in my head. 'I thought you were a cousin to Nessie?'

'Distant cousin to her, first cousin to Isla.'

I adopt a questioning expression.

'Yeah, you'll get used to that around these parts; everyone is related to everyone. Well, nearly everyone – there's very little fresh blood to choose from.'

As delicate, petite and feminine as Nessie and Isla are, Magnus is the complete opposite. He's rugged, with a weathered complexion, and could easily have stepped out from the cover of a farmer's weekly magazine, dressed in his no-nonsense woollen sweater, sturdy leather boots, and with his unruly mop of curls.

'I see. So, you're the farrier?'

'No. I'm a sheep farmer. I tend to the hooves of my own flock, but I reckoned horses and ponies weren't too different, so I started tending those too.'

I pause, half expecting him to turn the conversation around to mention my unfortunate incident the other morning. He doesn't.

'Thank you ... I feel quite foolish attempting to ride a bike after thirty years or more.'

'A flat surface would have been a safer bet.'

What a bloody fool!

I take a deep breath, grounding myself in the here and now, before extending a quivering hand towards him. 'I'm Verity ... occupant of Harmony Cottage for the next year.'

'As I said, Magnus ... nice to meet you.' He gently shakes my hand, igniting a tingling sensation that buzzes along my spine and gives me goosebumps.

I look up to find his brown eyes intently watching me. If I didn't know better, I'd say Magnus has witnessed my goosebumps.

'Stay here, I'll retrieve your bike,' he says, striding along the driveway. He picks the bike up by the central frame, as if it weighs nothing, and walks back to me before setting it down lightly on its tyres.

'Much damage?' I ask, staring at the bike, harmless now in its static upright position.

'A slight buckle in the front wheel, but nothing much. Come on, I'll walk you back and park this up against the cottage.'

I don't refuse his offer; I'm quite shaken up, though I'm not going to admit it. Floss stares up at me; I'm not certain if it's pity or sheer embarrassment on my behalf that I see reflected in her doleful eyes. Either way, it's expressive. As we walk, a rhythmical scraping noise fills the silence as the front wheel of the bike gently grazes the framework.

'Beautiful dog,' I say, as she trots at his heels. 'I think she passed me yesterday, when I was walking along the coastal path.'

'She would, she takes herself off on jaunts when she chooses.'

'Aren't you worried about her in the midst of the roaming sheep?'

'They're mine too. Floss is simply doing her inspection. It's what shelties do; they're Shetland sheepdogs.'

'Wow! So, the coastal sheep are yours, the sheep here are yours too – anything else?'

He nods ahead.

'Mmmm now, that can't be right because I already know Jutt belongs to Isla.'

'The cottage.'

'Oh, I see, that's also yours – and Isla's mum acts as caretaker.'

'She does. She's actually my aunt but, given our close ages, we don't refer to each other—' He stops talking on spying my quizzical expression. 'It's complicated. We're a big family with lots of offspring, and huge age gaps between siblings. My grandparents are long gone, but they used to live here when I was little.'

'And it's yours now?'

He nods, gesturing to the next cottage a distance away. 'Isla's family were given that one.'

'But you've never lived here?'

'Nope . . .' he pauses, before adding, 'it wasn't meant for me.'

The jigsaw pieces are rapidly fitting together. 'Do you live around here too?'

'Not too far away, but my flocks are spread over a fair distance so I tend to travel between them. Another reason why Floss regularly takes her leave and bolts off for a couple of miles to oversee their welfare.'

'Aren't you frightened she'll get lost or hurt?'

He almost laughs but reigns it in. 'Not this one, she's a fine girl; she knows her way home.'

We arrive at the cottage. Magnus leans the buckled bike against the drystone wall of Jutt's paddock. The Shetland pony pokes his black features over the five-bar gate and receives a welcome rub to his forelocks from Magnus.

'I appreciate your intervention – although, given the speed I was travelling, you might have hurt yourself,' I say.

He shakes his head, sending his curls into a frantic dance. I have no doubt that he'll repeat the story later – giving his family a good laugh at my expense.

'I simply grabbed you as you flew past. But you'll live – so I'll leave you to it. See you around.' He doesn't linger for a response but strides off, Floss at his heel, heading back towards his sheep paddock, where the flock impatiently wait at the fence.

I stare at his back as he retreats. His broad shoulders roll from side to side with each lengthy stride until he reaches the wire fence, grasps a supporting wooden stake and swiftly vaults over into the paddock, followed by Floss who lies down in the grass.

It's nifty actions such as Magnus's that separate the locals from us mainland folk.

Chapter Twelve

Wednesday 6 October

Isla

'Hello, I didn't expect to see you here!'

I look up to greet a new customer with a welcome smile. It has been a very busy, yet pleasant morning so far. His blond boy-band looks haven't changed in six months, though the tattoo peeking out from beneath his crew neck is new since we dated.

'Lachlan. Nice to see you,' I fib, wishing my ex-boyfriend hadn't chosen to enter The Orangery for a beverage. I'm not convinced the gallery is a location he'd be interested in.

'Are you working here?' he asks, looking me up and down a little too closely.

'Err, yep! Who in their right mind would be standing behind this counter if they didn't work here?' I say, tonging a batch of gingerbread into a display basket.

'Any chance of a freebie then? I won't tell your boss,' jests Lachlan, looking over his shoulder towards Pippa, a waitress busily wiping tables, her blonde ponytail swinging as she works.

'I don't think so.'

'Will she dock your pay if she finds out?'

'Nope. I'm the manager here – Pippa's actually the boss's cousin – but still, I wouldn't dream of bending the rules.'

'Pull the other one, it's got bells on! That lass is way older than you.' I watch as Lachlan laughs.

His reaction of disbelief highlights his cruel manner, which had so concerned my mum whilst I was dating him.

I cried for three weeks solid when he dumped me. My mum couldn't get me to eat, sleep or leave my bedroom. I messed up on two college assignments and had to retake an exam to gain the correct grade predicted by my lecturers, all because of this fella. Staring at his gawping mouth reminds me of the gaping hole I thought was left in my life at that time. Boy, if only I could have predicted this moment, I'd have been up, dressed and out with friends within the time it took him to pay me back the hundred quid I'd lent him. After several times of asking, of course.

'Are you serious? You're running this place?'

'Yep, so what can I get you? You can find the drinks prices on the main menu board,' I say, gesturing towards the large blackboard displaying my neat chalk handwriting.

'I suppose I'll have a flat white and . . .' He glances along the line of cake cloches and points to the basket of gingerbread. 'What are those?'

'Gingerbread Crispy ducks for the children – we've got a pet duck here at the gallery.' I'm quite proud of my little duck creations, complete with brown icing and a yellow beak.

'And that?' he asks, pointing somewhat like a child.

'Carrot cake.'

'That?'

'Lemon drizzle.' I anticipate he's stalling, so I name each cake. 'Shetland bannocks, teacakes and choux buns.'

'Just coffee, please.'

'That'll be one ninety, please.' I press the till screen and hold my palm out.

Lachlan eyes my gesture, pauses and only then reaches into his jeans pocket to produce two gold coins.

'Thank you.' I quickly hand him the change and begin

preparing his drink. I'm glad to be able to move away from his presence; I don't wish to chit-chat with a guy who, I now realise, treated me quite badly in our eleven months together. It's not sour grapes, I can assure you. More a growth spurt in my maturity, plus the removal of my rose-tinted glasses. I probably haven't ever made a flat white as fast as I make his. I'm eager to move on to the next customer, Old Niven, a smiley elderly gent who I'm distantly related to on my mum's side.

Lachlan hesitates for a fraction of a second, clutching his coffee mug and staring at me.

'You'll find sugar and wooden stirrers on the side cabinet.' I give a final smile and turn to welcome my returning customer.

'Isla. Can we talk?'

'Sorry,' I mouth towards Niven, who was about to give his order. I know he's partial to a warmed bannock, with a smidgen of butter, and a pot of tea. I turn to answer my ex. 'Lachlan, given the time that has passed, and the lack of contact or interest between us, I'd rather not, thanks.' Again, I attempt to turn my attention to my new customer.

Lachlan butts in. 'Look, I'm *sorry*. Is that what you want to hear?'

'I think she wants to hear my order, young man,' says Niven, much to my delight.

Don't you just love the old crumblies? They rarely mix their words but say it how it is.

Lachlan's expression drops at being verbally wounded by a stranger belonging to his granddad's generation. Niven raises his greying eyebrows at me as Lachlan shuffles along sideways, freeing up the main spot at the counter.

'A bannock, please – could I have it warmed through, with a noggin of butter? – and a pot of tea.'

I smile with satisfaction; I'm loving that some customers might establish themselves as my 'regulars'. Lachlan continues to stand and wait whilst I begin creating the order, much to Niven's amusement.

'Do you need further assistance, young man?' he asks my ex. 'I'll happily walk you to a table if you need me to.'

'Nah! I'm good, thanks,' says Lachlan, striding off towards the couches.

Frustrated, he plonks himself down on one that is facing the counter. I gather he intends to stage a one-man sit-in and watch me for a little while longer.

Verity

On entering The Orangery, I hastily drag Isla aside as she unloads the clean crockery on to the counter's shelving unit.

'Who is Magnus?' I demand, clutching her arm, refusing to let go of her sleeve.

Isla stares annoyingly at me without answering, her brow knitted into a deep frown.

'Magnus?' I repeat, shaking her sleeve as if reviving her.

'My older cousin. My mum and his dad are siblings, though my mum isn't far off his age. He inherited Harmony Cottage; that's who my mum helps out. Why?'

Confirmation. He wasn't lying.

I stare at her.

'Oh, dear God, no!' Isla exclaims.

'What do you mean "oh, dear God, no"?'

'You've got that strange, almost weird, dreamy expression . . . and your scary voice is suggesting to me that you and he have—'

'Oi, stop! I only asked a bloody question,' I say, releasing her sleeve, which she quickly straightens.

'But the way you were asking . . . it seems a bit . . . intense.'

'Behave yourself.' I stare at Isla, silently asking a million questions but voicing none.

I nip back through to the customer side of her counter and busy myself browsing the cake display. Isla is on my coat-tails, watching my every move.

'Anything else you wish to know? Or was it just the one question you needed answering?'

'Can I have two of these warmed, with a spot of butter?' I gesture at the pile of bannocks beneath their glass cloche. I'm trying to play this ultra-cool – or as cool as you can with a savvy teenager. 'And a latte.' I blush as her gaze meets mine. Sodding hell, the little minx is now playing with me.

'Bloody hell, he saves you from one disaster . . . and look at you, blushing like a nun passing the Ann Summers' window display.' Isla laughs aloud, as she readies my order.

So she already knows about the biking incident. Boy, news certainly travels fast around here – faster than me on a downward slope forgetting I have brakes! I busy my hands scrabbling for change in my purse.

Isla continues to talk. 'He's forty-five. A sheep farmer, though he's pretty handy at turning his skills to anything practical. He lives way off the coastal path in a bloody huge farmhouse and looks after his elderly parents, who used to tend the sheep before he did. He's happy to mend our leaky roof tiles, blocked drains or sort out car troubles. My mum keeps saying to us, "You two girls need to find yourselves a Magnus if you're going to be happy in life," though he doesn't know, as she says that part behind his back.'

Interesting. All-round good guy, by the sounds of it.

'And he's single – if you were wondering. Though I'm guessing you probably weren't thinking that, either.'

'No. I wasn't thinking that,' I lie.

'Sorry to have mentioned it then,' adds Isla, making no effort to take my handful of change.

The silence lingers.

'Has he ever been married?' I ask, as nonchalantly as I can muster, though my acting skills will never win me an Oscar.

'Nope. A near miss once or twice, when I was very little. I got all excited about the prospect of being a bridesmaid, only for my dreams of a hooped skirt and a tartan sash to be cruelly dashed. Gutted, I was.'

I can't help but smile.

'Well, well, well. Maybe there's time yet for a bridesmaid's dress!' teases Isla, flashing me the same wry smile as Magnus. And there's the family resemblance.

'Don't you "well, well, well" me,' I say indignantly, trying to claw back the upper hand. 'I've every reason to ask, given his actions yesterday.'

'And you feel the need to see him again to repeat your "thank you, Magnus"?' jibes Isla.

'Manners cost nothing.'

'I bet they don't. Look, all I'll say is what my mum says, time and time again: "It'll take a special one to turn our Magnus's head." So good luck,' says Isla, her voice altering to a serious, more mature tone.

'Your mum certainly has a lot of sayings when it comes to Magnus,' I quip, grabbing the proffered paper bag.

I spread out the crocheted blanket on the counter to admire my handiwork. Admittedly, I'm impressed. It took a little longer than I'd anticipated, as I'd made up the pattern. Amelia will be delighted with her gift, though I'll still be labelled the world's worst aunty, daughter and mother by my twin sister.

It's a simple square of intricate crocheting, embellished with a crocheted triangle as an ear, a circular black button as a beady eye, and a simple stitched kiss in rose pink as its nose. I was flummoxed by what to do for the sheep's tail, so after several – somewhat inappropriate – observations of their heavily soiled and claggy rear ends at the driveway paddock, early this morning, I've added a chunky but stubby white plait on the opposite side to the cute nose.

I giggle, picturing Amelia's delight. I can readily imagine my sister's renewed annoyance that my birthday offering will be a belated gift, given my remote location. I've searched online to discover that the postal service does very well; covering the distance will require just one or two additional days. I'd wrongly assumed that snail mail from this northerly longitude and latitude would take at least a month.

The blanket gift doesn't look much on its own, despite the hours of effort involved. I was such a practical little girl when I was growing up, always busy doing corking with a cotton reel or Fuzzy-Felt designs, engrossed for hours on end. I dash to my knitting needle selection as an idea dawns. Maybe I could make Amelia a beginner's knitting kit? Some chunky needles, a ball of colourful thick wool and an iron-on motif (though I recommend stitching it for a better finish, if customers ask). I am thrilled with my ingenious idea. I could make up similar kits for children visiting The Yarn Barn – everything you need to make a child's scarf, a headband or a mobile phone case.

I carefully fold the blanket, placing the beginner's knitting kit in the middle. I've already purchased beautiful paper decorated with dancing unicorns from the card-making lady a few stables along. Thankfully, she also sells Sellotape, brown wrapping paper and string, so it'll be ready for posting tonight.

'Morning,' calls Nessie, strolling in as I carefully fold the unicorn paper. Her hair is a vibrant blue, a change from the pink she was sporting at the weekend.

'I like the hair,' I say, gesturing to my own. 'It suits you.'

'I fancied a change. I've had shocking pink for a while now – I did it on a whim, as always. Anything nice?' She points to the folded gift paper encasing the blanket.

'A birthday gift for my niece,' I say, feeling obliged to show her my handiwork, rather than attempt to explain. 'I made it up as I went along really. Though the grazing sheep beside the cottage inspired the stubby tail.'

'Without the layer of shite, I see,' jests Nessie, admiring the gift. 'It's lovely. A new idea for a collection of gifts, or a one-off?'

I automatically fold the blanket whilst pondering her question.

'There's no reason why not. It was hardly difficult to make – and now I've made it once, a second one will whiz from my crocheting hook.'

'You could expand the range to include pink piglets with a curly tail – a wool-covered pipe cleaner would do – or rabbits with a pompom tail – those would probably be the easiest.'

'Or Shetland ponies?' I add, suddenly imagining Jutt as a soft crocheted blanket, complete with mane and bushy tail.

'A family of three sheep: large, medium and tiny lambkin?' suggests Nessie, her imagination firing as creatively as mine.

'How weird is that? One idea always leads to another. Thank you, Nessie – I owe you one.'

'No worries, it's how my mind works, I view everything on a creative level.'

'I thought earlier about children's knitting kits for total beginners. A couple of quid, pocket-money prices, is what I mean.'

'Again, perfect for little ones.'

'You don't think I'll be sued if a child harpoons their sibling with a needle, do you?'

'Probably, in this blame-game culture we live in – just put a disclaimer inside each pack, and mention it when selling. It might not be legally watertight but it should discourage your multimillion-pound law suit,' says Nessie, shaking her head at the mere thought. 'It's looking good in here, though, you've really got it organised. I can't knit for toffee ... but even so.'

Unbelievable, there's that line again – though I don't remark on it, as I'd fail miserably as a blacksmith.

'It's coming together nicely. Those display shelves are great because I can pack each section with a different ply, colour or brand ... but I'd like a free-standing display unit too. Ideally, something visually appealing that allows customers easy access. Buying wool is often a tactile purchase, customers are drawn to touching the yarn, stroking it, to feel its texture, durability ... I can't find exactly the right words to explain it ... but basically the truth is the yarn sells itself once it's been touched.'

'It sounds almost like it casts a spell.'

'Yes, almost. That's how I feel when I'm buying yarn. I can't wait to start knitting with it, knowing I'll capture and retain that wonderful feel whilst I'm making the garment. For me, it's missing that tactile sensation of beautiful wool, once the item is complete, which forces me to return, time after time, for another purchase and another project.'

'How tall are you thinking?'

'Sorry?' I'm taken aback by her question.

'The display rack – how tall?' Nessie eyes me suspiciously, waiting for me to catch on.

For a split second there, I thought she was on about men.

'About so high.' I indicate a fraction above my head.

A sparkle appears in Nessie's eyes as she takes in my gestures.

Chapter Thirteen

Nessie

'What are you making?' asks Isaac, as I step back from my work, scrutinising the last two hours of hammering.

'A display rack for Verity. She wants something unique but functional on which she can stack her wool. To be fair, I'm not one hundred per cent sure I've hit the brief.' I walk around the metal cone structure, not convinced by my efforts. 'I should probably have made a small prototype first.'

'Do you think?' Isaac puts aside the delicate wind chime he's been crafting and wipes his hands down his leather apron.

'I thought it would come together but it's proving difficult to imagine the finished design. Can you envisage balls of wool stuck on these prongs?'

'Mmmm, not really – but I'm hardly an expert on such things,' says Isaac, joining me to stand and stare at my new project. 'I didn't expect that blue hair would suit anyone, but you proved me wrong on that score this morning – so, who knows?'

'Thanks, I fancied a colour change. But this . . . this looks like a metal ribcage gone wrong,' I moan, returning my hammer to the workbench, and wiping my brow. I appreciate his comment but it lacks the whole-hearted conviction I need to hear. 'It doesn't bode well if I can't create something of use for a neighbouring artist.'

'It's hardly a disaster – just unfinished, from where I stand.'

What the hell would Isaac know? I never pass comments about his glassware.

'I did a quick sketch and it made sense, yet now it looks hideous,' I say, as Isaac scowls. 'Don't you think?'

'As I said, it looks unfinished. If you plough on with it, you might change your mind once it's complete. I assume these prongs fit somewhere?' he asks, pointing at the pile of pins lined along my workbench.

'They're supposed to be secured on each of the ribs at a slight angle, so Verity can display her balls of wool, one on each spike. The whole display will rotate, making it easy for her customers to browse her supplies. It seemed easy, but now it looks tacky.'

'It might be an idea to borrow some balls of wool – just to see what it looks like partly furnished,' Isaac suggests, trying to be helpful.

'Surely I shouldn't need to do that? Accurate measurements and metal struts should have been enough for me to create a functioning display unit –' I'm feeling exhausted now and close to tears – 'but nope . . . I haven't succeeded. Phuh!' I exclaim, in disgust.

'I think you need a boost, Nessie. Hold the fort while I go and grab you a strong coffee.'

'Thanks, but I'll need cake too.'

'Cake too,' repeats Isaac, leaving me to stare some more at my hideous creation.

It's just before closing when I nip back to The Yarn Barn.

'I've finished your display rack – just wondered if you'd decided where you want it, so I can deliver.'

'That was quick. I wasn't expecting you to drop everything else to accommodate my needs,' says Verity, jumping up from her knitting armchair.

'Mmmm, I needed a break from hammering toasting forks and horseshoes, to be honest. I bet I could make them in my sleep now. Isaac timed me the other day to see how quickly I could make one. Just under five minutes, if you were wondering. Come on, let's haul this display rack inside for you.'

When we reach the stable door, Verity seems gobsmacked by the wrought-iron creation standing on the cobbles. It's shaped like a giant ice-cream cone, but upended, with tiny spiralled prongs adorning the length of elegant vertical struts.

It takes a few minutes to drag it inside The Yarn Barn, positioning it centrally, taking pride of place, before we begin to fill each spike. With each ball of yarn added it comes alive in size and shape as the wool provides a soft curvy shape against the harsh black metal.

'I struggled with this earlier, it simply wouldn't behave itself when I was trying to bring my vision to life – so much so, poor Isaac bought me three cake slices to accompany my coffee.'

'Bless him for trying. Never mind, they'll keep overnight in the paper bags.'

'Are you joking! I scoffed the lot. I had such a sugar rush that this display rack was finished in no time – and now I'm actually rather pleased.'

'It looks like a Christmas tree!' exclaims Verity, as I step back to admire it.

'I hadn't viewed it as one, but yeah, pretty much the same shape and height. A wool tree, instead.'

'That's as pretty as a picture!' exclaims Verity, her grin widening by the second. 'Nessie, that is wonderful – you're so talented.' It even revolves when gently pushed to allow the customers to look at the whole range before deciding. 'How much do I owe you?'

I wave a hand, batting away her remark.

'No, seriously. I must pay. You've forked out for metal, then there's the time and attention you've paid to it.'

'Nothing, honestly. Just put up a sign clearly stating that Wednesday Smith created the display rack. I'm happy with that as payment. It'll show customers what can be achieved with a little thought and design. But thanks for the offer, that means a lot, Verity.'

'Are you sure, Nessie? So-called "love jobs" or "mate's rates" don't pay the mortgage, you know?' she says, looking at me dubiously, half expecting a change of mind.

'Believe me, I'm sure.'

I'm buoyed by her enthusiastic reaction, but I still can't quite silence the insistent voice that's been nagging away at me all day. Before I leave, I ask her the question that's been troubling me.

'Are you disappointed that sales have been slightly ...?' My sentence fades.

It's only the first week; surely we can't expect too much.

Chapter Fourteen

Verity

The rain is lashing against the patio window, a comforting sound when you're warm and dry inside. I sit in my winceyette tartan PJs, with a hideous green clay mask smeared over my face in an attempt to deep clean my dull complexion. It's not a beauty regime I adhere to but at just £1.75 from the supermarket, if it can reverse the ageing process it'll be worth it. The fifteen minutes' drying time was up thirty minutes ago, but I've decided to go for broke. The act of not smiling or frowning is unnatural to me. Dry clumps keep falling off on to my crocheting, reminding me that my face is never resting for long. It seems my expression always has something to convey, even when I'm alone. I grab my measuring tape to check the length of my crocheting, noting that I'm after a true square if I'm to mimic Amelia's original sheep blanket. It's worth a try, displaying one in the barn; if it sells, then all well and good. Nessie's creative mind has got me thinking about a whole range of farmyard animals.

I have no excuses as to why I haven't taken care of myself over the years. I might have had children to look after, but a cheap face mask whilst soaking in the bath, and an active lifestyle with a balanced diet of fresh fruit and veg, would have made all the difference. Instead, I've opted for comfort food, with a dollop of ketchup, and a quick scrub with Lux soap.

I hear my iPad make a ringing sound. Is it seven o'clock

already? I've lost an hour somewhere whilst crocheting the blanket.

I quickly fold my work away, tap the screen and accept the FaceTime call.

I'm greeted by a family portrait of three young men. I pinch myself, knowing they belong to me. Each face looks slightly different, with a trendy haircut and facial stubble, but there's a definite family resemblance around the nose and eyes. Anyone can spot they are brothers, alike yet different, which pleases me.

'Hi, fellas, how are you?' I say, talking at the screen but unsure where the actual camera is located. I can't imagine I look great, but I know my lads love me anyway.

'Hi, Mum, how are you?' asks Jack, taking the lead. 'Are you enjoying some "me time"?' he says, winking at me.

I'm a little disconcerted by his question. 'I'm good, Jack. How's the cooking going?'

'Not bad—' Harvey begins.

'If only someone knew how to set the cooking timer properly,' interrupts Tom, giving Harvey a hard stare.

'Harvey, are you not setting the countdown properly?'

'Something like that, Mum. It's hardly a crime, is it? They might complain but they ate the lot, so that tells you all you need to know.'

'My cooking mantra has always been, "When it's brown it's done, when it's black it's buggered!" A bit of burnt never did us much harm, did it?' I jest, still admiring how good-looking my lads appear on screen. Strong, healthy, vibrant, with decent manners and good teeth. I might not have been the best mum, never honed my skills as a domestic goddess, but the genes were pretty robust somewhere along the line. I selfishly refuse to acknowledge George's contribution.

'Burnt to a crisp would be a vast improvement, Mum. His offering was charred beyond recognition,' says Tom, squeezing his body into the frame on the bottom edge. 'We had to snap the corner bits off!'

'Snap them off – was it that bad?'

'Mum, don't ask. Harvey has failed to provide us with a decent meal on either of his duty days,' says Jack, elbowing Harvey in jest.

'I hope you made him wash up as a consequence!' I retort, pulling Harvey's leg.

'The actual baking tray is still soaking in soapy water, it was that badly burnt!' adds Tom, receiving a playful knuckle rub on his crown from a heavy-handed Harvey.

I want to cry. I couldn't be prouder. I could burst with pride that my boys are pulling together and looking after one another. To think that after a year's worth of detailed planning, I'd upped and left them, with just a sodding letter on the kitchen table – yet look at them now. If I'd have known they'd cope this well, I could have openly discussed my plans, without acting like a selfish mare. Though could my boys have kept my secret from Avril? Highly unlikely.

'Have you heard from Nan and Granddad?' I ask.

'Nan calls every morning at half six. Why do old people wake up so damned early?' complains Tom.

'Though Granddad is happy for us to call back an hour later after we've had showers and stuff,' adds Jack. 'Nan always asks if we're all up and dressed – we've learnt to lie to her each morning.'

'Aunty Avril keeps mentioning cousin Amelia's birthday ... do we need to get something and wrap it for her?' asks Tom, suddenly baffled at the prospect of buying a gift.

'Nope. I've made her a cute blanket, though your Aunty Avril will be miffed that it'll arrive late. I tried calling them a couple of times but they don't answer the phone. Are Nan and Granddad keeping well?'

'Yeah, they've started to go for a walk some afternoons – that's probably why they've missed your calls. Granddad's fine. Nan's still miffed with you, but I think that's Aunty Avril still stoking the fires. Nan keeps threatening to come round to do some dusting, but we told her we'd already done it,' says Harvey. 'Oh shit, I wasn't supposed to tell you that.'

'I don't care, Harvey. Seriously, leave the dusting till I get home, if necessary!'

'And you, what have you been up to?' asks Jack.

I spend ten minutes outlining the details of Harmony Cottage; I do a quick tour around the lounge by lifting and revolving the iPad screen. I give them a rundown about the gallery and how my little business is coming along. I feel quite at ease explaining to my lads what I've been doing. Though I fail to mention the bike disaster. And Magnus.

'I don't want any girlfriends staying the night – you know my house rules,' I say, feeling like a fuddy-duddy in this day and age. 'Unless I need to repeat the house rules, purely to clarify?'

'No, thanks, Mum,' says Jack, shaking his head, glancing at each brother. 'I believe you've written them on the fridge door.'

'We don't need a repeat demo with the courgette and a pack of three condoms, either,' adds Harvey, clearly wincing at the memory.

'Are you sure?' Not my finest hour as a parent but obviously not forgotten.

No one answers me. I assume there's nothing to report, or they've settled the issue of girlfriends sleeping over, prior to calling me. I've got nothing against Jack or Harvey's girls, both are lovely young women, but I know what I want for my lads; what I didn't have. I want them to have time to mature, become the men they wish to be, before they make decisions about their futures and family planning. Not that I haven't given them enough talks about the birds and the bees, but I also don't wish to give my neighbours anything more to gossip about. Damage limitation is probably the name of the game in my unexpected absence.

'Well, if there's nothing more, I'll love and leave you,' I say, blowing kisses to the screen.

'Love you, Mum,' calls Tom, waving like a toddler.

'Bye, call me if you need me,' I continue, not wanting to tap the screen to end the call.

'We will,' says Jack, casually nodding, obviously too old to wave.

'Sure,' mutters Harvey, always the quietest of the three.

Within seconds the screen is blank and my lads are gone.

Instantly, I burst into tears, for no apparent reason other than I've seen my three handsome sons: fit, healthy and coping without me.

I wander into the bathroom to grab some toilet roll and spy my dried, cracked facemask in the mirror. You daft mare! What the hell do I look like? Now I understand Jack's quip about "me time". He must have thought I'd been treating myself to a pampering spa evening at home – I wish!

I quickly scrub my skin and am left with a face that is blotchy and red – not the look I was aiming for at all.

Isla

It's quarter to eleven, I'm propped up in bed, reading a textbook for my business course, by the mellow light of my bedside lamp. I've said goodnight to my mum and sister who are watching TV downstairs, but still I feel hard done by, having to study after a full day at work. Today's routine meant I was up at six, washed, dressed and out to feed Jutt before working a long shift at the café. At the end of a busy day, I was collected by my mum, made dinner, ate dinner and cleaned the kitchen, visited Jutt, before showering and now studying! I bet neither of my best buddies, Fiona or Kenzie, are in bed reading how to balance a profit and loss sheet!

It's only been two weeks since I saw my friends, but it feels like eons. This is probably the longest we've gone without actually speaking; I don't count text messages – they're not proper conversations. I bet they've been out enjoying themselves; they'll have downed a couple of cocktails before nabbing a taxi back home and crowding into Fiona's mum's kitchen to make endless rounds of toast and yap until her dad declares, 'Enough, it's late.' Then Kenzie will nip three doors up the street to her own home where she'll sneak in, attempting to fool her mum she arrived home an hour ago.

I giggle at the image. How funny that we're all nineteen, yet they're out doing that and I'm doing ... I glance at the page of text to remind myself: 'depreciation of assets' and where to include it on the accounts sheet.

Tonight, studying feels so unfair. I'm tired and frustrated that more hours of my day are dedicated to work than play; no one said being an adult would be like this. I imagined it would be all fun and games whilst having money to do as I pleased. Instead, I'm curled up in bed with an accountancy book; Fiona and Kenzie would laugh their socks off if they could see me now. In fact, even Dottie would give a chuckle or two, seeing me sitting here like this.

I close the textbook in a huff, hearing the bulky weight of the pages slap together, and push aside my notebook and pencil.

If I hurry, I could shower, dress, slap on a bit of lippy and dash round to Fiona's place, tapping on the kitchen window in time for the first round of toast and Marmite. I should, it would make a welcome change. I push the textbook aside and flip the duvet back, swinging my legs over the edge of the bed. I could. All work and no play makes Isla a dull girl. I could surprise them and stay out until the early hours, then nip home and still catch a few hours' sleep before my alarm sounds. I could. I should. I would feel like the old me in no time. A good catch-up with my girls. A few laughs would do me the world of good.

You mustn't. A voice of reason kicks in.

I'd be tired and grumpy tomorrow, making it harder to complete my day, which would be tough. The reality of being a responsible adult swiftly returns. I hesitate for a second, before swinging my legs back into bed and smoothing the duvet down, as if locking myself in for the night. A big sigh escapes me as I pick up my textbook and turn to the correct page.

I look around the only bedroom I've ever known; its layout, familiar since childhood, is an eclectic arrangement of shelving units, an old wardrobe and faded wallpaper with a matching lampshade. It's comforting to be cocooned in my own little space, but there's more to the world than I've experienced so far. Anything is possible – as Jemima, my boss at The Orangery, proves each day.

I need to accept my responsibilities and study – otherwise someone else will gladly exchange places with me. I did promise at my interview that I was prepared to do whatever was required to be the best that I can be.

'Thanks, Granny,' I mutter aloud, grateful for that ever-present voice of reason.

Chapter Fifteen

Thursday 7 October

Verity

My twin sister, Avril, slathers her body in lotion after every shower, but it's never been my usual routine. It's not that I can't be bothered but when you're a busy mum, dashing from bed to bathroom to breakfast, lingering about in a state of nakedness while your moisturiser dries is not a feasible start to the morning. Never mind freeing up the bathroom to avoid teenage excuses for forgetting to use hot water and soap, made worse by their growing obsession with Lynx Africa and Old Spice. With three lively boys, my day needed to hit the floor running: Coco Pops, fruit juice and coffee before the arguments begin over who's nabbed whose socks. It didn't matter how much they'd grown, each day started with an unruly ruckus. But now, here in Shetland, with an entire cottage to myself and a daily reminder scrawled across the bathroom's vanity mirror, I can please myself. So slather I do.

I perch on the closed toilet lid and, for the first time since my first pregnancy, apply handfuls of fortified body cream to my stomach and thighs. As my hands gently rotate, I note the silvery stretchmarks spreading across my stomach, breasts and upper thighs, an amalgamation of three pregnancies. My 'life lines', as I like to call them.

Our Avril hasn't a single mark on her taut torso – or so she says.

I used to cream my growing stomach every day, yet still the tiny threads of silver decorated my skin post birth. I suppose they're a badge of honour; many women would wish to have such reminders of life. Though I never wore a bikini after having Jack, as I thought the marks were unsightly. I shouldn't have cared so much what others thought – who else, other than George, came close enough to see them anyway!

Body cream seemed unimportant while I was carrying Harvey, so I didn't bother. George and I had more important things to worry about whilst I was carrying our Tom.

The shape of my body has changed; there's a definite softness and riper curves, where once it was taut and defined. I might not be the size eight that I once was, but the stretchmarks are the only imperfections I have. They're probably the reason why this beauty routine ceased after baby one; it proved to be a waste of both time and cream for me.

I wait for ten minutes as my skin drinks in the moisture, appearing rosy and rejuvenated – it was obviously quite depleted and wanted attention beforehand. This is why I've never been one for beauty treatments. I can't justify sitting around doing nothing for any section of my day – unlike Avril.

I remember how Avril used to spend an hour a day practising scales on the piano – even on Christmas morning or New Year's Day. I kid you not! When it takes you until four in the morning to get three overexcited boys to sleep on Christmas Eve, the last thing you need is to be woken up at seven o'clock by your sodding sister and her piano scales. I could have killed her that year.

I sit and stare at the back of the closed bathroom door – this signifies me. I'm living alone, yet still I lock the bathroom door. Avril would never lock her bathroom door. She can't; my sister's lavatory hasn't a lock. Which is why, whenever I'm visiting hers, I regularly announce, 'I'm just nipping upstairs.' I bet she'd feel differently if she'd had three boisterous lads charging about the house every hour of the day. Amelia's so delicate and dainty; life must be so different raising a girl.

I chuckle at my own desire for conformity.

A locked bathroom door. Is that self-respect or a level of prudishness?

Am I a prude? I don't class myself as such. I can laugh at a smutty joke, deliver a swift innuendo and watch a Demi Moore film without flinching at her on-screen nudity.

So why am I sitting here?

I could go and put the kettle on.

Straighten the duvet on my bed.

Put a couple of slices of bread in the toaster while I wait ... sitting here waiting is ridiculous.

I stand, unlock the door and stride out into the hallway.

It feels weird.

I'm naked and walking around the cottage.

As I pass the hallway window, I spy Jutt the Shetland pony happily chomping away at his hay bale. The sky is a brilliant blue, the pony takes no notice of the fleeting sight of my wobbly flesh, so I continue to the kitchen and plop two pieces of white bread into the toaster before flicking the switch on the kettle.

Once the tea is made and the toast buttered, there seems little point grabbing my robe so I stand before the sink and eat my breakfast.

There's a bubble of laughter, which keeps lifting towards my throat, as I stand here eating in the buff. The crumbs are falling everywhere and sticking to my moisturised chest – but who cares? The old me would be fully dressed, eating her breakfast in a respectful manner for a workday morning.

I keep wanting to giggle.

I didn't think I was a prude, but maybe ... I possibly am. I'm not ashamed of my body. It has served me well in carrying my tiny babies and staying healthy, allowing me to work and provide for them, but this is so alien to me. I'm used to covering up, staying clothed, and I've definitely not shared my body with another for a long time.

A *very* long time.

Too long to even remember how long ago.

They've probably changed all the rules about sex without informing me. Those days of passion and frivolity are long gone, so it really doesn't concern me nowadays who puts what where – or how they even manage it.

George left when Tom was three months old, so a good seventeen years ago. Blimey! As I said, a long, long time.

I finish my toast, put my plate in the sink and brush away the stray crumbs as something outside flashes past the kitchen window, just at the edge of my vision.

I freeze.

I cautiously tiptoe towards the smaller kitchen window, trying to duck down below the countertop whilst craning my neck to peer out – all without showing myself.

There's no one coming up the driveway, and no one in either the pony or sheep paddock – phew!

A strong *rat-a-tat-tat* sounds on the wooden front door, making me jump. I sink to my haunches with no intention of answering.

I'm stuck. Curled in a ball, naked in my kitchen. I can't stand for fear of being seen through various windows. I can't enter the lounge or hallway for the exact same reason. I am visible from every direction. Why didn't I think to draw the curtains?

Worse still, if they're a local and know the entry code for the front door; I pray that they aren't too concerned about my well-being, fearing an emergency.

The knock sounds again, this time stronger and for longer.

'Go away, go away!' I whisper, eyeing the wall clock: eight o'clock. I need to dress and walk to the gallery before opening time.

What has my life come to?

I daren't poke my nose around the edge of the counter in case my visitor is looking through the large kitchen window that faces the front entrance. I've been crouched down on the cold tiles for two minutes, so I can't show myself now, I'd look a right fool.

I hear the sound of boots on the driveway, passing the smaller window above my head. Is the visitor peering in? Or departing? I simply daren't look.

I watch the second hand of the wall clock complete five laps before I lift my head to see if the coast is clear, vowing I'll never again leave the curtains open wide overnight.

Isla

It's just before nine o'clock as I climb the grand staircase of the manor, grateful that Dottie is showing me the way. I didn't mention how relieved I was when I spied her crossing the gallery's yard, arriving for today's dusting duties. Her blue eyes sparkled when I called her name. As I arrived for work, Mungo was scrubbing and hosing down the cobbles to remove the unsightly remnants of Crispy duck's droppings, a daily routine before customers arrive, but I hadn't wished to disturb him; you can never predict his mood.

'Thank you for accompanying me, Dottie. I'd have got lost in the corridors,' I say, referring to the rabbit warren leading from the age-old kitchen.

It seems strange that my interview bakes, which secured me the position in charge of The Orangery, were created in that kitchen, and yet I've rarely stepped through the adjoining interior door since we opened the refurbished café. This spacious old kitchen might come in useful one day; it now seems ancient to me, having got used to working amongst the stainless-steel mod cons.

'No worries. There isn't a problem, is there?'

'No, I'm having my first morning meeting with Ned and Jemima as part of our newly established routine. I've brought along the sales figures and the "waste book" for their inspection,' I explain, hugging the books to my chest as we continue to climb the staircase.

I dislike the gilt-framed portraits staring down at me, possibly passing judgement on my appearance. Huge tapestries hang from the walls; swathes of emerald-and-navy Black Watch tartan – the Campbell family's official tartan, I believe – drape the other walls as we make our way up to the third floor. It's beautiful and stately – don't imagine for one moment it isn't – but boy, it's an old residence. Much older than I remember from my interview, though I never climbed the staircase on that day. I'd have remembered my shoes sinking into such plush carpet.

I assume this is a little payback for the other day; I accidently on purpose forgot to charge Dottie for a tiny slice of cake. I can't imagine Ned would mind. I could never have charged my granny – her pension was never huge, and every penny counted. If Dottie needs to work at her age, charging her is out of the question. I'd simply pop it through as an imaginary entry for the 'waste book' – which we've hardly used, given the standard of service we offer. The odd piece of cake allegedly dropped on the floor is only a tiny white lie – but Ned will never know. Unless Dottie dobs me in, that is.

'Good lassie. Ned likes transparency where business is concerned. So tell it as it is, and you won't go far wrong.'

Her words provide some comfort for my jangling nerves. 'I'm a tad early but I'm sure they won't mind, will they?'

Dottie shakes her head. 'Tardiness is a pet hate, Ned likes early. He's crabbit when he's kept waiting.'

I like the third landing when we reach it; there are elaborate skylights overhead providing a great view of the morning sky. I bet when it's tipping down with rain it makes the best sound on the glass, much like The Orangery's glazed roof.

Dottie stops walking and points along the landing to a row of wooden doors. 'It's the door opposite the ceramic jardinière with the aspidistra plant,' she whispers, her little face beaming up at me. 'You'll be OK, I'm sure.'

'Thank you,' I reply, knowing I shouldn't be doubting my ability or my grasp of the figures at this stage in the week. I've been present for every hour of business since we opened, so there's nothing they can ask me that I can't or won't be able to explain. Though I'll choose my words carefully if they question me about Pippa; employee or not, blood is thicker than water.

I stride along the landing to the door indicated by Dottie, giving a strong rap on the wooden panel, then patiently wait until Ned calls, 'Come in!'

I enter in an apologetic manner, as if I wasn't expected, when I clearly was. The office is huge and bright, very modern in design and totally different to the rest of the manor. Jemima and Ned are seated at a long meeting table, with coffee mugs in their hands, both smiling at me.

After exchanging a brief greeting, I settle in a seat a little way from their positions: Ned at the head and Jemima to his right. I place my accounts books squarely before me – all very business-like, as my studies have suggested.

'So how are things going in the café?' asks Ned, eyeing my accounts.

'Very well, we've had a steady flow of customers on the opening days. We've recognised several returning customers too, which is lovely to see.' I expand by explaining the daily sales figures, the portion size and the controls I've implemented, plus show them the lack of entries in our 'waste book'.

'It's all looking very encouraging, Isla – well done!' says

Jemima, a beaming smile adorning her face. 'Can I ask how the waitresses are coping?'

I take a deep breath; I didn't want this question. 'Both ladies have proved very capable in the role, their customer service seems spot-on, and they both complete the rota of tasks each day . . .' My sentence tails off. 'Aileen seems very cheerful.'

'And Pippa?' asks Ned, glancing at Jemima.

'She's actually holding the fort as we speak. She's very polite to customers, but it's early days in terms of the team gelling together.'

'Mmmm, I see,' sighs Jemima. 'We'd like to be kept informed of how that progresses. Pippa needs to fulfil her role just as well as Aileen does. No taking liberties, OK?'

'Of course, yes.' I avoid meeting Jemima's gaze; I wish to be fair to everyone concerned.

There's no chit-chat, it is all very focused, and within ten minutes I've nothing else to add. I'm relieved when they bid me a good day, swiftly taking my leave. I close the door behind me and stand there for a second to gather my thoughts. It wasn't half as bad as I thought it might be. I didn't present myself as a gibbering wreck, and I answered every question.

I slowly make my way along the upper landing and am surprised when a smiley face appears from a doorway further along.

'How was it, lassie?' she whispers, wisps of grey hair wafting about her delicate cheekbones.

'All good, thanks, Dottie.'

She gives me a big thumbs-up and a wide grin before disappearing from view.

I traipse down the grand staircase, unaware of the staring portraits as I make my way back to The Orangery. What is Dottie's secret for staying so upbeat and hearty? I wonder.

Chapter Sixteen

Nessie

'Morning, Magnus, I didn't expect to see you so early,' I call, as my always loved but rarely seen distant cousin enters the forge soon after opening.

'Thought I'd show my face, to see if you've got any shoes ready,' he quips, his brown eyes sparkling with vitality and life.

'Really?' I give and receive a quick hug, as is our custom.

'Yeah, really!' He laughs, brushing a hand through his brown locks, the gesture slightly awkward.

''Cause a little birdy told me you might be dropping by, showing a keen interest in yarn, or such things.'

'Do I look like a guy interested in yarn?'

'Mmmm, maybe,' I say, opening my storage cupboard and withdrawing a wooden box. 'Here you are. I've made twenty, as I thought that would keep you going for now.'

'You thought right. A mixture of sizes, are they?'

'Yeah, the standard ones you always have. Though I've got time to make more, if you need them urgently.'

'I thought you'd be rushed off your feet in here,' he says, gesturing towards the two women browsing my wares a short distance away.

'I wish. I've made a standard set of wares and the odd piece has sold, so I've made a replacement or two, but nothing is flying out the door. Which is why I prepared your shoes; I can't afford to tie my money up in display goods.'

'Which all look great, by the way,' says Magnus with his usual wry smile.

'Thanks, but I'd rather see the back of them, with the cash in my till and me creating other products.'

'If things get tight, you can always give me a shout – you know that, yeah?'

I give his forearm a quick pat. That is what I love about our Magnus: regardless of his situation, how long it might be since we last spoke, or the distance along the family tree, he is always there for you. I admire that in a person.

'Thanks, I appreciate that. I'm letting the lack of sales bother me, and that's been affecting my mood the past few days.'

'It'll drag you down, Nessie. You've only just opened, so give it time. Rise above it and carry on regardless, like the warrior you are.'

'Boy, I haven't heard that phrase for a while.'

'Wednesday Smith, you're named after Woden, the god of war and protector of heroes, plus you have an association with the planet Mercury, so there's no fear of you not forging your own path in life.'

'Magnus, I could squeeze you. That's just what I needed to hear! Seriously, I've been moping around here for days now but, yeah, Wednesday Smith wasn't named after a pretty little flower but big burly gods!' A sense of pride wells up, deep inside. How the hell had I forgotten that? It might sound arrogant, self-important – even narcissistic – but it's a fact.

'Happy to help. Now, how much do I owe you?' he says, gesturing to the wooden box.

'Fifty quid in total . . . is that OK?'

'Of course it's OK. I don't expect ought for nought – you've got to eat, woman.' He pulls cash from his pocket and peels five tenners from the roll. 'And remember what I said: shout if needs be.'

'Thank you,' I mouth, as he hands me the cash and swiftly departs.

Verity

He walks in whilst I'm with a customer, discussing the eternal dilemma of choosing between beautiful coloured yarns. The only solution ever being to knit a duplicate jumper in the other colour.

He looks out of place, lingering beside the display unit browsing; it's obviously not his usual pastime.

'Thank you, see you again,' says the woman, taking her paper bag containing eight balls of 'Misty Heather'. No doubt, she'll be back next week for the same quantity in 'Silent Moss'.

'Hello, Magnus, sorry to keep you waiting,' I say, raking my hand through my hair nervously. For the first time in my life I want someone to think I left the cottage extra early to get to work.

'Morning, no worries. I was experiencing the same issue as your last customer: this one or this one?' He points to various shades of wool and shrugs.

I know he's pulling my leg, but still, it's quite witty.

'I'd suggest "Blue Haze" in preference to "Misty Heather", given your complexion and dark curls,' I say, playing along, though I instantly wish I hadn't as I feel a deep blush rising.

His gaze roves across my features, probably taking in my flushed cheeks, while I stand behind my counter, using it as a barricade behind which to hide. It seems hiding behind objects is my primary task for today.

'Anyway, I came to say that I've mended your bike and delivered it back to the cottage. I did knock several times but you mustn't have heard.'

Decisions, decisions. Do I come clean or not? 'Not' is the easier option, much easier.

I'd discovered the repaired bike leaning against the side wall of the cottage on leaving for work so had ventured to walk it to the bottom of the driveway before attempting to ride it along the flat coastal road. It had saved me a lengthy walk, for which I'm grateful. It had also confirmed the identity of my early-morning visitor, though since he owns the place he has every right to turn up unannounced.

'I found it, thank you. I must have been in the shower getting ready for work,' I lie, knowing my fading blush may well reignite before disappearing completely. 'I was going to ask Nessie to text you my thanks. I do appreciate it.'

'It was nothing, really. Your mishap caused very little damage to the wheel rim, and nothing to the actual spokes.' He nods as he talks, his gaze fixed on mine.

'I didn't realise you'd even collected it from the driveway, let alone repaired it and delivered it back.' I need to stop talking, I sound like motormouth even to myself.

'No worries . . . just don't do it again.'

He fidgets as silence descends. My stomach twists under his gaze. His Adam's apple lifts and lowers as he gulps. Without words being said, I feel it. Be it a telepathic thought or that elusive chemistry – a spark of connection – something occurs between us. How can two grown adults simply stand and stare like five year olds in a sweet shop.

Say something, Verity. Do something.

'How much do I owe you?' I say.

It's the most prosaic thing that I can think of. I'm sensing he won't charge, but still, it's good manners to offer.

'Nothing, honestly. I didn't have to replace any parts, simply remove the wheel and straighten it with a bit of brute force – it took minutes.'

'If you're sure,' I say, staring down at the countertop. Though

I can still clearly see his features as I look elsewhere, like an after-image that stubbornly refuses to go away.

'Verity . . . are you doing anything later tonight?'

My startled look conveys more than I wish.

'Sorry, I just wondered if you fancied going for a drink or heading out for dinner, that's all,' he says. Then quickly adds, 'If not, that's fine. No worries. I thought I'd ask; you being new to the area and such like . . .'

'Sure. I'd love to . . . like to, I mean.' Did I use the 'L' word? One sure way to scare off any guy.

'I'll call round for you at, say, half seven . . . we can grab a bite to eat down at the bistro.'

I'm nodding manically as he speaks, unable to control my mannerisms. Dating really wasn't included on my agenda for my gap year, but I suppose it's flattering if it happens. Technically, he's my landlord – which seems strange, though slightly inconsequential, given that all my dealings have been with Isla's mum.

'I look forward to it,' I say, edging my way back from the counter. 'And thanks again for fixing the bike.'

'My pleasure . . . catch you later. And, Verity, if you could put aside ten balls of "Blue Haze" I'd appreciate it,' he says, throwing me a wry smile as he leaves.

Isla

I'm grateful when my afternoon coffee break comes around and I slump into a chair at the first table by the door. It's my favourite table, with a view across the gallery's cobblestones, though on busy days, like today, when the door keeps opening and blasting a chill on to you, it's possibly the coldest spot in The Orangery.

I feel off-colour, having waited an extra hour to take my break as a result of Lachlan turning up unexpectedly. I didn't want him to see me sitting and relaxing at a nearby table, and have him think it was a subtle invitation to join me.

I cradle my coffee mug and watch the world go by, leaving Aileen to serve. I can see lots of people milling around, popping in and out of the stable doors and visiting the artists. Some have purchased items and are carrying the signature brown paper bags of the gallery, emblazoned with 'From Shetland, With Love' – one of Jemima's creative ideas, I believe. It saves the individual artists from forking out an additional expense, which some can ill afford.

I'd never thought about how difficult it is for them to get their products on show until I came here. The weaving ladies were saying they hardly sold anything outside of craft fairs because customers wish to touch and feel; they need to fall in love with the texture and design before purchasing. I imagined they'd simply visit an online shop to make their purchases, but no.

The door is pushed open by Levi, the local taxi driver, with his woollen beanie in place, as always.

'Afternoon,' I say with a smile as he enters.

He gives a sharp nod in reply. He's becoming a regular most days, though I've noticed Mungo often nips in for a break around the same time. Oh, here comes Mungo now, shuffling across the cobbles between the milling customers, his grey beard blowing in the wind. My legs will endure a second chilly breeze as he opens the door ... brrrrr, there it is.

'Afternoon, Mungo,' I say, as he pushes the door closed.

It's hinged at the top with an automatic soft closure mechanism, but Mungo insists on closing it himself. Something to do with his obsession about security down at the allotments, or so Melissa says.

Mungo raises a hand in my direction before heading for the furthest table beside the log burner; he and Levi have claimed it as 'their spot'. He'll wait for Levi to bring him his large white coffee.

There are a lot of people from the allotments at the gallery:

Jemima, Ned, Dottie, Levi, Mungo and Melissa. And yet not one of them supplies the café with fresh produce.

A voice in my head chastises me with, 'It is October, after all – what's left to harvest?' But there must be something they can provide, which would save me ordering it from the wholesaler.

I've no idea if allotments grow produce all year round, or not, but it'll be worth asking.

I'm on my feet, cradling my coffee, almost before I realise, and heading towards the rear table.

'Mungo, sorry to disturb you, but do allotments grow vegetables all year round?'

Both men look up as I rudely interrupt their conversation. They interact more like father and son than best friends.

'They can do – it depends on when you plant and how the weather is. Why?' asks Mungo.

'Have you any produce on your allotment right now?'

'I've got winter cabbage, some Brussels sprouts, beetroot, onions and a couple of rows of parsnips, though they might have gone past their best and be a bit woody.'

'And how about you?' I say, turning to Levi.

'Pretty much the same, with the exception of parsnips, though I've got some kale doing nicely in the polytunnel.'

'Any carrots?' I ask.

Mungo blows out his cheeks and rocks his body back and forth, before picking up his drink and ignoring my question.

Levi lifts his eyebrows high into his beanie hat.

'What?' I ask, glancing between the pair, sensing I've been stupid in asking. 'Don't carrots grow in the winter?'

'No carrots,' says Levi, once his eyebrows are sufficiently lowered.

'OK. And Dottie?'

'She only ever grows flowers. Her plot is virtually bare at this time of year,' explains Levi.

I notice Mungo is keeping out of the conversation, focusing on his coffee. Noted topics to avoid: keys and carrots. He really is a funny bugger at times.

'If I made an order for winter veg, would you be happy to supply it?' I ask.

A spark ignites in Mungo's features and he glances up at me.

'I could make a special allotment soup on one of the days – I reckon that would sell, being local home-grown produce.' I know Granny's recipe book has many soups dotted amongst the cake bakes.

Levi is nodding. Mungo appears interested now.

'I might suggest it at our daily meetings – I'll come back to you. Cheers.'

I leave them to their men's talk and head back to the kitchen, knowing my afternoon will be filled with bread-making and a stocktake of the dry stores.

Chapter Seventeen

Verity

Our meal at the bistro has been exquisite. And Magnus's company even more so. He arrived at the cottage bang on time and our evening went well, with endless chatter, some laughter and warm smiles exchanged across the table. Several times, I lost myself in his kind eyes; his gaze radiated a deep warmth. I listened intently as he explained about breeding Shetland sheep, being an expert on wool production, and being single for a while. He briefly mentioned that he lives with elderly parents and has a younger sister. I swiftly related my marital tale of woe, being a single parent to my three sons, and I managed to sidestep the conversation regarding me running away from my current responsibilities.

Magnus now links my arm in his as we slowly walk back towards the cottage in the dark along the coastal road. To our left, the sea dashes wildly against the rocks, sending an erratic arc of spray into the air as we saunter by. It feels strange to walk beneath the moonlight whilst occasionally being soaked by the landscape. Magnus's large frame shelters me somewhat, but even so, it's a new experience.

We're both feeling relaxed enough in each other's company to joke about our first encounter.

'Seriously, I must have looked such a prat ... half naked in my underwear, arms wide, clutching each curtain – it didn't enter my head to swiftly draw them again.'

'Mmmm, the funniest part was when you wrapped the one around yourself and continued to observe the sea view.'

My giggles cease as my hands fly to my mouth in embarrassment. My entire face flushes the deepest shade of crimson.

Magnus smiles before adding. 'You've got a fine figure, so please don't apologise.'

The cottage driveway doesn't seem long or winding enough as his hand takes hold of mine on the final stretch of our walk. Our palms fit tightly together. Our fingers entwine as one, which feels comforting, our joined hands hanging in the tiny gap between our hips.

The cottage looms before us, all too soon. I want to slow my step, but that would tell him far too much.

We stand in the amber glow from my hallway light. I stand expectant, my face upturned towards his, unsure how to proceed. It has been so long, I've lost track of the realities of a first date. Is a goodnight kiss still the indicator of a successful night?

His eyes search my features, taking in every detail: from my eyes to mouth and back to my eyes.

The silence grows.

My breath quickens. Do I move towards him? Or patiently wait?

'Thank you for a lovely evening.' I didn't realise I was about to speak until I heard my voice interrupt the tense silence. Idiot, stay quiet.

'I hope we can do it again sometime,' says Magnus, his gaze continuing to drift between my eyes and mouth.

'I'd like that.'

This is it. There's nothing else to say. I instinctively roll my lips together, ensuring they aren't dry.

'I'll wait until you're safely inside, if you don't mind.' Magnus indicates the cottage door.

I don't move. I wait. Is that it?

Magnus waits.

I wait.

His shoulders are fixed, his body motionless.

'Thank you, that's very . . .' I want to say gallant, thoughtful, something complimentary about his manners, but all I can think is: *where's my kiss?*

He gives a weak smile.

I slowly turn, hiding my disappointment, and open the outer porch door before looking back at Magnus.

I stand framed by the doorway, my hand on the doorjamb.

'And the door code?' he says, eyeing the inner door.

I turn away, swiftly punch in the code and push the inner door open by a fraction.

'I'm safely in, thank you,' I say, pleased that he's being so attentive. But I'm now standing several feet away from him.

'Right, I'll be seeing you, Verity. Thank you, once again.' In a flash, Magnus turns about and strides off into the darkness, disappearing within seconds.

I am stunned.

I let go of the outer door, allowing it to swing shut, as I stare fixedly at its wooden interior. My joyous glow dims as my mind replays the entire night in a montage of flashbacks. Our laughter, the wide smiles, the gentle touches of forearms as we excitedly talk. All those things happened, I didn't imagine the connection, yet there was no goodnight kiss.

As I close the inner door, I feel cheated.

Why be so attentive about my safety and yet stride off without a goodnight kiss? Obviously, he didn't enjoy the evening as much as I'd thought he had. As much as he said he had. He might say he wants to do it again, but he doesn't mean it.

What an act!

It wasn't as if I was going to ask him in for coffee. Who knows if coffee actually means coffee any more? Or is it like in my day,

when a late-night 'quick coffee' equalled chancing your hand at
extending a late night into an early-morning walk of shame? Not
that I ever lived like that – given I was pregnant by nineteen and
married within six weeks – but I remember how it was for Avril.

I bet Magnus is striding down the drive, as pleased as Punch
that he managed to get away from me and my expectant stance.

I close my eyes and visualise us standing outside the now
firmly closed porch door.

In my head, I position the human figures in close proximity,
reimagine his gestures, my lingering patience, the shuffling, the
awkward silence, my oh-so-obvious expectations for the end of
the night.

How embarrassing!

I kick off my shoes and slope off towards the kitchen, heading
straight for the kettle. Tea – my answer to everything. If it doesn't
lift my mood, it busies my hands, and the motion distracts me
from whatever is bothering me.

I mash my tea bag in the mug and reach for the milk as a
thought evolves: it wasn't a date. I took it as a date. Maybe it was
simply dinner between friends, mates – or merely acquaintances?

I drop the teaspoon into the sink with a clunk.

It wasn't a date!

And there's my answer.

Chapter Eighteen

Friday 15 October

Nessie

'Verity, what perception do you think your customers have before they enter?' I ask, wandering about The Yarn Barn, squeezing balls of wool with my freshly washed hands. Daily life at the gallery had evolved into a steady routine in under two short weeks, and I was eager to pick her brains.

'What a weird question!' says Verity, screwing her nose up. She's sitting quietly knitting in her cosy chair.

'Go on, say what you will. I'll explain in a minute.'

'I'd hope that before they come in they know what product I'm selling. They'd reminisce about warm cosy jumpers they've owned or knitted before. Maybe bring to mind particular colours, textures and smells that are all homely and comforting from their childhoods. Then I'd like to think they find all those things waiting for them inside The Yarn Barn and part with their hard-earned cash in order to bring back those feelings. Is that what you mean?'

'Exactly. Now, what do you think customers think about the forge before they enter?'

'It'll be dirty, smoky, grubby, soot everywhere . . .' She ceases talking.

'That's it exactly. You've hit the nail on the head, Verity. Customers are walking past the forge because they expect to get grimy or dusty when they enter.'

'But that's not actually the case, is it?'

'Nope. But their perception of what it will be like stops them nipping inside. They can hear me hammering, they can see Isaac blowing glass, but that's not enough to entice them inside to view and buy our goods.'

'Haven't you sold much?' asks Verity, looking up as she switches her needles over.

'Nope. Isaac's sales are fairly constant each day but low.'

'What are you thinking?' she asks.

I shrug. 'I haven't a Scooby-Doo. But I need to do something, otherwise I won't make enough to cover the rental.'

Pulling my cable-knit cardy tightly around my shivering frame, I peruse my display of goods laid out on the cobbles in front of the forge, trying to view them as a potential customer might. Firstly, there's the workmanship of each item. It's difficult grading your own work but I'm confident my smithing is up there with the best of them. That sounds incredibly arrogant and boastful, but I'm a natural. It's in the blood. Five generations ago, my great-great granddad lost his land as a tenant farmer so turned his hand to the one task he could do to put bread in his children's bellies. We've been blacksmiths ever since, except for my father, who made other choices. But even he can forge metal as well as the rest of us. He just never had the need or the inclination to do so.

'You OK, Nessie?' calls Isaac from inside the forge, as he cracks another beautiful fruit bowl from his blowpipe.

'I am. Just trying to figure out why I'm not shifting any of this stock.'

'You've made some sales, haven't you?'

'I have but . . .' I pause. I sound like a petulant child.

'But not quickly enough for your liking?'

'Exactly. I'm trying to figure out, is it my actual products or is it my display?'

Isaac comes outside and begins peering at the items.

'The quality of each piece is high,' I tell him. 'The aesthetics and decoration are pleasing to the eye and varied – I don't just do an odd swirl or a twisted loop. Look, I've incorporated delicate leaf and vine patterns, intricate hole-punching and latticework alongside the tradition designs. Yet I'm selling very little. I don't get it,' I say, picking up a hanging basket decorated with tendrils and vines.

'I can't see an issue with the quality or the designs, Nessie. I think you're being a tad harsh on yourself. Maybe your expectations are higher than they should be for the beginning of a project – it needs to build first.'

'What about the actual display then? Is there anything you can see but can't touch or lift, enticing you to study it further? Remember, I've got a few smaller bits on display inside.' I lead the way back inside the forge, keen to get another perspective.

Isaac scans the countertop, his gaze flickering over each item; I've made a fair few since my arrival. He was probably present at his bench during the creation of many of them.

He stands back, continuing to inspect. He's doing a bloody thorough job, I'll give him that.

'This might sound daft, but . . .' He glances up, as if unsure whether to say it.

'Please say – I'm looking for honest feedback.'

'It's all black.'

'It's all wrought iron and steel, Isaac,' I say, stating the obvious.

'*I* know that, *you* know that, but the average customer browsing in here only sees black metal objects. Any chance of you adding in some detailing with a silver-coloured metal – to highlight specific details, or give a different finish?'

I purse my lips, viewing the items with fresh eyes. He's got a point – every item is jet black. I feel like quoting Henry Ford but don't. Despite the delicate work and the intricacies that make each item decorative and homely, it remains black, which looks heavy and weighty, even if it isn't.

'Good man, that is exactly what I needed to hear!'

'You're OK with that comment?'

'Sure. I need to hear genuine feedback. What else in our homes do we buy in just one colour? Very little. Homes usually convey a rich spectrum of colour – some too bright for my liking – so the general public probably expect blacksmithing to have altered too. And it hasn't.'

'Phew! I thought I might have put my size twelves in it,' he says, wandering back over to his workbench.

'Any time you need an honest opinion, just shout,' I offer, with renewed spirit.

'Not likely! My glassware mimics every colour of the rainbow, much like your hair!'

I instantly return to work. I need to design a new range to include bronze, copper and brass, maybe a little aluminium and titanium, though I don't want to lay out too much cash. I need to rethink my designs, be they functional items like toasting forks or coat hooks, and spruce up the purely decorative pieces like name plates and door plates. How I'm going to do that in an instant is my next big challenge.

'Isaac, fancy a coffee?' I say, knowing full well it's my shout for getting the drinks in anyway.

Isaac nods as he collects a globule of molten glass, working it in his gloved hands to create a ball shape.

I exit the forge with a spring in my step. It seems so obvious; the public are viewing my wares with a restricted mindset. My task is to obliterate their narrow ideas and present beautiful items they can't believe have been crafted from metals.

I enter The Orangery; it is packed with people and happy chatter. I join the queue at the counter and view the sea of faces seated around each table – a quick calculation suggests there must be thirty adults present. Each one sipping a drink, purchasing a cake and lingering within the glazed café. Now, what can I create for each of them that would entice them to wander into my forge for a quick look before driving home?

I shuffle forward as the queue moves. I glance at the first lady on the nearest table, bottle feeding a baby reclining in a pushchair. She's in her early thirties, neatly dressed and fresh-faced. I'd suggest that her kitchen is all low-level lighting and glittery surfaces. I reckon she probably buys trivets to protect her work space from heated pans. Not black traditional ones, though – she'd want a delicate rose design in silver and copper to grace her countertops. Decorative, feminine as well as functional, that will be her key objective.

I shuffle forward again as the queue shortens. I note the elderly gent on the neighbouring table. The older generation mostly still have coal fires. He probably has a fireside set with pieces missing or broken, but he won't throw it out for fear of ruining a traditional set. He'd want it mended, if he's kept it for several decades. I suppose I could offer a mending service for one-off household items. There's an idea and a half!

'What's it to be, Nessie?' asks Pippa, wiping down the surface after her last customer has slopped their latte over the countertop.

'Two lattes, please, but hold all the sprinkles.'

'I can't see Isaac being a sprinkles kind of guy,' she giggles, grabbing two takeaway cups.

'You might want to confirm that when it's his shout to collect.'

'I doubt it. He rarely speaks to us in here.'

I shrug. Duly noted.

Pippa begins frothing milk, tapping, slapping and turning cups beneath chrome nozzles. In no time, I'm walking back to the forge carrying two piping-hot lattes.

'There you go, Isaac.' I plonk his cup down on his bench.

His eyes thank me; he currently can't speak as he is blowing a piece of glass. I return to my comfy seat and quietly sip my drink as he continues to steadily blow his long pipe, turning and working the growing bubble of glass on the end. It mesmerises me how a technique so simple as his breath can be controlled accurately enough to create something so delicate and beautiful.

I don't say a word. I've realised over the past few weeks that there are moments of concentration which flicker across his features as he works. The beginning of the piece seems to be vital, and when he's nearing the end too, leading up to the cracking-off task once the piece is finished. The in-between stages, which seem to depend solely upon controlled breathing, appear to allow Isaac to relax. I've seen several occasions when he's closed his eyes momentarily, only to open them wide as his brow knits with intense concentration immediately afterwards.

Isaac lays down his blowpipe and taps the bowl gently, catching it deftly as it falls into his hand below.

'That is quite amazing to watch. How big is the largest bowl you've ever created using that method?' I ask, as he places the bowl on his 'just made' shelf to cool and collects his hot drink.

'This big –' he extends his hands to demonstrate the size of a large football – 'which is a fair size to create when blowing because it takes it out of you, having to control your breath for so long. I've felt faint on more than one occasion.'

'Really? That happens?'

'Yeah, though a quick gulp of air settles you back down, but there's a chance the change in pace will affect the finished piece. It's not worth doing, as huge pieces rarely sell . . . well, that's what I find anyway.'

'Why's that?'

Isaac shrugs. 'Maybe folks are wary of having large glass items around their homes, especially with little children about – there are untold accidents waiting to happen. That and the price.'

It makes sense. It's funny how we've both got issues that hold the public back from purchasing our goods.

'The Orangery is packed. There's no way all those people have taken a nosey inside here this morning. I reckon we've had ten visitors in our first two hours.'

'About that. I've sold three pieces.'

'I haven't sold any. Which has got me thinking ... how do you feel about masterclass workshops? One-day events with participants actually working on a crafted item?'

'I think it depends how apt the teacher is,' replies Isaac, wearing a dubious expression.

'Mmmm, I may well pop a notice into the café offering a one-day taster session.'

Isaac eyes me cautiously before saying, 'Check your insurance first, and read the small print very carefully.'

Chapter Nineteen

Tuesday 19 October

Isla

'Do you come down here every day?' I ask, as Dottie unlocks the padlock and slides the metal bolt across, releasing the massive metal gate leading to the allotments. A busy couple of weeks have passed since I'd spoken to Mungo and Levi about winter veg. I'm determined to pursue the idea, so I've asked Dottie if I could accompany her on my day off. I'm happy to give up my free time whilst Dottie is working flat out on Ned and Jemima's forthcoming wedding at the end of the month.

'Every day – and have done for more than forty years. It's like another world,' she says, her smile reaching from ear to ear.

'And that's your get-up for here?' I ask, pointing to her wide-brimmed hat.

'Always. Come rain or shine, my trusty ribbon keeps it safely in place.'

I've never seen such a huge straw hat in my life, I didn't think they made such old-fashioned headgear any more.

Dottie closes the gate behind us and locks it. It's funny how she rattles the padlock when it's clearly secured. 'You can never be too sure,' she mutters, seeing me watching. 'This way.'

We spend the next few minutes walking along a dirt track from the gravelled car park, edged on either side by allotment plots. Each plot is fenced off for security but, boy, how different each one appears. There are neat ones, untidy ones, overgrown plots, plots with nothing but mud, carpeted plots, plots with army camouflage nets, garden chairs, complete bathroom suites as planters, tin baths as duck ponds; and in every direction, there are scarecrows or mannequin heads staring down from metal poles or wooden crosses.

'What's with the heads?' I ask, unsettled by those with missing eyes – until I spy those with freakishly painted eyes staring at me.

'They help to scare the birds away from your seedlings,' says Dottie, traipsing along the track at quite a pace for her age. My granny was the same; she never walked, simply galloped.

'And the carpet?'

'That helps to keep the weeds down on the bare earth you're not cultivating,' she says.

'And what's with the museum dedicated to Armitage Shanks?'

Dottie stops, turns and stares at me. 'You're full of questions, aren't you? That's to save wasting something that's still got plenty of life in it. Don't you think it's beautiful?'

'No.'

'You will when the spring comes, and Kaspar's urinal blooms with his nasturtiums. Stunning display, he puts the rest of us to shame.' Dottie continues along the track. 'Come on, chop chop, I haven't got all day for questions.'

A urinal? These people have lost the plot.

Within minutes, the track divides and curves like the cross section of a figure eight. We carry on straight ahead for a few steps before Dottie points and says, 'That's Levi's plot – the taxi driver. Mungo is next door. There's a new owner taking on this plot, though he's done very little since he collected the keys. And this one, this is Jemima's plot, or Old Tommy's as it was – the one with the front door.'

I stare. I've got nothing more to say or ask. Never in a million years would I have thought Jemima would have a front door as a gate – nor rubbed shoulders with the likes of these.

'Mine's the next one on,' says Dottie proudly.

I'm relieved to see that her plot has an ordinary gate and padlock. There are no unusual ornaments, staring mannequins or large flag poles; instead, there are tilled patches of earth with neat borders and a polytunnel beside which sit lots of beehives.

'You've got bees?'

'No. Ned has.'

'Ned ... as in Lerwick Manor Ned?' I ask.

'Oh yes. The honey in your display cabinets is his, you know.'

'I thought everyone was pulling my leg when they mentioned it.' I'm baffled beyond belief. How do they find the time?

'This is where Ned and Jemima met ... not quite here, more the car park, because it involved a skip ... but that's a story for another day. This way.'

I don't argue, I simply follow her along the pathway, which I note hasn't a speck of mud upon it.

On entering the polytunnel, Dottie begins pulling at the bunches of flowers hanging upside down from the wooden framework criss-crossing the tunnel roof. There are hundreds of bunches of colourful blooms.

'I was thinking a colour combination of pale lilac, orange and white. What about you?'

'Anything. It's not really my thing,' I say, before adding, 'I wasn't convinced it actually came from flower petals.'

'You can buy paper confetti, but dried flower petals are traditional – and my delphiniums give the best range of colours. I didn't want to use the boxes on display in the café – I want them to have freshly made confetti for their wedding day.'

I nod along. I'm not sure it matters; it'll end up being trodden underfoot, anyway. But then I'm particular about the spices I use in my baking. Other bakers aren't so fussy.

'The colours I suggested will blend nicely with the autumnal Hallowe'en palette they've chosen. I'd have quite liked Jemima to carry a bouquet of delphiniums, but that's out of the question at this time of year.'

'Are these all delphiniums?' I ask, developing a crick in my neck.

'All but a few favourites, which I grow purely for my vases at home.'

'You don't grow any vegetables?'

'No. Not one.'

'Not even carrots?'

'Isla, nobody grows carrots around here ... but that's definitely a story for another day. So, what's it to be? Equal quantities of colour – or are you leaning in favour of burnt-orange tones?'

'Burnt orange – it'll match the pumpkins being used for decorations.'

'Right you are. Her grandpop, Old Tommy, used to call her "little pumpkin", you know?'

Dottie stands back, pointing at various bunches; I fetch them down from the hanging rack with the aid of a sturdy wooden stepladder. She keeps assuring me it's 'quite safe' though every time I step on to it, I feel it wobbling like crazy. If I come a cropper whilst fetching dried blooms down from the ceiling of a polytunnel, my mum will not be a happy bunny.

'In the summer would you be able to provide bunches of delphiniums for the café?' I enquire. I feel cheeky, but if I don't ask I'll never know.

Dottie's cheeks instantly blush.

'I mean it. I'm not really sure what delphiniums look like fresh, but these stems seem quite tall. If we arrange them in a large vase as you approach the counter, they'll look quite fetching.'

'Isla, I'd love that. As long as you aren't yamse and demand all my best blooms.'

'I'll mention it to Jemima, though not until after the

wedding – but I can't see her having an issue with it. Fresh flowers in any setting give a wonderful feel to the place.'

On retrieving what must be the twentieth bunch of flowers, Dottie finally declares, 'We have enough!'

I thought we had enough after five bunches – but hey, what do I know?

Dottie holds open a hessian sack into which I stuff the dried flowers, blooms first. Apparently, it doesn't matter if the petals get a little squashed or even fall off the stems – that'll be happening soon enough anyway.

'I thought Jemima helped you to dry petals in the ovens of the old kitchen for confetti last year,' I say, puzzled as to why she's changed her methods.

'She did. It was very productive too, but I thought why not let Mother Nature do her work? She rarely gets it wrong if left to her own devices.'

'Who, Jemima?'

'No. Mother Nature.'

'I see.' I don't, but I'm sure my granny would have said something similar. That's what I love about the older generation; they have an unquestioning faith in things that I don't even believe in.

'Has Melissa still got her allotment?' I ask, as we traipse along Dottie's path, heading for the gate.

'Yes, it's the one across the way. When she first arrived, it was in such a state. The nettles were up to here –' she gestures to shoulder height – 'and the goat she hired to eat them got her into trouble and upset Kaspar. So then we all had to muck in, otherwise she'd have left for sure. Though she never made the broth that I suggested.'

'Broth?'

'Nettle broth – the best you can get, if it's made correctly.'

'Are you serious?'

'Ask Mungo, if you don't believe me.'

'I'm tempted to try.'

'I'll bring you some nettles. There's plenty at the back of my polytunnel.'

'Perfect. Let's get the wedding sorted first, and then I'll have a go at making soup.'

'I'm quite excited at the very thought,' says Dottie, as she securely locks her gate.

'Me too. Though is there any chance you can bring me a few dock leaves too, just in case?'

Verity

I turn into the driveway carrying two heavy shopping bags, to find Magnus busily tending to the sheep in his paddock. It's nearly two weeks since our dinner at the bistro, and I haven't seen hide nor hair of him. There's no chance of me sneaking past and safely reaching the cottage without him noticing me. I continue to walk, ensuring that my gaze focuses straight ahead, conscious of his presence a short distance away.

'Verity!' I hear his call but continue to walk, pretending I've not seen him. 'Verity!'

I stop dead, acting surprised, and fix a polite smile to my lips as a greeting. 'Hi.' I consciously don't say his name. I daren't. It makes him too real in my world.

'How are you?' calls Magnus, jogging across the paddock. 'Here, let me take those.' He vaults over the fencing and reaches for my bags.

'It's fine.' I don't release my grip.

His hands bunch over mine. 'Let go, you bugger,' he says, laughing, tugging at the handles.

'It's fine.' I'm not altering my grip. I'm not falling for that suave charm. Nor the allure of your lemon aftershave now you've come closer, I think to myself. Nor your strong muscular frame – which could easily lug these heavy bags, no problem – as if they aren't weighing me down and cutting into my palms.

'Are you OK?' Magnus steps back, tilting his head with a questioning gaze.

'I'm fine.'

'You've said "fine" three times now; I'll take it as a warning sign.'

I begin to walk.

Magnus catches up. 'Have I done something wrong?'

'No. I'm quite—'

'Fine! I get it. Fine, fine, fine and dandy,' he sings. 'So why am I feeling the permafrost beneath my feet and a chill factor of minus twenty?'

'Don't be daft. I've been food shopping, I need to sit down with a cuppa.'

I glance ahead at the cottage, willing it to draw nearer; unlike our bistro night, when I wanted our walk to last for longer.

Magnus stares at my profile, watching my every move. He's confused. Bothered. Irked. 'And this afternoon, what plans have you got?'

'I'm crocheting and chilling out.'

'And this evening?'

'I've bought a nice piece of steak for my tea.'

'And later?'

'Mmmm, there's a couple of things on TV that I wanted to watch – a documentary on the BBC.'

'Was I rude to you?'

I stop dead. 'What?'

'The other night . . . was I rude, ill-mannered? I thought we'd enjoyed a nice evening in each other's company?' His brow is deeply furrowed, his eyes narrowed and pained, his voice strained.

'I had a lovely evening, thanks to you. I'm just busy, that's all.'

Magnus purses his mouth before nodding. 'Are you sure you can cope with those?' He points towards my shopping bags.

'Yeah.'

'OK. I'll see you around, enjoy your night. Bye.' As the words leave his lips, he spins on his heels and jogs back towards the paddock. The flock waits at the wire fencing to welcome his return. Magnus vaults over the fence, returning to his duties.

I can see from the back of his head, he's miffed.

Oh well, join the club.

I continue quickly on my path, not wishing to be caught staring. I open the outer door and swiftly punch in the code to get inside, dumping the shopping bags in front of the fridge and starting to unpack.

I can't help but view Magnus through the window.

He strims the tall weeds edging the fencing, then straightens and secures the leaning fence post and, finally, examines the hooves of each sheep.

My mug of tea is untouched and cold by the time Magnus packs away his tools.

Not once has he looked towards the cottage.

Not once.

Which tells me all I need to know.

Chapter Twenty

Wednesday 20 October

Isla

From the safety of The Orangery, I watch as the crane lifts the duck sculpture high into the air. I'm not sure if the swinging action is deliberate, but it's making the assembled crowd wince as the sculpture sways precariously above their heads.

I can't see the look on Nessie's face, but I'm sure she's having kittens right now, standing outside the forge watching the proceedings. Is she wishing she'd opted for a smaller ground-based structure, set on a marble plinth, to highlight her talents? The constant swinging might imitate flying, but the steel ropes had best maintain a firm hold – otherwise Ned will be rebuilding his stone archway.

It's like car-crash TV; you can't bear to watch but you can't look away, either. I fear for the reputation of the MacDonald trio, with the eldest operating the crane. They are usually a sound bet where muscle and lending a hand are concerned, but today – well, today must be an off-day for all concerned.

I scan the stable yard; every artist is out on the cobblestones, staring up at the sky, bewildered by the operation. Even the man who whittles wood has emerged. I rarely see him outside his stable – he's definitely the most antisocial of all the artists. I don't think he speaks to anyone all day.

'Surely this isn't the norm for an installation?' says Verity, sidling up and joining me in front of the plate-glass window.

'Risky business, if you ask me, swinging it into place.'

'Exactly. All that was needed was an additional guide rope as an anchor point and that weathervane would have been in place ten minutes ago. Nessie must be on tenterhooks. Will the archway even survive?'

'If we capture its demolition on video, we could post it online. I'm sure it would go viral.'

'I dare you, Isla.'

'No way. I double dare you.'

'Nah, I'm older and wiser, it would be considered immature of me – but you, you'd get away with acting naughty around here. Ned would forgive you.'

'I doubt it,' I say, giving her a sideways glance before adding, 'but it would be worth the risk.'

'I'm off. They want it in place before the wedding, but my nerves can't take it. Can I have a coffee?' says Verity, heading towards the counter.

'Sure,' I say. 'I could do with one too, given that I've spent half the morning answering questions from their wedding caterers.'

'Are you not . . .?' she asks, leaving the question hanging.

'No way! It was a leap of faith, me taking on responsibility for the café, their wedding reception is out of the question. Jemima's arranged for an external catering company to provide everything, from the food to dining tables and chairs. I just wish they'd contact her with questions, rather than me; I've enough to do preparing the wedding cake.'

'Ah, that's so sweet.'

'I offered, and they jumped at it,' I say. I pause a moment, before adding, 'Are you OK?' I'm sensing there's more to her nerves than she's letting on.

Verity exhales, pulling a comical face. 'There's nothing like family to make you feel guilty for having your own desires, is there?' she says, slumping into the nearest seat.

I don't answer. I head straight for the coffee machine and prepare her favourite latte – on the house this time.

'My boys are fine with the situation, but my bloody sister is determined to keep rocking the boat while I'm away. She's failed in her attempts to berate me or talk me round, and it narks her beyond belief.'

'Do you think she might be a tad jealous of your gumption in actually doing what you please? She might not have the nerve to follow your example, but desperately wishes she did.'

Verity's head shoots up and she stares at me.

'I'm just saying. They reckon there's always a reason – I've only said the first thing that came to mind.'

'Isla, you little beauty. The truth might be simpler than I'd assumed.'

'Here, on the house,' I say, handing over her latte.

'You are an angel,' she replies, her mood entirely changed.

'I do my best!' I say, with a cheeky smile. 'Though if you care to mention it to Jemima, it might earn me a small pay rise.'

'Though not at the minute, I think she's got enough to deal with,' says Verity, as we watch the flying duck sculpture circle the archway, swooping erratically and nearing its final position.

Nessie

'Do you like it?' asks Isaac, following me back to the forge after a nerve-racking twenty minutes.

'I love it because I made it,' I say, needing a nip of something strong after watching the precarious installation completed by the MacDonald trio. I purposely stood away from the action to avoid getting involved.

'Ned warned them, "It's better to take your time and get it

right," which might explain the snail-pace execution,' he adds, following me the length of the forge.

'Could they not have put a lead rope on it to guide it? It might have saved my nerves somewhat.'

'The candle maker reckons your green hair might suggest Hulk tendencies. He was watching in case you got angry, but I reckon it's a lighter shade than Dr Banner ever achieved.'

Is that supposed to be a compliment? I ruffle my freshly dyed hair, almost in defiance. I haven't time to stand around justifying my hair colour; I've just downed tools for twenty minutes to be scared witless by a creation meant to delight and thrill. I had visions of the crane dropping the sculpture and it landing on the real, live Crispy duck, causing mayhem and unexpected trauma for the bride-to-be, Jemima. I begin to stoke my coal pit in an attempt to revive the fire and build up a decent heat that will see me out for another hour or so before I allow it to die down to ash.

'Nessie, any chance of a chat?'

'About what?' I ask nonchalantly, turning around to see Isaac's forlorn expression. What's up with him?

He falters for a nanosecond before saying, 'It doesn't matter.' He turns and strides back to his own workbench.

'Isaac?'

'Nessie, doesn't it look great?' calls Dottie, scurrying into the forge and interrupting the moment. She glances between us, before adding, 'Oh, sorry, I didn't realise you two were ... chatting,' indicating Isaac's vibe is clearly apparent; I didn't imagine it.

'It's fine. Come on in,' I say, tending my coals.

Isaac quietly settles at his bench and continues with a sketch he started earlier today.

'I just wanted to say, well done, lassie,' says Dottie, lingering by the door. 'It reminds me of the olden days when the original was still in place. A galloping horse it was, but modern times deserve modern flare.'

'Bless you, Dottie – I appreciate that.'

'OK. I'll be seeing you both,' says Dottie, giving a little wave from the doorway before disappearing.

'Sure. Take care,' I call, poker in hand, stoking my coal pit. 'Isaac?'

He looks up from his artwork and stares at me, as if his request for a chat never happened. Without warning, he puts down his pencil and stands up, abruptly announcing, 'My shout for coffee – what'll you be having?'

'The usual.' I watch as he swiftly departs for The Orangery, leaving me with the burning question: what's got under his skin?

Verity

I linger in the café long after the sculpture installation has been completed and widely admired, seizing the opportunity to discuss a business idea of mine with Isla.

'I couldn't possibly do that,' I say, taken aback at her generosity.

'Sure, you can. Nessie's had a fair bit of interest in her workshop, so I expect you'll get a good uptake. You can hardly accommodate more chairs in The Yarn Barn, can you? Bring them in here, it's rarely busy midweek, the group can settle in the far corner.' She considers for a moment, then adds, 'I might even ask Ned if we can offer a "Knitter 'n' Natter" deal of a hot beverage plus a cake for a set price. How does that sound?'

Having spied Nessie's poster advertising her 'One-Day Blacksmith Workshop' pinned to the café's display board, I'm running with the idea for a new weekly knitting group hosted by The Yarn Barn.

'Sounds bloody marvellous to me, but is asking Ned really necessary?'

Isla nods enthusiastically. 'I'm learning. First, you ask Ned. He listens intently, because it might sound like a lucrative idea but he's always cautious till he's weighed up potential drawbacks or issues. I think he's a "mull it over" kind of guy. Anyway, he puts you on hold, quite literally, then off he goes to run the idea past Jemima. Now, there's no hanging about with her. Jemima's switched on, she gets everything straight away. Ned then drops by to "unpause" you and your idea, so to speak, with a resounding "yes", whilst adding any savvy business details suggested by Jemima.'

'Pretending it's his idea?'

'Oh no, he doesn't undermine her in any way. They work as a team. She's his right-hand man, his Girl Friday, so to speak. He trusts her creative mind to fathom out any issues with the gallery, and he focuses on the land acquisitions and tenants.'

'You've got that pair sussed.'

'I have, but then I probably see more of them than anyone else here. I report back each morning, and they usually drop by during the day. Ned makes me nervous the way he scrutinises everything, whereas Jemima's pretty down to earth; they make a good partnership.'

'They say every pot has its lid,' I say, quoting my old nanna from my younger days.

Isla pulls a face. 'I haven't heard that phrase before.'

'It's obviously too "old school" for you young 'uns,' I say, collecting my belongings, needing to reopen The Yarn Barn.

'Not all pots have lids – or need them, nowadays,' says Isla, with a knowing look.

Cheeky bugger, though she's got a point. I haven't a clue what my generation say about dating or relationships – and any matching of pot lids is hardly my forte. I'm relieved Magnus wasn't brought into the conversation; I want to build genuine friendships at the gallery, not mere acquaintances who are only interested in one topic. I still feel awkward about my 'date' mis-understanding, so I can do without the reminder.

'Anyway, I'll ask Ned about the weekly group, he'll mention it to Jemima, and then I'll get back to you. Do you reckon four quid all in sounds about right for the special deal?'

'I'd happily pay that, given the size of your cake portions.'

'Shhh, I know. Ned's mentioned that a few times. I mark each cake before I cut it but, yeah, sometimes it goes wrong when I actually do the slicing. I end up with the odd door wedge – which Ned always spots as he walks through. I've thought about offering customers a doggy bag, if they can't manage the whole slice, but I'm sure Ned would say "it shouldn't be necessary if you portion it correctly".'

'That is a poor impersonation of Ned,' I say, teasing her deep, manly voice and furrowed brow.

'I know, but you get what I mean.'

I do, and with that I bid her goodbye, scurrying back to my yarns.

If Isla gets the go-ahead, I could start 'Knitters 'n' Natters' in a couple of weeks. I need to get a wiggle on and begin advertising.

Chapter Twenty-One

Monday 25 October

Nessie

It took a few days to settle my nerves after watching the installation of the duck sculpture, but the compliments I received were like balm to my flagging soul. Isaac hasn't repeated his request for 'a chat' so I assume it wasn't important. My inspiration and enthusiasm are sky high today as I stand before a group of six adults attending my workshop course.

'Welcome to the forge on this chilly Monday morning, I'm Wednesday Smith, the local blacksmith, known as Nessie. I'm hoping that for today you can forget about the world outside and simply learn about working with a hammer and anvil. We're not chasing perfection here; our focus is purely on enjoying creating something from metal. Your idea might start as a toasting fork and evolve into a coat rack over the hours – but who cares? As long as you go home with a finished item. Just remember: in blacksmithing there are no mistakes, only rapid design modifications!'

A titter of polite laughter erupts from the group standing in a semicircle in front of me, each wearing an aged leather apron and an anxious expression.

'There won't be any customers dropping by to browse, as the gallery is closed on Mondays, so we've got the place to ourselves. And, finally, don't look so scared; you're here to have fun!'

It takes much cajoling to perform the dreaded group introduction; some people hate speaking in front of others, but I learn loads about my participants. Mavis has purchased five coal shovels in recent years, but none have survived due to shoddy rivets. Kaspar desires a fancy wrought-iron planter to add some finesse to his allotment plot. Levi's after a bird feeder that will finally defy the local squirrel population. While Autumn, Paige and Jennie are open to suggestions; they aren't fussed what they create.

I exhale as they fall silent; I can't work miracles in eight hours, but I can definitely ensure that everyone leaves with something of which they are proud.

'Before we crack on, let me introduce my stable buddy, Isaac,' I say, gesturing over their heads towards my silent friend, busily colouring his molten glass. 'Isaac, give us a wave!'

Isaac obliges; the swift blush to his complexion suggests he wasn't expecting a mention. I've no doubt he'll get me back later. 'Isaac will be blowing glass throughout the day, so by all means wander over and take a nosey, but be very careful. Remember that today you're on the practical side of the boundary rope and not the audience side. So, if you could all gather around for one final section relating to health and safety ... after which, we will begin!'

I read the health and safety speech from a pre-prepared card; there is no way I can remember every detail, and I can't afford to slip up and have a personal claim made against me. It was Isaac's fabulous idea after hearing me practise yesterday and observing my failed attempts to remember each point. This way, my arse will be covered in every respect and, fingers crossed, everyone has an enjoyable day.

I check my watch: ten o'clock.

'We have one hour until our first tea break, which is perfect to introduce you to the tools and equipment you'll be handling today. You'll be working in pairs on the three anvils you can see positioned before you,' I say, drawing the group around the nearest anvil. I love how they're all eyes and ears, hanging on my every word. I've got a very good feeling about these mini-workshop days.

If today goes well, I might think about planning a three-day course – or even a five-day introduction course.

'I hope you enjoyed your coffee and home-made bannock; there'll be more delicious cake to accompany your afternoon break. I've no doubt Isaac will be joining us again?' I raise my voice.

'Yes, please, and at lunch too!' comes the hearty rejoinder from the far end of the forge.

'This morning, I've shown you two basic skills: heating and hammering. For this hour, I want you to have a go at doing it yourself. If we can master the basic skills before lunch, you'll be able to begin work on your chosen project this afternoon. It goes without saying that I'll be on hand throughout to assist. Gather round, folks, and I'll show you what's called "splicing".'

I pull on my heat-retardant mittens and grab a piece of iron, shoving it into the hot coals while I continue to explain. 'You're watching the process the entire time, so don't take your eyes off the coals. Let the iron talk to you, allow it to show you how hot it's becoming, and when it's almost a cherry-red glow, out it comes –' I keep my focus trained on the hot metal as I talk – 'and I'll be hammering it flat for stage one. Stage two, I'll cool it off in the slack tub and then reheat it before slicing the flattened head into two equal parts to create prongs . . .' I pause, watching the metal intently, before continuing. 'After which, I'll be bending each of the prongs to form a fancy design of a spiral and a geometric square, purely to show you what the metal is capable of. OK, now do you see how the colour of the metal has altered? That's what you're looking for.'

I'm a visual and kinaesthetic learner, so I'm hoping my method of teaching supports everyone in the group; I don't want anyone feeling left out or left behind.

I'm happy with the view: six eager adults in leather aprons, methodically hammering pieces of red-hot iron. Each appears to be comfortable wearing the safety goggles and mittens supplied. I continually glance around the forge, keeping an eagle eye on each one of them, ready to jump in the moment they need help or encounter an issue, but it's not necessary. I feel like a proud mother hen watching her chicks take their first tentative steps around the farmyard. I could get used to this. I'm enjoying sharing my working space with others. Explaining and answering some basic questions – which seem obvious to me, with my years of experience, but which to the untrained eye wouldn't be so obvious. I'm secretly pleased that the gender balance in the forge is slightly weighted in my favour; I was half expecting fewer females to sign up.

'Please shout if anyone has any questions or needs assistance in splicing – it's not an easy technique but it's doable, given the knowledge you already have.'

There's no answer, just six bodies happily focused on their hammering or busy supporting their partner to hammer, giving snippets of advice as they go.

I've charged a fair price of sixty pounds for the workshop, which includes all materials, use of tools, food and beverages throughout the day, plus constant supervision and teaching. Before me stands three hundred and sixty pounds' worth of happiness and not a penny less.

Today is a good day at the forge!

'You know each other from the allotments then?' I ask Kaspar and Levi, dunking more rustic bread into my second bowl of parsnip soup as we enjoy lunch in The Orangery.

'Yes, we've been digging down there for many years, haven't we, Kaspar? Everyone knows each other. It's a friendly community,' says Levi proudly.

'Most of the time,' adds Kaspar, wiping his bread around his empty bowl so fiercely I fear he might remove the glazed pattern.

'There's plenty more food,' I say, pointing towards the nearest counter section where Isla has placed our soup urn, platters of bread and a bain-marie of gorgeous tattie stew and dumplings. There's a glass cloche containing a giant carrot cake, and a huge jug of double cream too, for afters. Immediately, Kaspar and several others jump up for another helping. 'It all needs to go, otherwise it'll be my packed lunch for the rest of the week!'

'I bet folks have loved attending these workshops,' says Autumn, returning with a bowl of steaming stew.

'Actually, this is the very first one. I thought I'd try it out today and tweak it from here before taking it forward.'

'That's amazing. I would never have known. I'd have said you'd done this for quite a while.' She turns to Mavis, sitting beside her, who appears to be pondering the food selection from afar. 'She's so patient with us all, isn't she?'

'Definitely. I'd attend a longer course – be it a weekly night class, or even a five-day course,' says Mavis, getting to her feet, having decided on a little extra.

'Would you?' I ask, eager to hear their views.

'For sure,' says Jennie.

'And I would. One night a week or maybe a long weekend would suit me too,' adds Autumn.

I couldn't ask for better feedback, and it's only lunchtime – they haven't even started their individual projects yet.

Isla

'Do you know what would look lovely gracing the lawn come the summer?' I say to Dottie, leisurely staring out across the terrace gardens dressed in autumnal colours. 'Peacocks.'

Dottie looks up from mashing her tea leaves and stares at me. She rarely visits on Mondays, given that the other cleaning team 'secretly' attend the manor, but The Orangery is never out of bounds for a cuppa and a chat. It's a well-earned break for me, having spent all day icing the wedding cake in between baking bread and serving Nessie's workshop participants. I've never made a wedding cake before, and the thought of the happy couple posing for photographs beside my creation is overwhelming. I've followed Granny's recipe to the letter, not daring to alter anything for fear of the consequences. I'll die of embarrassment if they cut into the bottom tier and their silver knife comes away with claggy lumps of uncooked cake.

'Peacocks in Shetland?'

'Apparently, Ned keeps koi carp in the pond – so why not?'

'I can't imagine peacocks in Shetland – one gust of wind and the poor male would be lifted sky high like a feathered umbrella! He'd need rescuing every other day as he'd be blown over the allotment wall.'

'I think it would be beautiful seeing peacocks strutting across that lawn . . . and just imagine weddings! Seeing how smoothly Ned and Jemima's wedding plans are going – you could have a huge wedding marquee on that lawn too.'

Dottie shakes her head whilst adjusting her tea-strainer on the lip of her teacup. 'You've got more ideas than Jemima has,' she mutters, pouring her tea.

'Thank you, Dottie – I'll take that as a compliment.'

'I'm sure you will.'

I watch as she carefully pours her tea without spilling a drop. Adds milk, then sugar and stirs for an age. A routine my granny never rushed.

'Are you and Mungo thinking of making things official?' I ask tentatively, having heard my mum's recent chatter about their blossoming romance.

'I beg your pardon! You can leave us old ones out of your imaginary plans and fancies,' splutters Dottie, her teacup wobbling and spilling a dash of her tea upon the table.

'I think you make a fine couple – why not follow the trend and get married?'

'At our age? Get away with you, lassie.' She dabs the spilt tea with a paper serviette.

'I'm only saying, a nice big marquee, with peacocks roaming upon the lawn and lots of bubbles . . . it would make for some lovely memories for you two.'

Dottie shakes her head and focuses on sipping her beloved tea.

'I'd even say, if you asked Jemima—'

Dottie raises her index finger and silences me; it's a gesture my granny would do when I was younger. I giggle, heed the warning and finish my drink before I get my wrists slapped for being too cheeky towards my elders.

'Talking of Jemima,' says Dottie, gazing across the bare lawn, 'do you have any idea of what they'd like as a wedding gift? I've had a little whip-round, asking for contributions at the allotment and here at the gallery. Folk have been very generous, I've collected a fair few pennies.'

'You know them better than anyone. What would you suggest?'

'They've got everything they need in life, so maybe something symbolic or artistic? Something they can admire for years to come. They're not yamse people, they're grateful for what they've found in each other,' she says, her watery blue eyes sparkling with excitement.

'Given Jemima's delight with the weathervane, I'd suggest Nessie's your woman.'

Dottie's face creases into a huge smile. 'Perfect suggestion, lassie,' she says, quickly finishing her tea. 'I'll leave it for today – I can see she's got her hands full with the workshop – but later in the week, I'll nip over for a chat.'

Chapter Twenty-Two

Nessie

Our afternoon flew by as the attendees went at their individual projects with zeal. I'd included a thirty-minute design session to help them create a feasible object; the bird feeder and the allotment planter were a little ambitious for their current level of expertise. The group settled on four shovels and two toasting forks – though the design of Kaspar's toasting fork needed simplifying; I had no doubt that the fleur-de-lys wouldn't make the final article. Not today anyway!

Everything is going swimmingly; we've just thirty minutes to go before I close my first workshop, enabling the merry group to leave for home. I lap the three anvils constantly, observing and checking that each participant is handling their hot metal correctly whilst listening to the busy hammering ringing out from the forge. It makes my heart sing. I know Granddad wondered for a decade or two whether that unique sound would ever grace society again, fearful that the local blacksmith was a thing of the past. I glance around my workplace; everyone here is adding a tiny piece to the survival of this beautiful trade and … my thoughts are brutally cut short by a clatter and a guttural scream.

'*Aaghhhhhhhh!*'

I turn to find Mavis, standing bent double, her hand clutched between her denim-clad knees, wailing like a banshee and dancing on the spot.

Autumn, who I've teamed with her, is simply staring helplessly, alternating between her partner and the hot metal spinning about on the concrete floor and glowing a faint red colour.

I cross the forge in two strides, grab Mavis's hands unceremoniously and drag her to my slack tub, thrusting both her hands into the cold water and holding them in place. Asking questions would have lost precious seconds. I assume she dropped her metal shovel and automatically picked it up. When you're dealing with temperatures of 800°C, there's no time for delayed reactions or questions.

Isaac joins me within a nanosecond. Automatically the other two pairs cease working, and just stand and stare. They've felt the glowing heat all day; I assume they are imagining the worst.

'Keep your hands in the bucket – don't move, Mavis. Can someone fetch me a bucket of ice from The Orangery, please?'

Isaac hastily leaves the forge to tend to my request, grabbing one of my empty pails as he goes.

'It was my own stupid fault. I knocked it with the hammer and it fell to the floor. I simply didn't think, bent and picked it up,' says Mavis.

'When did you take your gloves off?' I ask, forcing her hands below the water line as she's unconsciously lifted them up whilst explaining.

'I couldn't hold the tongs properly, so I slipped one glove off just for a second and then . . .' moans Mavis, her breath becoming laboured as the pain is registering.

'So is it both hands, or just one?' I ask.

'Just my right hand.'

'Here.' Isaac returns, handing me the ice-filled bucket.

'Mavis, can you open your fingers and thrust them into the ice, please? We want maximum coverage, and as deep as you can, to ensure all the skin is being cooled. Isaac, can you call me an ambulance, please?'

Isaac's piercing blue gaze flickers to meet mine. He knows I'm crumbling inside.

This was my biggest fear – and to think we'd nearly made it to home time.

The flashing blue lights and swift arrival of the ambulance caused somewhat of a disturbance amongst the gallery's vendors who'd attended work on a Monday. Isaac has taken the other five participants for a coffee break, purely to empty the forge in my absence, whilst I stand before the open rear doors of the ambulance and watch as a paramedic examines Mavis's hand.

'Nessie, is everything OK?' asks Ned, approaching across the yard.

I refrain from sarcasm: time, place and all that malarkey. I calmly explain what happened.

His brow creases in a worried frown, causing the ridge above his nose to deepen.

'I didn't attempt to open her hands or even examine them – it would have been vital seconds out of the water or ice. The guys are taking a look now.'

'Your assumption is . . .'

'Deep burns . . . peeling skin, blisters . . . need I say more?'

'You're insured, right? Otherwise this could prove disastrous.'

You don't think!

I sigh, turn and politely smile at Ned. I get where he's coming from, but right this minute I can't think about the consequences. I just want to see the back end of this ambulance trundling along the drive towards the A&E department of the Gilbert Bain hospital.

'My main concern is Mavis. My second job is to complete the workshop for the remaining five participants and then, once the forge is closed, I'll gather my insurance documents together and notify them of an accident.'

'Good, good, if you need anything, just shout,' says Ned. He's satisfied his own nerves and is ready to return to the warmth of the manor.

The paramedic emerges from the rear doors of the ambulance.

'How's she doing?' I ask, knowing my mood is rapidly sinking.

'It's bad, but a quick trip to the hospital will have her sorted out and comfortable in no time,' he says.

'Mavis, are you OK?'

'Yes. Apart from feeling so bloody stupid. What a foolish thing to do. You'd told us all day not to remove our goggles or mitts, and what did I do?' She looks crestfallen. 'I'd only just cracked that hammering technique too.' She looks genuinely miffed at having her session cut short.

I begin to chuckle; I can't help it.

Mavis immediately follows suit. 'Seriously, Nessie – I'll be back to finish off my shovel. I'll need it for this coming winter; I'm not buying another one!'

'Oh, Mavis. I'm glad you're smiling but, seriously, my only concern is your hands. You're not supposed to touch the bloody hot stuff!'

'Right, we need to make a move,' interrupts the paramedic, glancing toward his duty mate.

'I'll notify your husband,' I say.

'I've already got Jennie to call. He's going to meet me there.'

'I'll call you tomorrow – I want a full report, please,' I say, feeling slightly better than I did a few minutes ago.

Isla

'Up you get!' I say, lifting Ella high to get her foot into Jutt's stirrup. She looks such a cutie in her tiny hard hat, strapped beneath her plump chin, and a tweed riding jacket. I once looked that adorable riding Jutt.

Little Ella is as eager as they come at that age; pony mad and only just entering primary school. What I wouldn't give to go back and enjoy a pony trek in the same manner, riding high while an adult gently leads the pony along the coastal path. I couldn't wait to ride a bigger horse, yet I was never happier than trekking with this old boy.

I give the Shetland an affectionate rub to his nose, causing his top lip to flutter. He's a good lad standing so still, he knows she'll be scared if he misbehaves. It's not as if he gets to be ridden more than an hour or so each week, which is a shame really because he is reliable in his temperament – very much a children's pony.

'Ready,' squeals Ella, beaming as she adjusts her hands upon his reins.

'Let's go!' I say with equal excitement, looping the training lead into my hand as we plod towards the paddock gate.

I can't help but notice that Magnus is shoeing the two ponies in the driveway paddock. I'm not one to gossip, but as my mum mentioned earlier, "He's definitely showing more interest in his flock at the cottage of late – he drops by most days." I only hope that Verity is happy with his newfound attentions. He might be family, but even I recognise he's a decent sort who wouldn't expect to be messed around. I'm sure Verity only has short-term plans to be in Shetland before returning home to her family. She's travelled a reverse route to most local folk; they were born here and many can't wait to leave. I give Magnus a cheery wave as we trek past.

Within no time, we're down the driveway and out along the coastal path heading towards the cliff top. The gentle pace enables Ella to relax and enjoy a steady ride. She's pretty capable, given her tender age. I correct her slouching posture, her newly gained habit of removing her boots from the stirrups, and praise her for the little bit of handling and control of the reins. She's definitely improving with each trek, though whether she'll have her own pony by this time next year is doubtful. Most parents are wary to fork out for a pony, paddock and upkeep, only to have the child's enthusiasm subside within months, leaving them with a pet pony but no rider. Some might say that's me, but I can't possibly allow Jutt to leave my life. I've had him for sixteen years – since he was a tiny colt and I was just three years of age. To look down at his blackened mane was the greatest view I could have wished for as a child. He could easily live another fifteen years, in which case I might one day be leading my own children upon his broad back. I smile. How weird would that be?

The sky is dark grey, with a smattering of dove-coloured clouds, while a blustery wind howls around our ears. We stand and look out across the Bay of Sound as the North Sea rolls and crashes upon the black rocks below. The retreating swirl of water offers a spectrum of blue hues, from light aqua to a deep navy, topped with the frosting of white spray. It's beautiful up here but desolate. There's very little light after dusk, and this path is treacherous in wet weather. Even the coastal path needs care and attention if you're out after dark, as there's no street lighting in these parts or along the surrounding lanes. I gulp, as a flicker of a story charges to the forefront of my mind. A little girl knocked over by a car whilst out playing after school. I shiver at the very thought.

Ella laughs as the grazing sheep scatter at our approach. I wouldn't want to be anywhere else right now. Outside of The Orangery, I'm in my element plodding alongside Ella and Jutt. I should probably do more trekking like this, enabling Jutt to have more human contact and regular exercise. And it's good for my well-being too. I don't know many youngsters any more; once your friends' siblings have grown up, there's a gap in your social network which I imagine doesn't get filled until your generation start producing their own offspring. I suppose I could advertise at work – after all, it's worked for Nessie and Verity – see if anyone is interested in children's riding lessons, though I'll need insurance. Two or three little ones wanting thirty-minute lessons would suit me nicely on my free days.

It might give me something to do outside of baking and business studies, which are starting to take over my every waking hour. I'm reaping the rewards of my commitment, but I don't wish to burn out and make myself ill, working too hard at a job I love.

Ella fidgets, Jutt stands proud and still as I gaze across the bay one more time. It's nothing short of a beautiful canvas that changes on the hour, every hour, depending on the weather, the season and the light. And I will never get sick of seeing it ... in which case, I need to start making additional plans for a lifetime here in Shetland.

Chapter Twenty-Three

Tuesday 26 October

Verity

As soon as I enter the bistro I wish I hadn't. My intention was to escape my cabin fever by seeking a comfy chair overlooking the turbulent sea, in which to simply read my book and enjoy a large glass of rosé. That desire is shattered the moment I recognise Magnus, with his mop of brown curls, his large hands cradling a pint glass, seated opposite an attractive blonde with a low neckline and full glass of white wine. Immediately I feel cheap in my freshly washed jeans and a slouchy hoodie; she's very attractive and, although she's sitting down, I can see she is certainly blessed with a figure to die for.

If no one had seen me enter I could have spun around and left, but the attentive barman has clocked me. I'll look foolish scuttling straight back out. My only hope is to remain invisible, as Magnus is deep in conversation.

'A large rosé, please,' I say, fumbling for my money, hoping to save time. I stand square on to the bar, attempting to hide my features by allowing my tousled hair to fall forward and mask my profile.

I'm grateful that the barman swiftly delivers; I wrap my fingers around the chilled glass and scurry towards the quiet snug area. Empty. My heart leaps. No distraction, no interruptions – and no Magnus.

I settle in the corner, restricting my view of the bistro's customers, and enjoy the panoramic view of the white surf riding the top line of the waves. My breathing softens, my body sinks a little deeper into the plush seats and I lift my feet up and curl them beneath my relaxed frame. I sip my wine and I allow my mind to drift into a hypnotic state.

I'm at peace. My family are happy and healthy. My business is growing with each passing day. All is well with the world.

'Can I get you another one?' Magnus asks, pointing to my half-empty wine glass, as he leans around the open doorway.

'I'm fine.' I watch as his eyes widen, surprised by my response.

'I'm trying to be sociable here, throw me a line, Verity.'

I feel spiteful now. 'A small one, then.'

'Rosé again?'

'Please.'

He disappears from the edge of the double doors so I return to my book, rereading the paragraph where Heathcliff sneaks a peek at his Cathy enjoying her new life. Vibrant images swirl before my eyes, as if I am peering at the modern world through a draughty window frame. Caught out in the cold, watching from afar and wishing I were on the other side. Was I ever on the inside enjoying the life I had, or have I always been on the outside making the most of what I see?

Three young boys, just babies when George left. And what did I actually do? Apart from dash back and forth between nursery school and primary school, racing to complete every teatime, bathtime, storytime and bedtime. How chuffed was I at successfully bundling them into bed before nine o'clock? It felt like an accomplishment in itself when they'd constantly climb out of their cot beds to begin playing Lego, on the hour, every hour, until the early hours. I'd wave a tired yet grateful goodbye to my parents as they took their 'extra pair of hands' home after their daily routine of supporting our evenings of family mayhem. More often than not it was my dad helping me out, though my mum often complained he 'wasn't that hands on with his own girls', but Dad justified it by saying that my three boys needed him more. Was that true? Or was my mum good enough to manage without a timetable of helpers on speed dial?

'Here you go.'

I jump as Magnus delivers my wine glass to the table.

'Thank you,' I say, cradling my book as he takes a seat opposite. 'Has your date gone?' I ask, glancing towards the main bar.

'Friend, actually, but yeah, she's gone home,' he says, offering a coy smile.

I raise an eyebrow. Pull the other one, it has bells on it! No friend wears her neckline that low for the benefit of another friend – well, not in my world, anyway.

He breaks the silence immediately, asking, 'What are you reading?'

'*Wuthering Heights*. I read it many years ago but wanted to reread it.'

'I don't read classics.'

'Not at all?'

'Nah. I can't see the point . . . especially those romantic ones.'

My expression creases in annoyance as he dismisses my choice.

'Sorry if that offends.'

I really must take charge of my expression.

'The way I see it, those books are like girl meets boy, girl fancies boy, girl moons over boy. Boy finally notices her, decides to chance his hand and then they enter that whole "will they, won't they, dare we, dare we not" situation . . . before they get it together and job done – book over. If you've read one, you've read the lot . . .'

My mouth drops open as he pauses to sip his pint.

'Unbelievable,' I mutter, as he lowers his glass.

'No, seriously, think about it: Austen, the Brontës and—'

I snap my book shut, ending his sentence.

'You don't agree?'

'No. I. Don't. *Wuthering Heights* defines a passionate and complex relationship, yet you make it sound like a twisted romcom, making it a waste of time reading it.' I sip my wine and calm my breath.

'Heathcliff is just a brooding menace who lets the girl slip through his hands before taking revenge. No decent bloke does that. No wonder he's haunted by the young girl's ghost.'

I quickly snatch at my wine glass and take another sip. How dare he summarise it as such?

Magnus is watching me, awaiting an answer.

I meekly glance over the rim of my glass.

His mild gaze swiftly turns into a stronger stare, before a twitch develops at his temple. 'Oh, I get it.' He swiftly sits back and turns to stare out at the sea raging beyond the glazing. 'My God, did they break their necks to bring you up to speed?'

I frown, unsure what he means.

Magnus shakes his head, his gaze roaming anywhere but my face.

'What?' I add, purely in ignorance.

'What?' Magnus puts his pint down, slamming it on the tabletop in his irritation. 'You know exactly what. I get it now. You've been awkward with me ever since we had dinner ... so who was it? Who's been gossiping?'

'Gossiping about what?'

His mood change is swift; I'm staying schtum, that's for sure. I'm not prepared for a modern-day Heathcliff to join my quiet drink.

'Don't give me that, Verity. You clearly know about the accident.'

My eyes widen, witnessing the deep pain etched into his features. What is he on about?

'Cease the act, because you're failing big time – your face gives you away at every chance. Someone has taken it as their duty to bring you up to speed about the death of my younger sister, not that it's any of their business. I bet they relished the tragedy of "how young she was" and how some lowlife "mowed her down" on the coastal road one night after dark. So you'll know it was a hit and run – she died there and then.'

I'm shocked to the core. 'I had no idea, no one has said a word. Magnus, I'm so sorry.'

His palm lifts, silencing my reaction. 'Save it, I've heard it all before.'

'Sorry, I honestly . . .'

His gaze is fastened on mine.

'And no one's ever been convicted?' I ask.

He gives a tiny shake of his curls.

'Were you close?'

'Yes, we were very close as youngsters – we thought the world of each other.'

'That's lovely to hear – that fact alone must bring you some comfort.'

He averts his eyes from mine. 'Some,' he whispers, almost to himself. He swiftly drains the last half of his pint and immediately stands up. 'Anyway, nice seeing you. Enjoy your book. Bye.'

'Good night, Magnus.'

'Take care as you walk back.' His parting words send a shiver down my spine.

Within seconds, he's gone, his hasty stride resounding on the wooden flooring.

I'm narked that he should take off so abruptly after downing his drink like that. If he's bothered about my safety, he could have walked me home. I sip my wine whilst silently spitting feathers; he's got under my skin and he wasn't supposed to.

I reopen my book, attempting to lose myself within its pages as the stormy sea continues to crash outside the panoramic window, echoing the second storm swirling inside my head.

Chapter Twenty-Four

Wednesday 27 October

Nessie

'Good morning!' hollers Isaac, on entering the forge.

'Is it?' I mutter, tending to my fire coals.

'Oi, lady, less of that attitude. What happened at the workshop was not your fault. The way you took swift action and handled the situation showed skill and professionalism, so less of your droopy lip.'

'Droopy lip? Is that even a thing, Isaac?'

'Yeah, given your mush this morning. Now, you've got five minutes to change your face while I fetch you a latte with sprinkles. Got it?'

I can't help but smile. He is such a genuine sort, standing there in his lumberjack shirt and woolly fisherman's hat.

'Got it!'

'Back in a minute,' says Isaac, scooting back out. He's crossing the yard but I hear him say, 'Morning, Dottie, yeah, she's inside.'

Within seconds, Dottie's smiling face appears in the doorway.

'We are honoured; we rarely have the pleasure of your company,' I say.

She totters towards me as I stoke my fire pit.

'I've got a favour to ask,' she begins.

*   *   *

'When Jemima mentioned sharing the forge and the rental, I wasn't too impressed,' I say, sipping my hot latte.

Isaac looks up, slightly startled; my honesty has a habit of doing that to others.

I continue before I chicken out. 'I'd said I'd think about it and I'd get back to her over the weekend. But the very idea of sharing dampened my excitement at joining the gallery. I felt cheated that someone else, a total stranger, would be creating beautiful objects in the space I wanted for myself. I asked if it was another blacksmith and she said, "No. A glass-smith – is that what they're called?"'

Isaac's sheepish expression cracks into a smile before acknowledging the possibilities within the title.

'But I can honestly say I wouldn't have it any other way now, Isaac. I was being selfish, possessive about my territory, when the reality is that you brighten my day . . . most days!'

'Do I now?' replies Isaac, eyeing me quizzically. 'Now there's a revelation.'

I pull a comical expression in a poor attempt at covering my embarrassment, though there's no chance of hiding my awkward stance here in the middle of the forge's floor.

'Pretty much. You were a star the other day. You buy me coffee when I'm not feeling it . . . and you've pretty much bumped me along for the best part of a few weeks now. Despite rubbing my face in it that you're doing so bloody well blowing your glass balls, angels and paperweights.'

'Correction. Christmas baubles, actually.'

'Balls, baubles, same thing. I'm so sorry if I've been a misery guts, if I've put a dampener on your new venture, and I'm sorry for whatever else I might have done in recent weeks. But, believe me, if Jemima phoned me up today and told me that you wanted to be my stablemate and split the rent, I wouldn't hesitate in accepting.'

'Cheers. Have you been drinking?'

'No! I've just been doing some thinking while you were out fetching these. It can't have been much fun listening to me moaning ... then the workshop happened and, well, the first sodding ambulance has been called to the gallery because of me. I've been melancholy and mopey ...' I drop my gaze to the concrete floor and sigh heavily. Looking up, I find he's still watching and listening. 'I honestly thought Monday was the beginning of something, but the risks are too high. We'd made it through practically the whole day, the group had been perfect, yet that incident still happened. It's scuppered me, it has.'

'Hey now – no you don't! That was a one-off. Mavis said herself she removed her gloves after you'd repeatedly told them all not to. She's not shouting about insurance claims or suing you, is she? No, it was an accident, and accidents happen, despite all the precautions, despite all the planning – that's why you have insurance policies in place.'

I'm hearing his words but they're failing to hit home. He's right: when I phoned Mavis this morning she totally accepted it was her fault. But regardless of who's to blame, I'm failing at what I love. The chances of living the dream, being a blacksmith and keeping my family traditions alive are simply kicking the bloody bucket before my eyes. I can't sell anything. The commissions aren't rolling in as I imagined. I can't even complete a workshop without someone getting injured. How bloody useless am I?

'So what's your plan, Stan?' asks Isaac, finishing his drink.

'Dottie has just delivered the plan for today. I need to be uber creative and just indulge myself, doing something I love. Forget about sales, rent payments and accidents. She's commissioned a wedding present which, given the ceremony's just a few days away, means I've got very little time left to design, create and complete it.'

'I'm sure you'll get it finished in time,' says Isaac, returning to his workbench.

'And you?' I ask, wishing to repay his kindness with interest.

'More Christmas baubles, methinks – get a head start before the festive season dawns.'

I shake my head; I can't plan that far ahead, because it scares me to think there's a chance I might not still be here.

Isla

I'm dead nervous as I climb the staircase of the manor. I don't mind the daily reporting, what I dislike is the route. The manor seems so old until you reach Ned's third-floor office, where you're surrounded by modern furnishings.

On reaching the correct landing, I'd never remember which is the office door if it wasn't for the ceramic jardinière placed opposite.

I rap on the door and patiently wait. It's routine now. I bring the sales book with me most mornings but he rarely asks to see it. Probably prowls around after closing and sneaks a peek then. Still, it's comforting to know I have the details, facts and figures to hand if he should ask a difficult question. It's one of the strategies that my business studies book recommends: forearmed is always the best way to conduct yourself. Jemima never asks me difficult questions; she's got a gentler yet insightful approach when it comes to business.

'Come on in!' hollers Ned.

I turn the handle and enter, to find them both seated at the meeting table cradling coffee mugs. I never bring my coffee, though there are times I wish I had when my throat goes dry.

'Morning, Isla,' says Ned, gesturing for me to sit down.

'Morning to you both,' I say, taking my usual seat.

'Morning,' adds Jemima, eagerly smiling at me. I think she senses that Ned makes me nervous.

I explain that we had an increase of fourteen per cent in sales compared to previous Sundays as we served an additional sixteen customers, which I feel is a true reflection of the steady increase seen since opening day. I managed to complete an observational study and believe that customers are occupying a table for about twenty-five minutes before we're able to clear and clean.

'That is very good to know,' says Ned, looking pleased and acknowledging Jemima's delighted reaction.

'Well done, Isla. That's fabulous news about the increase in numbers!'

'Measuring the turnaround time allows me to estimate the footfall for each day of the week, and even to manage the busy times when it appears we'll run out of tables – which we haven't, to date.'

'That's excellent forecasting, as it will affect the number of portions required to meet the demand. You can hardly whip up a cake in an instant,' says Ned.

'Actually, Isla pretty much can; it doesn't take you long, does it? I've seen her,' adds Jemima.

'I can respond to an emergency, but it isn't how I like to work, I'm more of a planner.'

'Of course, of course, but if needs must,' says Ned, 'it's doable.'

'Oh yeah, it's totally doable,' I reply.

'Is there anything you'd like to ask or suggest, based on the last few days?' asks Jemima, fiddling with the handle of her coffee mug.

'I wonder if we could introduce a purchase deal for a hot beverage and a cake, maybe a "sip and a slice" combo? Verity wishes to start a "Knitter 'n' Natter" group on a Wednesday afternoon. I was wondering if we could offer her group a comfy space plus an additional treat. It might entice them to return with their families at the weekend, which could generate sales for the other artists.'

'What are you thinking?'

'Four pounds – a saving of fifty pence. It doesn't seem a lot, but some families or individuals need to watch the pennies. They get to mingle and be social with the knitting group, and still get a little bonus.'

'I like your thinking, Isla,' says Ned, glancing at Jemima for confirmation.

'Thank you,' I say, grateful he hasn't rejected my idea out of hand. 'I think in the long run it'll boost sales and create more regulars.'

Ned sits quietly nodding, in a world of his own; I expect he does that during talks with his land tenants.

Jemima beams, she definitely looks content. 'Is there anything else, Ned?' she asks.

'Oh no, keep up the good work, Isla. The wedding arrangements shouldn't encroach upon your time too much in the coming days.'

'The wedding cake is finished, if you wish to see it,' I say proudly, as I push my seat back and stand up.

Instead of simply exiting, I continue to say 'thank you' like a fool until I reach the other side of the office door. I need to improve my self-confidence, as my newly gained business acumen seems to be paying dividends.

Chapter Twenty-Five

Thursday 28 October

Verity

'Have you seen Magnus?' I ask, oblivious to Isla's happy chatter when I nip in for a coffee break.

Isla's eyes widen in surprise; she was partway through a conversation.

'Sorry, that was rude of me. I didn't mean to interrupt.'

'It's OK. I'm good. I haven't seen Magnus today,' she says.

'Yesterday?'

'Yes. I saw him briefly in the distance. He seemed his usual self.' Isla falls silent as she cleans the chrome on the coffee machine, which seems to be her favourite job.

I wait impatiently, eager to hear anything else she has to say. Isla remains silent but continues with her task.

'And?' I ask.

Isla looks up again, surprised by my question.

I continue, regardless. 'And? Did he say anything? Mention anything?' I fight the urge to add, 'Did he ask about me?'

Isla slowly shakes her head; her gaze is fixed on mine as her hands continue their task.

'Bloody hell,' I mutter, looking out across the cobblestones, viewing the busy crowd milling back and forth between artists.

'Verity?'

I turn back to meet her expectant look. 'Don't worry ...

it's just me being stupid, forget it. Forget I even asked.' She's watching me carefully so I rearrange my expression by adding a smile and take an interest in the cake display, which seems more calorific than ever.

Isla's hands cease working. 'Don't tell me you've fallen for his charms?'

'Nope.'

'Oh, for a minute there I was about to say you wouldn't be the first. Our Magnus has a magnetic attraction . . . it's as if women can't help themselves.'

Not what I want to hear – but still, better now than later. All morning, I've kicked myself for ignoring him the other week when he was tending his sheep. I should have let him carry my shopping bags and invited him in for a cuppa, but oh no, I was happy playing the role of Miss Frosty. Then Tuesday night went pear-shaped at the bistro. I hadn't a clue about the family's tragedy, but I doubt he believes me.

'Thanks, Isla. I just thought he was interested, that's all . . . he seemed nice.'

'He is nice, don't think otherwise. He's always helpful, cheery, willing to help anyone in need, but when it comes to women . . . he doesn't fall at their feet and yet, he never seems to be short of offers.'

Great. Having now realised he's got under my skin and into my head, I have to somehow reverse the situation. I exhale, loosening the knot which has been growing in my stomach since our skewed conversation on Tuesday night.

I give Isla a smile, an unconvincing gesture to lessen her concern. 'Thank you.'

'You're welcome . . . don't think badly of him. My mum's not sure he'll settle down now, not given his age.'

Despite my earlier resolution to let Magnus go, my ears prick up on hearing this piece of information.

Chapter Twenty-Six

Sunday 31 October

Isla

'Can you believe they're getting married today?' I say to Verity, as we sweep the cobblestones as a two-woman dustpan and brush team. 'Engaged on the second of October and married on the thirty-first when, according to Dottie, they only met in the spring.'

'As Ned said at the proposal, what's the point in waiting? "When you know, you know."'

'Do you?' I ask, ceasing my sweeping task.

Verity straightens up to her full height, the large dustpan and brush hanging limply from her grasp. 'Yeah, I think so.'

'You're divorced, right?'

Verity starts to laugh. 'Yeah, but what's that got to do with the price of bread?'

'Nothing. I wasn't trying to be funny. But did you know?'

Verity ponders the question. 'No, I didn't know at nineteen. I simply did what I thought was the right thing, given that there was a baby on the way, but now that I'm older I think you do make an instant connection with some folks. I believe two people can gel in an instant, complementing each other's personalities and values – that's what I see in Ned and Jemima. He might be the lord of the manor type whereas she is your down-to-earth ordinary lass, and they met by chance, but them being together works, doesn't it? Remember, "every pot has its lid", as my nanna used to say.'

'Yeah, grannies say the weirdest things, don't they?'

'They do, but if they've truly lived, they've probably learnt a thing or two.'

'What do you mean "if they've truly lived"? They've all lived.'

Verity shakes her head. 'Nah, some of us go through the motions of acting and living every day, when really we're just existing, almost surviving, until we wake up and smell the coffee.'

I'm confused, what the hell is she on about?

'Are you pair going to stand and gossip all day?' cries Nessie, leaning against the door frame of the forge, wiping her brow with her usual cloth despite her vest top and bare arm combo.

'We've already swept half of this yard clean,' I holler back in defiance.

'Get a wiggle on and do the rest. I'm ready to reveal their wedding present,' banters Nessie, waving her cloth as she disappears back inside.

'She's a bugger,' giggles Verity, bending down to collect the pile of dust and debris I'd piled at my feet prior to our chat.

What was Verity saying before Nessie interrupted? Acting as if you're living without actually living? Is that what I do?

'Verity?' I glance down as she quickly fills the dustpan.

'Yeah.'

'Do you still act like you're living?'

'Not any more. I've done my share of wasting the years. I'm going for it big time, now my lads have grown. Bloody hell, Isla – I filled my deep freeze with home-made lasagne and pasties before buying an air ticket to start a brand-new business from scratch in a place I'd never visited. I reckon you can call that living the dream!'

I start to laugh. I love it when Verity goes off on one. I reckon I'll be like her when I'm older, but maybe without the 'wasting my years' bit.

'You are funny.'

'I'm honest, if nothing else.'

'Aren't you done yet?' calls Nessie, reappearing in her doorway.

'Come and bloody help if you're that desperate to be out here!' shouts Verity, waving her bristled brush in Nessie's direction.

'I would if I could but I'm busy making something beautiful,' retorts Nessie.

'Are you now!' calls Verity, standing to empty the full dustpan into the bin we've dragged along beside us. 'I suppose you're waiting for a clean stage on which to present your something beautiful too.'

'Yeah, so hurry up. I don't want the surprise ruined,' calls Nessie, remaining in her doorway and surveying the stable yard.

'I bet it's something spectacular,' whispers Verity, eyeballing me as we carry on sweeping.

'Probably. Dottie wouldn't have given her the task unless she thought Nessie capable of creating another masterpiece.'

'Isla, what's with all the pumpkins?' calls Nessie.

'Besides it being Hallowe'en,' adds Isaac, appearing at Nessie's side.

'Apparently, her granddad used to call her his "little pumpkin" so Ned thought it was fitting.'

'I hope Jemima agrees. I'm sure the wedding photographer won't want her in tears all afternoon, every time she spies them,' says Nessie, talking more to Isaac than me.

'She knows,' I say, before adding, 'she's asked for some to be hollowed out to hold candles for later tonight. It'll look pretty when the fairy lights are switched on, criss-crossing the yard. Though if Mungo tells me one more time, "Two pound for a pumpkin! What a bloody rip-off! I could have bought a packet of seeds for a quid fifty and grown 'em bigger than them tiddlers on my allotment plot," I'll throw one at him!'

*   *   *

I dash about non-stop from the moment my mum collects me from the manor's driveway until Dottie beeps her tinny horn; thankfully, I am ready.

'Remember to sing if there's music!' calls my mum, as I shout goodbye and nip out through our front door, clutching my box of petal confetti. Mum says that every time, regardless of whether it's a wedding or a funeral.

'Hello, Dottie, how are you feeling?' I ask, climbing into her tiny car. I've borrowed my mum's smoky-green interview suit to complement my auburn hair, which hangs loose for once. No hairnet required today.

'Very teary. I can't believe this day has actually arrived,' says Dottie, sniffing for good measure. 'I just wish his parents were here to enjoy it; they'd be so proud.'

'I'm sure they'll be present in some form, that's what my granny believed, anyway.'

Dottie dabs her cheek with a tissue before checking her rear-view mirror, indicating and pulling away from the curb.

I've only been in the main hall once at the Town Hall – during a school trip as a child. We'd filed up the stairs in a well-behaved crocodile, with our primary teacher counting us in and out of the room, as is their habit.

The sheer beauty of the main hall – a mixture of natural wood and intricate stained-glass windows – is breathtaking. The magic is created by the natural light streaming through the colourful glazing, creating a vibrant rainbow on the polished wooden floor. I've never witnessed anything so beautiful. Shetlanders often joke that the tourists come here sightseeing, visiting the treasures on our doorstep, but rarely do we get around to it. I wonder if the same applies to locals everywhere?

While we patiently wait, sitting in neat rows, Dottie keeps dabbing her eyes with a frilly hanky despite the current view being nothing more emotional than the nape of Ned's freshly shorn neck. We're all waiting and watching, wondering what the next thirty minutes will deliver. I bet the groom is nervous; Ned's side-stepping routine, which is making his kilt swing before the registrar's desk, is a giveaway.

Jemima's side of the room seems very sparse: just a handful of aunties and uncles, coupled with younger people who I assume are cousins. They all share a family resemblance of blond hair and pale skin, very unlike Jemima's colouring. I give Pippa a polite smile; she looks lovely in her feathery fascinator. My eyes search for anyone who has dark colouring like Jemima's, but there's nobody with her olive skin and dark hair.

Ned's side is filled with many friends, not a single seat remains unoccupied. I assumed Ned would wear his Black Watch tartan kilt, proudly reminding everyone it's the Campbell tartan, but I didn't expect his friends to oblige him. I couldn't name half the clan tartans, though I do recognise some familiar faces from around town. I feel honoured to have been asked to accompany Dottie. I understand that Mungo refused, as he doesn't like pomp and circumstance, unlike Dottie who's forked out for a new hat and matching handbag.

The lady registrar gestures for us to stand; her broad smile must be putting Ned at ease as the double doors slowly open. We all turn, eager to see our blushing bride. Jemima slowly enters upon the arm of an older man – her father, I assume, given their family resemblance and shared colouring. Jemima looks radiant in a white satin gown that gently flicks and floats with each step. Her sleek hair is tastefully decorated with a delicate tiara – she needs nothing more than the bouquet of thistle, Shetland sea pinks and ferns to enhance her look.

Dottie begins to weep tears of joy, whispering, 'How has she managed to get sea pinks? They don't flower this late in the year.'

'Florists can source anything with enough notice and at the

right price. Maybe they've been grown inside or under heated glass,' I answer, not entirely sure I should mention cash at a wedding.

Everyone's gaze is upon the bride as she slowly walks the length of the centre aisle. The vibrant rainbow effect from the stained-glass windows magically arcs from the floor and glides across the contours of her slender frame, colouring her stunning gown in a dramatic fashion.

Jemima and Ned exchange bright smiles and murmur a few words as she arrives at his side. Her father shakes hands with Ned before settling himself in the front row.

The registrar gestures for us to be seated.

And the ceremony begins.

This is so surreal. They've said their vows, signed the register and are now legally husband and wife. How can that be? With just a few simple lines spoken before a registrar! It seems utterly crazy that someone has the power to perform such a ceremony, transforming your life and status in one go!

We give a rapturous round of applause before the photographer begins directing the happy couple into numerous poses. Only a few minutes have passed and yet, for Ned and Jemima, so much has changed.

'That was b-beautiful,' I stammer, tears trickling down each cheek, as Dottie passes me a spare packet of tissues from her bag.

'I can't believe how happy they look – it's like a dream come true,' she says, dabbing her frilly hanky to her cheeks. 'If only his parents could be here, instead of me.'

I give Dottie an impromptu bear hug; she's such a selfless person, always thinking of others.

Nessie

Standing on tiptoe, I can just about peer between the shoulders of the two women in front of me and catch a glimpse of the wedding car drawing up beside the stone archway. The chauffeur climbs out and gracefully opens the rear door, standing aside to provide room for Jemima to exit.

A piper begins to play somewhere nearby and marches into view through the stone archway long after his bagpipes were first heard. The unique sound clears your sinuses, if nothing else, and I have to admit it unleashes a pang of heritage and pride, lending added poignancy to the occasion.

Jemima's dress spills from the seat in a waterfall of delicate white satin, the hem immediately correcting itself to swish about her pretty buttoned boots. She smiles at the waiting crowd, demurely clutching her wedding bouquet, waiting for her husband to walk around the vehicle from the other side. Ned appears, looking dapper in his traditional kilt and sporran, and swiftly takes her hand, giving it a gentle kiss. Their entwined hands nestle between them as they approach us across the cobblestones.

All morning, the artists have pulled together to ensure a lovely warm welcome on their return as Mr and Mrs.

Verity has strung her knitted bunting in autumnal colours between various stable doors. Many artists have helped to hang row after row of fairy lights, which look beautiful twinkling high above the cobblestones. The pumpkins have been decorated and piled high, creating a mellow glow from the tiny candles inside. As for me, I'm proud of our gift standing in the corner and subtly lit by carriage lanterns.

I'm desperate to witness the newlyweds' reaction, though I'm happily nestled amongst the crowd. Other artists will think it strange, but I tend to shy away from moments such as this. I'm easily embarrassed.

We all watch with a glint in our eye as the happy couple meander through the gathered crowd, receiving congratulations and handshakes as they go. A small party of relatives follow in their wake, nervously smiling and nodding politely, probably recognising a few of us from around Lerwick. I spy Pippa from The Orangery, looking grand in her fine feathered fascinator, though she doesn't acknowledge anyone.

I can't wait to witness their reaction; I'm so excited.

Ned suddenly stops walking, tugs at Jemima's hand and points to the corner by the green painted door. Their mouths drop open and the rest of the gathered artists are side-stepped as they swiftly divert their route for a closer look.

It took longer than I thought it would, but thankfully I managed to keep it under wraps. The two abstract bodies are entwined in a passionate embrace. The initials 'N' and 'J' are hidden at first, only revealed after closer inspection; the silver burnishing doesn't dominate but, once spotted, can't be unseen. His metal face peers down at her small frame, her chin lifts to receive a kiss.

Earlier, when Isaac and I heaved it across the cobblestones into place, all I could hear were the 'oooh's and 'ahhh's from a sea of smiling artists who'd helped to decorate the gallery's yard.

'Nessie!' calls Jemima, scanning the gaggle of artists. 'Where is she?'

I'm lip-reading, but it's easy to see Jemima's response. I sink down behind the front row of artists, glancing sideways at Verity. I'm not likely to charge forward through the crowd.

'Wednesday Smith, where are you?' calls Ned in a powerful, louder voice, surveying the gathering.

Eek! Not what I wanted. He's made me sound like a naughty schoolgirl being summoned by the headmaster.

'Wednesday!'

Verity winces at me as I reluctantly move through the crowd. My cheeks are burning as hot as my coals usually are. I approach Ned, shaking my head and pulling my cardy around my frame.

'This is absolutely stunning . . . I can't believe that you've been so generous to us. Wednesday – sorry, Nessie – we will treasure it for ever, won't we, Jemima? Thank you to everyone for such a beautiful gift.'

'It reminds me of Klimt's painting *The Kiss*,' says Jemima, pulling me closer for a hug, endangering her bouquet in her enthusiasm.

'That's what I was after,' I say, pleased that the original inspiration is alive in my interpretation. 'We thought you might like to place it in the gardens where you can enjoy it in private,' I mutter, recovering in time to receive a polite hug from Ned.

Chapter Twenty-Seven

Verity

I don't waste time flicking the hallway light switch on, before my mouth is on his. His hands rove about my waist and back, matching the impatience of my lips. I might have had two large glasses of vino but I'm fully aware of my senses – and his actions. I want Magnus; Magnus wants me. There's no quibbling about it. Our limbs are entwined and our bodies seem to be magnetically attracted to each other.

I was surprised to see him attend the evening reception, but he explained he's a tenant of Ned's, so it figures. We'd chatted non-stop after he sidled up to me at the bar.

I don't remember tapping the key code into the inner door, but we've tumbled inside the cottage and now we're surrounded by darkness. Despite our conjoined form, someone needs to make a decision: is it turn right towards the kitchen for coffee or left towards the bedroom? Our shuffled steps drift towards the right. Really? I honestly thought we'd have taken this to the bedroom; he's obviously being wise, cautious, a true grown-up, whereas I'm acting like a woman who hasn't had any attention since . . . I conceived Tom. Shit, that isn't the thought I need right now. My inner goddess pushes aside the lecture from Ms Common Sense, who reminds me that I'm not covered by contraception. I should be an adult, but I'm obviously not, as my sister frequently reminds me. Shit! I didn't need Avril to enter my thoughts, either. I've had a wonderful evening with a great guy, we've laughed, joked, talked about every topic under the sun, and right now we're in a passionate clinch that seems to be drifting back towards the left. Oh, here we go: decisions, decisions.

I meant to change the bed sheets earlier. And why did I leave the fresh ironing piled on my bed?

'Are you sure about this?' asks Magnus, still kissing me, as our fused shoulders bump against the closed bedroom door.

'Err, yeah. You?' His mouth distorts my words to a slur.

'Yes! Just didn't imagine this.'

'Oh . . . Oh!' I pull away, a flash of common sense suddenly flooding my conscience.

Magnus's fingers delicately trace their way across my neck, gently lifting my hair, tenderly urging me to return to our previous kiss. His mouth lingers tantalisingly close to mine; it's the smallest distance and yet the greatest expanse, filled with hot breath, unspoken tenderness and passion.

'Are you OK or have you changed your mind?'

'No. I'm just . . . oh, what am I . . . oh my God . . . I don't even know what to say or think.' I take in his features close up.

He's gorgeous. Different to any other man I've met, yet here I am on the brink of doing something I'd never succumb to in a million years, back home in the Midlands. Verity: always the mother, daughter, sister, aunty, smiley neighbour, reliable receptionist, never the lover, never the sexual goddess, so inexperienced in seduction, and certainly never wanton.

My breath catches in my throat, as his gaze takes in my roving stare. He can read my every thought and probably predict my next move. I feel his arm slacken about my waist, his fingers loosen at the nape of my neck. His body moves backwards by an infinitesimal amount, yet the tiny action might as well be a country mile.

'Hey, no worries. We've had a great night . . . I've enjoyed your company, so if we got caught up in the moment and that moment has passed, then it's fine. No pressure, nothing. I'm happy to call it a night. I've walked you to the door and you're safely inside.'

'Definitely safely inside,' I mutter, lowering my gaze.

My feet may rest between his widened stance but the distance between us is increasing by the millisecond.

'How about coffee?' I say, glancing up, embarrassment surging through my veins.

'Sounds good to me.'

I inhale deeply, as if trying to retrieve the heated passion of a moment ago. There's so much I want to say. Should say. Could say. Might still say.

'Verity, are you sure you're OK?' He gently hooks a finger under my chin and lifts it to secure my attention.

'I'm fine. Just a bit embarrassed … it's been so long since I stood this close to a man, I forgot how reactions and responses can ignite and, well … you know.'

He doesn't laugh, jest or tease. Magnus draws my face towards his and simply plants a kiss on the centre of my forehead.

'I understand. Coffee it is. Lead the way, madame.'

I hesitate for a second, before my chuckle of relief breaks the tension. 'Through here. Milk or not?'

'Milk with sugar, please,' says Magnus.

I illuminate the kitchen in soft light with a flick of a switch. I drag a chair from the table in passing – his invite to sit – as I head for the kettle. I hear the chair scrape the tiles as he sits down; his keys jangle in his jacket pocket as he drapes it across the back of the neighbouring chair. My mind is in a muddled fug, replaying the hallway scene. I busy myself, purely to balance my nerves, moving from kettle and tap to cupboard, to fridge and, finally, the cutlery drawer.

I eventually look at Magnus as I offer him the steaming mug and settle in the opposite chair cradling my coffee.

'Are you enjoying living here?' he asks, having had plenty

of time to contemplate his surroundings during my awkward, coffee-making silence.

'I am. I'm still surprised that I went through with my plans but I'm thrilled that I did, it's turned out better than I imagined. My lads are fine. My parents have come around to my way of thinking. I can cope with my sister being narked with me – after all, what's new there?'

'Do you not get along?'

'Yeah, we get along great, if I allow her to dictate what I should and shouldn't do in my life. It's how it's always been. She's the bossy, loud twin, I'm the quiet one.'

'She'll get over it.'

'Not any time soon, she won't. That's the thing with Avril, she can't cope with being sidelined. Whereas me, my entire life has been filled with setbacks so I'm trained to carry on regardless.'

'And your ex-husband – he's no longer on the scene?'

As Magnus listens, his eyes never leave my face. What's he thinking? This woman is chatting, burbling on about the failures in her life, thinking it's entertaining. Nope, you don't smile softly when you're hiding negative thoughts. His thoughts are warm. Just like outside the bedroom door: affectionate, caring and understanding.

'And you?' I ask, after a brief explanation.

'Mmmm, me. A simple question of never finding what I was looking for … if that even exists. My folks believe I'm too choosy: "There are plenty of nice girls in Shetland," they say. But it is what it is.'

'Don't you just hate it when everyone has an opinion about your situation? They should keep their beaks in their own back-yards.'

'Aye, they should.'

Silence descends again. We sip our drinks. We're eyeing each other over the rim of the mugs. The connection becomes stronger, as if all the unspoken words are flowing silently between us across the table.

I usually feel the need to fill silence, be it with a witty comment or the repetition of an earlier remark, but not this time.

His lingering gaze remains on me, without a flicker of self-consciousness or apology. I can't see his pupils but I can sense his arousal from the darkness of his eyes. I'm one to talk – I can't imagine my eyes reflect anything different. I watch him sip his coffee, unable to tear my gaze away from his face. I can almost feel the gentle pressure of his lips each time they meet the edge of the warm ceramic.

How weird is this?

Would he have snuck out in the cold light of dawn or remained all night? Would I have wanted him to stay?

My gaze falters, resting on his hand clasping the mug. Long fingers, neat nails with defined lines upon each knuckle – a hand free from jewellery.

'Magnus?' I say, putting down my half-finished coffee.

'Mmmm.'

I stand up and walk round the table before I can think of an excuse not to. I'm standing before him within a heartbeat.

His mouth tastes of sugary coffee as my lips re-enact our hallway embrace. His chair scrapes against the kitchen tiles, his hands return to my waist and I'm standing between his thighs.

I peel his hand from the small of my back and draw him up to his full height.

'Are you sure?' he mutters, his mouth on mine.

'Most definitely,' I say, leading the way towards the bedroom.

Magnus flicks the kitchen light switch as he follows my lead.

Chapter Twenty-Eight

Monday 1 November

Entry: 01.11.90
Bake: Shetland bannocks
Event: Ordinary day

Serving size: 24 individuals
Decoration: not necessary

Notes: The weather has turned chilly. My daughter made bannocks but they weren't as light and fluffy as I can make, so
I whipped up a batch in no time. My daughter gave hers to the
neighbour as a kind offering. It would have been kinder giving
their large family my new batch. As always, a little home-made
butter upon a warmed bannock tastes like heaven.

Verity

As soon as I open my eyes, I'm catapulted into remembering the
night before. There's no mistaking the unusual, heavy yet rhythmical breathing of the person beside me in bed. That all-knowing
sense that less than an arm's length away, beneath the warm
duvet, lies another naked body. A body that is still fast asleep,
given the late hour at which we ceased the intimacy of last night.

I daren't move my arm to check the time on my phone for
fear of waking him, so I squint at the blurred face of my bedside alarm. The clock's hands appear to be at six o'clock. Three
hours' sleep! What the hell! It's a bloody good job that the gallery

doesn't open on Mondays as there's not a cat in hell's chance of me functioning.

I lie perfectly still, staring at the daylight sneaking through the gap in the curtains. Jutt the Shetland pony will be wide awake by now, munching on his giant hay bale just the other side of the window. My three lads will be hitting the snooze button numerous times before dashing from their beds to make it to work or college, hopefully with their bellies full of breakfast – or possibly a McDonald's. A sudden thought strikes me. None of them had better be lying naked in a bed beside his girlfriend. Least of all Tom. I wouldn't be best pleased if he's acting up simply because he's had a free rein at seventeen. I'll be mortified if the neighbours sneak a peek of any young lady doing the walk of shame from my front porch. Though at twenty-three, I'd been married for more than three years and had two babies, so maybe I'm a bit quick to judge. Times have changed – obviously. Here I am, naked, lying next to a man who has seen every inch of my body with the lights on. I don't think George could have said that during our brief marriage.

I feel myself blushing.

I grasp the duvet edge a little tighter, as if to hide my nakedness. I certainly didn't clutch the duvet edge or hide beneath it last night. In fact, didn't we have to fish it off the floor at one point when we decided we needed sleep? I move my hand and feel a button; the bloody duvet is on upside down, for God's sake! Have we no shame! I stifle a giggle as an image of Magnus retrieving it from the bottom of the bed fills my mind. Did I really just lie there as bold as brass, without a care in the world, as he fished about at the edge of the mattress, pulling the jumble of fabric this way and that until the duvet eventually covered us?

I believe I did. I didn't hide. I didn't insist on the lights being off. I didn't even insist on the headboard and pillows being at the top of the bed – now there's a novelty.

I can't actually remember the last time George and I were

intimate but I can pretty much predict that my head wouldn't have left the pillow, or my back left the flat sheet, much to George's disappointment. And we were probably disturbed by a crying child waking from a nightmare, prompting me to hastily find my discarded nightdress in order to go and offer comfort.

Whereas last night . . . Bloody hell! There could have been a crying baby in a cot beside me, and still . . . I'm not sure I'd have been the perfect mother in such a situation.

I purse my lips to stifle yet another giggle.

The question is: what happens next?

Do I act all blasé – it was what it was? Or does this become a regular occurrence, as in 'friends with benefits'? Urgh! I hate that phrase. Not that it's ever applied to me before, but I can guess what's what in the modern age, despite being celibate for so long.

The light beyond the curtains is getting paler.

It's all well and good me making plans, but that might be it for Magnus; a notch on the bedpost and see you around. I doubt it, but I can't assume anything.

I snort at my own naïvety.

'Verity?' he murmurs softly.

'Mmmm.'

'Come here.' His hands reach out and caress my skin, pulling me backwards across the mattress and into a warm embrace of spooning. His stubbly chin grazes my shoulder as his lips find my ear lobe and his hands stroke my stomach.

My internal monologue ceases as my hand strokes his outer thigh; I believe I have an answer.

Nessie

The gallery is empty when I arrive on Monday morning. It's not surprising, given that everyone happily joined in with the wedding celebrations yesterday. They're probably embracing an extended weekend as a result.

My intention was to knuckle down to sketch a few designs for smaller, garden-sized sculptures, but the nip in the air has enticed me outside into the manor grounds. I don't wish to bump into the happy couple, but they're unlikely to be idly pacing the grounds deciding where their wedding sculpture should be positioned, so this gives me a chance to suss out the surrounding parkland.

I grab my parka from the boot of my car and set off along the gravel driveway, walking across the grasslands on the far side. I have no idea what lies on the furthest part of the estate, away from the manor house and gallery, despite driving through it each day – twice a day, in fact – and I've never thought to ask. As children, we'd never venture on to private property; we'd happily scrump about, making dens and hideouts elsewhere, but never here. Lerwick Manor was deemed too posh for the likes of us.

The grass nearest to the driveway is mowed regularly for a close cut, but it soon gains length and the terrain becomes slightly uneven the further you walk from the entrance gates. I look back several times, unsure if I should be traipsing around, but I'm doing no harm, just looking. The manor house and gallery appear idyllic from this viewpoint, almost chocolate-box twee, surrounded by acres of lush open pastures. Unused pasture. Unspoilt. And definitely under developed.

In the space of five minutes, I remain close enough to the manor to spy Isla walking up the driveway but far enough away to feel as if I've entered a new location unrelated to the manor or the gallery. A vast open space, longing to be used and enjoyed by the community.

I turn around several times, taking in the scenery beyond: purple mountains dominated by rain clouds, sheep grazing, and miles of dried bracken – which surely must be swathes of heather come springtime.

This is beautiful.

A location that could be home to an arrangement of artistic sculptures, with possibly a picnic seating area in time for the spring. I might ask if I could pitch a sculpture or two along the driveway – it would provide an attractive feature on the approach to the gallery.

A few large spots of rain splatter my parka. My time is up; I've seen all I need. I march back across the open pasture towards the forge, my head spinning with new designs. I spot Isaac driving through the gates; that'll be handy on a quiet Monday, as he's a fine one to bounce ideas off.

'What do you think?' I say, holding aloft the coat rack for Isaac's approval. I've sat for the last twenty minutes painting the decorative metal leaves a deep shade of emerald.

'Very nice, that makes a world of difference to the overall effect.'

'Fiddly, though. I much prefer wielding my hammer, rather than sitting down painting the completed objects, but I was inspired by my walk this morning.'

'That's what you need. A fresh perspective on things, creative ideas – and bingo! I bet that sells,' says Isaac, polishing a tiny glass duck he made this morning.

'Do you reckon?' I love his confidence.

'In fact, let's have a wager. I bet the coat rack sells within days – a week tops.'

'Hardly. I've had certain items since opening day!'

'It'll sell. You'll see.'

I sigh. His intention is kind; he means well, but first we need bodies to walk in through the door.

Chapter Twenty-Nine

Verity

Bang! Bang! Bang! The frantic hammering on the cottage door doesn't cease for a second as I launch myself from beneath a snoozing Magnus. Grabbing my dressing gown, I slip it over my nakedness, pinning it across my frame as I fumble to tie the satin belt. It's one thing to be caught still lounging in bed at ten o'clock, but quite another to appear only half decent. Eventually, I catch, wrap and secure the belt tightly, softly close the bedroom door and casually rake a hand through my tousled hair. If this is Isla, finally accepting my coffee invite, I'll be jiggered.

I open the inner door, then yank open the outer porch door to find a bedraggled figure – and it isn't Isla.

'Hello, Verity,' says Francis, my brother-in-law, his pale features peering from beneath his rain-soaked hood. His eyes widen, taking in my appearance.

'What the hell!' I exclaim, stepping backwards with the shock. 'What are you doing here?'

'Can I?' He indicates the interior of the porch. 'It's pouring out here.'

'Of course, come inside.' I shuffle backwards, not wishing to leave him standing in the rain, whilst wishing to die, given my current appearance.

'I'd hug you but, well . . . you can see.' I watch as Francis turns, reaching behind to claim a large suitcase.

'Are you staying?' I ask, still baffled that Isla isn't on my doorstep.

'Verity, it's been four weeks . . . someone had to come to talk some sense into you. And surely I'm a better choice than Avril?'

'Marginally,' I mutter, plodding along the hall towards the kitchen. I'm conscious that my naked body is concealed from my brother-in-law by the thinnest veil of fabric and secured only by a belt tie that frequently evades a firm knot. I assume he's following me. 'Coffee?'

I don't say another word while I make coffee. I'm fuming. I specifically asked for no interruptions. I wanted peace and quiet. But now, given the expression on Francis's face as he sits at the scrubbed table, having removed his wet jacket which is drip-drying beside him, I'm clearly about to hear an update from home.

'Are my lads OK?' I say, delivering his hot coffee and settling opposite him, pulling my robe across my chest and holding it tight.

'They are, absolutely nothing to worry about there, but . . .'

Here we go. I love Francis, he's the closest thing I have to a brother, but I'm shocked that he's been sent to do their dirty work and talk me into returning home.

'But what? Let's hear it.'

'Verity . . . this?' He gestures about the kitchen, his damp hair lolling in strands. 'What are you doing?'

I repeat the reasons I gave to Avril on my first morning here.

'But running away isn't the answer.'

'Isn't it? So far, I've had peace and tranquillity. I've been surrounded by animals, nature and silence – which, I might add, is totally bliss when you've grown up amongst my lot. I've had time to myself. Space to think. Time to reflect on my decisions. I've made new memories and started a business. Now don't tell me you've had time for all those things in the last month, because I know different, Francis. Back home, my life is non-stop – morning, noon and night – nothing less than fifth gear all the time. Not a minute to think; constantly scrabbling to complete one task before the next task comes my way. Your life is no different, in many respects.'

He rolls his lips awkwardly as I speak. I've touched a nerve. I swiftly continue for fear of interruption.

'There's nothing you can't tell me about my sister. I love Avril to bits, but there are times I'm not too sure if I like her that much. From day one, she's run you ragged from morning till night: "Francis, get this. Francis, get that." Bless your cotton socks, Francis, but seriously, man, Avril would drive a saint crazy with her constant demands and griping.'

His shoulders straighten, his jaw tightens. I've poked that nerve again.

'It's not what you want to hear. I know how loyal you are towards her, but I see what I see, Francis. You're a decent bloke, and yet my sister takes you for granted.' The words spill from my lips without me drawing breath. I sit back, unsure how he is going to react. I don't want to sound like I'm lecturing him, but the truth is the truth. Francis shouldn't be here to talk me into returning home; he should be one of my allies, given that he probably understands my situation more than anyone.

Francis sips his coffee.

'See, even now your loyalty towards her is honourable but, believe me, Francis, there is more to life than keeping my sister sweet. And I am not participating in this family pantomime any more. I should have expected this when they all went quiet – which I foolishly assumed meant they'd accepted my decision.'

Francis sits back in his chair, cradling his mug, and stares at me. 'You always seem so happy – I never realised that you felt so strongly about Avril.'

'It's not just Avril, it's the whole set-up. The twin comparison thing, being the family's token single mum, with constant interference because everyone assumes I can't cope,' I say, leaning across the table to reinforce my point. 'Did they ever give me the chance to try and cope? No!'

'Come off it, Verity – you needed their help at the time. Little Tommy was only months old when—'

'Back when the boys were tiny and George had just left, I was knocked for six by his decision, but not every waking moment since.'

'This won't make them back off!'

'Francis ... urgh.' I fall silent. I'm wasting my breath. I love him to bits as an in-law, but he's not listening. How can he? He hasn't walked my path.

We stare across the table at each other; there's no animosity between us, there never has been. Despite a peppering of grey amongst the blond at his temples, he's never lost the boyish good looks Avril fell for at first sight. This guy has been sent round to my house on a million occasions with orders from my family to cut back overhanging branches, unblock toilets or mend the puncture on his nephew's bike, without uttering a word of complaint. He's the son my parents never had, and I love him purely for that.

'Look, Francis, they see me as poor little Verity. George left me in debt holding three babies and in the midst of post-natal depression, if the truth be told. So my family took control and bailed me out. I bet that was the first thing they mentioned about me when you met Avril.'

Francis nods begrudgingly.

'And their mindset of rescuing me has never altered from that day forth, but now things are different. I'm older, wiser and, yes, still bloody useless in many ways. I can't fix a leaky pipe, wouldn't know how to change a car tyre, and I still have no idea when it comes to gadgets malfunctioning. But I need to be the woman that *I* need to be. Not the woman they view me as. I'm not some pathetic victim who needs rescuing every day of her life. Well, not now anyway.'

'Don't we all need family in a time of crisis?' he asks, his shoulders relaxing.

'We do, and I was grateful back then. But they take over the show, instead of assisting or asking me what I need. There are times when I wonder why certain family members mucked in. It probably made them feel a little better about themselves.'

'Now that's unfair.'

'Is it? Ask yourself why Avril feels the need to boss everyone around so much. Why does she issue a constant flow of sodding advice? It makes people feel better about themselves, Francis.'

'They thought they were helping you to be a good mum,' he adds.

'I didn't want to be a good mum, I wanted to be a *happy* mum. There's a difference – and my boys needed the latter not the former. "Good" mums go by the rule book, they're neurotic and obsessive about germs and brilliant whites. I wanted to be a happy mum who laughed, made memories, played in the mud and enjoyed the role of being a mum, despite the grey whites, the lack of money and winging every decision I ever made.'

Francis sips his drink.

'How was your journey, anyway?' I ask, after a lengthy silence.

'Probably identical to yours: same route but minus the warm welcome.'

'What makes you think I had a welcoming party? I arrived late, walked up the driveway alongside a taxi driver and found my own way in – so don't be hyping it up to the folks back home. And guess what? I've survived. But now, well, looking at the size of that there suitcase, I'm getting a funny feeling you aren't catching the next flight out of here.' I gesture over my shoulder towards his luggage in the hallway.

'Nope. I've brought all I need to stay for as long as

necessary – I can work anywhere with my camera, lens and my laptop. Don't you worry; a bit of freelance photography work will suit me.'

'At least Shetland offers plenty of scenic views and wildlife, which saves you a wasted trip,' I say, adding, 'I wonder whose suggestion this assignment was?'

'Mine, actually. Not everything that occurs in our household is down to your twin sister, you know.'

I raise an eyebrow.

He knows exactly what I mean. Avril is hardly meek and mild. She might come across as the woman who has it all neatly pieced together, the glowing beacon of motherhood, but she's not happy. Not unless she's dictating the rules of life to some innocent who, in her opinion, has chosen to go off-piste regarding the game of life. And in our family, that's me.

'Are they really annoyed with me?' I ask, curiosity getting the better of me.

'Let's put it like this: your mother has moved into yours, while Avril and Amelia are staying with your dad, so . . . go figure.'

My jaw drops. 'Are you serious?'

'Quite serious. Your little stunt has had wider implications than your lads warming up a few home-made lasagnes,' he says, adding, 'but still, you'll be home in no time, so then everything can return to normal.'

I glare at him over the rim of my coffee mug. If only that were true.

Francis watches me, he looks bemused.

'What?'

'Nothing,' he says, looking beyond me into the hallway.

'Seriously . . . what?'

'Morning!' calls Magnus, striding past the table, a white towel wrapped about his middle, heading straight for the kettle. 'Anyone for a fresh coffee?'

Typical Francis. The soul of discretion, simply bemused at spotting a semi-naked man appearing along my hallway.

'Magnus, this is Francis, my brother-in-law. Francis, Magnus . . . my new . . . urgh, who am I trying to kid? This is Magnus.'

'Hi.'

'Morning, Francis, apologies for . . .' Magnus gestures towards his attire. 'Are you OK for coffee or do you want a fresh one?'

'I'll have a top-up, cheers,' says Francis, simply raising an eyebrow in my direction.

This isn't how I imagined the morning after the big night before. I was expecting an awkward silence, lame excuses even, but as for a half-naked Magnus offering coffee to my brother-in-law – nope, not in my wildest dreams.

'My oh my, what will Avril say when you report back?' I say in jest, covering my embarrassment.

'She simply won't believe me,' mutters Francis.

Isla

'Morning, Mungo, what's it to be today?' I say, as he surveys the empty cake cloches; there's no point filling the displays on a Monday purely for the artists. 'I've just iced a cake, if that's what you're after.'

'What's fresh?'

'They are all fresh. I don't sell stale cake or pastries.'

'I don't want what you couldn't sell on Saturday,' he says gruffly.

This man really tries my patience. I automatically prepare his large white coffee in an attempt to soften his mood.

'Saturday's baking is long gone. I made this fresh this morning. They'll have sold by tonight, if the artists come in for coffee, and I'll bake another tomorrow.'

'What was freshly made today then?'

'A ginger cake, though I've got a lovely carrot cake that's cooling, having just come from the oven, if you'd prefer. I've prepared an urn of soup too.'

Mungo stares intently at me.

'Mungo, did you hear? Would you like a slice of carrot cake?' The look of disgust he delivers me is scary.

'What's the soup of the day?' he asks, stroking his grey beard.

'Pumpkin – with two noggins of bread. Fancy it?' I ask, pointing to the blackboard placard clearly stating my soup of the day.

'Pumpkin?' Mungo turns his nose up at the mention, before adding, 'Leftovers from the wedding.'

'I had to use what I could from the wedding pumpkins – the hollowed-out flesh would have gone to waste otherwise. It's very nice, Dottie's had some earlier.'

He grimaces before shaking his head. 'I'll have ginger cake,' he says gruffly, snatching up his coffee as I head towards the back room to cut him a large slice of cake.

One of these days I'll manage an entire conversation with that man without a trance-like stare halting us halfway through.

Chapter Thirty

Tuesday 2 November

Nessie

I wipe my brow – an occupational requirement with the constant heat – as I lean against the doorjamb and survey the quiet yard of the gallery. Despite it being a Tuesday, I can envisage the empty yard as if it were a typical trading day with customers nipping in and out of every stable apart from ours. I simply don't get it. I've visited each artist during a working day, I know what each is creating and know their items are selling well: the whittler is hunched over his bench, knife in hand, eyes down; he doesn't even acknowledge folk as they enter to watch him work. He's probably the most antisocial of the vendors here and yet he makes loads of sales. The weaving ladies are the total opposite; they natter to everybody who enters, hardly allowing them to leave without a creative conversation, a sale made or an order taken. I reckon some customers purchase goods purely to escape – and the fabrics they weave aren't cheap, either. The candle maker is more like us at the forge. He works his craft, prepares his wicks and dips his wax, sculpts and colours as required, whilst being sociable; nothing over the top, but you don't feel coerced into buying, you're free to browse and leave empty handed, though he doesn't ignore his viewing audience. Verity at The Yarn Barn also has a nice approach; she sits in the corner knitting, yet she'll chat and joke with customers when they enter, allow them to browse . . . 'mooch', I think she calls it, and then asks if she can help.

I'm not jealous. Well, actually I am a tad jealous, but I need to find the thing that'll draw them into the forge. We're as good as the others. I honestly thought the sound of the blacksmith's hammer would be a calling to people's curiosity, but nah. In fact, Isaac gets more attention than I do, so maybe it's a good job he's nearer the doorway than I am; they view him and then leave before venturing further in to see what I'm up to. If the customers aren't prepared to visit me, then I need to force my wares into their path whilst they're browsing elsewhere. Customer awareness is half the issue when selling crafted goods; I can't opt for online sales, like some of the others do.

I'm going to stand here until I come up with one solution or option, and then I'll dedicate an hour to trying it. Sixty tiny minutes taken from my day to focus on drumming up more footfall and raise awareness of my goods. Some might say it's a waste of time, but if I don't crack this issue, I'm history. Quite literally.

I can't afford not to find a solution. It's an issue I need to go at hammer and tongs! Excuse the pun.

Within ten minutes, I'm back at my bench busily writing down a list of items that have come to mind whilst viewing the gallery yard. My hand is speeding across the paper as if my life depends on it, which is fitting.

'Slow down, lady . . . where's the fire?' calls Isaac, lowering his blowpipe and expertly cracking the completed vase from the end.

'Shhhh, one minute, otherwise I'll forget!' I say, raising my hand but not my head to answer him. My list grows with each item; my heart is singing at the thought of each. 'There!' I stand tall and address Isaac. 'I've had the idea of creating objects that complement the other artists' creations, and hopefully they will agree to display them in their stable with a little card stating where to purchase them.'

'Good thinking.'

'A candlestick holder for the candle maker, a pipe rack for the whittling man, a scrolled wall-hanging brace for the weaving ladies, tiny support racks for the ceramic tiles made by the art teacher and displayed in the café, a cake stand for The Orangery and . . .' I stop reading as Isaac delivers a wry smile. 'Sorry, did I get a bit carried away with sharing?'

'Just a bit, but it's good to see you inspired and eager to create, given your mood the past few days.'

'My mood?'

'Yeah, you've been as grouchy as hell . . . Dottie would call you "crabbit", for sure. I was frightened to say anything, as your hammer is definitely larger than mine.'

My mouth falls open. I suppose I've been a bit overwhelmed by the additional worry I've been lumbering about, but I'll turn over a new leaf and start afresh. 'Sorry, these projects will take time to make, but if this list of ideas helps my business, then my worries might fade too.'

'Fingers crossed.'

He's so lovely, rarely complaining. Working alongside me can't have been much fun, but I'll treat him to a quick drink one night as a means of apology.

He returns my stare.

'What?' I ask, sounding like a confused child.

'What are you waiting for? Chop, chop, get to it!'

'Oi, I was basking in the glory of a mighty fine solution, so don't trample all over it.'

'Basking, is that what you call it?' Isaac laughs, returning to his own wares. 'I can read you like a book, and that wasn't basking.'

Yeah, it was. Or so I'll have you think.

Verity

'I'm impressed!' says Francis, as he turns around, eyeing the inside of The Yarn Barn. 'You've really put your heart and soul into this project. The family haven't envisaged this.'

'Bloody typical – "it's our Verity, so it won't be much cop!" Is that it?'

'They don't think that,' says Francis, glaring at me. Then he adds, 'You need to show them via Skype, or whatever you're using to chat with the lads. They'd be interested to see it.'

'Highly unlikely, but worth a try,' I say.

'And the blacksmith rustled this up, did she?' asks Francis, giving the wool tree a gentle spin.

'She's very creative.'

'And you "kept it in the family", so to speak, which will please the gallery owners,' says Francis, making himself comfortable in my armchair and pointing up at the tiny sign highlighting Nessie's talent for creating bespoke items.

'It's the least I can do.'

'I see you've knitted more animal blankets; Amelia loved hers, by the way, plus the little knitting starter kit – though she hadn't started it when I left.' He gestures to my farmyard of blankets displayed on the countertop.

'They're proving really popular and, given their size, they don't take too long to make, especially the family of three little pigs.'

'You could try zoo animals next: lions, zebras, though an aardvark might prove a stretch with those long snouty noses!'

'Woah, woah, woah, I've enough to do, thanks – my left hand's giving me gyp as it is with a touch of RSI from hours of knitting,' I say, rubbing the back of my left hand, which is becoming a frequent action.

'Just saying, helping where I can.'

'You do know you need to knit for thirty minutes if you pinch my seat?' I jest, pointing towards my knitting basket beside the chair.

'Stuff that! I'd wreck it in minutes. Knitting looks like cat's cradle with sticks!' He jumps up and straightens his jeans. 'Who's this?'

I turn to follow his gaze towards the open door as Crispy duck waddles in.

'That is the gallery's resident duck. Not my favourite customer, as he tends to crap everywhere, but he's harmless, I suppose. Shoo, ya little bugger,' I say, flapping my hands to direct him back out.

Quack, quack! argues the duck, as he totters back into the yard.

'Not your thing?'

'Hell, no! Nessie mentioned that Jemima has hand-reared him after she found him on her allotment last year. Everyone loves him. The little children seek him out on visits, but I can't see the fascination; though I'll admit he does look cute swimming in the stable's old water trough.'

'Careful, you might be getting attached.'

'Doubt it . . . I'd much prefer him with a serving of rich orange or plum sauce, mmmm!'

Francis shakes his head, aghast at my suggestion.

'I didn't know ducks crapped so much until I came here. They brush and hose the yard down every morning because of that duck. He's maturing; he was a mass of fluffy brown when I arrived but now you can see his emerald-green feathers coming through. Come on, let's show you the rest of the joint,' I say, flicking off the overhead lights. 'I might even treat you to a speciality coffee if Isla's still here, otherwise it'll be a DIY kettle job in The Orangery.'

Everyone knows if I'm present; my turquoise bike leaning

against the outer wall is a sure sign. Though today I've given Francis the scenic route by walking.

I securely lock my stable door, first ensuring that Crispy duck is clearly visible, waddling about the yard pecking between the cobblestones.

'Apparently, these were all run-down stables last year. Jemima and Ned struck up a friendship on the allotments adjoining his land, and this is the end result in a matter of months. Amazing, isn't it?'

'Quite. I suppose it depends how derelict the outbuildings were – but still, he's thrown a fair amount of cash at it to achieve this level of spec. The interior work hasn't ruined the exterior aspect, has it?'

We stand in the yard as I point at various stables, saying who's who. Some doors are securely locked; others are wide open, suggesting the resident artists have chosen a day of quiet creation without customers present.

The Orangery door is locked. 'She must have gone; never mind, it'll be a basic coffee, so don't expect a fancy motif in your froth,' I say, flicking through my keys for the right one.

'How come you've got a key?'

'Everyone has – the owners want us to use it as our canteen. There's an honesty box under the counter for staff, though I doubt everyone chucks in what they should. Do you want cake too?'

The heavy door closes with a thud behind us as I head for the counter, grab the kettle, fill it with water and throw some change into the staff honesty box. Francis wanders about the seating area, taking it all in.

'This is great . . . are these the same artists as the stables?' he asks, viewing the glass display cabinets.

'No. You can rent a shelf on a monthly basis, I forget how much for. The ceramics and textile lady, Melissa, she's a local art teacher, so she can't personally manage a rental all week. It makes sense, doesn't it? Isla sorts the cash sales at the end of each week. Melissa says she's doing quite well, regularly restocking an entire shelf. I'm not sure about the others.'

'There's even confetti for sale.'

'Yeah, thanks to the elderly dear who cleans the manor house. She grows award-winning delphiniums on her allotment plot; we used her confetti on Sunday for Jemima and Ned's wedding, which was a lovely touch. You really are impressed, aren't you?'

'I am. This is nothing like I'd imagined. Are they on honeymoon now?'

'No, what with the gallery venture just opening. I believe they're going away for a long weekend, later in the month.'

'And this . . .?' Francis points to the nearest wall-mounted blackboard advertising future events.

'Poetry open mics and comedy evenings – they're quite popular in town, so Isla wishes to host a couple here in the coming months, after hours, of course. Given the space, comfy chairs, plus the endless supply of coffee and cake – it's sure to appeal to some in the local community. I'm starting a knitting group this week too.'

'Truly inspiring, Verity. You're very lucky to be part of such a venture.'

'Here,' I say, offering him a mug of coffee and nudging a plate of ginger cake along the countertop, which I'd located in the chiller fridge. 'You almost sound convinced . . . aligning yourself with my thinking, perhaps?'

Francis takes the offered refreshments, as I collect mine and settle at the nearest table.

'I don't like how you organised it, I'll be honest. I'm not liking the three lads being left alone, though your mother has sorted that issue. But, having seen what I've seen, I've more appreciation as to why you want to be part of this.'

I sip my coffee, and smile. 'Excellent. Any chance you can convince the others?'

Francis gives me a sideways glance, as he tucks into his piece of cake.

'Any other questions?' I say, easing back into my chair and warming my hands on my coffee mug.

'What's the story between you and Magnus then?'

'I meant regarding the gallery.'

'I'm sure you did. I didn't. So, out with it.'

'There's nothing to tell. We've enjoyed a few drinks together, a meal together and now, well, now . . . things have moved in another direction.'

'Shagging.'

'Francis! How uncouth!'

'Come off it, Verity.'

'In all the years I've known you, I've never heard you speak like that. Don't you let my sister hear you, or you'll be in trouble.'

'Phuh! Not as much trouble as you when she catches wind of this. Your sister doesn't do "casual", remember that.'

'Isn't that the truth! She couldn't spell it, let alone live it, act it or accommodate it in her perfectly organised world.'

'You're being careful, like?'

'Francis, no! I love you like a brother but I'm not taking contraception advice from you. Enough talk . . . just drink your coffee and scoff your cake.' I baulk as his last two sentences replay in my mind, before adding, 'We need to determine how long you're kipping in my spare room; I opted for a year of independence, which certainly didn't include in-laws sharing my morning brew.'

Chapter Thirty-One

Wednesday 3 November

Nessie

'Morning! Thanks for coming,' calls Isaac as I enter the forge.

I'm arriving slightly later than usual, having got waylaid by Ned asking how Mavis's hands are. Thankfully, they've healed well in the ten days since the workshop.

'Oh, your hair's changed again!'

'Morning. What?' I'm puzzled. Did he just mention my new mahogany hair colour?

'Oversleep, did we?'

'No. I was waylaid by Ned asking for an update on Mavis's injuries. He's relieved to hear she's not claiming against my insurance. Bless her. She's taken full responsibility so isn't pursuing compensation.'

'It wouldn't have involved him, would it?'

'It could have, I suppose,' I say, before adding, 'but he and Jemima are like that – they're interested in everyone, aren't they?'

'True. Anyway, guess what's gone?'

I grimace. I'm not a guessing-game kind of girl.

'I said guess what's gone?' he repeats.

'Gone?'

'Gone. Sold. Purchased.'

I dash towards my counter display, looking for the painted leaves of the coat rack. It's not there.

'It's sold?'

'First thing this morning, to the first customer who came in. Plus, she wants three more the same but slightly different to give as presents. I've noted her name, address and phone number on your pad. She's paid half the cost as a deposit and said to call her when the others are complete.'

'Are you serious?' I hastily nip to my corner desk and find the note and forty-five pounds in cash. 'Isaac, that is unbelievable.'

'I told you it would sell. A touch of paint broke up the heaviness of the piece.'

I am gobsmacked.

'I nearly phoned your mobile to tell you but then had second thoughts. I reckoned the surprise might lift you for the day.'

'Isaac, that is so sweet. It has really made my day. It means I can start work on items that are virtually paid for already and will be heading out of the forge for sure.'

'Remind me, who won the bet?'

I begin to laugh. 'You did, Isaac, you won the bet.'

'Thank you very much, I have a good eye for spotting what's hot and what's not.'

'Have you really?' If nothing else, his wisecracks make sharing the forge worthwhile.

I work non-stop on the ordered coat racks with the painted leaves. I do my interpretation of the same design as before, but make each one different by altering the placement of the decoration and the shape of various leaves. Small differences, but nothing major to affect the overall appearance of the piece.

'It feels good to be creating items for a specific order,' I say to Isaac, as he tidies away for his lunch break.

'See, I'm not so great at that. I love to go with the flow when it comes to creating and then hope a buyer can be found. I feel nervous creating to order, in case I don't produce the item they envisage in their heads. There are too many opportunities for things to go wrong – or for happy accidents to occur, which actually on closer inspection enhance the piece somewhat.'

'Happy accidents – I like that phrase.'

'You have those, right?'

'All the time. I'll hammer something one way, think I've lost it or made a poor decision, only for it to work out perfectly well in the long run and be, as you call it, a "happy accident".'

'Are those all complete?'

'Yes, the lady is dropping by tomorrow to pay in full. I'll be in first thing, so I'll be here when she collects them.'

'I think she'll be impressed by the speed with which you've created them.'

'To tell you the truth, so am I!'

Verity

Five minutes ago, I was panicking as there was no one here, yet now there's a dozen people, bustling for a comfy spot in The Orangery. The chattering has started already as they remove coats and collect their knitting projects from various bags and rucksacks. I feel quite emotional. I pinned up two adverts – one in The Yarn Barn the other in here – and this is the result. I'm pleased that we've got two gents joining us: knitting has always been a unisex hobby, yet some think it strange when men knit. I've found they're more logical, sticking to the pattern without deviation, less inclined to tweak a little detail, to create something off the cuff – or should that be off the shoulder? – despite the pattern's instructions.

'Afternoon, everyone, I'm Verity, proprietor of The Yarn Barn. Please settle yourselves wherever you feel comfy in this section of the café. Isla is serving a hot beverage plus a cake of your choice for four pounds, so do treat yourselves. I've placed a selection of photocopied patterns on the middle coffee table in case anyone is interested in a new blanket project for the local Special Care Baby Unit. They're asking for knitted donations, so I thought we could make a collective contribution. If anyone needs help, advice or has a technical issue with their knitting, I'll be plonking myself down just there – once I have my cake!' There's a ripple of laughter as I point to the nearest wing-backed chair, bagsying it for my own creature comforts.

It takes no time before there's a pleasant hum of contented chatter, accompanied by the clink of coffee cups, plus 'oohh's and 'ahhh's complimenting the delicious cake selection. I'm quite taken with how folk have simply shown up and dived into an afternoon of knitting. A roar of laughter occurs every now and then, causing others to look up with an expectant expression.

'You've done very well to get a gathering this size on your first week, don't you think?' says the willowy blonde seated to my right, who I recognise but can't quite place. 'A friend of mine went to a group once where she was the only knitter to attend, so she felt obliged to stay and keep the lady company. She never went back.'

'That was my biggest fear,' I say, adding, 'you're Melissa, aren't you?'

'Yes, I'm Melissa. I create the ceramics and textiles in the display cases over there. I don't usually knit but thought I'd drop by.'

'Very nice, I'm glad you could join us. I hear you're getting plenty of sales?'

'Yes, I'm having to restock the cabinet each week. I work part time, teaching art at the local college, so the display units are perfect for me.'

'Excellent. And what are you knitting?' I ask, noting that she's casting on in pale lemon wool.

'Well, I'm attempting a matinee jacket ... though looking at the pattern I think I've bitten off more than I can chew,' she says, shaking her head.

'For you?' I say, subtly eyeing her torso for signs of a bump.

'It's early days, but I couldn't help myself.'

'There's nothing as lovely as hand-knitted babywear. Here, pass me your pattern – let's take a look,' I say, gesturing towards her paper.

She swiftly hands it over, and I can see she's gone for traditional baby knitwear. It's not that difficult – but for a novice, which I assume she is, it'll look like a baffling code of initials, numbers and brackets. This is the part I enjoy the most: teaching others a simple craft, helping them to become better knitters, and sharing ideas. Melissa leans in as I decipher her pattern; she'll have mastered the few fancy stitches in no time.

'Do you know what each of the abbreviations mean?'

'Not really,' says Melissa, giving a chuckle.

'But you know how to knit garter stitch.'

'Oh yeah, my granny taught me when I was little. She was a big knitter.'

There's that lovely line again. I love it when someone says how their granny taught them to knit. Much like Isla and her baking, it links the generations through memories and just goes to show that the traditional skills never truly die.

I happily spend the next ten minutes talking Melissa through her pattern and then sit back as she confidently begins to knit her first few rows, before returning to my own project: a cardigan for display purposes.

The time flies by and, before I know it, two hours have passed and we're packing our knitting away, grabbing our coats and bidding each other goodbye with a cheery 'see you next week'.

'Excuse me, can I ask if you're hiring knitters?' asks an elderly gent, who earlier had a gaggle of happy ladies encircling him.

'Not yet, but there's definitely scope to consider it in the future,' I say, knowing full well that to offer customers a knitting service would definitely add to my business. I couldn't possibly do it single-handed.

'Could I leave my name and address? I'm very good at intricate cabling and traditional Highland knitwear, which is always very popular,' he says, adding, 'I live fairly close by and can usually get an adult jumper finished in under a week.'

'That's fabulous . . . and you are?' I ask, clocking his beautiful arran jumper with highly intricate cabling from waistband to crew neck.

'Niven McAllister, at your service,' he says, a twinkle coming to his eyes.

'Well, Niven, can I ask you to come across the yard with me so I can jot down your details? I am certain that I'll be needing your knitting skills very quickly. Sales have taken off like nobody's business, but not everyone can knit the garment they fall in love with. This way.'

I'm intrigued that such a quintessential gent has a penchant for knitting, but that's the beauty of this hobby, we can each sit cosy and snug within our own four walls and create beautiful garments to share with the world. I just hope that I'm still as active as he appears to be, and still knitting, when I reach his age. He must be ninety, if a day.

I spend the next half an hour happily chatting with Niven as he inspects my supply of yarn; I seem to have gained his approval and he's certainly acquired mine.

Chapter Thirty-Two

Isla

'Come on, Jutt,' I say, as we walk the main coastal road a little after dusk.

It's not the best time to exercise him but I have no other choice given the time of year. The clocks have gone back, which means the sun is setting whilst I'm still at work, but we're staying safe with my fluorescent vest and Jutt's matching high-vis cuffs which wrap above each hoof. You can't miss us walking on a bleakly lit road.

Mucking him out isn't such an issue; I've got an electrical source cabled into his small stable. I can easily do that after we've exercised. It's a pity that I can't accept trekking lessons any other days than Mondays and Tuesdays – and then only if I choose not to attend the gallery during my time off. Simply another restriction I have to consider whilst juggling work, my business studies and family commitments. It's a good job my mum picks me up each night, otherwise I'd need a bike like Verity, or lose thirty minutes a day walking home from work.

Jutt plods along, his mane bobbing with each stride, his lead looped securely in my palm. It's not ideal doing this each night but it gives him some variety, affording him a change of environment and offering a harder surface for his hooves.

A dark car dashes past us, closer than I'm happy with; Jutt and I are quite bulky walking side by side. They could have given us more room. Bloody idiot.

I watch the red brake lights flare in the distance. Mmmm, going too fast for the bend in the road too. Some people haven't got time to live.

We continue on our way, turning in at the driveway leading to the cottage and home for Jutt.

Parked at the top beside the cottage is Magnus's car; there's no sign of Floss, so he's not tending to his sheep. I smile. Verity will be pleased, despite her questioning his whereabouts the other week. My mum keeps asking if I know anything, but I haven't squealed. It would be wrong; Verity's my friend.

We traipse past the parked car, unlatch the gate and go through into the paddock. Jutt scampers off to frolic as soon as I release his bridle lead, whilst I head straight to his small stable for a mucking-out session.

Verity

'What you're saying is that it's sex, and that's it!'

'*Shhhh*, keep your voice down, Francis is in the lounge. What I'm saying is why rush things? I ... we ... enjoyed ourselves and each other's company, so why does it have to become all formal?' I quickly turn to the kitchen counter to slice onions in an attempt to avoid this discussion.

Magnus had only dropped by to make sure I was OK after the other morning. He shifts in his seat, causing the chair to scrape on the tiles.

I continue to chop, allowing the cutting action to fill the growing silence.

'So, is that enough for you?'

'It's nice.'

'Nice?'

'Yeah, nice.'

'Great.' His tone is thick with sarcasm.

I remain schtum. I'm not ready for this. I'm not up for an argument, let alone an in-depth discussion of where we are after one shared night.

I'm done slicing, so I hastily grab another onion from the fridge to continue my act.

'What you're saying is that this is it? Me, you, a drink sometime, a meal on occasion, and possibly sex if we both feel like it. Nothing more. Nothing meaningful, no connection. Basically, no strings attached—'

'Excuse me, I think the other night proved we certainly have a connection, Magnus,' I interrupt, not daring to turn about to fully involve myself in this unexpected conversation. 'Isn't this all a bit heavy and rushed after one night?'

'You know what I mean. I'm interested in you, yet you're opting for casual – like the "friends with benefits" cliché. No dating. No courting.'

'I think you'll find they're the same thing.'

'No, they're not. Dating is simply getting to know someone; courting is more serious.'

Things have obviously changed since my time with George.

'Don't tell me your lads don't date girls and decide with each date whether to take it further or not?'

I stop chopping and turn around to face him. 'Not really. Our Jack has been with the same girl since school. I can't imagine at fifteen he separated the two – maybe one just evolved into the other?'

'Exactly. That's hardly a conscious decision, but there's a difference, Verity. And that's the discussion I'd like us to have. I've dated lots of women but I haven't courted, as such. My last two relationships pretty much fizzled out without either of us deciding otherwise.'

'So, you want courting?'

'No, I want us to start dating. Getting to know each other properly.'

'What's this then?' I gesture with the knife between us.

'This seems to be us chatting half-heartedly while you make dinner for yourself and your brother-in-law. Something I'm not entirely sure I should be witnessing, given my desire to get to know you outside of your domestic role.'

My mouth falls open in disbelief. 'Francis moves out in a day or so to the B&B up the road. I'm simply trying to be hospitable, providing him with an evening meal; he'll incur enough expenses staying elsewhere, as you well know.'

Magnus continues as if I haven't spoken. 'No offence, but after our night together I seriously thought we'd discuss what happened between us in an adult fashion and take it from there. You seem to be avoiding the topic, wrongly assuming I'll happily fall into the trap of being up for a night of passion whenever you call the shots – and that isn't what I'm after.'

I turn back to continue my chopping. I'll need something else in a minute or I'll have a mountain of sliced onion. I could busy myself slicing the mushrooms, I suppose. I collect the tub from the fridge and repeat.

I like Magnus, very much. I haven't felt this comfortable alongside a man for years. The sex was great. The affection, tenderness, and even his concern that he hasn't heard from me, are all new to my world. I want more of that, but I can't commit. I hadn't planned on this happening. I came here to find independence, not a similar existence to the one I left behind; which is why I've asked Francis to organise digs elsewhere. I love him as a brother, but I don't need intrusion from my family.

'Verity, are you even listening?'

'I'm listening. I'm trying to cook as well.'

'Maybe cooking isn't the focus right now.'

'But I've just stood here and chopped all this.' I step aside to reveal the chopping board.

'And there's the issue, Verity. I think you're so wrapped up in doing your own thing, making up for lost time, proving to your family that you're now independent and standing on your own two feet, that you haven't even realised that, actually, I'm asking for more of you than you're prepared to give.'

'What?' Where's this coming from?

'I don't want some "shag buddy" situation where I drop by a coupla times a week. Call it old-fashioned, but right now I'd quite like two adults to make an effort to get to know each other and see if anything develops.' Silence descends as Magnus slowly stands, slides his chair under the table and collects his car keys from the window ledge. 'Have a think about it and let me know.'

I'm dumbstruck. What the hell was that?

I watch as he leaves my kitchen. I hear his boots as he walks along the hallway, followed by the opening and closing click of the inner door.

'Magnus!'

No answer.

He's joking, right?

I expect him to reappear at any second, jesting that he's pulling my leg.

He doesn't.

Instead, I hear the thud of a car door slamming shut, then the throaty hum of an engine revving. His headlights shine into the kitchen, illuminating a section of the far wall, as he slowly reverses down the driveway.

Did that just happen?

I stare at the two huge piles of chopped vegetables. Francis had better be hungry, otherwise what the hell am I going to do with this lot?

Chapter Thirty-Three

Thursday 4 November

Nessie

'Morning!' I say, entering the warm stable. 'How's tricks?'

Whittling man looks up from his work, a startled expression flitting across his weathered features; he has a knife in one hand, a chunk of wood protruding from the other. He doesn't answer but gives a curt nod, his piercing blue eyes – the telltale Scandinavian heritage of this area – boring into mine from his hunched position on a three-legged wooden stool, which I presume he crafted himself.

'Anyway, I wanted to offer you this,' I say, holding a metal pipe rack out for his inspection and, hopefully, acceptance. 'I was wondering if you might like to display your carved pipes on it, alongside a small card stating that I made it.'

He places the wood carefully on the floor, then slowly chews the inside of his bottom lip before taking the offered rack. I watch as he twists and turns the object, his gaze scrutinising every join and weld.

'How much?' His voice sounds as gruff as he looks.

'Oh, nothing. I thought it might be useful to you – and, in return, useful to me if customers wish to purchase one, or are simply intrigued to know what else I make.'

'I see.' He offers it back to me, collects his chunk of wood from the floor and continues to whittle. Curled shavings fly off as he slices the sharp blade back and forth across the surface grain.

Does he not understand? Is he thinking about it?

I stand and wait, unsure of what to say or whether to leave. Is that it, am I dismissed? I turn my pipe rack over in my hands, viewing it afresh, as he did a few seconds before. The joins are neat, the lines are clean, and I've kept the decoration to a minimum, assuming it was something that would appeal to men. I assume it is still mainly men who enjoy a pipe nowadays, though a female smoker wouldn't be offended by the intricate scrolling detail along the back panel.

I watch him as he works: head bowed, back and shoulders hunched forward, his elbows resting on his splayed knees and his hand repeatedly working the blade against the fresh wood. Surely he gets backache sitting like that? How long do I need to wait before I speak?

'Are you not interested then?' I mutter, almost apologising for my presence.

He ceases carving, looks up from below a furrowed brow and stares at me. 'Do I look interested, young lady?'

'Well, no, which is why I'm asking. Everyone else has been most accommodating with the items I've made for their crafts, yet you seem indifferent, almost insulted, that I dared to venture in here and offer you a display rack free of charge. Essentially, that's all it is. It hasn't cost you a penny, in time or effort . . . and those pipes –' I gesture towards his countertop where eight pipes sit neatly in a row – 'don't you think they'd look better presented on a rack, so the customer can view the detailing more easily?'

'Nope.'

'I thought racks such as these were how smokers kept their pipes at home.'

He shrugs before carrying on with the task in hand.

I can't quite believe this. How many folk would refuse a

freebie nowadays? Not many. In fact, the opposite usually occurs: offer anything free of charge and you've soon got a stream of people requesting it; everyone wants something for nought in these times.

'So sorry to have bothered you. I'll leave you in peace.' I turn on my heels and swiftly leave.

I realise that I haven't made an effort to get to know him over recent weeks. But surely being part of the same gallery should make us want to support each other in any way we can? Obviously not.

I march across the cobbles, the pipe rack swinging from my clutches, and enter the forge in a fug of self-righteous anger which even Isaac has yet to behold.

'Oh dear, like that, is it?' he calls, looking up from his workbench.

I stop mid-stride. 'You know the whittling guy?'

'Yeah.'

'Well, he's a tit!'

Isaac's eyebrows lift, his jaw judders and he begins to laugh.

I continue. 'I offered him this –' I hold aloft my pipe rack – 'and all he does is inspect it before handing it back to me without a word, then he continues to whittle as if he can't possibly lose a precious moment of his day to converse with me.'

'Reject it, did he?'

'Rejected it ... me ... us, the whole bloody concept of the gallery community, if you ask me. How can he sell as much as he does when he hasn't got the manners he was born with?'

'Folk aren't buying his manners, though – it's his woodworking talent they're after.'

'In that case, I seriously don't get it. We are so welcoming to every customer that comes through that door, yet I'm struggling to sell ... and you, well, you're doing much better, but still. Old moody chops over there sits on his stool, barely lifts his head, yet has his goods flying out the door. Go figure!' I say, finally slumping down at my workbench to stare across the forge at Isaac. 'And he really needs to sweep up each day – there's a sea of wood shavings covering the floor.'

'That might be an attraction for some – the smell is quite alluring, don't you think?'

'No. No, I don't. I think he's a lazy craftsman – and ignorant for good measure.' My steam is all blown out, and I'm now deflated after what had been a good hour of my day.

'And the rest of them?'

'Well, they couldn't be more pleased with a freebie; the weaving ladies virtually insisted on paying for theirs, but I stuck to my guns. "No, a simple card explaining where customers can purchase one is sufficient for me." Bless them – not like old misery guts over there. Can you believe it?'

Isaac smiles and nods. 'Yep, I can. Not everyone has your outlook or vision; they do what they do, and nothing more. If I were you, I'd let it go, focus on the good eggs who want to support you, and leave the likes of him to do his own thing.'

'Too right. Bugger him and his wood whittling. He obviously doesn't take my craft seriously.'

'Coffee?' asks Isaac, climbing down from his stool and stretching his back.

'Yeah. Can I have some cake too? A big piece.'

'Got to you that much, has he?' he says, heading for the door.

Isla

'What's the special today?' asks Niven, finding his reading specs to peer at the counter's blackboard.

'Nettle broth – I made it fresh this morning, and it's selling like hot cakes.'

'I'm not sure about these new age recipes.'

'It's not new. It's as old as the hills. With two noggins of bread to accompany it, you'll be full until teatime.' He's the first person to waver, every other customer has jumped at the chance of tasting it. 'Would you like to sample it before you decide?' I ask, not sure where that suggestion came from.

'Could I have just a spoonful?'

I'm taken aback by my own suggestion, let alone his reaction. He never chats, even though we're distant relatives; some folk simply aren't interested in maintaining family links and keeping in touch. Mum says, 'He's one of the older generation who keeps himself to himself'.

'Of course.' I nip through to the kitchen, looking for a small container; an egg cup would be perfect. I scour the plate rack, the mug rack – wanting something to jump out at me as being suitable for a mouthful to taste. I turn to view the paper merchandise; we bought plenty of samples but didn't reorder everything for opening day. I spy the ketchup cups: perfect. Tiny paper vessels that seemed too fiddly for everyday use, but they'll hold a mouthful of soup to sip. I return to the counter, open the soup urn and ladle a tasting sample into the paper cup.

'There you go, Niven – try that. Mind, it'll be hot. The nettles were freshly picked this morning by Dottie off her allotment. You know Dottie Nesbit?'

Niven nods, taking the offered sample.

Butterflies are fluttering in my stomach – I can't believe that such a simple solution came straight to mind. If I leave a pile of ketchup cups – tasting cups – close at hand beneath the counter, we could offer a sample to anyone who is unsure. It suggests a firm belief in our foods, almost a guarantee of their quality. We're so confident that we'll let you try before you buy!

I try not to watch Niven slurp the soup, but it's difficult not to note his reaction as his taste buds are awoken by the earthy yet vibrant taste.

'Oooo, now that is lovely! Quite delicious. Yes, I could eat a bowl of that … with bread, did you say?'

'Two chunks: white, brown, rye, wholemeal or sesame seeds.'

Niven's eyes widen as he surveys the wicker bread basket before him.

I hastily grab a soup bowl and ladle, then serve a generous helping of the steaming soup and deliver it to Niven's tray.

'And a pot of tea?' I ask, knowing his usual order.

'Please.' He beams a contented smile.

I might try the same tack with Mungo, if he nips in for lunch.

Having made his pot of tea, I turn to the till, ring in his order and take his payment.

'Are you OK carrying that?' I say, not wishing to suggest he can't, but the man has a walking stick to contend with.

'I'll be fine, as long as I take it slowly. I walk everywhere, you know.'

'I've seen you. Many a time we've passed you when we're out in the car and my mum always says, "Niven's as fit as a fiddle thanks to walking."'

'I've walked all my life.'

With that he hooks the walking stick over his wrist as he collects the tray and shuffles towards the nearest table. He does take it slowly, but he gets there without slopping his tea or soup.

I collect my dishcloth and wipe down the countertop. My granny would have been exactly the same; she was a tough old bird like the rest of her generation.

Nessie

I thrust the piece of hammered metal into my slack tub amidst a rising cloud of steam, ready to discard it on the trash pile.

'That's the third time today I've messed up hammering a basic piece. What the hell is wrong with me?' I say, more to myself than Isaac. 'In fact, what's been my excuse for all the things that have gone wrong this week?'

'Are you having a bad day?' asks Isaac, mixing coloured powders in a small dish.

'A bad day. A bad week. A bad fecking year!' I snap, throwing the cooled metal on to my waste pile, causing a clatter of metal to resound about the forge.

'Coffee?'

'Coffee? Gin? A full-time job elsewhere – you decide.' I know where this outburst is heading, even if Isaac isn't fully up to speed. 'I don't know why I bother.' My voice breaks on the final word.

I should offer a warning bell for evacuation when moods like this descend upon me, but so far Isaac hasn't witnessed the full-blown, maximum pixilation, Dolby surround sound version which is brewing within and will ignite upon him uttering a single kind syllable.

'Hang on – that sounds rather a defeatist attitude for such a talented woman.'

Wrong tack, Isaac.

'Don't be nice to me . . .' I mouth as tears loom, blurring my vision. I'm trying so hard, doing everything I can, and yet I feel dreadful. Useless, in fact.

'Hey, hey, hey. What's all this? You're usually a little fire-cracker, not weeping like this.'

Now I can't see him at all, he's just a blobby shape moving across the forge towards me. I'm in danger of dissolving into a quivering mess, when a warm gentle hand rests upon my shoulder.

'Come on, take a seat and dry your eyes. What's brought this on?'

I grab my usual cloth and frantically dab at my cheeks and eyes, sniffing and snotting in turn, which doesn't feel good from my side and probably looks much worse from his.

'I just can't keep doing this day in and day out . . . I love what I do, I'm giving it my all. By continually failing, I'm actually tarnishing my family history. How can I . . .?' I couldn't articulate my final word, so Isaac has no hope of making any sense of it as he steers me towards my wooden stool. I automatically climb up and sit there in misery like an upset child, minus the wounded knee, before continuing. 'And you deserve to share your workspace with a successful business not one that must be bringing you down mentally . . . and possibly affecting your sales too.'

'Don't you worry about me; I'm doing just fine. Sales are decent, revenue is ticking along nicely, and I've had a few commissions come through online, so please don't give my venture another thought. That's simply adding weight to your own troubles.'

I nod, accepting his kind words. 'I feel so vulnerable, but how can I keep battling on when every day is wearing me down?'

'I get it. Eating is pretty essential in my life, along with paying the mortgage, the bills and affording the odd luxury, here and there.'

I sniff, taking back a little self-respect, having dabbed my eyes dry. My shoulders cease quivering as I let out a deep breath. 'Sorry.'

'Don't give me sorry . . . you're just having a wobble – it happens to the best of us.'

I raise my eyebrows in a comical fashion. I can't see him repeating this performance any day soon.

'Not that I do the teary stuff, but maybe I should. It might surprise you to walk in here one day and I'll be the one with a wobbly chin, protruding lip and clutching a hanky,' he kindly jests, playfully bumping my shoulder with his knuckles.

'I can't see that happening,' I mutter, a smile breaking across my tear-stained face.

'You never know,' he adds.

'Thank you, anyway. I feel slightly better now, having shown myself up.'

'You haven't shown yourself up at all. You probably thought it would be easier, nearly plain sailing – but it isn't, is it?'

I shake my head.

'I never cry in front of anyone,' I mutter.

'Well, I'm honoured then,' he says softly.

I'm starting to feel stupid now that my tears have dried and the emotions have passed. My cloth is a mixture of tears and snot, so I'm unsure which section remains clean.

I say the only thing that comes to mind. 'I need coffee. And cake.'

Chapter Thirty-Four

Verity

The Yarn Barn has been busy all day. It's amazing how quickly my display garments sell once the crisp autumn weather turns to November damp. Today, the same customer purchased all my children's jumpers and four crocheted animal blankets. I've opted for a quiet night in front of the TV, with a fresh ball of wool, and I've invited Francis over for company.

He goes to speak, then shakes his head before changing his mind.

'What?'

'Nothing.'

'No. Go on – you can be honest, you won't offend me.'

'Growing up as an only child, I assumed that siblings would have their moments, their arguments and skirmishes, but nothing serious, nothing monumental. But since joining this family . . . I've had that idea well and truly squashed. I never thought sisters would act like this.'

'All families argue, Francis.'

He shakes his head. 'Not like you pair.'

I pout.

'Honestly. I've spent enough time in other people's families, amongst friends and relations, to know what the reality of family looks like. But this family . . . you've taken it to an Olympic standard where the sniping is concerned. It's sad.'

I mouth the word 'sad'.

'It's the very reason—' He stops, then withdraws from the conversation by sipping his coffee.

'Go on. Like I said, you won't offend me.'

'No.'

I watch him intently. I suspect his drink is too hot, but he still drinks it – otherwise, he'll have to continue his train of thought.

'I don't hate her as much as she belittles me,' I venture.

He puts his mug down on the tabletop with a slight thump. 'She doesn't hate you. You said it yourself, there are times when the two of you don't like each other, but Avril doesn't hate you, Verity. She'd be mortified if she thought you believed that.'

'I'm not convinced,' I mutter. 'I don't blame you for not wanting to waste your breath.'

'It wasn't about that.'

I give a little snort, sure that he is lying.

Francis tilts his head, capturing my gaze. 'No, seriously, it wasn't, Verity.'

'It's OK, I guess it must get tiring listening to the same argument between the same women, going around in circles for evermore.' I drain my coffee mug and stand up.

'Verity, we haven't had a second child because Avril is adamant that she's not going to force Amelia into the same situation that you and she have created. That's what I was about to say.'

My expression drops.

'Exactly. My wife doesn't want another child because of her own relationship with her twin sister.' His eyes glisten before he gulps. 'Nothing to do with me, our marriage, our financial situation, or even Amelia.'

'Us?'

He nods.

I slump back down into the armchair. 'Oh, Francis. I'm sorry. I just thought that you'd both decided one baby was enough . . .'

My words fade as he slowly shakes his head.

'Nope. My wife doesn't want to cause our daughter the pain and upset that she's endured by having a sibling. Personally, I think it's ludicrous, but Avril is dead set against it, despite everything she sees within other families. Your three lads are a fine testament to how supportive siblings can be. Whereas I vowed never to have a single child, given my upbringing; I was always longing for a younger sibling. But one of us has to compromise, and it looks like it'll be me.'

I feel quite ashamed. 'I suppose every guy wants a boy,' I say, filling the silence.

'Not really. Another girl would suit me fine,' he says, without hesitation. 'I want my daughter to have a younger sibling. But the more you girls keep slating each other, the chances are looking pretty slim. Plus time is running out, given Avril's age.'

'Amelia's already six,' I add.

'I know. It would be nearly a seven-year age gap if Avril agreed . . . that's not what I wanted, either.'

'And Avril know this?'

Francis nods.

I'm lost for words; I had my boys, Avril had her girl. It never entered my head that their family life wasn't as rosy as she'd always made out.

Nessie

I sit back from the table, having enjoyed a midweek roast with the family – my first in eons, given my working hours each Sunday. It feels good to be surrounded by loved ones after my meltdown earlier.

'How's things diddling at the forge, lass?' asks Granddad, seated beside me.

'So, so.'

'Oh, that good!' he chuckles, exchanging a concerned glance with my father, who is seated at the far end of the family table of five. 'I'm not sure that's the answer I was hoping for.'

'Nor me, Granddad, but that's how tricks are. I'm making a whole range of goods in iron and steel, but they simply aren't selling. Call it a trend or a phase but the footfall isn't coming through the forge. I've popped a few heavy items on display in the yard outside, so customers can get a taste of the selection before entering the forge, but it's not working.'

'Won't they be pinched?' asks Mum from the opposite side of the table, her furrowed brow suspicious of everyone.

'Not if I place only bulky items outside, such as decorative planters, coat stands – they'd struggle to pop one inside a jacket or a pocket, wouldn't they?'

'Seems uncalled for, to me,' she adds, standing to clear the plates.

'Seems a necessity, to me . . . if I'm to find my footing in the gallery. Honestly, Mum, the other artists have got customer sales coming out of their ears, but little old me, well . . . I'm standing by, waiting for any sign of customer interest let alone sales. Granddad, there are days when I feel guilty in case I'm affecting Isaac's potential sales with my very presence.'

'Now don't be daft, lassie. I've never met a wealthy glass blower in my life,' says Granddad, shaking his head and handing over his empty plate to Mum. 'But I've met many a comfortable blacksmith.'

'Seriously, there are days when customers enter the forge and purchase virtually all Isaac's goods in one transaction. It blows me away, but it frequently happens. What I wouldn't give to be in that position,' I say, pulling a hound-dog expression.

'So, what's the answer then, lassie?'

I shrug.

'Don't you shrug. We Smiths have been in bigger pickles than this and survived. What you need is a novelty draw – something that brings the punters in, allowing you to showcase your talents and letting them leave with a memory.'

'Granddad, with the best will in the world, I have tried everything in these past few weeks.'

'You can't have done, otherwise you wouldn't be in this slump. Now, buck your ideas up, otherwise the likes of me will be pinching your anvil from under your nose!'

Chapter Thirty-Five

Friday 19 November

Isla

Our morning briefing finishes almost before it has begun. Sitting at the meeting table, I'm taken aback when Ned doesn't ask questions about sales and Jemima doesn't ask, 'Is there anything else?'

Today, it's Ned who finishes the meeting as I gather my sales books after another successful week.

'Isla, just a word before you leave – as you know, we're going away for a long weekend. We've made sufficient arrangements so there's nothing outstanding businesswise, but in case of an emergency we'd like you to notify Dottie and Mungo as your first port of call. Whether it be staff sickness or, God forbid, another accident occurs in the gallery.'

It's perfect timing; as the last two weeks have proven, daily life within the gallery occurs without a hitch like a well-oiled machine.

'I'm happy to do that – I have their contact details in The Orangery.'

'Excellent stuff. Anything from you, Jemima?'

'Nothing.' She beams at her new husband.

'That's all for today, Isla. We'll see you when we're back home.'

'Have a wonderful time,' I say, instantly taking my leave.

I berate myself as I nip down the grand staircase; who's not going to enjoy themselves on their official honeymoon? Doh!

*   *   *

'Did they tell you about Edinburgh?' asks Pippa, as soon as I arrive back at the café.

'Their honeymoon, yes.'

'Obviously, they don't trust us to be away for any longer than a weekend – that's the thanks you get around here,' says Pippa, wiping the coffee machine over.

'I don't think that's the reason, Pippa. The gallery has recently opened, we've got Christmas in a matter of weeks, and now's the perfect time for artists to push forward with their craft sales. For them to disappear for a week or two to the Caribbean really isn't the best idea.'

Pippa shrugs.

'We'll be fine, and they'll be back before we realise they've gone. It's not as if they're always breathing down our necks every day, are they?'

'That's what you think,' mutters Pippa, continuing to clean.

I head towards the rear kitchen on a mission to find a new bake in Granny's recipe book, Pippa's remark ringing in my ears. I want to experiment with something new for this weekend.

Verity

'We need to talk,' I say on entering the sheep barn, which smells deliciously of freshly laid straw.

Magnus appears unperturbed by my sudden appearance en route from work. Apart from brief conversations while he busily tends to his sheep paddock, I've actively avoided him in recent weeks. He's dressed for work in a chunky jumper, corduroys and wellingtons, and is guiding five sheep from one end of the barn to the other, past numerous filled sheep pens, using a section of metal fencing as a driving shield. Floss lies outstretched on the nearest oblong straw bale.

'Aye, we do.' He continues to guide the flock but quickly darts sideways to block the route when a brave maverick decides to separate from the others.

'So, I was thinking . . . if you'd like to come over tonight, we could have a glass of wine and maybe a chat.'

'Tonight?'

'Yeah.'

'No can do, busy with these here sheep.'

'Oh.' He's thrown me. I hadn't anticipated a 'no'.

'Tomorrow night, then?'

'Same situation.'

'When, then?'

'Now's fine by me.'

'Here?'

'The sheep don't interrupt or gossip, if that's what you're worried about. I can keep working and we can chat as you wish.'

'But it's not as I wish, is it, Magnus? It's as *you* wish. You're the one who wants the big discussion defining what we're doing and how we're doing it. Not me. I'm quite happy.'

He continues to drive the sheep through the straw-lined corridor towards a pen at the bottom end, neatly closing the open gate once the final animal is safely inside. Then he puts down his fencing shield and sits down on the nearest bale of straw.

'So, you're fine with chat, dinner and bed, followed by shower, breakfast and bye?' he asks.

'Didn't I seem fine? I enjoyed our time together – what more do you want?'

'Any bloke can act like a friggin' stud for the night and leave, freshly showered, in the morning. There's plenty of those everywhere, be it here or on the mainland.'

'Are you spoiling for an argument, or are you going to allow me to explain?'

'Go on then.' His broad shoulders sink a fraction.

'I thought we were on the same page. I was enjoying the freedom that my new situation awarded us – I mean me. Yes, me.'

'Freedom?' he repeats, the word barely audible.

'Yes, Magnus, freedom. I hate to highlight the situation, but for the last two decades I have had to juggle taking sole responsibility for my children, with paying a mortgage, and bills and my ex's debt, and worries and decisions and a whole load of shite that I shouldn't have shouldered alone, but I did, because I had no other choice. I was enjoying – *am* enjoying – your company, but also enjoying the distance between us on days when I didn't choose or want . . . you know what I mean . . . to see you.'

Magnus gives a knowing nod.

I hastily continue. 'What I'm trying to say is that the last time I was allowed this amount of freedom, I was just thirteen and thrilled to be handed a front-door key to come and go as I pleased. Just five years later, I had to grow up. It's a trap I fell into when I was vulnerable, I just never got around to untangling myself. Whereas with you, there was no one telling me to do anything . . . I decided for myself. No emotional bargaining, no boundaries, no kowtowing. Forgive me for saying it, but I kind of like being free to do as I wish!' I didn't mean to end on a note of exclamation, but I'm feeling fired up, so I went with it.

'I see. So "to do as you wish", as you've so eloquently put it, actually is a plus point where you're concerned?'

I blush profusely, but I don't care; I'm in this conversation too deep to back out now.

'Basically, yes – and I'm sorry that you're wanting more, or aren't satisfied with the arrangement, but for the first time in my life, I am doing exactly what I choose to do.'

'And me?'

'I can't answer that, Magnus. I've been honest; I like you, a lot. But I can't make promises regarding the future. At the minute,

I'm here in Shetland. But in a year's time, I plan to return home to my boys.'

Magnus sighs heavily, slaps his thighs and stands tall. He pulls a batch of paperwork from his jacket and begins analysing it intently.

'You're not going to say anything in response?'

'Not at the minute, I need time to think.'

'OK.' It's my turn to sit down beside the outstretched sheep dog. I can't believe a creature can lie so flat – her jaw resting on the straw, framed either side by huge paws – and actually be alive.

Magnus begins checking ear tags and counting each sheep inside the pens. There are five in each, and I count sixteen pens lining the interior of the barn.

'Why aren't they outside? It's hardly bad weather.'

'They'll be staying inside for the next month.'

'Why?' I ask, wishing to restart our conversation but curious as to his current task.

'Each pen is assigned to a different ram for tupping. I need to have the right ewes in the correct place before I introduce the four boys. There's no room for error if I want healthy lambs next spring.'

I wince; it sounds so calculated.

'Don't look like that. I keep my potential mums nice and calm after the event; it ensures more live births. It's easier to keep an eye on them in here than when they're roaming the coastal pastures.'

'Lucky girls, they'll get kicked out into December's snow.'

'You'll be surprised how mild it is here.'

'What – in ten-foot snow drifts?'

'You're in for a shock. The warm air current drifting from the Gulf of Mexico protects us from such harsh weather.'

Is he pulling my leg?

'Seriously, there'll be plenty of winter storms, with ferocious gales and lashing rain, but the snow drifts rarely happen.'

'And you'll put these ewes, hopefully pregnant by then, out in the winter storms?'

Magnus nods, a wry smile lighting his features. 'These are sturdy little creatures, that's precisely what they've been bred for. Their fleece is second to none in protecting them from the elements. I do my daily rounds of feeding them out on the pastures. You wait and see, you'll be in awe at how they cope.'

'But first they need you to match-make on date night?' I say, squirming at the thought of mating sheep.

'It's taken hours getting this barn ready for some loving, I can tell you.'

'That is so wrong.' I giggle, feeling the blush creeping up from my chest.

'Wrong, eh? If anything, these ewes have got this mating business sorted, compared to us humans.'

'Urgh!' is my only remark, as my cheeks burn and Floss rolls her eyes in judgement of me.

Chapter Thirty-Six

Isla

'Hi, I'm Fiona and this is my best friend, Kenzie. We've been searching for weeks for our missing friend Isla. Do you know her? Have you seen her?' calls Fiona, her thick eyelashes fluttering like butterflies with each word, as I scurry along the pavement to our meeting point outside The Thule. 'We're assembling a search party, complete with police helicopters and trained sniffer dogs, but you have a slight resemblance to the girl we love. Is there any chance you're called Isla?'

'Stop it, lady! I feel bad enough as it is, but I've been dead to the world every evening after a full day at work. I'm here now, so let's hear less of your banter and more of your news,' I retort, giving each of the girls a bear hug and really meaning it.

'Oooo, she's back!' squeals Kenzie, raising both arms above her head in celebration.

'I'm back!' I holler, instantly forgiven for neglecting my two besties. 'And, boy, have I got loads to tell you pair.'

'I'm dying to hear it all. We've missed you, girl, but first I need gin,' says Fiona, rummaging in her handbag for her purse before we've even entered the bar.

I link arms and the three of us squeeze through the bar's entrance in search of gin.

'What's the news?' asks Kenzie, flicking her thick mane over her slender shoulders, before reaching for her bulbous glass. 'I bet it's not all hairnets and scrubbing burnt potato pans at The Orangery.'

I swallow my first sip of chilled violet gin. It tastes amazing after what seems like eons.

'I'm loving it, though it's hard work. I constantly feel out of my depth, but the couple I work for are soooo lovely. Actually, Jemima is a darling, but Ned scares me a bit – though I can cope, knowing she's on hand.'

'Posh-nosh kind, are they?' ask Fiona.

I lose sight of half her face as she raises her wide cocktail glass. 'Sex on the beach' caught her eye whilst at the bar ordering our gin.

'He is, she's not. She's one of us, seriously. They went on their honeymoon to Edinburgh today, but she wouldn't be out of place here.' I glance around at the crowded tables filled with young people. 'Jemima's a creative sort. Her mind sees everything in a different way to others; focusing on possibilities and opportunities. She's ace as a boss.'

'Look at you with a girl crush,' says Kenzie, gently nudging my elbow. 'You'll be having her babies next.'

We choke and splutter on our drinks, collapsing into our usual trio of giggly friendship banter. I couldn't have got through secondary school or catering college without these two by my side – or at the end of a mobile.

'I can't imagine finding the love of my life out of the blue, it's like a fairy tale come true. Talking of which, you'll never guess who's hanging around The Orangery like the gallery's cat?'

'Lachlan!' they squeal in unison, both performing the hand-flapping action of excited females.

'How do you know?' I'm shocked beyond belief.

'He told us. Was it last week or the week before? He was in here bragging about how he pops in every day, just to say "hi" to you, and you're all "swoon",' giggles Fiona, glancing towards Kenzie for confirmation.

'The lying git! I hardly have time to stop for my coffee break, let alone sodding swoon over the likes of him.' I'm disgruntled that his overinflated ego should make him lie to my friends.

Both Fiona and Kenzie sit open-mouthed, hanging on my every word.

'That's not what he's telling folk, Isla. He's saying you're "begging for it",' adds Kenzie, her words confirmed by Fiona's nodding head.

It takes me ten minutes to put my ladies straight about that fact! 'Wait till I see him next, the cheeky sod,' I say, feeling het up by his lies. 'He has a short memory – we dated and he dumped me!'

'In the cruellest manner,' adds Fiona, talking into her wide cocktail glass whilst sipping her drink.

'Yet he thinks he can walk back into your life. Phuh!' finishes Kenzie, a disgruntled look etched into her perfect brows, as she snatches up her gin glass from the marble tabletop.

My mum's right; being back with my girls, amidst a never-ending flow of laughter, banter and sharing, feels like the best thing in the world. And the only thing I need in my life, right now. The boys – or rather, a man – can definitely wait.

Nessie

I feel like a thief sneaking around in the dark, cautiously feeling my way across the cobbled yard in the pitch black, armed with a large flask and my keys to the forge. I ask you: what's the point of lying in bed staring at the ceiling worrying? I might as well be here working. So here I am, early for work. Jemima and Ned are away enjoying a well-deserved honeymoon, so it's not as if I'll give them a fright prowling about at midnight.

I quickly unlock the forge door and nip inside, closing it behind me in a flash. I snap the lights on like a child scared of the dark – which I'm not, but it feels more comforting. Isaac's workbench is as it should be: clean, organised and prepared for tomorrow. I glance at his wooden rack of recently finished items; I think he likes to keep them close before parting with any new designs. Lucky bugger, having all the fun at the minute. He certainly has the Midas touch; customers can't get enough of his glassware. Fingers crossed, his luck wears off on me sooner rather than later.

My fire pit is stone cold so I begin my ritual of building my tinder pyre. If I make it well, it might see me through the whole of Saturday too. Isaac won't know if I've arrived an hour early or eight hours early – so what's there to worry about?

Within no time, I'm in the zone, hammering and twisting metal to produce the intricate designs for a coat stand. It isn't my finest piece, but standing at six feet tall it demonstrates the versatility of metal and showcases its beauty in a modern style. Not everything has to look heavy and raw; if I paint it a bright colour maybe it'll catch someone's eye for a sale. Anything for a sale. I'll happily make more sodding weathervanes if it encourages people to start browsing and buying my work. The last thing I want is to admit defeat and be forced to quit this—

I stop mid-action to listen.

Nothing.

I thought I heard something outside on the cobblestones.

Probably that bloody duck lingering about. Why they don't put him on the rear lawn to live simply baffles me. The amount of crap he deposits on the cobblestones . . . someone will break their neck sliding on it sooner or later, and then—

There it is again.

Friggin' Crispy duck! I'll crispy duck him, with a side dish of shredded iceberg lettuce, some noodles and a rich orange sauce if—

And, again.

I put down my hammer and tiptoe to the doorway, pushing it a little way open, which is hardly helpful; I'll need to open it fully to get a complete view of the yard. I remove my goggles and peer round the edge of the wooden door: the gallery yard is empty, with no sign of movement, just long lingering shadows. No duck. No humans. No worries.

I linger by the forge door, daring myself to holler 'hello' like every victim in a horror movie, forgetting to abide by my own advice – 'Don't call out!' – usually shouted repeatedly at my TV screen.

'Hello?'

No answer. I'm grateful there isn't a set of cellar steps down which I could venture for a further look.

I repeat my call once more, before returning to my anvil.

'Nessie Smith – you're losing the plot!' I mutter to myself.

'Morning!' calls Isaac, bang on eight o'clock. 'Bloody hell, it's warm in here.'

'Hi. I couldn't sleep so thought I might as well come in a bit earlier.' It's not actually the truth but, hey, kind of.

I continue to stoke my fire pit as Isaac readies himself for the day ahead, hangs up his jacket, starts lighting his own furnace and collects his apron.

I glance at my workbench; there's enough work to suggest I'm early, but not too much on show to suggest I've been here for hours. I've pushed the completed coat stand to the rear of my section. I'm pleased with the final finish in duck-egg blue – it could take pride of place in any modern hallway or young lad's bedroom. I couldn't tell that I've worked for hours, so hopefully Isaac won't notice either.

'I'll go grab the coffees, shall I?' I say, as I'm partway to the door, wrapping my cardy around my shoulders.

'Are you sure?'

'Yep, sure as I've ever been,' I say, over my shoulder, in desperate need of caffeine to perk me up.

Chapter Thirty-Seven

Saturday 20 November

Isla

'Isla, there's a guy out here asking for you,' says Pippa, a wet dishcloth in her hand, gesturing to the front of house.

'What does he want?' I ask, irritated that I can't be left in peace to complete the icing of a freshly baked opera cake. It'll need chilling before going on sale later today.

Pippa shrugs before returning to her task of clearing tables.

I quickly wash my hands before following Pippa's path. The second I reach the counter, I regret it; I should have known. Lachlan is leaning against the till counter, his hands plunged into both jacket pockets, staring straight at me.

'Hi, Lachlan, did you want something?'

'Yeah. Can we talk?'

'Mmmm, not really. I'm busy preparing cakes.'

'It'll only take a minute.'

'Lachlan, this really isn't appropriate timing for me.'

'When, then? Later tonight? Tomorrow?'

I shake my head. I heard enough details from Fiona and Kenzie last night to quench any curiosity regarding his intentions.

'I didn't mean that, I meant . . . this . . . us. It isn't the appropriate timing for me and my life. I was happy sharing my life with you when we were dating, but you decided you didn't wish to be with me. Dropping by, asking to speak to me, the constant questioning, and now this – you're actually preventing me from doing my job. And I need to focus on my job. I'm not looking to get back with you, Lachlan. Sorry if that sounds harsh, but it's just how it is. OK?'

'No. Not really.'

I'm taken aback by his forthright manner. I glance towards Pippa, who has ceased wiping her tables and is obviously listening to our conservation. I'm glad she's present. It's not that I'm frightened of him; more a case of having a witness to our conversation, given the sudden change in his tone.

'Isla?' calls Pippa.

'Yeah.'

'Do I need to fetch Isaac?'

I sidestep, creating more distance between me and Lachlan, whilst presenting a confident stance to Pippa.

'It's not necessary, Pippa.'

'What do you take me for?' says Lachlan, turning around to face Pippa.

'From what I hear, you need to get the message: she's not interested,' says Pippa, before resuming her task.

Lachlan turns back to me, clearly narked that she should have interrupted a private conversation.

'Look, Isla, we can go out for a bite to eat, grab a drink or two and just chat.'

'I'm happy being single and doing my own thing with my career. I've a lot on my plate at the minute, what with this place and my additional studies – I've very little time to spend socialising.'

'Isla?'

'Lachlan, please. I need to finish my cake. Pippa will see you out. Bye.' I return to the back room.

I feel awful; his face looks crestfallen. I hear Pippa cajole him towards the exit. I imagine he's not best pleased, but that isn't my issue. I collect my icing bag, attempting to pick up my task where I left off, but my mind is elsewhere: mainly on Lachlan. Am I shooting myself in the foot purely to prove a point? Am I even proving a point? I'd happily remain back here, decorating my cake, even if my Prince Charming showed up. I smile. That thought only confirms I'm doing the right thing in my life.

'Are you OK?'

I turn to find a concerned Pippa leaning against the doorjamb. 'I'm not sure I'm comfortable with that young man turning up like that,' she says.

'Don't worry, he's harmless but persistent.'

'Mmmm. Mention it to Ned, just to be on the safe side.'

'No.'

'Jemima, then.'

'Nope. I'd prefer not to. And I'd prefer it if you kept it to yourself too, Pippa.'

She gives a curt nod, which doesn't convince me.

Nessie

'Nessie!'

I hear my name called. The syllables are there but they're muffled and muted, sounding miles away, as if I'm being called through a haze of fog or under deep water. I stir to find Isaac leaning over my bench peering at me.

'Are you OK?'

'Fine, fine, always fine,' I say sleepily.

'You were fast asleep.'

'I wasn't ... just resting my eyes for a second, that's all ... thinking of a new design,' I lie, trying to revive myself without actually shaking myself awake in front of Isaac.

'Like that, is it? You're embracing the art of meditation in order to bring forth creative ideas?'

I want to die with embarrassment. I'm rarely comfortable falling asleep in front of family members, let alone Isaac. Was I snoring? Have I got dribble attractively oozing down my chin, or crease marks etched into my cheeks?

'Do you want me to fetch you a coffee?' he asks, as a humorous expression threatens to burst forth, dispelling his air of concern.

'I don't need coffee.'

'Just a bed and a warm duvet, by the state of yee,' he mutters, nudging my elbow.

His action causes my chin support to drop. I perform an undignified head jolt, my eyelids flutter with heaviness; his kind face is blurry and my whole body jumps at the sudden action.

'Coffee, now, fetch,' he orders. 'Otherwise, I think it's home time for you.'

I ease myself from my wooden stool. I feel dopey, like a sleeping child awoken at the end of a long wedding reception and manoeuvred towards the family car waiting outside in the cold. I just need a back seat to curl up on, somewhere cosy to drift off till we reach home. But Isla's espresso coffee shots are my only option.

'Nessie!'

'Sorry, yes, I was lost in a world of my own,' I apologise, as Isla waves two takeaway coffees at me. 'How many shots did I ask for in mine?'

'Three . . . which I think is a lot for one drink,' says Isla, concern etched into her features. 'Are you OK?'

'You know me, I'm always OK,' I reassure her.

I collect my order and scurry out, hoping three shots don't taste as bitter as I expect, otherwise my coffee grimace might ignite Isaac's suspicions.

Isla

'See you tomorrow,' I call after Pippa as we leave The Orangery for the night.

'Bye,' she calls, dashing towards her parked car.

I pull the door closed and rummage in my handbag for my keys. Not there ... or there ... I think frantically – where could I have left them? – as my fingers scamper around the interior of my bag, checking for any rips in the lining.

Across the stable yard, mellow glows spill on to the cobble-stones from several open stables as the artists busily work after hours.

I can predict their actions: the whittling guy is hunched over his lathe, the candle guy is dipping a rack of candles into his vat of wax, and the constant rhythmical ring of hammer upon anvil filling the night air, signals that Nessie is still busy at work.

Where are my keys?

I widen the mouth of my bag, continuing to look. They've got to be here somewhere. My mum will be waiting at the bottom of the driveway; I'm usually there by now.

Sod it!

I nip in to ask the whittling man, at the nearest open stable, 'Hi, can I borrow your keys for a second?'

He looks up, gestures to his countertop.

I quickly retrieve his keys, instantly finding the one I need. 'Be back in a second, promise.'

I run outside, cross the cobbles, swiftly lock the entrance door and return his keys.

'Thank you, I owe you a favour,' I call, as I dash for home.

There's a huge moon above, providing a tranquil light across the manor's surrounding grounds. I begin the trek along the gravel driveway. It's not a long walk, just a few minutes, but tonight I'm hot-stepping it, causing the gravel to spray up in my wake – a piece slips inside my shoe, which is a pain, as it bites my heel. But I'm not stopping to fish it out, I'll do it in the car.

I'll be home in ten minutes, showering in twenty and tucking into my dinner within the hour. My plan is to study for the remainder of the evening and get a grip on the next chapter of my accountancy book.

I'm in a world of my own until I hear the crunch of gravel behind me.

I whip around to view an empty pathway; simply my mind playing tricks. I take a few more steps ... but again, I hear a crunch or a snap. What's behind me: a fox, a badger or ... Lachlan? Instantly, I berate myself for being so unkind. I might be annoyed but I shouldn't think badly of him. He's only trying to build bridges. I need to start growing up and maturing a little faster than I am. My granny would have said, 'You can't go through life thinking badly of everyone,' and she's right. How I miss her words of guidance, which always provided comfort in every situation.

'Isla.'

It's barely a whisper carried on the breeze, but there's no mistaking it. A low voice calling my name, over and over.

I stop walking. I'm not far from my collection point. My eyes have adjusted to the surrounding darkness, I can make out the dense shrubbery, the shadows of Lerwick Manor behind me, but I can't see another human being. Just hear them.

I'm not scared. I'm certainly not going to show any fear, but I kick-start my strides into a gentle jog that develops into a pounding run. I might as well reach my mum's car sooner rather than later.

Within seconds, I'm at the car. As soon as I touch the door handle, I wrench it open and dive into the passenger seat.

'Hi, my darling. How are you?'

'I'm good, Mum,' I pant.

'You ran?'

'Yes, I felt cold when the wind cut through my bones.'

'It's hardly a gale, Isla – just the lightest breeze imaginable.'

She's right, I used the wrong excuse.

But what does it matter? I'm safe.

Chapter Thirty-Eight

Sunday 21 November

Nessie

'What are you doing?'

His voice makes me jump out of my skin; I didn't hear the door open.

'Isaac?'

He's leaning against the wall at the far end. He inclines his head, awaiting an answer.

'How long have you been standing there for?'

'Long enough to have caught you red-handed at two o'clock in the morning. As I said, what are you doing?'

'It's necessary if I'm to survive until the new year, or you're going to need a new stablemate!'

'So, you came back?'

'Meh, not quite.' I turn away to hide my guilt.

'You never left for home?' His surprised tone says it all, his expression simply reinforcing it.

'I had every intention of going home. But you left, and the yard fell silent . . . what the hell am I going to do there, anyway? I might as well be here and produce something, rather than sitting at home staring at a TV worrying. I can sleep tomorrow without the fear of losing custom.'

'Oh yeah, makes perfect sense if you wish to work yourself into the ground. And what about last night?'

'Ach, you know about that too?'

'Mmmm, a certain little bird told me you literally overdosed on espresso shots. No wonder you were dashing to collect the coffee orders – three shots in each drink, wasn't it?' He peels his frame off the wall. 'You falling asleep was kind of a hint. I'm not stupid, Nessie. So, tell me, is it proving productive, or are you simply knackered throughout business hours because you're up with the owls and the larks?'

'Needs must, Isaac.'

'No. They don't.'

'I have to make the most of Jemima and Ned being away – how can I do this once they return from their honeymoon? I can't. Though maybe I could if . . .'

'I'll give you another couple of days working in this fashion before you start feeling ill, your body begins to fail, and for what? To prove to your family – or is it to yourself – that you are worthy of doing this?'

'Oi. You're out of order!' He's touched a nerve; we both know it. I glare across the forge, my temper glowing white hot like my fire pit.

We stare angrily at each other, like two cowboys in a western film about to draw their guns at either end of a deserted gold-mining town. I'm not prepared to avert my gaze; his next comment could be the spark I need, be it fight or flight.

Isaac removes his jacket, casually rolls his sleeves up and saunters across to my section. I continue to stare, ready to draw my imaginary gun. If he thinks he can give me another lecture on the back of that remark, he's got another thing coming.

'What needs filing or polishing then?' he says, surveying my workbench where an array of items, finished and part finished, await my attention.

'Are you serious?' I ask sheepishly.

'Yep, give me a task to do and show me how to do it.'

I haven't the energy to refuse his kindness. I select an ornate door plate and hand it to him along with a large rasp file.

'I need the jagged edges removed from these sections . . . here and here,' I say, pointing to the edges. 'You'll find it easier if you secure it in the vice on the far side of the bench.'

'Gotcha! And when I've done this one, do these other four need the same treatment?'

I nod, as a sense of relief washes over me.

'Perfect, I'll get cracking then.'

I return to my fire pit, using the tongs to gently turn the iron strip which had been my focus before he entered. My mind is whirring thanks to his comment. Am I slogging my guts out to prove a point to my family – or to myself? However angry it makes me, I can't honestly answer that question. I've longed for this venture to be a success, but when will I accept that it might not be? Does my dream have a sell-by date? Will I wake up one morning and simply chuck in the towel? Or will my efforts drag me down, ruining my health and driving me crazy chasing something that will never exist for me? My father might have been the wisest one in turning his back on the industry and securing a solid job in order to feed and clothe his bairns. At this rate, a family of my own will never exist, let alone face the prospect of going hungry. Maybe I should be grateful for small mercies?

Our silence is filled by Isaac's rhythmical rasping and my methodical hammering. It's like an industrial symphony blending in mid-air – much like my apology should be.

I glance over my shoulder at my new apprentice. He's hunched over the wooden bench, scrutinising the rough edge he's smoothing.

'Nessie, do you remember what colour your hair was when we first met?'

'Bright pink.'

'And then?'

'Electric blue, I believe. Followed by luminous green.' I roll my eyes towards the oak-beamed ceiling at the memory of that disastrous colouring.

'It made you look like the Grinch from the back – which probably wasn't your aim.'

'You cheeky bugger! I admit it went a bit wrong, which is why I re-coloured it within days.'

'And now your current colour is?' He gestures towards my pixie cut.

'Warm mahogany. And your point being?'

'You'll be opting for gothic black next, if your sales don't pick up.'

'I won't,' I protest, feeling miffed that he should bring my appearance into my daily work. 'Stop staring at me; I feel like a fourteen year old with dyed ear lobes, a scrubbed but stained forehead, and school tomorrow.'

'I think you need to rethink a return of the pink. Not that I'm telling you what to do, but I think there's a definite link between your mood, your outlook on life and your barnet.'

Surely not.

'Isaac?'

'Yeah.'

'Thanks for helping me,' I say, turning to greet his beaming features.

'You'd do the same for me, wouldn't you?'

'Yeah, I would, actually. Though let's be honest, you don't need my help.'

'Right now, I don't. But things can swiftly change with the traditional crafts.'

'Nah.' I shake my head, returning my focus to the twisted metal I've just plunged into the slack tub.

'Wait until January, and you'll see: they'll attempt to haggle over any glass baubles that remain unsold. I'll be lucky to sell a decent-sized vase as I'll be competing with the January sales in town. I might as well take the entire month off and design new glassware. But I won't, I'll be here working alongside every other artist who'll be struggling to make the rent.'

'At least you have festive wares to sell. I'm up against the usual issues, plus nothing I make is fancy or Christmassy enough to be specific for the season.'

'So, create something! Get your imagination spinning, Nessie. Surely it's not too late for you to design a new product and then push it like crazy – we've got weeks before Christmas. The Yule Day celebration will bring a new flush of customers. Folk will still spend money on last-minute items they think they just have to have!'

'It's that easy, isn't it?'

'Err, yeah, actually it is.'

I love how everyone makes my venture sound so bloody easy. Hammer this, hammer that . . . and bingo, I'll be flying high, customers rolling through the doors, cash sales and card payments bombarding me.

'Stop muttering to yourself, it makes you sound cranky. Right, when you were little, did you play the word association game? Let's do it. I'll start: Christmas.'

I flick a bemused glance over my shoulder. Has he lost the plot?

'Come on, stop being so mardy. I'll say it again . . . Christmas.'

'Holly.'

'Ivy.'

'Poison,' I say.

'Dior,' he says, to which I am impressed.

'Gift.'

'Present.'

'Ribbon.'

'Glass bauble.'

'That's cheating, relying upon your own goods. Tree.'

'Wool.'

'Wool? What the hell?'

'It's legit! "Tree" made me think of the display stand you made for Verity – it looks like a wool tree in the middle of her ... what's up?'

'You are a star!'

'Nessie, what's wrong?'

'Give me a minute to think ... what if I craft a larger version of her display stand ... but instead of having spikes, which is how she secures each ball of wool, I make each fancy spike into a hook, then families can hang items ... decorate them with baubles, lights or tinsel.'

'Plus, they get to keep the tree year after year, whether it be inside the house or outside in their garden.'

'Their garden – yes. They could even use it to support other climbing plants during the year ... then it reverts back to being a decorated Christmas tree each December.'

We work throughout the night, moving productively from one project to another, while my brain buzzes with the designs for tomorrow's creation: Christmas trees.

By the time six o'clock in the morning arrives, I'm ready to call it quits. I'm happy to clean up while Isaac takes a breath of fresh air and stretches his back in the silent yard. Several times during the night, I wandered outside to enjoy the serenity of the early hours; the stillness is verging on magical.

'Nessie, come and take a look at this.'

'In a minute ...'

'No, now! Come and take a look.'

I'd prefer to clean my tools and be heading off home before any other artists arrive and I have to dodge their curious looks. I can do without becoming the talk of the gallery.

'Nessie!'

It's no good, he's going to insist. It's easier to comply than to fight.

'What?' I say, as I reach the stable door.

Isaac is staring up at the sky. 'Look.'

The heavens display velvety hues of blue and steely grey, with a silver moon appearing amidst a smattering of twinkling stars, making for a truly beautiful canvas stretching far and wide above our heads.

'Worth seeing?'

I throw him a sideways glance; he knows me so well.

'Go on, admit it . . . that is beautiful.'

My attempt to stifle a laugh fails miserably. 'OK, I'll admit it – that sky is something else. And yes, you were right to insist I came out to view it. There, I'll admit it, so there's no need to gloat, Isaac Jameson.'

'Oooo, full name use. I must have rattled someone's cage!'

I laugh, as a faint childhood memory bursts from nowhere. 'Do you remember how Mrs McBride always included your middle name when calling the class register?'

'Being Isaac Archibald Jameson, I certainly do remember! Boy, did she have a way of turning you to stone in one glare before the nine o'clock bell.'

Archibald! Ha, I'd forgotten that. Though it doesn't sound quite right. Somewhere deep inside my head a bell begins to ring.

'Actually, wasn't there more to your name than Archibald?'

'No.' His response is a little too quick.

I eye him carefully; I'm right, there was more. Wow! I've actually remembered something from our schooldays, apart from the tears and the bullying.

'I could swear you had other middle names . . . like . . .' I can't for the life of me remember, but the expression on Isaac's face is worth pursuing. 'Yes, I remember you had the longest name in the class.'

'Ha, ha, two can play your game, Wednesday Elspeth Smith – and don't you forget that!'

My mouth is open wide. How has he remembered that? I left in year six.

Isaac is belly laughing as he peels himself away from the brickwork and returns inside. 'We need to get out of here.'

'I'll get you back, don't you worry!' I call after him, ignoring his common-sense remark.

'Believe me, I'm never worried,' comes a voice from inside the forge.

Ooo, now that does sound ominous.

Chapter Thirty-Nine

Tuesday 23 November

Verity

I watch the sea roll and crash against the black rocks of the cove. It's my second free day and I simply cannot settle.

I could clean. Tidy each room. I could, but I can't be bothered. I could walk the blustery coastal footpath, but I don't want to. I could settle with a coffee and figure out the intricate knitting pattern for the collar of my new display piece. I could contact home later tonight for another family get-together and chat, but there'll be nobody home at present. I could do many things, but I simply haven't the inclination.

Instead, I've been pacing up and down the cottage non-stop for the past ninety minutes in search of something to calm my inner self. But nothing grabs my attention.

'Where's Magnus?' I ask myself, pressing my forehead against the patio glass to stare at the cove beyond. It has been days since our 'chat' and I haven't seen hide nor hair of him. He said he wanted time to think – but surely this is long enough?

I fish my mobile from my pocket.

Do I call? Do I text first? Would he care? Would he answer? Have I waited too long? Or not long enough?

'Get a grip,' I mutter, shoving my mobile back into my pocket. I wouldn't stand for one of my lads pining over a girlfriend, yet here I am wasting my free days achieving nothing – and it's all over a grown man.

A knock at the front door awakens my spirits.

Finally!

My smile disappears on spying Isla through the hallway window; she's dancing on the doorstep, obviously cold. Instantly, I feel mean for not taking delight in her unexpected arrival.

'Hello, come on in,' I say, opening the door wide.

'I thought I'd drop by, as you've invited me on so many occasions and I've refused. But look, I've made us a cake.' She holds up a hessian bag. 'You can give me your honest opinion on this, plus something else.'

'Oooo, is this another original creation?' I say, stepping aside to welcome her indoors.

Isla kicks her boots off in the porch before proceeding through to the hallway. I hadn't asked, but am grateful for her considerate action.

'Not really ... more a combination of Granny's recipe book and a modern twist.'

Within minutes I've made a brew, found side plates and handed Isla a large knife with which to do the honours.

'A traditional Christmas cake with a twist, try it and see,' says Isla, cutting me a large slice of the loaf-shaped cake. 'It'll need to get Jemima and Ned's approval – and you know what a stickler he is for tradition.'

I pinch off the corner once I'm handed my portion. It has the texture of Christmas cake, but the appearance is somewhat paler. And the taste is totally tropical.

'Is that coconut I can taste?'

'Yes, I've used tropical fruits rather than the traditional ... too much, too little, too way off the scale?'

'I like it, but I wouldn't be so keen if I was wanting a traditional slice of Christmas cake, with icing and marzipan. No offence.'

'None taken. I skipped the decoration stage to focus on the taste of the cake.'

'It's quite refreshing, actually, and not everyone likes heavy fruit cakes.'

'Do you reckon it would sell alongside a more traditional cake then?'

'Definitely. I can't see Ned accepting this version otherwise.'

Isla nods. 'I'll go in with that suggestion then. Fingers crossed they'll like it after I've added orange-flavoured marzipan, and iced it too.'

'I'm impressed, if that holds any significance.'

Isla seems pleased with the compliment and finishes her slice of cake in record time.

I linger over mine. 'Are you OK?' I ask as she stares about the kitchen.

'My gran taught me to bake in this kitchen, though it didn't look like this back then,' she says, glancing over at the cooker top.

'Yes, sorry. I forgot that your gran is also Magnus's. Has it changed much?'

'Loads. Magnus has gutted this place – likewise, my mum with our cottage – but it brings back memories sitting here.'

I let her reminisce. At last, there's her reason for refusing my coffee invites: memories.

'Anyway, I'm being cheeky asking, but what do you think to these?' Isla snaps out of her trance, pulling a selection of slimline cards from her bag. 'They're prototypes as such, but each contains a recipe from my granny's book. She'd like them to be shared with others. I wondered if Jemima would get them printed professionally and display them on the counter for customers to browse and take home to try.'

I take the offered cards, flicking through them to scan each recipe.

'They're traditional and not difficult to make – a child could create them. Actually, I did – most days, after school.'

I like the concept, and I'm sure the Campbells will, too. 'A photograph on each would be nice; customers like me who don't know the traditional recipes gain confidence by seeing the end result.'

'Good idea. I could ask Francis, though he'd probably need to charge a fee.'

'Photographing food is not his thing. What about someone local? Try asking Melissa, she's got an eye for colour and composition. A decent phone may be all she needs to snap an image.'

'Yes, I'll ask her before I put the idea forward to Jemima and Ned.'

'I can't see Melissa refusing you, Isla.' I hand back her stash of recipe cards, which she shuffles before returning her attention to her cake plate.

'No Magnus today?' she asks, pressing her index finger on to the plate and collecting every last crumb.

'Not today.' I don't intend to be cryptic, but I'm not baring all.

Isla stops fishing for crumbs and looks up expectantly. 'You haven't had a falling-out, have you?' she asks, sounding generations older than her years.

I can't help smiling. 'No. He's busy breeding sheep in his barn, apparently.'

'Oh yeah, he does that every year. He likes to pen them into groups and then . . . way-hey!'

'Isla!'

'No, seriously, he's got this computer programme that tells him about genetics and biology and stuff . . . so that he can't make errors with inter-breeding certain sheep. All very complicated, my mum reckons. It must work, as he gets a fair price for his fleece.'

'Magnus sells his fleece?'

Isla pulls a quizzical expression. 'Err, yeah, what do you think he does with it?'

'I've never thought . . . I just presumed they were for meat.'

'Meat! Don't let Magnus hear you saying that about his beauties, or he'll have a fit!'

'Sorry . . . but can't you eat them?'

'You can, and other farmers breed for meat production, but Magnus is more focused on grazing for conservation – and the fleece.' Isla tries to stifle a belly laugh, which makes talking difficult. 'Seriously, they're his babies.'

I shuffle in my seat, uncomfortable at the turn of our conversation. If there's one thing that has the potential to interest me in the coming months as I become established at The Yarn Barn, it's fleece.

'Sorry, call me thick, but why has he not mentioned this?'

'Don't ask me, maybe you two are too busy for such discussions,' teases Isla, sipping her tea to help clear her throat.

'Excuse me, I'll have you know that—' I cease talking, and my sentence lingers, incomplete.

Over the edge of her mug, Isla raises her eyebrows, before taking another gulp. 'You were saying?'

'Never you mind what I was saying – in fact, you need to skedaddle. I need to talk fleece with Magnus.'

'Don't you just hate it when friends ditch you midway through coffee for a fella?' jibes Isla, collecting the remains of her cake and plopping the used knife into my sink.

'Mmmm, and I just hate it when so-called friends casually drop details that could potentially have a massive impact on improving my business!'

'Good luck with negotiations . . . he's not an easy one to

haggle with,' says Isla, nipping along the hallway to retrieve her footwear.

I watch her traipse down the driveway, absorbed in my own thoughts.

Should I call Magnus or not?

Chapter Forty

Wednesday 1 December

Bake: Honey cake
Event: Boxing Day morning, 2010
Serving size: 12 slices
Decoration: Left plain (no icing)

Notes: Little Isla, my youngest granddaughter, came over wearing her new baking apron — she wanted to sleep in it last night but her mother refused. She cried herself to sleep — she's such a cutie-pie. I showed her how to bake a honey cake, as easy as child's play. I had one remaining jar of honey from the Lerwick Manor estate, so I told her stories of my younger days and the family at the big house as we baked.

Isla

'Morning, Nessie, any chance I can borrow your keys for a second?' I ask, sheepishly, hoping she doesn't ask why.

'Sure, but why?'

'I dashed from the house without mine,' I lie, as she digs about in her dungarees pockets for her key ring.

'Here. I think The Orangery keys are the gold-coloured ones.'

'Cheers, Nessie.'

'Any chance you can bring them straight back?'

'Absolutely.' I make a swift exit.

I have no intention of keeping her keys; how embarrassing if

I lost these too. It's more than a week since my own keys went AWOL. I nip across the stable yard, hoping that Jemima and Ned don't cross my path; they often appear from the green door of the manor, which they use as their main entrance. My hand shakes as I unlock The Orangery's glass entrance door. Once inside, I dash behind the counter and flick all the lights on to illuminate the silent café, which feels eerie at this time of day. I've yet to get used to the transformation that occurs once the artists start arriving to collect their morning coffees and breakfast treats; from that moment until minutes before closing, the place is a hive of continual activity, and this hour or so of serenity seems like a figment of my imagination.

I don't even remove my coat before heading back to the forge; I don't trust myself after my irresponsibility with my own keys.

'Cheers, sweet,' says Nessie, as I return her keys.

'Thank you,' I mouth, turning on my heels and dashing back before Jemima or Ned have a chance to walk through The Orangery and find I'm absent.

'Morning,' I say cheerily, on entering Ned's office for our Wednesday meeting, clutching a cake tin. I've spent my two days off at home racking my brains, trying to work out where I've left my keys.

'Morning, Isla,' says Jemima, looking up from stirring her coffee. She's been looking refreshed and happy since returning from Edinburgh.

'Morning,' says Ned, leaving his desk to join us at the meeting table. 'Everything seems shipshape in The Orangery . . . anything unusual to report?'

'Not to my knowledge.' I hurriedly change the subject. 'I've made something a little different, so I wondered if you'd like to try it before I put it on display, ready for the Knitter 'n' Natter group later.' I slide the cake tin across the table before settling in my usual chair, removing my café account books from under my arm.

'Sounds promising,' says Jemima, reaching for the tin. 'Can we ask what it's called?'

'You'll know as soon as you taste it,' I say, blushing – which could be an element of guilt over my missing keys.

An 'oooo' escapes Jemima's lips as she removes the lid of the cake tin, retrieving two slices of the golden-brown cake.

'This seems naughty at breakfast time,' she adds, in what seems a poor attempt to cover her eagerness.

'Possibly, but is it ever too early to snaffle cake?' I say, wishing I'd popped a third piece in the tin, though I've already nibbled one slice.

Both of them take a bite, then stare at the meeting table while they chew and ... like twins, their heads shoot up as their taste buds ignite and recognise the flavour.

'Honey?' exclaims Ned, through a mouthful of cake.

'That is gorgeous!' confirms Jemima.

Ned swallows his bite before speaking. 'You've made this from my honey ...?' His words fade, as if his ego isn't bold enough to allow the thought to evolve.

'Yes. I thought, why not? You can add most things to cake if you balance the ingredients. I reduced the moisture from other ingredients in favour of the honey. I think it's worked quite nicely, so is there any chance I can pop it on sale?'

'That is amazing, Isla. Ned, I think the decision is yours,' says Jemima, finishing her cake slice and licking her fingers noisily.

'That is unbelievable. I would never have imagined the taste would be so subtle, yet so defined. It's a definite "yes" from me. Well done!'

I sit back in my chair. I don't know what we discuss for the remainder of our meeting: probably the usual sales, any waste logged, and the latest customer numbers. Jemima seems preoccupied with finding every last crumb in the cake tin, and Ned seems distracted.

I leave our daily meeting, feeling as if I'm floating on air. I glide down the grand staircase and return to The Orangery.

Grabbing a blank mini-blackboard display, I make a new sign: 'Ned's honey cake'. I even draw a picture of a honeypot with a tiny buzzing bee to display beside our new addition; I've no doubts it'll make Jemima laugh.

Nessie

My melancholy mood, which has lingered about me like a dark cloud, has finally lifted.

'Morning, how are we?' calls Isaac on arrival, removing his jacket and readying himself for the day ahead.

'Good, thank you. I've spent the last two days eating, sleeping, counting my blessings and colouring my hair. New month, new me. You?'

'I can see. It's shocking pink. Very pretty.'

I accept the compliment; it feels good taking time out and sprucing myself up ... back to the original me. I haven't come this far simply to come this far!

I've spent the last week refining the initial design for my wrought-iron Christmas tree, based on Verity's display rack. I need to modify the revolving element and enhance the overall finish with more twirls and swirls, providing suitable hooks on which festive baubles can be hung. And a sturdy base, obviously – the wheels I used for Verity's aren't necessary.

'Isaac?'

'Yeah?' He looks up eagerly, his features brightened by the renewed flow of energy running through the forge.

'Will you make me a set of glass baubles to grace my display tree?'

'I wondered when that question was going to arise. Sure.'

'Something a bit special, like.' I give a wink, knowing I'm being cheeky in asking.

'How many?'

'Would you say eight or ten?'

'Ten.'

'Sorted then.'

'Any colour?'

'Festive colours – each unique, with swirls, bubbles and gold thread.'

'You don't want much, do you?' teases Isaac, searching his store cupboard for coloured powders. 'You might want to fix a ready-made gold star or an angel to the top – it'll save losing the bugger, like my family always did – and then your tree will be good to go.'

'Isaac, I owe you a drink, my man. Your suggestion is perfect. I'll be able to create trees of various sizes, from huge eight footers down to teeny-weeny desk-sized ones for the local office workers.'

'Glad my childhood games have proved worthy of repetition.'

'Isaac?'

'What?'

'I promise to repay your help, come hell or high tide.'

'I know you will, I've got a memory like an elephant.'

Verity

It's been a tough day at the gallery. My Knitter 'n' Natter group gets larger each week, so I was relieved when Francis nipped off straight after our evening meal, and Magnus accepted my invite for a quiet drink.

'What do you mean, Niven's collecting a project?' asks Magnus. He's sitting at the kitchen table cradling a wine glass and looking bemused.

'Exactly that. Niven knits, and he's collecting an order that a woman has bought and paid for in full. He's going to knit her garment in the required size.'

'Is that even a thing?'

'Er, yeah. Lots of customers browse the yarn, show an interest in a particular colour and a pattern. Do you think we let them walk out because they can't, won't or aren't able to knit it themselves?'

Magnus shrugs. 'I haven't a bloody clue.'

I smile.

'What?' he asks.

'I quite like that you're more surprised by the project than the fact that a man can knit. I think that's sweet.'

'Sweet? Verity, I reckon there's a damn sight more men around here who can knit than you'd imagine . . .' He pauses, before adding, 'Me for one.'

'You can knit. No way!'

He's instantly offended, as his mouth drops open in mock horror, and he widens his eyes. 'I'll have you know I learnt to knit as a child, my granny taught me.'

'Good old granny, eh – all these grannies have certainly done their bit to keep my business alive and kicking around these parts.'

'Well, who taught you to knit?'

'Guess?'

'Your granny.'

'Yeah. There's not so much difference between Shetland and the mainland after all, is there?'

'So back to old Niven . . . the woman's bought the yarn and the pattern, and then he simply collects it and knits the size she asked for?'

'Yeah. As simple as that.'

'And you charge her for his time.'

'Pretty much. It's not a fortune, but it's a nice earner if it's what you do while watching TV of an evening. He'll never be rich from it, but he says he likes to create things for others and it means he keeps up the skills he acquired as a youngster.'

Magnus nods, and rolls his bottom lip.

'And that means what?'

'Nothing, really. We're related, way back, but he's always kept himself to himself. He's one of those guys that everyone knows but rarely mentions or asks after.'

'I got the impression he didn't have much family.'

'He hasn't. He never married. Never had children. Other than seeing him out walking, I don't see him around that often.'

'You'll see him even less at the minute; this is the third customer order he's been offered since joining my weekly Knitter 'n' Natter group.'

'Good for him, keeping his hand in and doing what he enjoys.'

'I like him. He collects his parcel as soon as I call him, and so far he's returned the finished garment before the due date. Both customers were delighted with his knitting. Win–win as far as I'm concerned.'

Magnus reaches for the wine bottle to refill our glasses. I watch as his steady hand pours my drink before filling his own glass.

'What are you smiling at?' he says, shaking the dregs from the bottom of the bottle.

'I really can't see you with a pair of needles and a skein of wool,' I say, trying not to giggle.

'Is that funny, eh? I've got news for you . . . you haven't seen me do a lot of things in this world. Don't you write us Shetland guys off as useless; we are far from it!'

'Sorry.' I can't help myself; I've seen him swing sheep about, and throw hay bales around the barn, but to imagine this burly guy, cosy in an armchair and knitting, now that's something I really need to see.

'I'm talented when it comes to knitting jumpers, and I'm an expert at cabling, I'll have you know.'

'Oh my God, please, I beg you to stop – that's exactly what Niven said.'

Chapter Forty-One

Thursday 2 December

Isla

'Hi, Verity, any chance I can borrow your keys to open up?' I ask, poking my head around her stable door.

'Sure. Here you go.'

I almost snatch the keys from her outstretched hand and dash across the yard to open up as quickly as I can. I don't feel I can keep asking Nessie to borrow her keys; I was hoping I'd have found my own by now, but no such luck.

I swiftly unlock the main door, illuminate the lights and nip along to the rear storeroom. Once inside, I begin peeling off my coat as the single lighting strip flickers to life. Instantly, I stop short and stare at the floor-to-ceiling shelving units.

Someone has been in here since I closed up last night.

I slowly remove my arm from my coat sleeve and hang the garment in my usual spot.

The tins, bottles and boxes are immaculately arranged in lines and rows, just as I left them last night, but I can smell an aroma. I sniff the air; there's a musky smell like the final notes of aftershave or heavily fragranced perfume.

Is Ned checking up on me?

Why would he do that? It seems so underhand. If the guy doesn't trust what I report back during our daily meeting, surely there are better methods of checking than sneaking around after hours. I get that it's their investment and I'm at the helm, but seriously, they either trust me to run the café or they don't. It's not as if age is a fail-safe method of getting everything right in life, it's just a number.

I've got a good mind to mention it, but I daren't rock the boat. I love my role here. I don't want to play into his hands if he's planning to get rid of me. I may be fairly young in years but my granny always said I had an old head on my shoulders and a mature attitude. Surely, that alone counts for something in life?

I close the storeroom door, making my way back towards the front of house. I reach the counter area, blindly focused on returning Verity's keys to The Yarn Barn, and find Jemima looking about the seated area.

'There you are. I called but you didn't answer. How are you?'

'I'm fine, thank you – and you?'

'Good, thanks. I was wondering if you could bake a Victoria sponge for us to share down at the allotment, to celebrate Dottie's birthday. She's been a bit down lately since a close friend passed away, and we thought . . . Isla, are you OK?' Jemima tilts her head, peering closely at me, a quizzical expression dawning.

'Fine. Thank you.' My fingers are clasped around Verity's keys, hiding the key ring; I suspect Jemima knows mine has a cupcake design.

'Are you sure?'

'I'm sure. Is there anything particular you want for decoration, or is a simple dusting with icing sugar sufficient?'

'I'll leave that to you. I'm sure Dottie will be thrilled, whatever you do; she's always praising your baking.'

'That's sweet of her. She reminds me of my granny – they went to school together, apparently.'

Jemima's face lights up, her quizzical expression chased away. 'That's lovely. If you can put the cost through as a staff miscellaneous – I'll sign for the details and mention it to Ned.'

'Sounds lovely. Leave it with me, Jemima, I'll let you know when it's ready,' I say, happy to help but conscious of my earlier thoughts.

Is this another test or a genuine request?

Nessie

I silently praise myself for nabbing a comfy armchair before the staff meeting starts, and saving one for Isaac. The other artists pile through the doors of The Orangery, eager for the best seats. Isla and Jemima stand behind the front counter, handing out hot drinks and gesturing for attendees to help themselves to a slice of cake.

'I'm glad we arrived early, it looks like the lemon drizzle cake has all gone!' says Isaac, his eagle eyes trained on the remaining selection.

'I'm grateful for a pitch near the log burner more than anything, Isaac – the cake slice was a bonus.'

'Like you would have wanted the slab of fruit cake,' scoffs Isaac sarcastically, knowing my weakness for sticky-gooey cakes.

I want to agree but can't bear to acknowledge that he knows me really well in such a short time. I can't make such observations about him – or could I?

'Do you even know why Ned's called this meeting?' I ask, attempting to steer away from negative thoughts.

Isaac shrugs. 'Mungo mentioned something earlier about announcing plans, but you know Mungo. Everything is urgent, yet he's always short on detail.'

I agree. The guy is a wealth of knowledge, in a manner of speaking. But try to wheedle the exact details out of him, and he'll always falter.

'They'd best not be announcing the closure of the gallery – it can't possibly be in trouble financially, given the footfall through here,' I say, finally airing my worries.

'I doubt it. Get ready ... Ned looks as if he's about to start.' Isaac sits tall in his armchair.

I continue to slump into the softness of mine. I think I'll begin to cry if Ned announces a planned closure, though pigs might fly past the glazed skylight too, but until I know I can't settle.

Ned taps a teaspoon against an empty glass, making a *ting-ting* sound and calling attention from the chattering artists.

'Thank you for attending; I do appreciate you taking the time out from your affairs to be present. I'll keep this short and sweet as I realise it is after business hours.'

I glance at Isaac as my stomach lurches. I feel sick.

'Jemima and I wanted to confirm that we have agreed to hold the local Yule Day celebration here, on the twenty-third of December. We'll be advertising details in the local papers as of tomorrow. We'd like the stable yard to be our main hub of activity by erecting market stalls for the day, enabling visitors to browse your wares without having to crowd into each of your stables. A market layout will encourage more visitors to attend, whilst also providing you with two areas of sales – indoors and out. We are asking for volunteers who can assist artists by manning a stall. I know we already have interested parties from the local allotments association who have agreed to help throughout the day.'

I exhale slowly, pressing my index fingers to my middle fingers almost in a meditation pose. Isaac shifts in his seat; my sideways glance lets him know that I'm content on hearing the announcement.

'It goes without saying that we want you to make the most of the day, promote whatever wares you currently have or can make before then. We'd like to encourage a festive celebration of the season. I realise it's very close to Christmas but folk still buy – until the final hour on the twenty-fourth, right?' He glances at Jemima for confirmation. 'They still do that, right? Or is that just me in previous years!'

A titter of laughter ripples in recognition of his recent promotion from bachelorhood to married man. Jemima's face is a picture as she slowly shakes her head in response.

'Anyway, produce what you can, make it your day to promote your traditional crafts. Hopefully, we'll have a runaway success on our hands and this can be logged in the diary as an annual event. But if we don't go for it, we'll never truly know, will we? Are there any questions?' Ned observes the sea of faces before him.

No one responds. Ned's announcement is good news – and I, for one, am feeling hugely relieved – but it'll mean a lot of extra work.

'OK, one last thing before you go. We'll have a company attending to professionally dress the gallery for the festive season so you won't need to lift a finger in relation to decorations. And I do believe we have some new gallery gift tags ready for December. That's all from me, have a good evening.'

The artists swiftly disperse, chatting in small groups.

'It looks like I'll be blowing Christmas baubles from now until then. I was hoping to have a break, but I can't risk running out before the big day, can I?' says Isaac, unlocking the forge door as we swiftly return to collect our belongings before heading home for the night.

'Lord knows how many Christmas trees I'll have made by then.'

'An organised event like this, with lots of visitors, could be a make or break situation, spotlighting your talents and boosting your sales. Don't you give up before the twenty-third.'

'It's nearly a whole month away, Isaac. How am I going to survive until then?'

Chapter Forty-Two

Verity

'Say that again?' I ask, unsure if I'm dreaming.

I've been rudely woken by my ringing mobile as I doze on the sofa while Francis makes himself handy by cooking tonight's dinner.

'I. Said. Tom. Is. Missing!' repeats Avril, in a staccato fashion. 'We were wondering if he's arrived in Shetland?'

'When? What? How?' My brain turns to mush, much as it did during my pregnancies, rendering me incapable of handling the basic tasks in life.

'I take it that's a "no" then,' she stutters.

A pause develops. This can't be happening.

'From the beginning, please,' I snap, frustrated by her lack of fluency in a crisis, in addition to the confusion of my own thoughts.

'We assumed that you might have known of his whereabouts before we did.'

'For the love of God, Avril – the details, please!' I retort impatiently. My heart rate is now rocketing off the scale for a woman my age.

'Jack arrived home at six to find a note on the kitchen table saying he'd taken forty quid out of the food money and that he'd be in touch in a day or so.'

'And?'

'That's it. Nothing more.'

'Have you called the police?'

'No.'

'Avril, my son is missing!'

'Did we call the police when you left a note?'

'That's different.'

'How? Please explain.'

'Tom's seventeen.'

'He's a sensible seventeen, though.'

'And I'm not?'

Silence.

'Avril!'

'Verity.'

'Are you suggesting that my youngest son has more nous at seventeen than I've accumulated in over four decades – because if so, you're out of order!'

'He's definitely more mature, I'll give him that. You upped and offed, leaving your kids to fend for themselves!'

I want to explode on hearing her comment. I want to rant and scream at my sister. Act up and swear down the phone line that I am not the bloody liability this family seem to think I am. Boy, there's nothing like a supportive family, is there? And this is nothing like a supportive family!

'You cheeky mare!'

'Verity.'

'Seriously? Your remarks prove just how little respect you have for me as a human being, let alone your twin sister. Obviously, I'm nothing more than a glorified teenager who can't survive a second without the likes of you directing her life. I must be such a frigging burden to the lot of you. Well, don't you worry about me, not any more!'

The lounge door opens, framing Francis who is wearing a wipe-clean apron depicting a map of Shetland and holding a wooden spatula. His expression is distorted by the lack of light in the dusky lounge.

'I'll tell you what: give all the details to a mature adult. I have one right here,' I say to Avril, quickly offering my mobile to Francis. 'Tom's gone missing. Take the details, would you? I can't stomach speaking to her a minute longer.'

Francis takes the offered mobile as I snatch the spatula from his grasp.

'Avril? What's going on?' I hear Francis calmly ask.

I dash towards the kitchen and attend to the stove.

'What did she say?' I ask.

Francis enters the kitchen, placing my mobile on to the table. I've kept my cool for the last ten minutes only by stirring the pot of chilli con carne, which saves my hands from violently shaking.

'He's left a letter. He's taken some money, clean clothes and that's it. They think he'll be heading up here to be with you. But with just forty quid to his name, how's that going to happen?'

'Exactly, he can hardly hitch-hike. He's obviously taken the hump with the other two and decided to sofa surf at a mate's house for a night or two. Maybe their parents will accommodate him before he heads back home. It's what I would do, if a friend of Tom's turned up unannounced.' I check my mobile screen: empty and lifeless. 'Though I'd have the manners to contact the parent, purely to let them know all is well, even if I'd been sworn to secrecy.'

Francis leans against the wooden countertop before grabbing his spatula and resuming his original chef's duty.

'She's upset that you said—'

I raise my hand to interrupt his lecture. 'Woah, hang on a minute. You didn't hear what she said beforehand. Told me that Tom has more common sense than I have. Is she having a laugh?'

He doesn't bite. Instead, he switches the conversation back; Francis respects my view, sometimes.

'They've called all his mates – no one's seen hide or hair of him.'

'They must have. They're covering up for him, like he's asked them to.'

'Or he's sleeping on some park bench or in a shop doorway,' mutters Francis, staring at me intently.

'No.'

'It's possible.'

'*No!*'

I grab my mobile, tapping the screen frantically. Francis watches me intently as he stirs the pot. I return his stolid gaze as I wait for a connection with Tom and the sound of ringing fills my world. Uninterrupted ringing – the worst kind.

'Now what?' asks Francis.

'Jack or Harvey will know where he is . . . they just will.'

'Are you suggesting Avril didn't think to ask them?'

I cut off my call to Tom and try Jack's number.

'Mum!'

'Jack. Where's Tom?'

'We don't know. Hasn't Aunty Avril just called?'

'Yes, but you know what she's like, always bossing people around when—'

'Tom's been gone for most of the day, Mum,' says Jack, adding, 'the woman next door saw him leave at ten o'clock this morning.'

My gaze instantly shifts to the large kitchen clock. I make a quick calculation. 'That's nearly nine hours ago!'

'Exactly. We've phoned everyone . . . no one has seen him.'

Panic kicks in. There has never been a time in my life when any of my sons doesn't know where the others are. Even when they were off down the quarry messing about in the water – somewhere they'd been banned from going – they'd give me a sheepish look. Even when I had to punish all three for lying to me and covering up for each other, they always knew. This is a first for me. I don't know where Tom is – and they didn't know, either.

I feel sick.

I thrust the phone towards Francis for the second time in twenty minutes and dash along the hallway towards the main bathroom.

My reaction is instant.

I repeatedly retch whilst clinging to the white porcelain before sitting back on my heels, my forehead clammy, as I dab toilet paper to my mouth.

'Are you OK?' Francis appears in the bathroom doorway.

'Phew! I can do without this.'

'Maybe he is hitch-hiking his way to be with you.'

I turn about and stare in horror. 'Thanks a bunch, Francis! Like that's what I want my teenage son to be doing with just forty quid in his pocket.'

'Sorry, what I mean is . . . oh, who knows what I mean? Look, Tom's a sensible kid. He isn't daft regarding drugs or girls. He looks older than he actually is. My bet is he'll be home by morning.'

'And if he isn't?'

Francis shrugs. 'Looks like you might be making a quick dash home in search of your son.'

'Why couldn't I have my time out, like I planned?' I ask, offering him my hand so he can help pull me up from my kneeling position with my head over the toilet bowl.

'Because you're a parent . . . we're not entitled to such luxuries once we've put another little person on to this planet.' Francis swiftly hoists me up.

'Is that so?'

He nods.

I run the cold tap, splashing water on to my clammy face before staring at myself in the basin's mirror. My eyeliner mantra – written on my first morning in Shetland – stares back at me. 'Do as I wish and please myself!!!'.

'Look, this is all I wanted,' I say, gesturing at the mirror. 'Just time to be me, before I return to the clan. And now . . . disaster.'

Francis hands me a face towel. 'If writing it on a mirror ensured it happened, human beings the world over would never see their reflections again.'

I sigh. He's right. Some things in life require far more effort than we ever imagine.

'Anyway, this chilli is more than ready . . . or would you prefer some toast to settle your stomach?' he asks.

'Toast, please.'

His broad frame disappears from the doorway. He's got a heart of gold; I know he's a decent sort who I can rely on. Francis is a fair match for our Avril, yet still their life is complicated.

I glance at the vanity mirror. I know what Francis would write on his mirror. But that bundle of joy isn't arriving any day soon – thanks to me and my twin.

Chapter Forty-Three

Friday 3 December

Isla

As soon as my lunchtime arrives, I slump into Verity's armchair, and watch as she fusses about The Yarn Barn unpacking her latest delivery of wool. I'm happy to drop by, knowing she's had a major upset and is worrying about her son. Secondly, The Orangery is overrun with the professional designer and her team brought in to add festive decorations to the wrought-iron conservatory.

'Do you reckon Ned wanders around here after we've all gone?' I ask.

Verity glances over her shoulder whilst popping balls of wool on to her tree display. 'Hardly. I imagine he's got better things to do. Why? Do you?'

'Mmmm, I do.'

Verity turns to stand before me, looking at me quizzically, ready to listen.

'Some mornings, when I arrive at The Orangery, things have been moved or changed slightly – not significant things, but just enough for me to notice. I suppose you'd know if someone nipped in here after you'd closed up.'

'Sure. We each have our quirks and habits. For example, I'd notice if this display was pushed further along the floor space – do you mean that kind of thing?'

I nod. I need to come clean. Confess to what has happened, and then I'll be able to share some of the details.

'I've lost my keys.'

'Have you!' Verity's eyes widen. 'Have you reported it to Ned?'

I shake my head. 'I daren't. He'll think I'm a childish idiot – it'll prove I can't be trusted with the responsibilities of a fully grown adult. I've looked everywhere, here and at home, for days.' I daren't admit it's nearer two weeks.

'Days!' screeches Verity, dropping the wool back into its delivery box before drawing nearer to me.

I have her full attention now, whether I want it or not.

'I've been borrowing different keys from various artists each day to unlock and lock up each night. No one has clicked yet.'

'Mmmm, I think Nessie has. She mentioned to me that she sees you nipping across the yard to various folk and back again at the end of your shift.'

'She's spotted me then, but she's the only one.'

'You need to tell Ned, it's only right.'

I want to cry. I know that's the right thing to do. Why have I left it so long?

Verity continues. 'Do you think he's clocked you?'

'No, I think he's checking up on me outside of our daily meetings. He's probably checking that I'm not lying. But some of the stuff that he's touching or moving doesn't make sense. My mum reckons our daily meetings are a safety net – like them overseeing my work because I'm so young to be doing this job.'

'Surely, if he's checking, it would be your daily sales book? You've got a wastage book too, haven't you?'

'Yes, but we waste very little. It's not the admin stuff, it's the food in the dry stores, in the back room. Sometimes, I find the armchairs have been moved. And this morning, I found the magazine rack emptied on to the floor.'

'That's never Ned! Why on earth would he do that?'

I'm about to answer when a customer arrives to collect an online order that Verity has put aside. I sit quietly in the corner, mulling over my own situation, whilst the lady becomes quite excited at collecting balls of wool. Her hands repeatedly squeeze the soft bundles of multi-coloured yarn. She sniffs it. Brushes it against her cheek, then coos over the fluffy texture. Verity carries on chatting as if it's normal matter-of-fact behaviour – I think it's weird. The customer is jigging about on the spot like an excited three year old; she appears torn between wanting to chat and needing to dash off home.

Verity removes the wool from her clutches and carefully parcels it up before bidding her a good day.

The lady exits at a trotting pace.

'What's wrong with her?'

'Sorry?'

'All the jigging about and squeezing looks slightly suggestive.'

'She was just excited ... and eager to get back home and make a start.'

'What, at knitting? Are you serious?'

'You've seen nothing until you've seen me in that state, Isla. You might laugh, young lady, but the texture and smell of some wools literally send me into seventh heaven. I can't wait to cast on, and knit row after row, feeling such beautiful wool slipping through my fingers.'

'Weird people,' I mutter.

'Look who's talking; you can't even knit!'

'Knit shmit, I wouldn't ever behave like that if I could.'

'We'll see about that. Tomorrow lunchtime I'm going to teach you how to knit.'

I pull a face, unsure if I want to learn.

'You'll be able to cast on and complete a basic garter stitch in no time, so don't pull a face.'

'In return, I'll teach you how to make traditional Shetland bannocks.'

'I'm up for that. It's a deal.'

'OK. Deal.' Reluctantly, I prise myself from the armchair. My lunch break is over, all too soon.

'Don't forget, I think you need to tell them about the keys.'

I nonchalantly bat away her comment. I was trying my hardest to escape without Verity reminding me.

Chapter Forty-Four

Nessie

It feels strange being out on the town, even more so to be dressed up and wearing high heels instead of steel-toecapped boots. My upper arms are killing me from non-stop hammering of wrought-iron Christmas trees.

'I'll be as stiff as a board by tomorrow,' I say to Isla, as we stand awaiting our drinks at the busy Waterfront bar.

'It'll be worth it come Yule Day; did you see Jemima and Ned's reaction when they toured the gallery and viewed the festive decorations? They were ecstatic.'

'It looks amazing – like a winter wonderland. Where do you even source a real Christmas tree that big for the courtyard? It couldn't have been cheap, organising a company to professionally decorate every inch with garlands and fairy lights. I've seen social media influencers decorate with less.'

'Did you notice they'd even popped a festive Santa hat on the weathervane duck?' says Isla, giving me a broad grin.

'I don't begrudge the owners anything; from what I hear, they've both worked their socks off to achieve this. But when your hands disappear completely into a luxurious, diamond-glint-on-snow-effect garland swathing your doorjamb, you know they didn't skimp on the price. And as for the garland of mistletoe hanging in The Orangery ... well, have you ever seen anything like it?'

'Never. I've only ever seen a token sprig before. From what I see from the catering accounts and general footfall, the gallery is doing better than they expected.'

'And it's only been open just over eight weeks!' I say, as the barman finally delivers our espresso martinis. 'I can't imagine they'd go back on the decision to convert unused stables into a thriving business.' I raise my glass. 'Cheers, Isla.'

'Yes, cheers.'

I gratefully take a sip of my drink; it has been a long day.

Isla continues, 'Can you picture what it'll be like come the Yule Day celebration? With Christmas tourists and the locals dropping by to visit Santa's grotto and see the spectacular dec-orations – it'll start a new tradition, which will probably get bigger and better each year.'

'Mungo reckons they've booked real reindeer for the grotto for Yule Day. They'll be advertising their very own tours of the illuminations next,' I say, quickly taking another sip before adding, 'Sorry – that last remark might have sounded catty, it wasn't meant, honest.'

'No worries, I didn't take it as such. Are things picking up for you?' she asks, as we move away from the bar towards the nearest empty table and drag the heavy velour chairs closer to each other before settling.

'Not yet. I had a meltdown the other day and totally lost the plot amidst tears and snot – and a kind stablemate.'

'Ah, bless him. Isaac's lovely, isn't he?'

'Yeah, a true gent.' I spend the next few minutes explaining how he bundled me on to my stool, talked some sense into me and then promptly fetched me a very large latte with extra cream and sprinkles.

'He didn't say a word at the counter.'

'He was a real trooper. I owe him one, though I doubt he'll need it. Funny, isn't it?'

'Human nature is weird, though. I see so much from behind

that counter. Like yesterday, a woman came in and ordered three cakes and three different coffees, then sat by the window overlooking the lawns and scoffed the lot. Seriously, I was shocked. I expected her friends to walk in any minute and join her, but no. I mean, full marks to the woman for having what she wants, but she must have hollow legs to consume that much in an hour.'

I begin to laugh, not so much at the anecdote but at Isla's expression; she's such a lovely person, so open, so fresh and unspoilt.

'Isla, you're so funny.'

'I don't do it on purpose. Next time you're feeling blue, come and visit the café for thirty minutes. I guarantee you'll see something funny – if not the customers' eating habits, then Pippa.' Isla rolls her eyes towards the ceiling. 'She really gets on my nerves with her "I'm Jemima's cousin, you know. Do I really have to clean the backsplash behind the coffee machine, again?" Yes, Pippa, just as Aileen and I do each day, too.'

'Is she work-shy?'

'She hasn't reached the bare minimum of work-shy standards yet. Ned's clocked it, though whether Jemima's on the case, I'm not certain, but ... oh no. Don't look now, but here comes Lachlan. Don't invite him to sit ...' Her sentence fades as the young buck wanders nearer, stands between us and virtually turns his back on me to speak to Isla. Nice manners.

I raise my gaze to stare at the back of his black leather jacket for a few seconds. But when he doesn't move aside, I tap his left shin with the toe of my shoe. 'Excuse me. Girls' night out. No fellas allowed. Sorry.'

Isla giggles at my remark. He growls an apology in my direction.

'Heard it all before, mate – but sorry isn't good enough to secure you a shout – nor a drink – tonight, so excuse me,' I say, nudging my chair a tad closer than I usually would to Isla and squeezing him out of the gap.

'See ya,' grumbles Lachlan to Isla, sloping off to stand beside the bar and flashing me sporadic death stares from under his lowered brow.

'What is his problem?' I ask, unsure if Isla realises he's actually quite unpleasant despite his good taste in young ladies.

'Well . . .' Isla begins, leaning in closer.

I gladly sip my drink for the next twenty minutes as Isla tells me her tale of woe about his supposed cheating and two-timing antics. All of which occurs under the watchful eyes of a scowling Lachlan, who is propping up the bar and getting in the way of the glass collector's counter area.

'And what have we here?' says Isaac, strolling by with a group of mates.

'Ladies enjoying the fruits of their labour!' I say coyly.

'Funny you should say that, because Ned dropped by after you'd left. He asked me to pass on the message of "yes, OK" if I saw you before he did. Does that make sense to you?'

'You're joking, right?'

Isaac shakes his head.

'Seriously, you're not just pulling my leg?'

'That was his message. He said he'd try and catch you tomorrow. But he's busy till late afternoon and thought you'd want to know first thing in the morning, so could I pass on his message? I simply said yeah.'

'You haven't a clue what it's about, have you?'

Isaac shakes his head.

'The Christmas trees, my wrought-iron ones . . . I've asked if he would consider commissioning me to line the driveway with giant ones, complete with fairy lights and angels, as a decoration for Yule Day. And you're telling me he said "yes" to my suggested commission!' I'm up and out of my seat in a flash, hand raised, about to gleefully high-five my messenger.

Isaac goes in for a hug; angling his body into my freshly showered underarm. I'm mortified as we both stop mid-flow, realising our error, unsure what to do next.

Isaac steps back, delivering his palm for an afterthought high-five. 'Congratulations, Nessie. That'll take the sting out of the coming few weeks.'

His interruption invariably makes my night, but our awkward moment will be hard to forget. Why would he go in for a hug when it felt like a high-five moment?

'Ladies, what's it to be? I'll send over two more.' His index finger gestures between our near-empty glasses on the table.

'No, we're fine. Honest,' I say, knowing that such a kind gesture is costly.

'Come on, I can afford to buy my gallery buddy a drink.'

Isla looks sheepishly at me, as if uncertain whether she should answer or not.

'Isla, don't look at Nessie before answering. I can afford a couple of cocktails, ladies. If you don't say, I'll only ask the lad behind the bar what you had, and send them over. So you might as well tell me.'

He's got us there. I give in and accept, which sends him straight to the bar to catch up with his mates.

'Ah, he is lovely,' swoons Isla.

'I'll put a good word in for you, if you like,' I say, not sure if she is interested or not.

'Nope. I'm staying away from blokes at the minute. I got seriously burnt dating Lachlan. I said to my mum, "I'm focusing on my career and establishing myself before anything or anyone pushes me off course." It's tough enough juggling the day job alongside the business course I've started.'

'How's that going?'

Isla dives into detail about her assignments, her study notes and her tutor feedback. I love seeing folk enjoying what they're doing, brimming with life and vitality. I wish I could regain just a little of her sparkle – maybe my sales might improve if my aura does.

I'm so absorbed in her talk, I quite forget that Isaac is on his way over, so I jump when he returns carrying two espresso martinis.

'Ladies,' he says, pushing a glass towards each of us. 'Enjoy!' With a swift wink, and our thank yous ringing in his ears, he heads back to his friends.

'Lachlan would never have done that,' says Isla, glancing across at his now vacated spot at the bar.

'Let that be a lesson,' I say, clinking my cocktail glass against hers. 'Isaac hasn't a bad bone in his body.'

'He's single, right?' she asks, watching me over the lip of her wide glass.

'I believe so, though we don't tend to talk about our private lives at work, so I couldn't really say. He's never mentioned a specific girl's name, or said anything about his home life, in passing.'

'Mmmm, there's your chance then.'

'No, Isla. Like you, I've enough on my plate keeping my head above water. I can do without complicating things with Isaac and then working alongside him, making it as awkward as hell.'

'You've got a point there. Could you imagine it: flame-throwing hot coals at each other inside the forge?' giggles Isla, clearly imagining the possible carnage.

'I can't imagine that but, yeah, it wouldn't be right for either of us,' I say, glancing across the crowded bar towards the gentle yet burly guy who kindly talks me round most days.

Isaac looks up and our eyes meet.

Bloody typical.

I give an awkward smile, which he instantly returns. He is gorgeous. Stop it, Nessie – it's all too much.

Verity

'You're where?' I stammer, unsure whether to laugh or cry with relief.

'I'm at Dad's,' repeats Tom.

'My dad's?'

'No, my dad's.'

'George's?' I holler, in surprise.

'Err, yep, Mum. Unless there is something you need to tell me and him,' jokes Tom, as only a teenager can at such a pivotal moment.

'What the hell made you go there?'

'He's my dad.'

'I know that, Tom, but he hasn't bothered with you since he left, so I'm surprised that you even knew where to find him . . .' My words slowly run out of steam as a random thought takes shape. 'Unless you and he have been having contact behind my back?'

I know the answer before he speaks.

'Aunty Avril said you wouldn't be happy; she promised not to say a word, if I didn't.'

'Whoop-de-bloody-doo for you and your frigging dad. I thought you'd be honest enough to talk to me about such things – but, oh no, off you toddle. I'm guessing Aunty Avril didn't have any qualms about helping you make contact?'

'Actually, she said—'

'I don't want to hear what Avril had to say!' I lie. I could kick myself; I'm more than interested in what my sister had to say on this topic.

'I won't tell you then. Dad made me phone to say I'm safe and sound. Nothing bad has happened to me, and I'll probably be here for a week or so.'

'Did Jack know?'

'No.'

'Did you tell Harvey?'

'Nope. Why should I?'

'They're your brothers!' I exclaim.

'You can't talk. You wouldn't let me finish my earlier sentence, and now you're lecturing me about telling the other two. Get real, Mum.'

I'm gobsmacked. My three boys are as tight as they come; true brothers in every sense of the word. Come hell or high water, they will have each other's backs for life – regardless of partners, future families, commitments – it won't matter. My boys will be there for each other. Or maybe not.

'Mum?'

'Yeah.'

'Dad wants a word.' Tom's gone before I have a chance to answer or think.

'Verity?'

His voice sends shivers down my spine, like it always did. That rich, deep tone is the equivalent of velvet: irresistible, soothing and luxurious as every word rolls from his tongue.

'Errr . . . yes,' I answer, lacking in eloquence.

'Rest assured the lad can stay here for a few days. I think he just wanted some time away, like you on your jollies.'

My "jollies"? Such a whimsical word. Or is he trying to undermine my reasoning? He's had enough time to himself over the years!

'To be fair, you're suggesting a few days, yet Tom mentioned a week or so; neither duration sits right with me. I'd prefer that he returns to the family home with his older brothers, thanks, George.'

'That's not what the lad wants. OK?'

'He has a name,' I say narkily.

'Tom would prefer to stay here, OK?'

I'm not agreeing. It doesn't matter how many times he repeats 'OK', I'm not agreeing. I want my son back at home with his brothers.

'But Tom needs to be—'

'Thanks, Verity, I'll ask Tom to text you each day, purely to let you know that he's fine.'

The line goes dead from his end.

I stare at my phone screen.

He's got a bloody cheek. Seventeen years after walking out on me and three babies, he decides to take charge and be the considerate one.

'What?' asks Francis, entering the lounge to find me growling at my blank phone screen. He's returned to Harmony Cottage to consume last night's reheated chilli.

'My bastard ex-husband has decided he now wants to play daddy, so Tom will be staying at his for a few days while I'm away on my jollies!' I rant. 'They can't even agree on the time scale!'

Francis settles in the armchair and listens while I pace back and forth, denouncing George's irresponsible attitude, his absence of parenting and lack of communication.

Francis's calm exterior never falters.

'And now he thinks he can tell me what is happening ... as if!' I finally fall silent to draw breath.

'Tom OK?' asks Francis.

I falter in my stride. 'Yes.'

'That's all that matters.'

I stare at my brother-in-law. His direct gaze doesn't leave my face as he watches the irritation caused by George's resurfacing fade away. He and Magnus have similar qualities; Magnus would have uttered that line.

'You're right. Tom's fine.'

Francis is rarely wrong. I can't help but admire his logical thinking and his calm manner – a testament to his endurance since marrying my sister.

'Text Jack to let him know and then we can get back to eating dinner – this chilli won't last another day.'

'You're well versed in this role, aren't you?'

'Mmmm, you could say that.'

'Oh Francis, we all know what Avril's like.'

He gives a wry smile, but remains silent and as loyal as ever.

Chapter Forty-Five

Saturday 4 December

Nessie

'Did you have a good night out?' asks Isaac, strolling into the forge.

I'm busily engaged in stoking my fire pit. His morning greeting, before peeling his coat off and slinging it towards his cubbyhole of belongings, is almost like daily déjà vu. If I turned around to find him doing anything different one morning, I'd probably fall into my own fire – though I suppose he could say the same about my morning routine.

'I did, thank you. Isla suggested it after seeing the festive decorations go up. She's quite good fun when you get to know her, despite the age gap.'

'Did you go on to anywhere afterwards?'

'Are you kidding? I was ready for my bed after three cocktails ... thanks for our drinks, by the way, that was really generous of you, as they aren't cheap.'

'Still, I got to treat two colleagues, which all adds to the fun of the fair.'

What's he playing at?

'What's that face for?' he says, starting to ready his furnace for the day.

'You. Talking like that. "Fun of the fair" and all that ... it sounds like you're up to something.'

'Me? I'm not up to anything other than minding my own business, readying my tools and, hopefully, blowing some delightful glass baubles. Don't you recognise a happy mood when you see one?'

I give him a sideways glance whilst prodding my coals one last time; I'm finally satisfied that they are burning nicely.

'You're up to something, Isaac Archibald Jameson, it's as if you've got the devil in you today.' The school register memory instantly returns. 'That roll call of names still doesn't sound quite right for Mrs McBride, you know.'

'Bugger Mrs McBride, she was eons ago; the woman's probably pushing up daisies by now.'

'Ahhh, don't say that – she was nice. Coffee?' I say, heading towards the door.

'Yep, large latte with an extra shot, please.'

'An extra shot?' I say, wrapping my cardy across my front and pinning it tightly beneath my elbows, before joking, 'I'm not made of money, you know, but I'll let you off, seeing as you bought me a cocktail.' I exit the forge, just as an icy blast of December air whips past the stable door.

'Nessie!' hollers Isaac, from inside.

I stop dead before answering. If he's going to bump the cost up with a chocolate brownie, I'll pretend I didn't hear him. 'What?' I say, poking my head back inside the forge.

'You scrub up alright, gal. Mighty fine indeed,' says Isaac, striking a match to light his gas-fuelled furnace.

'Oi, keep your eyes to yourself.' I disappear hastily from the doorway before he sees me blush.

Boy, he's certainly in a good mood. I'll let that last remark go over my head. I traipse to The Orangery in a world of my own; not sure what I'm to make of today's Isaac. Isaac Archibald *blah blah* Jameson – yes, there were definitely some other names read out by Mrs McBride.

Isla

'What are you doing, Isla?' asks Pippa, finding me with my shoulder pressed to the side of the upright fridge where we keep the fresh milk.

'I'm looking for my recipe book – you haven't seen it, have you?'

'Your old granny's book?'

'Yeah.'

'No.'

I stand upright and roll my shoulder back into place. 'I've looked behind every piece of bulky equipment and storage, yet I swear it was on the side . . . right here . . . when I left last night.' I tap the stainless-steel countertop beside the milk fridge.

'You've moved those?' Pippa points to the tall stack of storage boxes in which we keep the café's supply of paper serviettes.

'Yep. And the cutlery drainer, the wire plate rack, the giant mug rack and the electric mixer,' I say, pointing at each item in turn.

Pippa's eyes grow wide at the size of each piece of kitchen equipment.

'I'm now knackered, and still without my granny's recipe book.'

'It can't have gone far,' she says, which is what I've been telling myself during the last forty minutes. 'I don't know how you've moved all this on your own, you'll put your back out.'

'I know, but both of you were busy serving customers. At least I won't be needing any exercise for days to come.'

'It can't have gone far – there's only a few of us who come through this way.'

'So where is it, Pippa?' My voice cracks as my brain jumps ahead, delivering the thought that Granny's recipe book might be lost for ever.

'It'll turn up when you least expect it,' says Pippa, heading out to the front of house to serve a customer arriving at the counter. 'At least you've got the displayed recipe cards to work from, if needs be.'

'A handful of printed recipe cards can't replace Gran's wealth of experience and culinary knowledge,' I chunter after Pippa has left the kitchen. 'As if!'

'You go through, round, under and off, OK?' says Verity, as her nimble fingers flick and fiddle with two needles and a ball of pink wool.

This wasn't my intention for my lunchtime, but it has distracted me from searching.

'No way.'

'Push the needle in there, yarn sweeps around, then bring the new stitch back under and off on to the other needle.'

'That is witchcraft for sure!' I retort. All I can see is a blur of movement and not the 'basic steps' Verity keeps reminding me of.

I've stood in front of her and behind her, watching intently. She's sat in front of me and behind me, with her arms wrapped about my shoulders as a means of showing how this evil hobby works. Knitting isn't easy, despite what Verity keeps saying.

'Here, take the needles and just try. Repeat it in your head if you have to: through, round, under and off.'

I attempt to mutter her instructions but the needles feel weird, the yarn is catching on my fingers, and the loops I've made aren't big enough for the other needle to slip through. Verity stands back and watches me, a quizzical look adorning her features.

It takes a further fifteen minutes for me to complete a single row.

'Did you mention it to Ned?' asks Verity, after a lengthy silence during close observation.

'Yeah. This morning.'

'And?'

'And nothing. He didn't say a word.'

'I'm on about the missing keys, Isla.'

'And so am I. He didn't say a word.'

'Are you sure he heard you?'

'He heard alright; the hard, cold stare he gave me immediately turned me to stone. Jemima ushered me from the office faster than I could walk, so I never heard his opinion on my carelessness. Apparently, they're thinking of calling a locksmith, but Ned doesn't really want the expense. Jemima is going to come and talk to me later.'

'It was the right thing to do.'

'I'm well and truly in the doghouse now, aren't I?'

'It was the mature thing to do. Only a kid would have continued to beg, borrow and steal keys from the other artists each morning.'

'Oh, thanks for that remark,' I snap.

'You know what I mean, you touchy mare,' says Verity, comically wagging her index finger at me in a motherly manner.

'I do. I just don't want to hear it.'

Chapter Forty-Six

Verity

'Are you sure? I don't want to put one of your girls out purely for my selfish impulses,' I say, hoping he's buying my apology. I should have gone straight home but was eager to turn my hand to something new.

'Save the lip service, you don't give a bugger that one of my girls has got to run about naked for the winter. You want what you want, regardless of her blushes,' jests Magnus.

This man can see straight through me in every possible way.

'Sorry.'

'What colour are you thinking of experimenting with?'

'I just need a fleece, Magnus.'

Magnus shakes his head and walks to the first pen, surveying the flock. There's every colour imaginable upon these five creatures, even one which looks too much like a panda to be an actual sheep.

'Dear ladies, we need to educate this one, don't we?'

'Excuse me!'

'Pipe down with the "excuse mes", just listen and learn,' he says in a sing-song voice. 'You wouldn't want the jet-black fleece, because how could you dye that pale lemon? I reckon if you're unsure what you're aiming for, then the paler the fleece the better. So we'll rule out the dark beige, the russet and the light brown. I suggest you opt for a pale cream.'

'Pale cream?' I say, beginning to laugh as he points to each sheep in turn, rubbing its nose or its back end in a comforting manner at being dismissed.

'Yeah, and I don't think this cream girl is pale enough, but I know just the right one. She's up here.'

'Magnus, surely cream is cream.'

'Ouch, ladies, just listen to her. Can you not see the difference between this fleece and that one?'

I view the neighbouring pen, where he points at two bulging clouds nibbling at their mound of hay. Both are cream coloured, but I'll admit there is a huge difference in the shade.

'Damn you, Magnus, you know bloody everything.'

'Mmmm. I'd actually prefer you to have the paler fleece, as she's an older girl; she didn't lamb last spring, so it won't be out of order to shave her now and keep her inside amongst my delicate mums. She can cope without a fleece, that way.'

'OK, that sounds fair to me. I'd never sleep at night knowing I'd caused discomfort to a sheep, having nabbed her fleece out of season.'

'OK, Bracken it is.'

'Bracken? You don't name your sheep, do you?'

'Oh yeah, they're all called Bracken – apart from the pandas, of course.'

'Of course, because that would be bloody stupid.'

Magnus laughs as he enters the pen and makes a grab for the identified Bracken. He literally bundles her up and off her feet while she's happily nibbling hay. Her bulky frame is rolled up against his thighs and torso; he holds her tightly to his chest as he exits the pen.

'Isn't she heavy?'

'They look heavier than they actually are – they're bulky more than anything – but watch her hooves, if she catches you you'll know about it for a week.'

I scurry backwards from the upturned sheep, who is surprisingly clean underneath, given the heavily soiled back ends that have become a daily sight whilst living at Harmony Cottage.

I follow as Magnus strides down the corridor of pens, each sheep eyeballing the chosen Bracken, who is unceremoniously carried legs akimbo towards the shearing area, which I've never noticed before. Magnus flicks a switch as he passes the equipment, then drags a hand-held shaver from the wall clasp. As he pulls the shaver, a concertina of plastic tubing unfolds from the rafters and slides across, allowing the electrical wiring to stay out of the way of the sheep's legs and Magnus's frame. I'm mesmerised by his swift movements as he tumbles the sheep towards the hay-strewn floor; his big hands turn and twist her this way and that as the shaver noisily buzzes and she is disrobed in a methodical fashion. Admittedly, there's a moment when I feel my skin prickle and I get a flashback of our time together between the sheets.

'Verity, are you OK?'

'What?' His words break into my thoughts.

Magnus is staring up at me with a coy smile adorning his entire face. 'Your gentle moaning will spook my sheep.'

Shit, how embarrassing!

I plonk myself down on to the nearest hay bale, attempting to hide my blushes. I obviously got lost in an imagined moment of something that has absolutely no chance of ever bloody happening again.

Within five minutes, Magnus has returned a naked Bracken to her original pen, before returning to the shearing area to clip and clean, then flip and fold the fresh fleece into a neat bundle.

'Any idea which plant you're going to use to create a dye?' asks Magnus, binding a length of string around the parcel and handing it to me.

'Not a clue. I only had the idea this morning whilst walking the coastal pathway. I noticed there's still quite a lot of foliage of various colours amongst the bracken,' I say, emphasising my choice of words. I don't let on about my previous conversation with Isla.

'It might be late in the year, but you'll still find loads of native plants hidden amongst the bracken. They'll give you a range of colours, from neutral shades through to a touch of pink and purple, if you mix and match or attempt a double-dye job.'

I grimace. I have no idea what he's talking about.

'Have you never dyed anything before now?' he asks, witnessing my expression.

'Yeah, plenty, when the boys were small. Those stray red socks in the family's economy white wash were always planned.'

'You can dip-dye the wool as many times as you want; the fibres will absorb fresh colours and enhance certain tones each time. The results can be quite spectacular.'

'It sounds like you fancy trying your hand at such an experiment.'

'I wouldn't say no, even if it were simply helping out. The fleece will need washing and spinning before you can even think about dyeing it. I'm happy to lend a hand; it's like venturing into the unknown, because you can rarely predict the end result.'

'Thanks, I'll bear that in mind,' I say, attempting to retain a nonchalant air as I cuddle my newly shorn fleece.

Nessie

'Nessie, have you seen my recipe book recently?' asks Isla, entering the forge after her usual home time. A quick text to her mum had probably rearranged her collection time.

I stop hammering at my anvil and straighten my frame.

'Your leather notebook?'

'Yes, that's the one.'

'I couldn't honestly say, Isla. I haven't noticed it, but then I don't look for it. I'm so used to seeing you with it . . . it merges into the background, like wallpaper.'

Her expression instantly drops. 'I can't find it. I've looked everywhere in the last twenty-four hours. I used it the other afternoon but now, urgh!'

'It'll turn up, don't worry. You probably took it home without realising and left it there. Tonight, you'll kick yourself when you find it sitting in your room.'

'I hope so. If I've lost the most precious book I have ever owned, I'll be gutted, heartbroken.'

'You don't think that Pippa has got her own back for grassing her up to Jemima?'

'Nah, she might not like what I said, but I reckon she knows herself pretty well. She might be lazy but I doubt she's that mean,' says Isla, joining me at the anvil. 'I was hoping to make a special cake for the Yule Day celebration, but without the exact measurements I'm stuffed.'

'Surely the basics of a fruit cake don't change – there must be a staple list of ingredients on which all cakes are based?'

'You'd think so, wouldn't you? But not the one I'm planning on making. I was going to prepare the dried fruit and spices in the coming days so I can make the cake whilst catering for Francis's photography workshop. If I'm here all day, I might as well do something useful and of interest for myself, but now . . . what's the point?'

'Have you ordered the ingredients?'

'Yep. It's all stashed in the rear storage room . . . which is why I'm desperate for Granny's recipe book, to check the correct weights . . .' She sniffs before falling silent.

'I assume you've looked everywhere?'

'Yep. I've even scouted around Ned's office, thinking I might have left it there after a morning meeting.'

'Behind your fridges and moveable cupboards?' I say, attempting to help.

'Yep, I've pulled all the fixtures and fittings out of position, just in case.'

She looks pretty downhearted, her eyes are red-rimmed, and that cheerful smile is eclipsed by a doleful expression.

'How are you going to cope, if you never retrieve it?'

'Please don't. I can't go there!' Isla gulps at the very thought. 'I'll be devastated, Nessie.'

I blink and in a split second her face crumples as tears spill from her lashes. I put down my hammer and bundle her into a bear hug. The poor lass, she's worked so hard, in such a short time, to master her skills and cope with the pressure of running a new business.

'Now then, come on, don't give up like that. We all have blips in our working days, and you misplacing your granny's book is just a mishap. I've no doubt that in the next day or so it'll show up out of the blue. It might be at home, in your mum's car, or sitting amongst a pile of magazines in The Orangery. You'll probably laugh when you find it. I do stuff like that all the time.'

'I've. Looked. Every. Where. Nessie. Honest. I have,' sniffs Isla, dabbing her sleeve to her eyes. 'I've searched and searched. It's gone.'

At the very mention, she erupts with further tears. There's no reasoning with someone when they're this upset; I simply hold her and gently rub her back until the emotion has passed.

'I promise you, Isla – this isn't the last you've seen of that cookery book,' I say, with conviction.

Isaac glances up at me from the far end of the forge, and I can imagine his thoughts.

'Do you think?' she says, exhaling deeply and calming herself.

I release my tight hug and she straightens her skewed hairnet and apron.

'Yeah, I do,' I reassure her. 'I reckon your granny will bring that book back to you, one way or another,' I say triumphantly, knowing how a flicker of hope can bring a renewed sense of purpose to a flagging soul.

'Thank you, Nessie. I hope you're right. I'd best get back.'

'Any time, Isla.'

She dawdles towards the exit, passing Isaac but not acknowledging his presence.

The silence lingers long after she's left.

'You shouldn't promise what you can't deliver, you know,' says Isaac, after an age.

'Mmmm, some hope is better than nothing.'

Isaac shakes his head, whilst continuing to work.

'It's no different to when you give me a coaching talk when I'm having a down day.'

'That's not hope; that's fact, Nessie. No one who works as hard as you do will ever fail at anything in life.'

I blush; he says the nicest things.

'Ah, right. And here was me thinking you were feeding me any old bull.'

Isaac shakes his head and, without raising his gaze, says, 'Hardly, my dear.'

Chapter Forty-Seven

Monday 6 December

Isla

'Morning, Francis, how are you?' I say, holding The Orangery door wide as he approaches carrying numerous metal boxes, allowing a blast of cold air to race inside too.

'Good, thank you, as long as I don't drop these!' he says, sweeping through the doorway and heading for the nearest table to offload. 'I've stretched my arms for sure. I should have completed two trips to unload the taxi, but his meter was still running.'

'I take it that's costly equipment then?' I say, allowing the door to swing closed.

'You can say that again. My wife, Avril, would have a fit if I still spent on photography what I used to before our daughter arrived.'

I peer inside as Francis undoes two metal clips; each gives a snappy sound as it flicks up and back. The interior is padded with pimpled grey sponge; various large lenses are nestled in separate compartments.

'Is that how they have to be stored?' I ask. Seeing how carefully they're protected, I'm unsure they'd be damaged even if he dropped them off a cliff top.

'They're delicate items. You don't want scratches or serious knocks to your equipment, it buggers up your images.'

You learn something every day. I watch as Francis opens the second case with an identical interior, this time containing a camera.

'Do you want a coffee?' I say, having seen enough. It's not my thing, but I appreciate that others care about their interests as much as I do about cake ingredients.

Francis digs into a pocket, I hear the change jingle.

'Don't be daft, it's on the house, all part of your workshop.'

'Are you sure?'

I don't answer but simply make his usual double espresso, wincing that anyone with taste buds can consume it. I might make them for customers all day long, but I can't handle the caffeine hit myself.

'Here,' I say, placing the half-filled cup beside his paraphernalia. 'Jemima has agreed to a warm buffet for lunch, given the change in the weather. I simply need a suitable time for laying it out ready for your guests to help themselves. There'll be hot drinks on arrival, a mid-morning break with cakes, the warm buffet for lunch, with a mid-afternoon drink plus cookies. Does that sound alright?'

'Sounds perfect. If you serve the break-time drinks in takeaway cups, we'll take them outside with us, as we'll be trekking round the grounds looking for suitable snapshots.'

'That's doable. Saves the dishwasher being on non-stop, too. If you need anything in between, just shout and I'll see what I can do. Jemima's interested to see how today goes; we received great feedback after the blacksmith held a similar one-day course a while back. The Orangery is always empty on Mondays, which is perfect for workshops such as this.'

'She's got her finger on the button, hasn't she?'

'Definitely. I'll leave you to it.'

'Cheers, Isla.'

I check the clock as I return to the kitchen; he and I have

forty minutes before his photography guests arrive needing their first beverage. That gives me enough time to focus on weighing out my ingredients for my Yule Day cake. I'm 'guesstimating', given that I still haven't found my gran's book. It's going to be a whopper of a cake, as Jemima wishes to share it with as many of the locals as she can. She's suggested I send any leftover cake to the local retirement complex. Leftover cake – who is she kidding?

I've got a better idea.

It's comforting to hear the friendly chatter of the photography folk whilst working in the rear kitchen. They're discussing the entry rules for a calendar competition organised by the local tourist board. They welcomed the hot drinks on arrival, alongside which I served a plate of bannocks that were nearing their shelf life; it wasn't what Jemima had asked for, but it saves wasting them.

I'm surprised to see Levi attending the course, given that he turned up for the blacksmith's workshop, too. Though I'm not surprised to see Mungo here, alongside his buddy.

I organise an array of glass dishes, lining them up carefully on the countertop. Here lies the magic for my celebration cake. Sometimes, I can't believe that mixed together, along with a touch of heat, these humble ingredients will produce a beautiful cake. If I'd been taught science in the same manner, I'd have taken more of an interest. Though I wouldn't want to do anything else with my days other than bake, so maybe things happen for a reason. Though without Granny's recipe book for guidance and weights, I'm on a wing and a prayer.

I secure the mixing bowl on to the giant mixer. Ned might unnerve me with his posh, aloof manner, his obsession with budgets and portion size, but I have to hand it to him; he didn't skimp on decking out this place. I'm nineteen, straight out of catering college, yet I've been handed a brand-new kitchen to play in. It's a little frightening that I've also been awarded several part-time waitresses to serve front of house. I don't know what I'll do if one of them needs speaking to about a serious matter; I'm yet to reach the age where I feel comfortable addressing older people. I've still got a lot to learn. I just hope the waitresses continue to pull their weight, being extra nice to customers and turning up on time for their shifts. They've appreciated the odd slice of cake I've sent home for their families to enjoy; it's better than it going to waste in the bin.

I begin adding the ingredients to the giant bowl and start the mixing paddle. I love how the contents swirl and lap around each other as the paddle rhythmically moves, blending and binding the textures together. My granny would have loved this. Though she would never have used such a machine; everything was mixed by hand with her large wooden spoon.

A childhood memory comes to mind: 'Which do you want, the bowl or the spoon?' I always got the chance to choose first, she had the other. Given the sheer size of this particular mixing bowl, I'll never select spoon again in my life!

I tip in colourful citrus peel, halved cherries, nuggets of walnuts, brazil nuts . . . and watch as they sit proud for a split second before the mixing paddle swirls them into the creamy mixture. I must remember to tell Jemima that we'll need to display a 'nut allergy' label when offering the cake to the customers – we can't risk someone having a reaction.

Eventually, the stainless-steel countertop is empty of my glass measuring bowls; everything is included, even the nip of whisky Ned said I was allowed to put in. How he ever thought I'd agree to make it minus the best bit is beyond me. Thankfully, Jemima laughed her head off at his suggestion and he quickly apologised. I suppose it's early days for them, too; each getting used to the other's ways and expectations. How lovely, though, to have found each other and for the two halves to complement each other so well; she really is the yin to his yang.

I sigh.

What I wouldn't give to have a relationship like that when I'm ready. Not yet, I'm happy focusing on my career, building my reputation as a baker, catering manager, whatever they wish to call it. But one day I'll settle down and enjoy another aspect of life. I wouldn't say no to what I witness between Ned and Jemima.

I flick the 'off' button and smile at the creamy mixture before me. Maybe the best relationships are nothing more than the right ingredients measured and mixed to complement each other, like the perfect recipe; like when one chooses the bowl and the other the spoon.

Chapter Forty-Eight

Tuesday 7 December

Nessie

I drop a pile of new merchandise tags on to Isaac's workbench as I pass.

'What are those?'

'New gift tags purely for the Christmas season. Jemima's handing them out around the gallery and asking for the usual gift tags to be removed and replaced with those.'

Isaac eyes the gilt-edged scarlet labels before selecting one.

'I quite like them, though I haven't many items from which to remove the usual blue tags, have I?' I say sarcastically, staring across at my array of finished goods, each with a blue gift tag declaring: 'From Shetland, With Love'.

'From Shetland, With Love At Christmas,' reads Isaac, inspecting his new tag and swinging it by the gold thread. 'Are we to save the removed ones and reuse them, or discard?'

I shrug. 'She didn't say. I just happened to walk by, so I saved her the job of dropping in here to deliver them. Why?'

'It seems a waste to be changing tags each season, just for the sake of a small detail.'

'A crucial detail, some might say, given the marketing aspects, especially for those who export their goods around the world. Verity received an online yarn order from Saudi Arabia the other day. Can you imagine opening a gift box and this –' I swing the Christmas tag back at him – 'being neatly presented. It's a finishing touch that leaves a lasting impression.'

'I suppose.'

I watch as he gathers up the new tags and puts them aside.

'Are you not feeling it?' I ask.

'I get it, don't think that I don't, but . . .' he glances towards his display rack of glassware and baubles. 'I've got all these to change, if I'm to comply with their small request.'

'Phew,' I say, seeking to lighten the mood. 'For a moment, I thought we had anarchy occurring at the forge – and it wasn't initiated at my end.'

Isaac throws a smile over his shoulder as he busies himself checking the temperature of his furnace. He says nothing more, but continues to work.

'Are you doing anything Thursday evening?' asks Isaac, tidying his workbench.

I'm sweeping the floor after yet another late finish. 'The usual – dinner, TV and early to bed. Why?' I ask, glancing up from the debris and dust billowing before me.

'I'm heading out to Sumburgh Head to view the Northern Lights, just wondered if you fancied going.'

'Yes!' I literally jump at the chance.

'Would you like a moment to think about that?'

'Not necessary. My dad used to insist every year that we should spend one night camped in a cold muddy field staring up at the skies hunting for the faintest tinge of green. Though he always called them the Mirrie Dancers,' I say, suddenly feeling warm and fuzzy with childhood memories.

'I was aiming to arrive for eleven o'clockish, I could pick you up on the way. It gets pretty cold, so you'll need to wrap up.'

'Isaac, that is the best idea I've heard all day!'

'Sorted. Let's get out of here, then.'

With a renewed burst of energy, we're done and dusted for the day and locking the forge door in record time.

'Night, Nessie. I'll see you tomorrow,' says Isaac, swiftly departing for his car. 'Dig out your long johns ready for Thursday.'

'I will.' There's no fear of me risking the cold, not after the memories I have of frozen fingers and toes during my childhood.

Verity

I stare round the kitchen. It's clear, despite my pretence, that I have no idea what I am doing. I've had a long day ... with very little to show for it.

'Do you need a hand?' asks Francis, attempting to make a coffee whilst wafting away the flying fibres filling the air like dust motes.

He's dropped by, expecting an evening meal, and I'm nowhere near finished.

'I should have opened a window, shouldn't I?'

'You should have given it up as a bad job two hours ago. What exactly are you trying to do, Verity?'

'Were you this encouraging with your workshop attendees?' I ask, before adding, 'To dye the fleece before drying it, so a local lady can spin it into a skein of wool for me.'

Francis turns and stares. 'Are you strapped for cash?'

'No. Whatever gives you that idea?'

He gestures around the kitchen: the buckets of water, clumps of soaking fleece, the pile of wet bath towels thrown in front of the washing machine.

'All this for a ball of wool?'

'Oi, not just any ball of sodding wool! Wool hand-dyed by me, using plants picked by me from the picturesque coastal path – true bona fide Shetland wool.'

'When you put it like that, I can see the price tag going through the roof.'

'You get what you pay for,' I murmur, attempting to roll up my water-sodden cuffs, without success.

'And do you advertise that the amount of sheep crap in every ball of wool may vary in content?'

'Francis, that's gross.'

'If you're strapped for cash to buy yourself some wool, just say. But this . . . well, this looks like a cottage industry gone sadly wrong. How long have you been at it?'

'Five hours, plus an hour foraging for plants. Which is why you need to pedal into Lerwick and grab us a last-minute fish supper. I'm not cooking at this late hour.'

'That'll be expensive wool, if you're going to cover your time, effort and still pull a profit.'

He's right, but I'm not confirming that. I can do without our Avril crowing over my continued incompetence.

'Oh, ye of little faith, Francis.'

'What the hell do you call that shade?' asks Magnus, as I hold aloft a sodden clump of fleece from the bucket.

He's dropped by because his curiosity was tweaked after stopping and speaking to Francis as he pedalled towards town.

'Stop laughing; it is not funny. It's taken all day and I've ended up with . . . well, this . . . fifty shades of sheep shite!'

'You're telling me. My sheep Bracken kindly donated her fleece so you could make something beautiful, yet you've decimated it and colour-matched it to her soiled claggy arse. I've a good mind to ask for it back so I can return it to its rightful owner, but looking at that . . . well, there's not much point.'

I plop the fleece back into the bucket and watch as a grown man is bent double in my kitchen, coughing, spluttering and choking at the sight of my hard work.

Magnus slaps himself in the middle of the chest, saving me from doing it.

'Next time, wash and dry the fleece, then have it spun into tidy skeins of wool before dyeing it. It won't resemble roadkill in your chosen shade!'

'Next time?'

'Exactly. If I'd known that was to be the end result, I'd never have agreed to shear her.'

Chapter Forty-Nine

Thursday 9 December

Isla

'Well done, Isla. Francis was chuffed to bits with how his photography workshop went on Monday. The feedback forms specifically mentioned how lovely your warm buffet was, the availability of hot beverages throughout the day and how delicious the cakes were. You've done us proud,' says Ned enthusiastically, continually glancing towards Jemima as he offers me praise. As if being guided by her reaction; checking he's doing it right. I might not be the only one winging it around here. 'Is there anything you'd like to add, Isla?'

I quickly unfold the paper containing my notes; I'll go blank otherwise.

'We've supported the blacksmith's day and now a photography session. I wondered if we could follow the same agenda with other events in The Orangery?' I look up to witness Ned and Jemima exchange a glance. I hastily continue for fear of interruption. 'You could hold poetry open mics, karaoke nights, host wildlife enthusiasts, ornithology groups, landscape painters, creative writing workshops, charity quiz nights, floristry masterclasses – and I could even take on a small group of cake decoration students.' I quickly fold my piece of paper, expecting both Ned and Jemima to chime in with a series of excuses as to why such ideas wouldn't be viable or profitable.

Neither one says a word.

'They're just ideas. I don't mean to cross a line, but I thought if I made a suggestion, other people could benefit by using The Orangery on days when the rest of the gallery is closed.'

'I'm impressed,' says Ned. 'I like your thinking. Why don't you leave your list with Jemima? And we'll discuss it further.'

I slide the paper across the meeting table. At least he's given me a chance to share my ideas. Which seems fair. I'll shoulder Ned's excuses and his rejection later.

I return to The Orangery with a spring in my step. It seems childish but receiving praise for something I love doing is simply the best feeling. Why can't every day start like this one has? I'll need to thank Francis when I next see him. I've no doubt Jemima will be onboard regarding my ideas for other 'workshop events'. My mind goes into overdrive with potential ideas.

I stop short on entering the café: Lachlan.

I head straight for the counter, as I would when spotting any customer enjoying their drink, but I sense he's there to see me. To watch me. To attempt to . . . urgh, it's bloody creepy.

'Isla!' he calls as I pass.

'Yes,' I say, spinning around, but intentionally not changing my route.

'Any chance of a chat?'

'Can't, really. I've got lots to do.' I feel slightly cruel, not engaging. But I'm not going to be browbeaten into meeting his desires.

He had his chance, months ago. He might be regretting how it ended, but this ship has well and truly sailed.

'I'd appreciate it if I could be left to decorate this cake for the next few hours,' I say to Pippa and Aileen. 'Thursday mornings aren't the busiest, so if I can crack on now it'll be all hands on deck by lunchtime.'

Both ladies nod in agreement, though Pippa sighs heavily.

Here was me thinking she'd have jumped at the chance to lead the show for a while.

'Who's in charge out of us two, then?' asks Pippa, suddenly coming alive.

'Is that necessary?' asks Aileen, looking bemused.

'It might be,' comes Pippa's answer.

'Ladies, you both know what's what around here, so can we not just get on?'

'Humph!' sighs Pippa, staring out across the terrace and the leaf-strewn lawn.

Aileen rolls her eyes, declaring her thoughts about Pippa.

I fill my piping bag to bulging with white royal icing; I love to feel the hefty weight between my hands as I decorate a cake. Delicate icing is one skill I struggled to master. Each attempt ended in sheer disaster; I was trying too hard. Now, I allow my hands to drift along the pristine surface, guiding the nozzle; I find it quite relaxing. I can see the desired pattern for this celebration cake in my head, though maybe jotting it down as a working reminder wouldn't hurt. But I've started now, I don't wish to stop – and I can always scrape it off if I go wrong.

I keep one ear cocked for the goings-on in the café. Why can't some women get along with others? It's almost as if Pippa feels the need to dislike every female, as if they were a personal threat to her livelihood. I'm glad I'm not like that. If anything, I welcome the input and advice from other women. Observing Verity with customers, Nessie's buoyant manner, Jemima's innate kindness and creativity, they all enrich my life as I learn from each, in turn.

Oh, and Dottie, I forgot little Dottie! I love her spritely manner as she totters back and forth across the gallery yard, ensuring everyone is happy. If my granny were still alive, I bet she'd be like

Dottie. Melissa was right, her allotment is "spick and span" – not a single weed to be found.

'Have you just finished icing that?'

I jump on hearing a male voice beside me: Ned.

I step back from the cake, my piping bag held aloft and turned skywards, before answering. His voice has zapped me straight out of my icing zone; my heart rate will recover in a second.

'It doesn't take long once you start. It's really just a case of keep going and . . . *ta-dah!* It looks great, doesn't it?'

'It certainly does.'

How long has he been standing there? I bet he thinks I'm rude not speaking to him.

'Anyway, how can I help?'

'Yes, sorry, I dropped by to give you this – it's just arrived in the mail.' Ned hands me a shop-bought thank-you card, its envelope resting beneath. I flick open the front and read the tiny writing, certain phrases jumping out at me: 'superb baking', 'swift service' and 'Shetland bannocks like I've never tasted before in my life'.

I look to Ned for an explanation.

'The lady attended the photography workshop with Francis O'Connell the other day,' he says. 'She was obviously very impressed, so we think you should have this, as you've earned it.'

'Wow! I'm touched that a customer actually put pen to paper, to praise me.'

'I'm glad you're pleased. Well done, Isla.'

Within seconds, Ned's gone and I'm left holding the card. Two lots of praise in one morning, I'm on a roll!

No one at catering college ever mentioned how good this moment would feel. I slip the card into my apron pocket; I'll Blu-tack it to the office wall later as a reminder.

Nessie

Isaac reverses the car so the tailgate faces out to sea off Sumburgh Head. There are several other vehicles scattered about the car park; a short distance from us, three occupants sit on car bonnets or deckchairs. Tonight, I ignore the mighty lighthouse, looking beyond into the night sky. The faintest green haze can be seen in the distance on the horizon.

'Grab those blankets before you settle yourself,' says Isaac, pointing to the rear seats of his car as he opens the tailgate up high. 'You might not want to move once you get comfy.'

'There's a fair few here, are you expecting company?' I jest, collecting the pile as instructed.

'No. Just us. You'll be surprised how many you'll need, as thick as they are.' I watch as he arranges a cushion pad along the edge of the tailgate, covering the paintwork and stretching partway back into the boot area. He takes the top blanket from the pile I'm holding and opens it before spreading it over the cushion. 'There . . . a wee cosy seat to save your legs from going numb. Are two blankets enough for you?' he asks, lifting two more from the pile.

'Given the various layers I'm dressed in, I'll be surprised if I need additional blankets.'

Isaac laughs, gesturing to my remaining stash. 'They're yours, you'll be needing them later, I'm sure.'

I shuffle into place on the edge of the open tailgate, my legs dangling over the bumper like a small child in a high chair. I watch as he unzips his puffa jacket, wraps a large tartan blanket around his middle from chest height, creating a long skirt, before securing the zip and settling on to the cushions. He leaves a decent gap between us.

'Quite an art, that,' I say, smiling at his preparation.

'I drove up the other night too but it was a waste of time; the lights were so faint, you could hardly see them. I was frozen within two hours.'

'Given your nifty swaddling style, from the chest downwards, I doubt you'll freeze,' I say, opening one woollen blanket and casually draping it about my shoulders before folding it around my front.

'I've brought coffee supplies just in case,' says Isaac, nodding towards a couple of flasks stashed behind us. 'There's biscuits, cake and crisps, as well as sliced pizza – which probably isn't hot any more.'

'Quite a picnic, thank you.'

'I don't usually bring so much, but I didn't know what you'd like,' he says, staring out across to the horizon. 'The lights are already more defined than the other night. Fingers crossed, we'll get a proper display tonight.'

We sit in silence watching the sky slowly change in a graceful manner like shimmering dancers trailing veils across the night sky. It's mesmerising to observe the various shades of green ripple across the dark sky as if tumbling towards us, casting aspects of pink, orange and purple to merge and mix around the edges.

Our silence is comfortable. Each content with the company of the other. I don't feel the need to chat inanely, filling time. Sitting side by side on the tailgate feels normal, as if we've done this many times before. My mind is clear, my breath steady and my worries gone. It's like meditation; a calmness has slowly descended, anchoring me to this moment in time.

'Have you ever seen anything as beautiful?' I whisper, not daring to speak louder for fear of breaking the spell.

'Nothing. It amazes me every time,' he replies, his gaze focused on the shimmering lights.

*　　*　　*

We sit transfixed until three in the morning, the provisions consumed; our goosebumps remain, despite the warm heavy blankets, and our breath billows into clouds. It's strange, seeing Isaac's breath disperse in the air, having watched him control this invisible force whilst using a blowpipe.

'Are you ready for the off?' asks Isaac, unzipping his jacket to release his blanket wrap.

'I am, though not really,' I say, knowing my bed is calling me but not wishing to leave this night behind. 'I could stay right here right now in this moment for ever – it's so beautiful.'

'Life doesn't allow that, though, does it?'

'Sadly not. Our days are filled with business worries, paying bills and drama – in reality what I need is this ... tranquillity, calm and pure beauty.'

Isaac turns to face me; his blond hair and pale features create a striking, almost haunting, appearance. The glistening light in his eyes dances erratically, scanning my upturned face.

My breath stalls. My heartbeat quickens.

Our silence returns as neither one of us moves. We each stare, absorbing the other's presence. My insides knot, as if an invisible thread has been woven between us and firmly secured by the intimacy of silence.

Finally, I exhale.

Isaac inhales deeply.

'Anyway, let's get going,' he says, awkwardly shifting and jumping up from the tailgate.

Our moment has passed. I breathe differently beside this man.

'Anyway,' I mutter, echoing his words, unsure of what I actually mean.

Chapter Fifty

Sunday 12 December

Isla

'Isla, Ned wants to see you in his office,' calls Pippa, on replacing the telephone's handset behind the till counter.

'Did he say what for?' I ask naïvely.

'He's hardly going to tell me, is he?' says Pippa, pulling a face.

I get that she doesn't much like being a waitress, but personally I think Ned was foolish employing Jemima's cousin. Melissa and Dottie reckon there's no love lost between them – but still, don't take it out on me.

I remove my apron and drape it on the side counter before heading over to the manor. I've already had my daily chat, though admittedly Ned wasn't present. There have been several times when he's been 'out on business', attending to emergencies with his land tenants. I can't imagine what this is about; I've never had two meetings in one day.

I push the green door leading into the manor pretty hard, as the bottom edge sticks on the floor tiles. Once inside, I wipe my feet; I don't want Dottie chasing me. I hotfoot it through the winding corridors to the grand staircase, then avert my eyes from the paintings staring down and possibly criticising my presence in such a posh house. I'd love them to know that my beautiful cakes have helped save this manor, their previous home, from being handed over to a tourist trust – admittedly, in a very small way, but still, they have.

On reaching the third floor, I walk the length of the corridor and rap on Ned's office door, sounding more confident than I feel.

Surprisingly, I don't have to wait as he calls out straight away. 'Come in!'

'Hello, Pippa said you wanted to see me.' I enter, half-expecting the same routine as each morning.

Instantly, I sense it isn't the same. Ned is sitting at his desk; Jemima is pacing the floor before the fireplace, nibbling her thumbnail as she glances over at me.

Ned doesn't stand, Jemima doesn't stop walking, and neither of them asks me to take a seat.

'Isla, I'd like a word, if I may,' says Ned, his gaze direct. This time, he doesn't glance towards Jemima for confirmation.

'OK.' I stand before the side edge of his desk. I imagine it's like being summoned to the headmaster's office, though that never happened to me.

'Can I ask you, what are these?' Ned swiftly opens the top drawer, pulls out my bunch of keys, then places them on the desktop before closing the drawer.

My keys.

Ned frowns. Oh, he's not happy.

Jemima has stopped walking; she's not happy, either.

'They're my keys.'

'Are you sure?' he asks, still staring.

'Yep. Those are mine. That's my wooden cupcake key ring.'

Ned swivels around in his chair to face Jemima, who simply stares back at him; not a word is said, no gesture or grimace, and yet a conversation passes between them.

I glance from one to the other, expecting either one to speak. Nothing. Jemima slowly turns her back towards us and faces the large marble mantelpiece. Her shoulders seem rigid.

Ned turns back around to face me. 'Isla,' his voice has softened in a fatherly manner. 'Do you know where I obtained these keys?'

I shake my head. I can't lie. I think I've done enough of that recently.

Ned glances at Jemima's back, which is now ramrod straight, before continuing.

'These were offered for sale in a local pub – the price tag was five hundred pounds!'

My eyes widen.

'Which pub?' I ask.

'Which pub? Are you serious, Isla?'

'Sorry, what I mean is ... if it's the pub that I'm thinking it might be, then I might know who was trying to sell them.'

'Oh really, because my first question is how did some lowlife get their hands on a bunch of keys belonging to my estate? Secondly, are you aware that these keys contain the master key, which opens all the artists' premises, plus The Orangery?'

I gulp.

'Sorry.' It's the only thing I can think to say.

'Sorry? Sorry isn't good enough, Isla. I'm going to need a detailed explanation as to how my land tenant was offered this set of keys at such a price – potentially enabling some scallywag to do us over by breaking into every area of this development ...' He pauses, before adding, 'I'll say, so you fully understand the significance of your answers, your future here depends on the information you provide.'

My mouth drops open.

I look towards Jemima, who remains unchanged in her stance.

'Now, I'm a fair person, and I realise you are a young person who might wish to call a parent to attend while you explain. If so, then please go ahead and phone them.'

'I don't need to call anyone,' I say.

Ned stares at me, and Jemima speaks. Her voice is slow, controlled; she's as angry as Ned is, plus I think she's been crying.

'Isla, there are times in life when the best thing to do is to follow the suggestion that is made to you. I don't think you need to call anyone, but I would like you to call someone you trust so they can sit with you whilst you answer my husband's questions.'

'OK. Can I call Verity to join us?'

'From The Yarn Barn?' asks Ned.

I nod. I suppose I could have chosen Dottie, but she's not always around for more than a few hours a day.

'If that's what you want, then go ahead. Jemima, can you phone down to The Orangery asking one of the ladies to nip across to Verity and ask her to come up?'

Jemima moves from the fireplace to the phone. I remain where I am, not daring to move. Ned's not raging, he's not shouting, but I can tell by the set of his jaw that he is fuming inside. I wonder which tenant called him? Did they pay the money?

'Why don't we settle while we wait for Verity to join us?' says Ned, indicating the meeting table.

I don't sit in my usual middle seat; this isn't a usual meeting. I sit at the far end. Ned settles in a seat partway down one side – not his usual seat, either.

I don't know where to look. I've never really been in trouble before, whether it be at school, college or home. I don't like how this feels. I've no intention of making matters worse. I'll be gutted if Ned terminates my contract or takes steps towards altering my role as a result of this. The last few weeks have been the busiest and best weeks of my life.

I watch Jemima chatting on the phone. Her eyes are red, confirming her tears. She replaces the handset, blows out her cheeks as if stressed and then joins us at the table. She doesn't sit down but remains standing. I'm actually upset that I've upset her. She's been so lovely to me. She's kept it professional, but I know deep down she's tried really hard to support me.

'They're going to nip across to Verity, it shouldn't take long.'

'I don't think she'll know where to come to,' I say, recalling our previous conversations.

'That's a point. I'll go and meet her,' says Ned, standing up.

'Are you sure?' asks Jemima, with a doleful expression.

Ned gives a curt nod before leaving the room. Jemima sits down heavily into his vacated seat.

'Sorry,' I say.

Jemima sighs, resting her elbows on the table and cradling her chin in her hands. She looks exhausted.

'Look, I don't want to say much without the others present but I'm really surprised, Isla. Please just tell him the truth, that's all I can suggest.'

I nod. I know she's my boss – part of the management team – but she feels like a big sister watching out for me.

We sit in silence. I want Ned to hurry up, but at the same time I don't want him to arrive back. I can't have it both ways. I wonder what the ladies in The Orangery are doing. Hopefully, continuing as if I were present in the back room baking.

Verity

'Is there something wrong? Has my gallery rent not gone through on the direct debit?' I say, approaching Ned as he stands on the doorstep of the green door, waiting for me. I'm glad I've locked The Yarn Barn as I have no idea how long this will take.

'Nothing of the sort. There's no issue with your rent . . . it's more a private matter, come in and I'll explain.'

I've never entered the manor before, though I've heard Isla mention bits and bobs as she traipses through for her daily meeting.

Ned barges the door with his shoulder. 'The bloody thing

sticks, it needs sorting,' he mutters, pushing it wide and allowing me to enter.

We're in a dimly lit corridor, very old-fashioned, with tiled floors and high ceilings. Ned leads the way through a series of corridors decorated in a similar style.

'We've had to call Isla in for a chat but we'd prefer a third party to be present, purely so she can speak freely and confidently, without feeling . . . what's the word?'

'Intimidated?' I suggest, knowing how my three lads might feel chatting with their bosses.

'Well, yes, it's as good as any,' he says as we reach a massive staircase.

'Is this about the keys?'

Ned halts as he's about to step on to the first stair. He turns, sighs and nods. 'Yep – her keys, to be specific.'

I pull a knowing expression and nod as we climb the staircase.

'Right, so she's told you. OK, well . . . obviously, things have developed a little further and I need to hear Isla's explanation. I'm not good at handling such matters. But Jemima is gutted – she really believes in the young woman – so I haven't any choice but to lead this, however difficult it proves to be. My wife's spent the last hour in tears.'

'That's a shame. I'm sure Isla can explain.'

'I hope so, it's pretty serious.'

I don't know how many flights of stairs we climb but I'm out of breath by the time we reach a landing with skylights. I could do with a breather at the top but cover it up and continue to pace alongside Ned.

'Just in here, Verity,' he says, indicating a door on our left.

'Thank you.' I enter to find Jemima and Isla seated at a meeting table.

Ned's right; Jemima looks terribly upset: ashen-faced and red-eyed.

'Hi, Verity,' says Isla, from the far end of the table.

'Hi ...' Jemima musters a single word, and sends a weak smile my way.

'Verity, thank you for agreeing to join us. If you'd like to take a seat beside Isla, we can make a start,' explains Ned, in a fatherly manner, settling in a chair beside Jemima.

I take a seat; I'm pretty sure whatever has happened is a big misunderstanding, but this feels tense.

'Purely to bring Verity up to speed, I'm going to recap what happened this morning,' says Ned, glancing between Isla and Jemima. He spends several minutes explaining details about a pub, a tenant and the offer of five hundred pounds in exchange for Isla's keys.

Once he falls silent, I realise why I've been called to assist.

'Before we continue, let me just say that Jemima wants to be present but she feels she needs to stay neutral, given the nature of this discussion. She feels responsible for everyone who she supports in this gallery. Isla, she's had nothing but fabulous things to say about you since we employed you. After the interviews, I was concerned about your lack of life experience, I'll admit that. Your baking skills and willingness to learn shone through, which clinched the role. You've been so creative with ideas and suggestions, and supportive towards everyone here. Jemima ... actually, I'll correct that, both of us have been delighted with how you've managed The Orangery. Isla, can you explain about your keys, please?' asks Ned, falling silent.

'My keys went missing. I know I should have said, but I honestly thought my keys only gave access to the café. I knew that every artist had a key to The Orangery to gain access on days when it isn't open but I didn't know that mine gave access to their stables. I searched everywhere but couldn't find them. I kept assuming I'd come across them in the café, in the rear stock-room, or maybe they'd slipped down the side of the fridges, so each morning I borrowed a different artist's key to gain access. Each night I borrowed another artist's key to lock up. The days simply went by and . . . well, I didn't find my keys.'

'And you didn't think to mention it?' asks Ned.

He's remaining very calm, but he's not impressed at all. He keeps glancing at poor Jemima, who's cradling her chin on the backs of her hands whilst staring at the wall ahead, listening intently.

'I did . . .' Isla looks at me, before continuing. 'Verity said I should say as well, but I didn't.'

'You told me that you had, though,' I say, wanting Ned to know everything.

'I shouldn't have lied to you either, Verity. I'm sorry.'

I sit back, listening to her answers.

'So, you carried on as if it hadn't happened. And then what?' asks Ned.

'That's it. Nothing else. Apart from when Melissa's sales money went missing, but I replaced the twenty quid without saying.'

'You replaced it?' asks Jemima.

'Yeah, I thought you'd think I'd taken it otherwise. I hadn't, but . . . you know.'

'You're telling me you genuinely don't know who had the keys?' Ned asks.

'Yeah. Exactly that.'

Ned's gaze drops to the tabletop. I can see he's thinking before continuing. 'My tenant – and I trust this guy, I've known him for years – tells me that the seller was bragging that you were in on the scheme and were pocketing half the cash. Buyers were being told that you'd checked every door to ensure that every key opens and locks where necessary and were guaranteeing access across the development. Is that not true?'

I'm gobsmacked. I turn to view Isla's reaction and, boy, what a reaction. Her mouth is wide open, her eyes even wider, her complexion is ashen, much paler than Jemima's. Isla is frozen like a statue.

Jemima turns her head and stares along the table, viewing Isla and assessing her reaction.

'Isla, you need to answer me, please. I'm trying my hardest to get to the bottom of this,' encourages Ned, who looks to me as Isla remains silent.

'Sweetie, you must answer him. Your position here might depend on it,' I say, rubbing her forearm as a gesture of kindness.

'Exactly, Verity, that's how big this is,' says Ned. 'Potentially, we could have seen every artist burgled; they'd have lost every product, material, tool, personal belonging kept inside their stable. The Orangery could have been emptied of all the catering equipment, not to mention the personal safety of anyone who intervened to prevent such a burglary taking place.'

'Was he called Lachlan?' mutters Isla.

Ned nods.

Isla's hands fly up to cover her mouth, as tears spill over her lashes.

'I'm so very sorry. He wants us to get back together and I don't want to. I had enough last time. He seems really nice at first but he doesn't know how to behave. He thinks that he can date you one minute then drop you the next. I was really poorly when he dumped me. My mum said I should learn my lesson, and I did. Honest, I did. He showed up here one day and asked for a discount on his coffee, and I said no, I didn't want him coming back. But he kept coming back every few days to chat to me. I kept saying I had work to do, I was busy running the café, but then he'd come in every day and ... the keys went missing ... but worse than that ...' her sentences are interrupted by huge body-racking sobs. 'My. Granny's. Recipe. Book. Has. Gone. From. The. Storage. Room.'

I wrap her into my arms and let her cry.

Jemima releases a deep breath she's been holding for the last ten minutes, and Ned relaxes as I gently rock Isla and let her cry on my shoulder.

There is silence, apart from her sobbing.

I'm angry. Angry that this young woman has been tricked by this boy. My lads were taught to treat people with respect – obviously, this young man doesn't do that. How she's coped without her granny's recipe book is quite an achievement. I'm surprised it's taken her until now to get upset about its loss.

Isla

I feel like an utter fool. More so when the police arrive to take details. I should have told Ned about the keys straight away. I should have told Lachlan to sling his hook. I was just trying to be kind. It can't be easy on a guy's ego if the girl he likes doesn't reciprocate his feelings. All my days, here I go again, putting others first. I know first-hand how it feels; he dumped me, rejected me months ago, and still I allowed this to happen.

I straighten the chairs and coffee tables, giving the café the once-over before locking up. It's way past my usual home time; no doubt my mum will be curious and start asking questions as soon as I step into the car. I won't lie, I can't. She'll hit the roof to think I was so stupid.

'Are you nearly done?' asks Jemima, popping her head around the door.

'I am, thanks,' I say, taking in her appearance. Jemima looks how I feel. She's really taken it to heart. 'I'm so sorry to have upset you.'

'We need to get this sorted, and then hopefully things can move on.' She bites the inside of her cheek, as if stopping herself from saying more. She lingers by the door, waiting.

Has Ned sent her to watch me lock up? Have I completely blown their trust?

I flick off the main light switches and find the new key Ned has provided, just for The Orangery. Apparently, my original bunch is being photographed in Ned's office.

I pull the heavy door to. We both stand outside, surrounded by the chilly night air, as I swiftly turn the key in the lock. A satisfying clunk is heard before I withdraw the key.

'Goodnight,' I say.

'Good night, Isla. We'll see you on Wednesday.'

I sigh; I needed those extra few words, otherwise I wouldn't have slept for days. I've a million thoughts running through my head: what were the other ladies told? Where is Lachlan right now? Did that tenant really threaten to punch his lights out if he didn't hand over the keys for free?

Jemima nips across the yard towards the green-painted door. I imagine matching my steps with hers; picture the sticking door, the walk along the tiled corridor, up the grand staircase and . . .

A figure steps from the shadows as I reach the stone archway at the entrance to the stable yard.

'Bloody hell!' I yell, my hand flying to my mouth.

'Sorry, sorry. I didn't want to leave without seeing you were OK,' says Verity, as my heart settles back in my chest.

We begin walking along the driveway, Verity pushing my mum's bike.

'I'm not sure, to be honest. Ned called the police, so I had to speak to them, but Jemima just said "see you on Wednesday".'

'That's good news; I thought you were history back in the office.'

'You and me both. Given the up-coming Yule Day celebration, I'm glad I've completed the cake ahead of time. But still, it messes things up with the upset I've caused.'

'Have they included Mungo in the police discussions?' asks Verity.

'Nope. Thankfully, Jemima said he would hinder the situation with his obsession about keys and safety, so not a word to him.'

'Right, best you get home, then bath and bed with plenty of rest, ready to face the coming week. If the waitresses ask questions, which they will, just tell them it's linked to me ... and Ned's asked you not to discuss it for my sake.'

'Verity, that's good of you, but it would be another fib and I don't—'

'Look, if you don't, you'll have them gossiping about you and jostling for your position. Make life easy for yourself, blame it on me. They won't question it, and you can have an ordinary week.'

'Thank you, I owe you one.'

'Bloody right you do!'

I can see my mum's car waiting at the bottom of the driveway. I'm now nervous at seeing her, let alone explaining.

Verity gives me an awkward hug as we part company. The bike's handlebars twist as she leans it against her hip to wrap me in her arms.

'It'll be OK,' she whispers.

I grab the handle and open the car door.

'Hi, Mum ...' Here I go.

Chapter Fifty-One

Wednesday 15 December

Nessie

I scurry to my own end of the forge on hearing the sound of his boots on the cobbles. I've just made it in time to stand before my fire pit and busy myself building my tinder pyre, when he enters.

'Morning!' calls Isaac, in his usual cheery manner. 'Are you running late?'

'Me? No,' I say, aiming for a nonchalant tone and quickly turning back to focus upon my task.

'But you've only just arrived, right?'

'No.' I don't look up or turn around at his questioning.

I hadn't planned on him being five minutes early, but he knows my morning routine. His arrival each day must seem like Groundhog Day, as I'm always standing in the same spot doing the same task.

'How come you're behind then? You've usually got your coals lit by the time I walk in.'

I shrug. I want to laugh, as he hasn't noticed, but that will ruin the surprise – which is hardly the greatest surprise, but still, I did my best to help him out.

'Nessie?'

'Yeah.' I sneak a glance across the forge to see his baffled expression. 'Am I such a stickler for routine that you can almost pinpoint my arrival time by working backwards? Bloody hell, I need to get out more.'

'No, it's just that you always arrive bang on time, then you're methodical in doing the same routine . . . and, yes, when I walk in you are usually stoking a fire, not building one.' Isaac is turning about on the spot, he knows something is up, or different, or . . .

He stops, having spied his display rack of vases, bottles and baubles, each displaying a new Christmas tag.

'Bless you, you've changed the gift tags for me.' He is standing stock-still, his coat halfway off his shoulders, surprise etched across his features. 'That was very kind of you.'

'You're welcome. You seemed somewhat miffed at the prospect of switching them over, and I know you haven't had time. So I reckoned I'd do you a favour – to repay all those you've done for me.'

Isaac removes his coat and nods. 'Fiddley stuff like that with my fingers is just a pain in the arse. It was bad enough when I had to loop each one in the first place, but to have to remove and then replace them – I just thought, *urgh!* Cheers, Nessie.'

'No problem.' I turn back to my fire pit and continue to build. It took me all of ten minutes with my nimble fingers, but I get where he's coming from. 'My good deed for the day has paid off nicely.'

'Well done. I'll gladly pay you back with a good laugh.'

'What?' I'm confused.

'Isaac Archibald . . .' he pauses, smirks before continuing, 'Balloch Clyde Drummond Jameson is here at your service!'

'I told you!' I burst out laughing as I regress to my seven-year-old self in Mrs McBride's morning registration.

'Damn my parents and their devotion to Scotland!' hollers Isaac, puffing out his chest and standing tall like a Scots Guard.

'I remember now, it was the A, B, C, D sequence the other kids used to giggle at,' I add, between bouts of laughter.

'Believe me, I'm grateful they didn't continue along the alphabet further. I might have ended with a Wallace, or even a Zuill.'

I can't look at him as he struts about, exaggerating his pose for comic effect.

'Sorry, but it's my default move when I need to make others laugh. But you, dear lass, appear to be in an impish mood. Have I wasted a valuable resource in revealing the truth?'

'Thank you, but think of it as paying it forward; repeating such details will always do wonders for my mood.'

Isla

'How dare you?' I'm seething, he's the last person I want to see on a quiet night out.

There he sits, all loud and proud, amongst a group of his mates. I'm across the floor of the pub in seconds; the poor barman only just took my drinks order before I stormed off.

'Isla, come and join us!' wails Lachlan, obviously drunk, given his slurred tones.

'No bloody way! You've got some nerve showing up in here – or is that because you can't nip to your local? I hear someone promised to kick ten shades of crap out of you over your wheeler-dealer antics after you stole my keys.'

Lachlan is on his feet, and somewhat sobered up, before I can say another word.

His mates stop their jeering and banter to stare at us, now standing toe to toe, Lachlan staring down at me, me staring up at him.

'All because I wished to stay single. You giant prat!' is all I say, before heading back to the bar to collect my round of drinks.

I don't care that I've just made a show of myself in front of half my neighbours. I smile at the barman, who looks utterly baffled, hand over the cash and spread my fingers around the three tall glasses before heading back to Fiona and Kenzie.

'Isla?' He steps into my path.

'Seriously, unless you want me to call for the doorman, I suggest you move out of my way. Don't ever speak to me again.'

I'm relieved when Lachlan steps to the side, freeing my path.

I focus straight ahead, concentrating on not spilling the drinks, and return to my table of friends.

Chapter Fifty-Two

Tuesday 21 December

Verity

There are afternoons spent with friends, which you don't want to end. You want the company, the witty banter, the camaraderie to continue hour after hour. Deep down, you want the result to be an afternoon spilling into an evening and overflowing into whatever naturally occurs next.

This is one such afternoon.

I've collected my freshly spun yarn from a local spinner, after Magnus kindly donated a second shorn fleece.

My entire kitchen is yet again covered in buckets of hot water, though there are no fleece motes dancing in the air this time. I'm armed with a pair of wooden tongs, which I keep being told were an incorrect purchase – 'Next time, buy the metal tongs.' If there is a next time.

I'm enjoying his company; sharing our space, time and his knowledge. Earlier, on the coastal path, Magnus had happily explained the colour properties of various plants, despite their dormant state, the late season and the falling snow.

I was tempted to restart 'our conversation', push for an agreement defining our time together, but ... something is slowly evolving. Could this be the beginning of a mature adult relationship? It doesn't feel like the 'young kicks' of yesteryear, alongside George. There's an aura to Magnus's presence, an unexplained connection I simply can't deny. It's as if he's gently guiding me towards a safe harbour in life, as Floss does with her flock.

Magnus relieves me of my incorrectly purchased tongs and dips them into the first bucket, clasping and lifting the soaking contents.

'And that, lady, is how you dye wool ... properly.'

Before me is a glorious skein of purple wool which, despite being wet and hanging limply from the tongs, has a variety of pinkish hues running through it. I could name thirty knitting patterns that would show such a yarn off to perfection.

'You bastard!' is all I can mutter.

He plops it back into the water and moves to the next bucket, to repeat the action and display yet another gorgeous skein of wool, expertly dyed by a sodding sheep farmer.

'It's in my bloodline. And some folk around here haven't got that luxury, have they, Verity? Fancy comparing it to your fifty shades of sheep shite?'

'No, I threw that out as a bad job.'

'Really?'

'No. I lie. I dried it, as any delusional woman would, thinking it couldn't possibly be that bad – and everything looks better when it's dried, right?'

'And did it?' asks Magnus, moving along his production line of perfectly dyed skeins, each more beautiful in tone than the previous bucket.

'See for yourself.' I nip into the hallway, poke about under the staircase for a holdall and return to the kitchen, where I ceremoniously unzip it before dragging what looks like a dead carcass from the bag. 'I was thinking of burying it under the small patio – but as you know, this isn't my cottage or patio.'

'Bleeding hell, woman. I suggest we get a spade and do just that. It's worse dried than it was wet!'

'It might look better when it's spun into skeins of yarn,' I say, with renewed hope.

'The Shetland women can work magic with their spinning wheels but miracles take a little longer, Verity.' He lets out a glorious belly laugh.

I really can't say how long we laugh together; Magnus sporadically tonging his glorious yarn from each bucket and me, when I can stand up straight from laughing, methodically colour-matching my attempt against his.

I also can't say how long we kiss, when Magnus reaches the final water bucket. I know the wooden tongs fall to the floor, my disastrous fleece is trampled underfoot and we christen the lounge, shower and bedroom for longer than it takes to dye wool.

Isla

'What's this I'm hearing about you trading your keys in with some criminal sort?' asks Mungo, charging into The Orangery as soon as I open.

Here we go! I knew this moment would arrive. I was hoping for a quiet Tuesday filled with solitude and baking, admiring the gentle snow falling artistically upon the cobblestones.

'Morning, Mungo, how are you this beautiful day?'

'Don't you try and change the subject with me, young lassie. Ned has told me everything, and I'm surprised that you, of all people, would do something such as this.'

'Trading? I didn't trade anything with anyone, despite your understanding, Mungo.'

Mungo begins to unpack his theory, but I switch off. There's no convincing some people, they're not interested in the truth, just the drama.

'Can I get you your usual?' I ask, grabbing a large takeaway cup and a lid.

'I haven't time for coffee, I need to investigate the key situation for Ned.'

'The police did that over a week ago; he went straight over your head to the boys in blue,' I say, waggling the coffee cup before him.

'Why didn't you say anything? You could have trusted me. I would have sought out this young man and spoken to him, man to man.'

'Mungo, how? I didn't know he'd taken them, let alone that he'd been using them to sneak about this place and . . .'

I cease talking as his expression defaults to shock.

'What! He came in here after hours?'

'Didn't Ned mention he'd been prowling around the buildings?'

'No. I. Did. Not. Know!' snarls Mungo.

'I need to stop talking.'

'Actually, you need to start talking. My role around here isn't just as a handyman. I've got a lifetime of skills regarding security – and you, young lassie, need to start taking notice of what I've been trying to tell you.'

'When?'

'When what?'

'When did you mention security stuff to me?'

'Loads of times. In fact, every time I come in here. Levi can vouch for that.'

'Mungo! That's unfair and you know it!'

I'm fuming at that allegation, but out of habit I find I'm making his usual large flat white.

Mungo clocks my busy hands and falls silent.

Chapter Fifty-Three

Yule Day celebration, 23 December

Isla

'Isla!' calls Jemima, from the rear kitchen area, whilst I pipe festive Santa hats on to a tray of freshly made Crispy duck gingerbreads.

'Yes!' I reply, popping a silver sugar-ball pompom on each, waiting for a question to follow . . . but it doesn't.

She's not usually one to holler, so it must be important.

'Jemima, did you call?' I say, making my way through to the back section.

She's standing in the rear kitchen staring; instantly, I know what she's spotted.

'How come there are two cakes?' she asks, pointing to the two celebration cakes standing before her on the countertop.

'Ah well, you suggested that any leftover cake could be sent to the Happy Days sheltered housing complex, but I know that there won't be any leftovers, having learnt from past experience. I've made the second, smaller one as a gesture of good will at Christmastime.' The words tumble and trip from my mouth.

Jemima looks at me, before returning her gaze to the cakes. They are identical in every way, apart from size.

'I'm happy to deliver it during my lunch break so the old folk can have a slice with their afternoon tea.' I need to stop talking; it's purely nerves, knowing how much I've messed up recently.

Jemima is silent. I'm trying to read her expression. There's been no animosity or grudge held since my key clanger. Thankfully, our thriving relationship has continued, as if that sorry incident had never occurred. She's probably considering the costings: budget, time and effort. I'm fighting the urge to justify my interpretation of her original instructions.

'I made them both on the day of the photography course, so it's not as if I've done any overtime. They both cooked in the same oven, which was already on for the main cake, so no additional cost there, either. Simply the additional ingredients; and they'll need reminding about nut allergies.'

Jemima's hand flies to her chest and she gulps. 'Isla, these are beautiful. You're right, I did suggest the local retirement home, if there were any slices left over, but if it tastes as good as our wedding cake it'll be eaten in no time. Many of the elderly residents won't be able to attend the gallery to join in our Yule Day celebration – and now, they can. What a lovely gesture.' Her eyes brim with tears.

I'm still in her good books.

'If you wanted to go the whole hog to include the older generation, you could always deliver one of Nessie's giant Christmas trees and pitch it in their front garden – that's the main view from their communal lounge window.'

'Isla, you have a heart as big as a bucket,' cries Jemima. 'Go and ask her if there's one we can lend them for the week – I'll go and ask Ned to arrange a trailer for delivery.'

I dash from the kitchen, leaving Jemima slightly overcome and still staring at the cakes. I double back with a question.

'What if Nessie hasn't got a spare giant Christmas tree?'

'Ask her to select one from the driveway; guests won't notice one missing in our line-up.'

The layer of crisp snow makes it slippery underfoot as I scurry across the cobblestones, weaving between the artistic folk busily organising their craft stalls.

I find Nessie, as always in dungarees and T-shirt, displaying her bare arms, stoking red-hot coals.

'Phuh! It's boiling hot in here,' I exclaim, as the heat hits me like a wall.

'No one has ever said that before,' chides Nessie, turning from her coals.

'Ha ha. Anyway, Jemima has sent me to ask you if you have a spare giant Christmas tree plus decorations, which we can have delivered to the local Happy Days sheltered housing complex.'

'A spare? Like I didn't make enough of them in the last three weeks,' says Nessie.

'Don't shoot the messenger,' I say, adding, 'and if you haven't got one to spare, could you select one from the driveway, which folk won't notice is missing?'

Nessie grimaces, ceases stoking her coals and pops her blackened poker into its rack.

'How do you remove a Christmas tree from the double row of Christmas trees lining the driveway and not have anyone notice the gap?'

I shrug.

Nessie looks about her, as if there's a spare tree hiding in her forge.

'Whose idea was this? Jemima's?' she asks.

I gulp.

'I might have known you'd be behind it, given that the older folks are benefitting.' She purses her lips, shakes her head. 'You owe me one.'

'Yep, I know, duly noted.'

'Come on, let's take a look before Mungo arrives with his trailer to complicate matters.'

'He won't complain, not today. He's readying himself for a delivery of reindeer to accompany his Santa role in the grotto,' I say, repeating a snippet of gossip courtesy of Pippa. 'Apparently,

Ned has said if they mess in the grotto straw, Mungo gets to shovel it up and keep it for his allotment plot.'

'A bonus present for Santa, eh!' says Nessie, grabbing her cable-knit cardy as we exit the forge, heading for the driveway.

'I reckon you can remove this top one just here. Its location nearest the stone arch isn't the best spot to have positioned it; its absence will probably go unnoticed. Any gap further along the driveway would look like a blinding howler,' says Nessie, striding around in the snow, her hand shielding her eyes from the winter sunshine as she inspects her beautiful guard of honour. 'I assume Jemima wants them to have the baubles too?'

'The whole shebang. It's coming back in a week or so.'

'Ah great, we'll store it for them until next year, shall we?'

'*Nessiiiiiie*,' I say in a comical fashion at her display of Scroogeness.

'Sorry, I'm simply too jiggered to care.'

I know what she means; we're all on our last legs, with a long day and night ahead of us.

Verity

The gallery looks amazing: throngs of happy locals have gathered, dressed in bobble hats and gloves; the artists stand behind their craft stalls lining the cobbled courtyard, and the winter wonderland is complete with a layer of fresh snow underfoot.

I'm grateful that Dottie has been assigned to give me a helping hand for the day, though I've asked her to hold the fort inside the barn rather than out here in the chill. I'm happy that she'll be warm and toasty with the electric heater and a comfy armchair. The afternoon light will quickly fade and a night chill will soon descend upon the proceedings, despite the blazing fire beacons strategically dotted around to offer comfort and heat.

'Have you seen this?' says Francis, appearing from nowhere and thrusting a paper calendar beneath my nose.

'Er, no.'

'Look!' He quickly turns to the final two pages, each displaying a beautiful photograph: the first a stunning shot of Lerwick Manor in the early-morning mist and the second of Nessie's duck weathervane complete with his festive hat. 'Levi's shot was chosen for November and Mungo's for December – you can't ask for better than that. Full marks to them both!'

'That sodding duck gets everywhere,' I snort, shaking my head.

'Hopefully, the gallery and Nessie benefit from the free advertising,' says Francis, closing the calendar. 'Jemima needs to request a pile of these from the tourist board to display or hand out in the café.'

'If I see either of the guys I'll congratulate them, but full marks to you too, Francis – you encouraged and inspired them.'

Suddenly, a bell begins to clang and, in unison, all those gathered turn towards The Orangery to find Ned ringing a handbell furiously; much to Jemima's surprise, given her expression and her reaction of gloved hands pinned over her ears.

'Ladies and gentlemen, I feel honoured to welcome you to The Stables Gallery at Lerwick Manor. We're here today to celebrate Yule Day, a tradition dating back centuries, in which our local community would come together to enjoy the music, food, entertainment and delights on offer. Here at the gallery, we're home to some of the finest traditional crafts provided by extremely talented artists for you to enjoy today. We have traditional music from local fiddlers and drummers in the marquee across the driveway, refreshments and food are available inside The Orangery, but, most importantly, Santa has made special arrangements with Rudolph, his chief reindeer, to collect him later tonight – so there's no issue with tomorrow night's big delivery drop.'

A titter of laughter lifts from the adults. The children stare, wide-eyed at the very mention of Santa.

'We're also delighted to be joined by our friends from the Shetland Community Choir and the Lerwick Brass Band, who are collecting for local charities, so please dig deep and give a donation.' Ned points towards the ensemble gathered beyond the stone archway. 'So, without further ado, I officially declare our Yule Day celebration well and truly open!' he announces with a flourish, not a moment too soon.

The gathered crowd applaud generously before dividing like a sea of knitted woollen hats, heading in various directions, as the carol 'In the Bleak Midwinter' magically fills the air. Instantly, a lump collects in my throat at the mere sound of the brass band and the choir's harmonious voices. Luckily, I gain a customer straight away, happy to browse my knitted goods and the small selection of dyed wool, courtesy of Magnus.

Isla

'What can I get you, Santa?' I ask, as the large fella with the grey beard and red suit becomes my next customer.

'Can I have a ploughman's, please?' asks Mungo.

I glance up, surprised that he'd ask such a question, today of all days. I've been run ragged, serving and baking decorative Yule cakes most of the day. He knows what's on the menu, and yet he's taking advantage of his current status.

'It's not on the menu, but I could rustle you up a selection of cheese and crackers, if that's what you fancy, Santa. A pickled onion or three, some sliced beetroot and . . .' I pause, on seeing his eyes light up. Well done, me, securing my place on the 'good girl' list! 'I've even got a jar of pumpkin and turmeric chutney, if you fancy a bit on the side.'

Mungo glares at me from beneath his wig of grey curls. Here we go again, just when I thought I was doing so well, another almighty fail in my communication with Mungo.

'Did Jemima make it?' he asks quietly.

'No. I did.'

There's a long pause while he considers.

'Go on, then.' Mungo's grey beard lifts in a weird double nod.

'Sit down and I'll bring it over to you,' I say, knowing full well that I've just made a breakthrough of sorts and will be fist-pumping the air once I'm out of his view in the rear kitchen.

Chapter Fifty-Four

Nessie

There's a definite nip of excitement in the air, as the Yule Day celebration commences and the attending crowd swells. I've happily spent a few hours manning our craft stall, selling both my goods and Isaac's glassware. Isaac has taken control of the forge and has given numerous demonstrations of his craftsmanship and answered a million questions from interested observers.

For today is like no other. Today could save my business from the faltering start that I've had to endure. For even more precious reasons, today will be a dream come true.

'Nessie!' calls Isaac, from inside the forge. 'Are you ready to switch?'

'Ready when you are!' I holler back, undoing the money apron I've been wearing most of the day and handing it over to Isaac as we switch duties.

'I'm glad to get out of the heat,' he sighs, appearing at the door.

I hurry inside, tend to my fire pit and take delight in the knowledge that I'm about to have the time of my life.

'Yee ready, my lassie?' says Granddad, briskly entering, undoing his shirt cuffs and removing his white shirt, which I'm sure my nan ironed fresh this morning, only for him to throw it aside.

'I am. Are you ready to take a tanking from your granddaughter?' I say, removing my cardy and likewise throwing the garment aside.

'Phuh!' he hisses through his teeth, chattering to himself as he straightens his braces and ensures his white vest is tucked in.

I notice Isaac poke his head around the doorjamb and give me a fleeting smile on seeing the elder blacksmith undressing, preparing for his toil. Isaac's a big bloke in his build, but even he's impressed. Granddad's physical frame is extraordinary; he's nearing eighty years of age, but you'd swear his body was several decades younger. He's got bulging muscles where other blokes have knotted gristle. His taut, pale skin is flawless, with no deep wrinkles, no sagging or sallow appearance, but plump, solid and healthily robust.

'A fine pair of biceps, eh, Isaac?' I call.

'If that's the end result of smithing, I might switch professions!'

'Lad, this is nothing. These arms were as thick as my wife's thighs on the day we got married. And she's built like our Nessie here – solid, like.'

'Oi!' I glance open-mouthed between the pair. 'Mind the cheek!'

'I was only saying. Your grandmother's thighs were ...' He gestures with both hands.

'We know ... you don't need to show us, thanks. I can see how this is going to be.'

My granddad wraps a loving arm around my shoulders and pulls me close. 'Today is going to be grand. I never thought I'd be smithing alongside my girl.'

'Didn't you think I'd qualify?'

'No, it's not that. I never thought we'd get the chance, but this forge is perfect. I'd have quite liked working here myself.'

'Which anvil do you want?' I ask, gesturing towards the three anvils I've got standing around my section.

'Listen to you, offering me an anvil.'

'You're the guest, you can choose. That one there is your very own ... you might choose to work on your old faithful.'

Granddad gives me a coy smile. 'Do you seriously think I didn't clock her the minute I walked in! Nah, our days of working together are done, she's all yours. I told you that, the day I handed her over; my love affair with that beauty finished the last time I struck her with my hammer.'

'Boxers make a comeback – can't blacksmiths?' calls Isaac, leaning through the doorway and watching us.

Granddad shakes his head. I've heard this speech before, so I busy myself getting him a set of tools.

'There's no going back, lad. The way forward is the next generation when you're a smith like me. Though I never thought it would be the girl in my family who'd have the iron in her blood, I can tell you that. She's wielded a hammer since she stepped from her pram.'

I can hear Isaac laughing, which is what Granddad likes. He spent his career working alone, with very little interaction with others, apart from his customers when they collected their goods from his forge.

'Choose your weapon, Granddad,' I say, pointing between my two other anvils. To the untrained eye, they both look exactly the same but I know he'll have a preference based on girth, height and – if I dare say it, though it's not a complaint – location in relation to our potential audience.

Granddad walks around each anvil, gently touching it, attempting to rock it, to identify any unevenness in its standing. Neither moves, both have been rock solid since I've been here.

'This one!' is his final declaration, no reasoning given, but I suspect the free floor space and distance from his fire pit might be the deciding factors.

'What are we making?' He's no longer interested in exchanging pleasantries or generational talk with Isaac; he means business.

'Whatever you wish.'

Granddad casts a nonchalant eye across my display items:

a hanging basket, a toasting fork, a filigree wall panel and a decorative grille for a fire hearth. 'I can make that lot with my eyes closed,' he chunters, producing his aged leather apron and tying it about his thickened waist, proudly announcing, 'Still fits!'

'I should think so – it has bloody ties a foot long! That's like saying your scarf still fits each winter,' I jest, before turning towards the handful of visitors who have congregated before us as our audience. 'Welcome to Smith and Smith!'

'Ready?' asks Granddad.

'Oi, cheeky. This is my forge . . . I ask if you're ready.'

'I thought the rule was age before beauty?' retorts Granddad, winking in the crowd's direction.

I ignore their titter of laughter and point out my cabinet of tools, my slack tub and, of course, the fire bucket and extinguishers, should anything go wrong.

'Happy?'

Granddad smiles, his chest expands before he answers. 'Very happy, my lassie.'

'Crack on, then – you've got an hour to create something beautiful.'

The man doesn't wait another second; he's off selecting his metal, his tools and probably which of the many designs stashed in his head he'll be using to show the younger generation that he still has the magic touch.

'I take it this anvil's mine?' comes a voice from behind the crowd.

I look up from my hammering to view my dad, unbuttoning his cuffs and removing his shirt to reveal his white vest.

'What are you doing here?' I exclaim, moping my brow with my usual cloth.

'What's it look like? Haven't you heard, our family has more than two talented blacksmiths?' hollers Dad, crossing the rope barrier that acts as the audience divide. 'What are we making?'

Suddenly, I'm overcome with emotion, but I manage to whisper, 'Family history, Dad.' After which my throat snags.

I want to cry but I refuse to be the emotional one hammering an anvil.

Isla

I stand before the glass door, gazing out at the crowds milling about the courtyard enjoying the delights of Yule Day. I can't believe how busy we've been. Myself and four waitresses have been run off our feet in The Orangery; there were occasions when we struggled to clear the tables of dirty mugs. I hate to think how many times the dishwasher has been put on and instantly unloaded before it's even had time to dry properly.

Mungo tells me the lane is blocked with a line of parked cars, as our makeshift car park couldn't cope with the attending numbers. The artists' goods are flying from their stalls into brown paper bags – which is incredible, given how close we are to Christmas Day. I've caught glimpses of Ned and Jemima flying between the gallery and the manor house; neither one has stopped for a bite to eat, ensuring that everyone else is happy and well catered for.

Before me is one huge happy scene: artists, families, tired children and a snaking queue waiting their turn to visit Santa. Crispy duck waddles through the snow, in a world of his own, pecking at the covered cobblestones and settling beneath a craft stall when the threat of being stepped on arises. He's no more than a glorified litter picker always on duty!

'Isla?'

'Yes.' I turn to find Pippa squirming before me; I sense she's about to ask a favour.

'Any chance I could go?'

'Go? Go where?'

'Home.'

'Home?' I'm conscious that I'm repeating everything she says.

'It's been a long day, which is nearly over, and I just thought if I could get off, then maybe . . .' She doesn't finish her explanation but leaves it hanging between us.

'I'd prefer you to stay, Pippa,' I say, hoping I don't have to say anything more.

Pippa chews her lip and considers the situation; I see her cogs whirring ten to the dozen as she stares at me.

Her attitude prompts me to assume more authority than seems necessary. 'Maybe I should run your request past Jemima.'

'But . . .' she falters.

'We're all tired, Pippa. How about you grab a coffee, take ten minutes – you'll feel better afterwards.'

Pippa goes to speak but thinks better of it before walking off.

I'm sure I'll be paying for that little discussion in the near future. This is the downside of employing relatives; some always want to take that little extra advantage compared to others.

I return to the counter, collect an empty tray and begin clearing tables of dirty crockery.

'Isla, can I have a word?' says Lachlan, standing up from the nearest armchair.

Here we go again. I plaster a smile on my face, place the heavy tray down on the nearest table. I may as well be polite; there's no point me lowering myself to his gutter level.

'I am busy, but . . .' My speech falters as he produces my granny's book from inside his zippered jacket.

'I want to return this.'

The recipe book lies on the table between us, as if nothing more needs to be said. I daren't touch it. He might pull it back, out of my reach, if I do. Or it might disappear, like a mirage.

He nudges it towards my hands, which are hanging limply at my sides.

'I'm so sorry. I did it purely to get back at you for refusing my suggestions of a date. I wanted to cause you upset and this ... seemed the easiest thing to take.'

'Do you know how much this means to me?' I say, taking the offered book.

'I'll admit it, I do.'

I grasp the recipe book more firmly as my irritation towards him ignites within me. 'And yet you still took it!'

Lachlan nods, his gaze averted from mine.

'Words fail me. I honestly thought ...' My rant dissolves as my self-respect reminds me that this lowlife isn't worth another second of my time. 'Thank you for returning it.' I turn and leave, heading for the rear storeroom where my tears of joy and bitter frustration can flow freely without a witness. I feel bad for assuming Pippa had taken it.

Standing with my back against the closed door, Granny's book clutched to my chest, I sob as if there is no tomorrow. It's the kind of sobbing that as a little child causes you to hiccup afterwards for ages.

I want my granny. Right here, beside me, telling me everything will 'come out in the wash', as she always did. She could make anything better. Yet now, a mere four years since she passed, I'm hiding in a storeroom crying my heart out. And what was I even about to say to him? 'I honestly thought ...'

What was the end of that sentence going to be?

'... you were someone I could care for.'

'... someone I could forgive.'

I sigh, clutching the book a little tighter to my chest; I thought I'd lost Granny's recipe book from my life for ever.

Nessie

'Nessie, there's a letter for you, it was delivered to the manor by accident. Jemima tried to nip it over earlier, but you were busy hammering alongside your family,' says Isla, as soon as Isaac and I enter for a cheeky coffee break.

The café is bustling with happy families and noisy chatter. Thankfully, no one is waiting to be served. We haven't got long; we've locked the forge door and left Levi manning our market stall and, hopefully, selling our wares.

'Interesting,' I say, automatically suspicious.

'It looks pretty official, not like the kind of letters I receive,' adds Isla, rummaging below the countertop and retrieving a white envelope addressed to me.

'Oh, look, Ms Wednesday Smith – full name usage, so it must be important,' mocks Isaac, glancing over my shoulder.

'I doubt it,' I say, taking the proffered envelope and playfully thwacking him with it as he orders our coffees. 'Probably high-class junk mail, if there is such a thing.'

The quality, texture and paper finish are instantly apparent. My index finger works the gummed seal as Isla works her magic creating our two lattes.

'It's busy in here,' mutters Isaac, observing the crowded tables as we drift towards the end of the counter.

'Mmmm.' I remove the folded letter, which matches the envelope in colour and paper quality.

The embossed crest on the headed paper ignites my interest. My brain can't focus; my gaze skitters about the page, picking out odd phrases: 'Lerwick Town Hall', 'committee', 'public library' and 'requests an audience' all jump out from the text, bamboozling my mind for fear of misunderstanding. My breath quickens.

My hands begin to shake. I can't read it properly. I don't understand what they're asking. Or suggesting!

'What's wrong?' asks Isaac, peering over my shoulder as my flustered state becomes apparent.

'I don't understand. Here, read this to me.' I thrust the letter at him without waiting for his reply.

Dear Ms Smith,

The heritage committee of Lerwick Town Hall are interested in commissioning your artistry and talent for two installations within the local vicinity.

The first project is to redesign, create and install the upper-floor railings in our public library, situated on Lower Hillhead. The current installation is a plain, functional rail for the health and safety of our users. We wish for you to redesign this feature as an aesthetically pleasing decoration, befitting its valued heritage. It was formerly St Ringan's Free Church, prior to the conversion now housing our library.

Secondly, we wish to commission a weathervane for the Town Hall, similar to the recent installation at The Stables Gallery, Lerwick. A Shetland pony is the desired motif, whilst all other design features are open to your creative flare and interpretation.

The committee requests an audience with yourself to discuss both projects in the coming weeks. A suitable appointment can be made via our main office, quoting extension number 2011.

Should you have any questions, please don't hesitate to contact me.

Yours sincerely,
Moira Halcrow

Isaac stops reading, folds the letter and offers it back to me.

'Are you kidding me?' I shriek, overflowing with excitement and energy.

'No. I've read it word for word. Congratulations ... that's two successful events in one day. You deserve—'

Isaac doesn't finish his sentence.

I can't explain what comes over me – except, deep down, I do know. My hands instinctively caress either side of his face and I plant the heartiest, most energetic and enthusiastic kiss I can muster upon this gentle but burly guy. A spark of connection ignites us both, before it gently smoulders and steadily grows as his lips respond to mine. Much like my fire hearth each morning, the flickering heat gently increases, taking a firm hold without fading or faltering, each second creating an established flame which draws its energy from both of us until the temperature soars and a white-hot passion is openly revealed.

I'm breathless when we eventually part. My cheeks burn red hot as I step backwards and attempt an apology, amidst the whistling and good-humoured hollering from the general public.

'Bloody Nora!' squeals Isla, staring in amazement from behind her counter.

I'm blushing for Scotland, but I don't care.

'Don't say a word.' Isaac's index finger lifts to gently rest upon my mouth, silencing my stammering lips. 'Please, don't apologise, Nessie ... accept it as a happy accident beneath the mistletoe.' He lifts his index finger from my lips to point up at the sumptuous garland swinging above our heads.

That's three good things today. I can't take my eyes away from his face.

His every word is steadily crafting this one defining moment, as if I'm a delicate glass vessel being created by his enchanting breath.

Chapter Fifty-Five

Verity

Despite the blanket of glistening snow, I've had a very successful day selling many garments and all of Magnus's hand-dyed wool. My body aches; I haven't done anything that equates to such tiredness – except for constantly smiling, serving customers and answering numerous crocheting questions – but nevertheless I feel done in. I should jot down an order for the wholesaler to replace today's stock, but all I want to do is sink into a deep bubble bath, and sip a very large glass of white wine. Afterwards, I'll wrap myself in the largest, fluffiest white towel. Once dry, and only then, I'll pamper my skin with a well-deserved lotion, containing royal jelly and exotic perfume. That thought alone will get me through the final hour if I keep adding to the details.

I'm lost to my daydream as I slowly pack away many of the yarn decorations that I lovingly pinned to the front of the stable this morning. It's like packing the Christmas decorations away: I'll regret not folding the knitted bunting in a neat manner the instant I need to unravel it in the future; but I'll curse relentlessly and attempt to blame someone else.

Everyone in the gallery courtyard is busy socialising whilst politely attempting to tidy up their pitch without looking as if they're closing, which might trigger the remaining customers to leave. That sneaky tactic of leaving out one sample of each item whilst packing the rest away. I can see Nessie is struggling, given that her items are big and bulky; she can hardly nip inside carrying a four-foot wrought-iron Christmas tree, complete with glass baubles, without being spotted. She was overcome with joy earlier when her granddad and father joined her in the forge. I gave her a huge hug and hope the New Year brings a renewed energy to her business. She could do with a roaring start come January.

As I pack away my stall, the festive spirit continues as customers and their families mix and mingle, browsing and buying, all the time bumping into old friends they haven't seen for ages. Every conversation starts with an exclamation and ends with a promise to visit soon.

I watch as Isla hotfoots it, collecting spent coffee cups, crumpled serviettes and paper plates from flat surfaces, dropping them into her large bin-liner like a mum clearing up after a kid's home birthday. Dottie's helping her tidy at a slower, steadier speed.

A knot of emotion clogs in my throat at the thought of family. This is the dangerous stage of Christmas: the 'oh so near but oh so far', with just days to go. Two days might be enough time to grab a cheap flight home to see my lads. My parents. Even my sister – though I doubt she'll be too happy to see me. A flying visit home would be wonderful: check how they're coping, iron out any niggles, plus give and receive big sloppy kisses before heading back on Boxing Day, or possibly the day after.

But would I? That's the big question.

Would it cure my homesickness? Or would it knock my current mindset – my decision to be here in Shetland – off kilter? And that would be a shame. I've worked so hard – grown so much, from my 'mum' role into my 'me' role – that surely I can't risk the chance, even if it's the smallest chance, of heading home and then not returning.

I carry the packaged box of knitted decorations into my stable and plop it down before the counter when a sudden movement, from someone seated in my armchair, makes me jump.

'Niven! Oh my days, you frightened me. Are you OK?'

He's sitting amongst the shadows, his features half obscured, his shoulders set square.

'I'm good, thank you, and you?'

'Jiggered, I know that much. Having a little sit down, are we? Getting the life back in your legs before you walk home?'

'Something like that,' he mutters.

I busy myself, purely to prevent me standing and staring.

'I've always walked, you know,' he muses.

'Have you. Did you never pass your driving test?'

'No. Didn't fancy it much, even as a young man. Everything I needed was around here, within walking distance, so why bother?'

'That's one way to look at it, I suppose.'

'Except for the once. One night, I borrowed a car and drove, just the once. Everyone around here knows that.'

'Lost interest after that, then?'

'You could say that. After all, walking isn't a bad way to move about this earth.'

There's a clipped tone to his voice, a faraway distraction, which alters each word, each pronunciation; not his usual conversational flow but, hey, we all have our moments.

'Sometimes the basics in life are the best,' I say, starting my closing-down routine. First I check the electrical switch for the overhead heater is off.

'It's like knitting, isn't it?'

'Come again, Niven?'

'You learn all these fancy stitches to create beautiful patterns but then, once in a while, you notice how beautiful a simple garter stitch can be.'

'You do. You can't get more basic than garter stitch, Niven.'

I check that my cash box is safely hidden under the countertop.

'Yet all along you avoided it for being what it is ... basic.'

Where is he going with this?

I check that blasted duck hasn't settled in the far corner behind the wool tree.

'Niven, that's me nearly done. Do you need a hand getting up or are your pins sufficiently recovered?'

'I'm good, all good.' He shuffles forward in the seat, places his large hands upon the armrests and gives a big push, forcing his body into a crooked but standing position. He then slowly unfolds to reach his true ramrod stature, as stage two of the process.

'All good, I see.'

'Always good, Verity.'

I watch as he shuffles towards the door, his steps steady and slow, but sure-footed, as always.

'It's been lovely sitting in here,' he says, 'quietly admiring the various yarns – such a happy place, filled with beautiful crafts.'

'That's lovely of you to say.'

'Bye, Verity.'

'Good night. Mind how you go!' I call, relieved that he is fit and well, but with a niggling concern. Had he taken bad? Felt overwhelmed by the crowds, or did he simply want to be amongst the Shetland yarns?

I give the stable a final once-over before flicking the switch, pulling the door to, and setting off to fetch the remainder of my sample goodies from the stall outside.

It's begun to snow again as I cross the cobblestones; it's been threatening to all evening.

'Now that's lovely!' exclaims a woman's voice.

'Bit pricey, if you ask me,' comes a reply, as a hand flicks the price tag back and forth.

I glance up, smiling politely at the pair of women, obviously mother and daughter, in their matching bobble hats. I could really do without a difficult customer at the very end of a long day.

I'll only go home disgruntled and sharp-tempered, ruining my night's sleep and ensuring the same mood for tomorrow. I don't want that; Magnus and Francis certainly don't.

'I much prefer shop-bought knitwear, I don't see the fuss about handmade, hand-crafted, hand-knitted,' continues the woman. Does she assume I'm deaf? 'Just a bloody good reason to whack a ridiculous price tag on it – the kids grow out of it before they've worn it properly.'

I need to answer her, correct her – put her straight, put her right – whilst she continues flipping and fingering the price tags on my samples.

'Actually, hand-knitted garments are—' I begin, looking up and staring directly at the complaining woman.

She's got a scarf wound about her jaw and nose, a bobble hat pulled low over her brow. But those eyes, almond-shaped eyes, with short stubby naked lashes, like mine . . .

The woman stares directly back at me, almost challenging.

'Avril! Mum!'

My scream must have rung out across Shetland, as the recognition kicks in of who is standing before me complaining about my goods. I scurry around the stall to receive the biggest hug I've ever needed in my whole life. I'm sucked into a vortex of puffa jackets, gloves and tears, muttering, 'How? When? What the hell?'

'Surprise!' whispers Mum into my ear, as a whole load of arms and bodies crash into the family scrum.

My head shoots up to see my three lads' faces beaming at me over the top of my sister's sobbing shoulders as she wails, 'We've all missed you so much!'

'My lads!' I make a feeble attempt to release myself from Avril's grip but fail, forcing me to awkwardly reach out and pat each son from my confinement.

My dad stands beside Francis, who's snuggling a tired Amelia into his puffa-jacketed chest, standing a step or two aside from the group, and watching the scene unfold; his eyes are glistening ever so slightly.

I can't catch my breath. My heart is beating so rapidly, while my brain attempts to make sense of it all and catch up with what seems like a dream come true. 'What the hell are you all doing here?'

'We're here for Christmas,' says Tom, craning his head to look at me.

'You haven't brought your bloody father, have you?' I ask, unsure if I could feign delight at that little surprise.

'Yeah, like our dad's ever gonna give up his holidays to spend time with us,' chides Tom, shaking his head as if I really should know better than to ask.

'Oh, has there been a development between father and son?' I ask, glancing between Jack and Harvey for confirmation.

'That's one way of putting it,' quips Jack, wrapping a protective arm about his little brother's shoulders.

I'm instantly saddened by the prospect that George has yet again caused our sons pain, but it's a lesson in life which Tom had to learn. I know the older lads were tiny when we split, but both have memories of how family life was with both parents; Tom has only memories of me, alone, struggling to raise them. I look at his doleful eyes straining to portray happiness. I know that particular look; I once wore that mask permanently.

'Never mind, babe, we'll talk, if you wish.'

Tom nods.

'But first, I need to pack the last bits of my stall away – have you seen inside The Yarn Barn?' A series of headshakes confirms my next duty. 'Come this way – though mind you don't step on a sodding duck, or let him into my stable.'

I spend the next fifteen minutes, having put the lights and overhead heater back on, giving a detailed show and tell to my gathered audience. I watch with pride as they wander about, chatting, joking and trying on display garments, until there's nothing else to do but close down again, and lock the stable door.

I've asked a million questions in the meantime: Francis negotiated the air fares, Mum and Dad appear to have paid, the boys seem to be obliged – though their girlfriends are apparently "well jel and not friggin' happy" ... oh well. Amelia is so tired her bottom lip is protruding – which won't end well, unless we get her to bed pronto. Which sends me into another spin.

'You are all going to have to top and tail regarding sleeping arrangements,' I announce, rather formally, pushing my bike along the driveway towards their hired people carrier, as if leading a Boy Scout troop on a jamboree.

'Sorted!' calls Francis. 'The guys are staying with you at Harmony Cottage, the rest are staying with me at the B&B.'

'Oh Francis, you have been busy.'

'You haven't accepted a penny towards our evening meals over the past few weeks, have you?'

'No, but ...'

'Well, there you go.'

'She charges us board money!' exclaims Harvey, from the rear of the group.

'That's being a good parent and teaching you an essential lesson in life – nothing comes for free, your uncle Francis knows that already.'

'Let's hope so,' calls Avril, exchanging glances with her husband.

Isla

'I'm trying to explain – won't you at least hear me out?'

'No. I won't. Why should I accept your offers of a date because it suits you, eh? Tell me that. I was happy to date you months ago, but in your opinion, I wasn't good enough. You didn't even pay me the courtesy of discussing it at the time, you simply upped and offed and chased another girl. Now, I'm supposed to be gracious and afford you time to explain. Lachlan, you take the biscuit, you really do. I've just landed myself a job where I'm punching way above my weight and skill. I need to focus if I'm to grow, to gain experience, to study and become the rounded and knowledgeable baker I wish to be. I can't afford to waste my precious leisure time – which provides a balance to my working life – on a guy who blows hot and cold, as he chooses, and then steals from me, thank you very much.'

Lachlan's bottom lip simply drops lower and lower on hearing each sentence. I'm not trying to hurt him or put him down. But for a guy who thinks he's so clever, he really doesn't understand the basics in life. I haven't sufficient hours in a day to focus on my career whilst being continually let down by a guy I can't rely on. I know what I want at this stage in my life, what I want to achieve, and what dreams I'll be chasing in the next stage of my life. Sadly, Lachlan's not part of my picture.

'I wouldn't hold you b-back,' he stammers.

'It's not a case of holding me back . . . but a case of me being free to decide, to seize the moment when it arises. Call me selfish – I get that it sounds that way – but, at nineteen, I know what I want, right now.'

Lachlan's features come to life. His lips are pursed, his eyebrows flicker and his nostrils flare as he snorts in disgust.

'Isla Henderson, I've got news for you. The likes of me can do a damned sight better than the likes of you. You might think you're all that . . . with your job bossing folk about at The Orangery. But it's basically a glorified café, when all is said and done. I saw you the other night, walking your "My Little Pony" along the coastal road in the dark – what a saddo! Save your breath lecturing me. You'll be needing it, the next time I see you in the pub. You'll be begging me to take you back. And guess what my answer will be!'

Lachlan turns on his trainers and strides off across the gravel driveway towards the parked cars.

I walk back towards the cobbled yard. I'm not surprised or hurt by his words; I've known Lachlan Gray for a long time. I haven't a moment to waste on him and his kind. I'm going to build the future I dream of.

In the distance, I hear a car making a wheelspin. Typical Lachlan.

Chapter Fifty-Six

Christmas Eve

Verity

On arriving at the gallery, I'm greeted by a tearful Pippa, serving coffee and snivelling as artists collect their regular orders.

'Are you OK?' I say, concerned that the two guys before me didn't say a word regarding her tear-stained appearance. 'Where's Isla?'

'Haven't you heard the news?' Her ashen face stares at me.

My baffled expression provides an answer, as my heart skips a beat.

'Niven, old Niven who knits for you – he was run over last night as he walked home from the Yule Day ... and ... they ... didn't ... even ... stop ... to ... help ... him.' She struggles to form each word through her tears, whilst her hands busily make my toffee latte.

'No, that can't be true, Pippa.'

'It is. Honest. Jemima phoned me first thing this morning, asking if I would cover Isla's shift and open up. Verity, I wouldn't joke about something so serious. He died at the scene. The police are out combing the stretch of road ... I've seen the blue-and-white tape where they've ...' Pippa crumples into a mass of sobbing.

'I spoke to him only last night, as he was leaving here ... he spent some time sitting amongst the yarns and admiring their colours.'

'It seems so surreal ... and to think he died not far from where—'

'Pippa, should you be here?' I interrupt her, as sobs escape from her tiny frame.

'I want to be here. He's no relation to us, but he was always nice when he dropped by, wasn't he?'

'Pippa, it's a half-day opening – folk can survive four hours without—'

Pippa raises a palm to silence me. 'I'll be fine, I want to support Isla the best I can ... I let her down yesterday.'

'You'll make yourself poorly, being this upset and trying to serve customers.'

'Nope, I'll be fine. What's terrible is it's just like when that young girl was run over, all those years ago, while out playing – virtually the exact same thing, apparently. My mum remembers it all. The older brother was gutted. It'll bring it all back for him – and over Christmas, too.'

Magnus! My hands fly to my mouth, holding in the shriek of pain I know he'll feel at such a reminder.

'Pippa, I've got to go. Sorry,' I say, turning on my heels and leaving my half-prepared drink in her capable yet shaking hands.

I run from The Orangery, re-entering The Yarn Barn in haste, and grab my mobile. I must speak to him; I can't erase any of the pain he'll feel when he hears about this latest tragedy, but he has to know that I'm thinking of him. I'm here to talk, if he wishes.

His mobile rings out – no answer.

I instantly cut the call and redial, as if two nanoseconds can change the outcome. Again, no answer.

I talk myself out of calling for a third time. My missed calls will register on his screen when he gets to his mobile. I'll offer support the best I can, despite a house full of family, but I will manage; manage is what I do best in life.

I close my eyes. Inhale deeply, hold my breath, before exhaling noisily and desperately. When I open my eyes, Nessie is standing in my doorway, an expression of clear concern hammered into her ashen features.

'Have you heard?'

'About Niven, sadly yes.'

'Can I have a quick word about Magnus?'

Isla

I feel awful. This is my second encounter with the police in just under two weeks. What is my world coming to? As I enter Lerwick's police station, I can't help but glance at the decorative lintel stating AD 1875, as if the weight of time presses a little heavier on my conscience as I pass beneath it.

The stone building looks daunting, with its prominent brick fascia and weathered pillars guarding the entrance, as steadfast as the officers on duty protecting our little community around the clock.

I've never felt so guilty in all my life; not even the time when I didn't muck Jutt out for three days after a teenage strop, or when I copied my maths homework from the clever kid on the front row whilst walking to school. Before disappearing through the impressive entrance door, I give my mum a small wave. What if I'm thrown into a bare cell over the Christmas holiday? What if I never see her again? I'm bricking it as I enter the lobby area.

It's empty. Not that I was expecting a huddle of police officers studying a timeline of the crime on a whiteboard. But I didn't expect empty, either – not given the news and current circumstances.

I'm not sure whether to press the button for assistance, or simply run back to my mum's car. Thankfully, I don't get the chance to decide, as a uniformed male officer appears, his fiery red hair cropped short.

'Can I help you?'

'I'd like to speak to someone regarding the accident on the coastal road late last night, in which Niven McAllister was run over.'

'And subsequently . . .' he pauses, eyeballing me, as if unsure whether I know the fatal outcome.

'I know, he died.'

'Take a seat, and I'll be with you in a few minutes,' he says, quickly disappearing back into the other room.

I settle in the suggested chair and read the array of community notices on the board opposite: drugs hotline, drink-driving awareness, winter road safety campaigns, even a scam awareness poster. I didn't know Lerwick had so much going on. There's a pile of calendars neatly stacked on a small display table, the usual white spiral strip holding each month in place. They're freebies from the tourist office; my mum usually hangs one in our pantry at home. I heard Francis mention the annual competition to his workshop attendees. I take the top calendar and begin flipping through, admiring the local images depicting Shetland in all her glory. I halt on reaching October's page; a beautiful image of pumpkins and carriage lanterns arranged on cobblestones. I know that scene! I scour the bottom edge for details: courtesy of Melissa Robins. Well I never! She didn't even attend Francis's photography workshop. Though with her recent news about the baby on the way, and her husband relocating back home, she'll have little or no time for hobbies.

The officer reappears. 'If you'd like to come this way?' he says, gesturing me to follow.

I feel sick with nerves. I shove the calendar into my handbag; it feels like stealing, under the officer's dutiful stare.

'My mum will use it,' I mutter, guiltily.

Entering the dark corridor and being shown to another seat feels significant. I'm not wanting to cause trouble, or waste their valuable time, but I need to confess: it was my fault.

The decision is then theirs to make, not mine; whatever happens next, it will be out of my hands.

Verity

I close the connecting lounge doors, as if glass will prevent my lads from hearing my rage and relief at seeing Magnus enter my kitchen, some twelve hours after I called his mobile.

'You've got a bloody nerve. I've been worried sick all day. Then you stroll in here without a sodding care in the world, as if I'm supposed to make you a coffee and then listen to the details. I've been sick to my stomach with worry in case you're somehow responsible for Niven's death – and even now, you stand there staring at me, not saying a bloody word, not one sodding word, Magnus!' My negative thoughts and fears gush forth in one go.

'I'm waiting for you to draw breath,' he mutters, in a low voice.

My mouth continues to work avidly, but I'm saying nothing. I glance towards the lounge, and through the glass I see Tom perched on the edge of his armchair whilst Jack motions for him to 'stay where you are'.

I could scream in anger. Cry with relief. I'm exhausted from trying to fight away all the nasty, evil thoughts which have churned through my head all day. Was he detained in custody? Did he do it as revenge for his sister's death? What kind of bloody maniac am I mixed up with? My questions have been endless, growing darker with each passing hour. Yet here he is, in the middle of my kitchen, dressed in his everyday attire – brown corduroys, a chunky jumper and muddy wellingtons – with those bloody unruly curls, and staring at me as if I'm the one who's lost the plot.

'Verity, have you quite finished?'

'No. I. Have. Not. OK?' I'm seething inside. I've been here before, with a man deceiving me, behind my back, for countless hours every day. Expect the unexpected, that's what men have taught me.

'Please sit down. Do you want a glass of something for your nerves?'

'No. I want to know where you've been all day.'

'OK. I am assuming you've heard the sad news about Niven. Yes?'

I give a curt nod. My eyes glisten at the very mention of his name.

'I assume by your reaction someone's informed you that his accident occurred on the exact same stretch of road as Marina, my sister's.'

He's never said her name before.

I nod, words failing me as my stomach twists and turns, waiting for the punchline.

'I've been busy helping the police with their enquiries.'

I gasp involuntarily and instantly regret how pathetic I am, as my imagination jumps ahead of his speech.

'Stop it! You're upsetting yourself with these wild thoughts. Please listen. Last night, whilst waiting for Floss to return from one of her solo walks, I witnessed a car being driven erratically at high speed past our farm. I heard the collision and went to investigate … there was nothing anyone could do for him. It's taken hours, but I've given a statement explaining what I saw. I'm not involved as such. And there's no question of seeking revenge, as far as I'm concerned. After I'd finished at the police station, my parents needed my support and some comfort, given the upset it reignited for them. I hear the police have pulled young Lachlan in for questioning.'

'Isla's Lachlan?'

'I believe that's actually the issue. They're not together. They argued again last night and he drove off in a temper.'

'And he knocked Niven over, then left the scene?'

Magnus grimaces, saying nothing. He simply stares at me, chewing his bottom lip in that goddamn irresistible way he does when he's working out what to say.

'Who knows? It might be purely an accident, unrelated to my sister's death. I've explained that there's a distant family tie to Niven – we're second, third cousins or something – but the same applies to Lachlan. Around these parts, we're all from the same bloodline if you trace our ancestry back far enough.'

'Was he drunk, or just reckless after another rejection?'

'Only Lachlan knows that. But there's hardly any lighting along that stretch, there's no pavement, and enough twists and turns for a Formula One racetrack.'

'Oh Magnus, I'm so sorry that you've had to relive such horrible memories. Honestly, I'm so wrong for even thinking that you could be responsible.' My words falter as I see his expression change. 'I need to shut up. I'm not painting a very supportive picture, am I?'

The lounge door opens. Tom pops a concerned face through the gap; his teenage shoulders are squared, his puppy eyes fixed upon Magnus in a defiant way.

'It's alright, me and your mum are cool. There's no argument happening here. She's simply been frightened by my silence, and her imagination has spun itself into knots.'

'Mum?' Tom's eyes are fixed on me, questioning Magnus's words.

'He's right, love . . . I imagined something terrible, and now I need to calm down. You can come and sit in here with us, if it makes you feel better,' I say, before adding, 'Magnus here, he's not cut from the same cloth as your dad.'

Tom hesitates, before deciding to join us.

'Seriously, take a seat. I'm not here to upset your mum, not by a long shot,' Magnus reassures him.

I glance from Tom's silent features to Magnus's. I have no idea what Tom has encountered while staying at his father's house; he's definitely staying schtum on that topic. But as his stance relaxes I see that Magnus has just earned brownie points in Tom's world.

And mine.

Chapter Fifty-Seven

Christmas Day

Nessie

I'm hardly awake and out of bed when someone begins hammering on my front door. I can see the bulky outline through the frosted glass as their knuckles connect, rapping heavily on the glazed window.

It isn't the familiar outline of family, to whom I've opened the door a million times, but someone unexpected.

'Isaac?' I say, taken aback when I open the door. He's the last person I expected to see, especially given the blustery backdrop of falling snow.

'Merry Christmas, Nessie. I just wanted to drop this off,' he says, offering me a square cardboard box the size of my palm. 'It's just something little, but I wanted you to have it today.'

'Come in,' I say, embarrassed that I'm in my dressing gown, but probably with less flesh on show than when I'm smithing.

'No, I'm fine. I'm on my way to see my parents.'

'Can I open it?' I say, conscious that I haven't bought him a gift.

'Sure.' He looks eager to witness my reaction, so I'm praying I like it.

I lift the lid, revealing a glass bauble nestled within a layer of padding.

'You've made this.' I hook my finger through the gold thread and gently lift it out of the box.

He nods eagerly, a coy smile adorning his features.

The bauble is clear glass; inside it, a wispy swirl of white mimics snow surrounding a delicate Christmas tree, topped with a tiny gold star. My breath snags in my throat: it's utterly beautiful.

'Oh Isaac, you made this for me?'

'Yep, one of a kind – especially for you, Nessie.'

'Isaac, it's so beautiful. All made from glass?'

'Yep, just like the other four hundred I've made since October. I wanted you to have something unique, matching your personality and our friendship.'

'I feel bad, I didn't think to—'

He interrupts me. 'Don't be, please. I'm happy to settle for that drink you keep promising me, sometime in the new year.'

I'm taken aback.

'You know … the one you owe me for talking you around on down days, fetching you coffee and cake on hopeless days, and generally being an all-round nice guy who happens to share inspirational ideas every other day of the week.'

'You're right. I know that guy. I do owe him a drink, and I'll happily pay my debt of gratitude come new year.'

'Excellent. I'm pleased to hear it. Right, I'll be off … I just wanted to deliver your gift and wish you a merry Christmas,' he says, stepping backwards along the pathway as he speaks. 'Enjoy yourself, and I'll see you at the gallery in a day or so.'

I'm transfixed by his gesture. He is the nicest guy I have ever had the pleasure of meeting, and he has definitely supported me more than anyone during the past few months.

'See ya,' says Isaac, raising a hand in farewell.

I wave. 'Isaac, thank you,' I call, as if wanting him to stay longer.

'No worries.'

I watch as he strides along the section of pavement towards his parked car. 'Isaac!'

He stops, turns around and waits.

'We work well together, yeah?'

'Yeah. We're bloody amazing in that forge.'

I have no time to think of the consequences before the words leave my lips. 'Maybe the new year will bring more . . . for us.'

His face cracks into a beaming smile. 'I have every confidence that it will, Nessie.'

I wave goodbye, close the front door and go into the lounge; to give my beautiful new bauble pride of place on my wrought-iron Christmas tree.

Oh my God, have I just suggested what I think I have? Given that my smile is as wide as his, I think I must have done!

Verity

It has snowed all day. The early-evening sky provides a stark navy backdrop, enhancing the beauty of the falling flakes. There's a diamond glint twinkling in the heavens, whichever direction you look – I'd say it was picturesque, but my sons have just destroyed the perfect image with their size ten boots. Having stayed indoors all day, enjoying the harmony of a Kendal/O'Connell family Christmas – thanks to Francis's last-minute trolley dash around Tesco on Christmas Eve – my lads were dying to be set free.

Magnus pulls his woollen beanie low over his brow, taking in the raucous sight unfurling before him.

'In our family, this is as traditional as the children leaving a mince pie and a carrot out for Santa and Rudolph,' I say, gesturing towards the pony paddock, thankfully minus its usual inhabitants, who are safely stabled. 'On the years we actually have snow in the Midlands, that is.'

'Mum, I thought the snow drifts in Shetland would be massive, but it's not that different to home. Is it, Harvey?' shouts Tom, thrusting a handful of snow down Harvey's jacket collar, much to his sibling's annoyance.

'You little git!' cries Harvey, trying to empty his jacket whilst chasing Tom across the paddock into a blanket of untouched snow.

'Whoa, Jack. Help me!' cries Tom, as he darts in a zigzag route to outmanoeuvre his offended brother.

'Charge!' cries Jack, joining Harvey in chasing after Tom.

'Mind Amelia!' I shout after the trio, trying to avoid tears before bedtime as the little one quietly rolls the beginnings of her snowman with my dad and sister. I can do without our Avril having a barney with me, today of all days. I feel responsible for keeping the peace between us, given Francis's recent confession about the only-child situation. A show of family solidarity might go some way towards mending our sisterly rift, and it might change Avril's mindset regarding another baby. I owe Francis that much, after his recent support.

It has taken all my powers of persuasion to talk Magnus into joining us for the evening, after spending a traditional Christmas Day with his elderly parents at the farm. He was eager to meet my entire brood but didn't want to tread on people's toes, given my lengthy absence, or intrude on much-needed family time. Though the sight of my sons terrorising each other at the far end of the paddock in a tumbling pile of testosterone, amidst a spray of flying snow, proves that not much changes with my brood.

'Are you OK?' asks Magnus, standing behind me, wrapping both arms tightly about my shoulders. He hooks his chin over my shoulder as he twists to view my face.

'I am. You?'

'Very happy, thank you.'

Our eyes meet and we stare intently at each other in a moment of stillness. We seem to have found our compromise: together.

'I'm so sorry about yesterday and my terrible accusation. It seems utterly absurd today that I should entertain such a horrible thought about you seeking revenge, but . . . I can only put it down to shock and past experiences.'

'I get where you're coming from.'

'Do you? Really?'

'Yeah. You put two and two together and came up with a million crazy ideas, based on our lack of understanding of each other, no knowledge of the specific circumstances – and possibly, occasional snippets of information which others have mentioned.'

'No one's been gossiping, I promise,' I add quickly for fear he'll think badly of Isla or Nessie.

'But I never explained about Marina's death, did I? I avoided the conversation and allowed other people to fill in the blanks for you. Yesterday your mind took over, and the end result was truly ridiculous. My family will never truly know if Niven was responsible for her death. We've never once suspected him, but now . . . thinking of the words he repeated so often about driving – just "the once, one night" . . . who knows what he was trying to explain or confess, for all these years? Either way, the poor chap didn't deserve to die like he did.'

'You might be a giant of a guy but you're caring, loving and haven't a nasty bone in your body. That should have been enough to know you wouldn't be involved.'

'Loving?' Magnus smiles.

'Stop it, I'm being serious. I was consumed by an inescapable fear of impending doom, created by your lengthy silence. The last time I endured such a day was seventeen years ago, with the boys' father. That night he buggered off without a care in the world, and left me holding three babies!' I glance over to see my three babies now boisterously burying their uncle Francis deep in snow, before continuing, 'I thought I'd lost you yesterday. I felt that ache deep inside, knowing I'd wasted time. I should have invested effort in your dating scenario, allowed a natural intimacy to develop. And now, well, I've a newfound respect for what you originally wanted and I refused, back then.'

'Out of fear, you mean?'

'Yes, I'll admit it. Out of total bloody fear of getting hurt all over again. Every bloody fear I've ever had has been moulded into a cast-iron bubble in which I've encased myself and yet, I knew deep down ... that you ... you with your sheep-shearing skills, your cable-knitting talent and your gorgeous sheep dog were capable of punching your way through my armour.'

Magnus plants a gentle kiss on my cold cheek. He didn't need me to say it aloud, he knew all along.

'Are you pair going to stand there all night smooching?' shouts Avril, looking over while Amelia and my dad roll yet another snowman's body to sit alongside the wonky-looking figure they've already created.

'Smooching – is that what you call it?' I ask, wondering which decade Avril's terminology is derived from. 'I think you'll find we've been more than smooching.'

'She's lying, Avril. We've only just started dating ... I've only just met the family!' calls Magnus, his tone light and comical.

'Are we doing this your way then?' I ask.

'We've being doing this my way since the day I mentioned it.'

'Oh, have we now?'

'Yeah. Didn't you notice all the times I left early without giving in to your wanton charms?'

'How do you explain the wool-dyeing afternoon then?'

'Well, having seen your innate skill at producing fifty shades of sheep shite yarn, I simply couldn't resist, could I!'

I burst out laughing.

Boom!

A huge snowball smashes against the front of my padded jacket, covering both me and Magnus in icy flakes.

'You little buggers! Who threw ...?'

Boom!

Another snowball lands, this time hitting the side of Magnus's beanie.

The war cry of 'Snow fight!' fills the air as we are bombarded from every direction. Magnus releases me and we both frantically grab handfuls of snow and prepare to defend our little corner of the paddock.

It doesn't take long before I've lost all sense of who I should be throwing snowballs at and who's on my side: the rules seem to have gone adrift in the excitement. I just know that I'm a happy mum, having a wonderful time with my lads, plus my official new date.

Suddenly the air is filled by the sound of a clanging saucepan being beaten with a lid.

The action stops and we turn to stare at the cottage.

'Come on, enough now! Time for our cold turkey buffet,' announces my mum from the doorstep of the cottage, before returning inside. Bless her, she hates the snow, so she offered to prepare the food.

My three lads charge up the driveway to get inside first. You'd think they'd still be full from the roast turkey dinner with trimmings I'd produced earlier; they must have hollow legs.

'Mum, what's the door code?' calls Tom, kicking off his boots in the porch to stand before the inner door.

'Three, four, six, five and hash,' shouts Magnus.

'Shush!' urges Avril. 'You don't want everyone knowing.'

'I bet half of the shoppers in Tesco know it,' quips Francis.

'More than half,' corrects Magnus, as we plod up the driveway towards the cottage.

'I never imagined Shetland would have a Tesco,' mutters my dad, as we reach the doorstep.

I smile at Magnus as the family erupt into the usual tourist discussion.

'I can't believe there's not that many trees,' says Jack, pulling off his boots.

'I was expecting to see ten-foot snow drifts at least,' adds Avril, waiting to remove hers.

'I can't believe . . .' We all turn in surprise as little Amelia speaks. 'That Shetland ponies live here!'

'Oh sweetheart, they certainly do!' I say, stroking her rosy cheek.

We cram into the hallway, having fought for space to remove our boots and outdoor clothing. The conversation continues as we enter the kitchen where platters of food cover every surface.

'I can't believe Mum expected us to live on lasagne for a whole year!' says Harvey.

'I can better that! I can't believe Mum scrawled a mantra on her bathroom mirror!' says Tom, a cheeky grin adorning his face as he grabs a plate.

'Oi, stop taking the mick. I'll have you know, that's helped me some mornings.'

'Yeah, but not any more. I've changed it! Go look.'

All their faces turn to stare at me, awaiting a reaction.

I nip out to view my bathroom. What's he done?

I pull the light cord, and there on the mirror – instead of my first morning mantra, which has been wiped clean – is a big love heart with the initials VK and MS enclosed within it, and from the vanity light hangs a gallery label declaring 'From Shetland, With Love At Christmas'.

A bubble of emotion lifts from my chest; I want to cry happy tears. I switch off the bathroom light and return to a noisy kitchen.

I haven't done too badly raising three lads on home-made lasagne: with decent manners, good teeth and a cheeky but loving sense of humour.

Isla

I'm utterly exhausted. Having spent the entire day at the stove cooking and baking for my family, I simply can't settle. My mum's fast asleep in the armchair and my sister has disappeared to her room to read. I know they're grateful; they cleared every plate and dessert dish I placed before them. They even banished me from the kitchen whilst they cleaned and tidied every surface, which I appreciate.

But now, it's only eight o'clock and the day appears to be over. There's no Christmas night partying for our family this year, out of respect for Niven. The bloodline might be fairly distant but my mum wants to do the right thing.

I could start munching the Turkish delight, unpacking the toiletry boxsets received as gifts, or even do an hour of business study before climbing into bed. Though should I really be studying on Christmas Day? It seems a little sad; I bet my friends Fiona and Kenzie aren't having this debate.

I stare at the TV, feeling glum at the prospect of the same films shown in rotation from last year. And probably scheduled for next year, too.

Next year. Boy, that sounds ominous, given how momentous this year has been. I left college, attended an interview and landed my first dream job. Lost my gran's recipe book, caused a whole load of upset over stolen keys, and then had an almighty showdown with Lachlan. Though having been charged with 'causing death by dangerous driving', he's got a very difficult time ahead. I wouldn't want that on my conscience.

My gaze falls to the oxblood leather cover of Gran's book, which I've brought home for fear of it going missing again. I shouldn't be letting it out of my sight, given its worth.

Irreplaceable, that's what it is. I possibly shouldn't be ferrying it back and forth to work each day, either.

A sudden thought strikes me. I scramble from the sofa and dash upstairs to collect my laptop from my bedroom. If I type each of her recipes into a Word document, the ingredients plus methods, I'll be able to print my own useable, affordable and replaceable version, should the same dilemma occur. A hundred pocket pouches and an A4 file is far more durable for my everyday needs.

As I settle at the kitchen table with the screen loading, I berate myself. This feels like a lightbulb moment. Why haven't I thought of this before?

'Isla, are you going to bed any time soon?' asks my mum groggily, entering the kitchen at three in the morning in her dressing gown.

Instantly, I feel bad for disturbing her night's sleep.

'Just a couple more recipes and then I'll have finished this section, Mum,' I say, blurry-eyed yet eager to continue typing the honey cake recipe. 'I promise.' I flash her my sweetest smile and blow her a kiss, knowing she's half asleep, almost zombified, and needs to return to her bed.

The kitchen door slowly closes and silence resumes.

It's been therapeutic sitting here and working alone into the night. The smell of spices and oven-baked bread fills my senses as I type. The wave of contentment eases my jittery nerves after recent events. I've been lost within an imaginary world for hours; despite being surrounded by my mum's modern fixtures and gadgets, the room has an uncanny resemblance to my gran's kitchen. It's as if I'm back at Harmony Cottage as a little child, straight from school, standing on a chair to reach the countertop, with my pinny neatly tied, rubbing butter cubes into sieved flour. My gran is standing at my right shoulder, watching and guiding. Correcting and praising me. The memory feels so real that, with a glance to my right, I'm expecting to see her gentle smile. Instantly, my disappointment crashes like a wave upon the rocks. But as the tide seeps back via the crevices to join the ocean, I know deep down she'll always be present at my right shoulder.

'I'll be here all night if I don't get a wiggle on and type faster,' I mutter, giving myself a metaphorical shake as tears threaten to fall.

I take a deep breath and continue to type; my fingers dance across the keyboard. Not only have I typed up a wodge of Gran's recipes but I've jotted down a couple of feasible ideas, which I intend to suggest to Jemima and Ned during our next morning meeting.

Firstly, given the attraction of Crispy duck, who draws in the visiting children, would they consider me relocating my pony, Jutt, into one of their paddocks? It might be a nice way to introduce horses and ponies back to Lerwick Manor. Who knows? It could be the start of an animal petting farm – I think Jemima would like that idea.

Secondly, the calendar photographs of Lerwick Manor used by the tourist board should be enlarged, framed and proudly displayed in the café. It wouldn't cost much, but I think Melissa, Levi and Mungo would be dead proud.

I smile whilst rereading my brief notes.

And finally, though I daren't write this idea down for fear of getting my hopes up – but the more I think about it, the more I know my gran would love it – could her tried and tested bakes be shared with a wider audience of budding foodies?

'Isla! Bed!' shouts my mum, banging on her bedroom floor.

Mmmm, I might organise and run a successful café, but I still need telling when I'm overstepping the boundaries.

Epilogue

Saturday 1 January – Hogmanay

Nessie

As the final notes of 'Auld Lang Syne' fade, I cease miming to words I've never learnt. The happy circle encompassing the ballroom unclasp hands, hug and then offer a round of kisses before finding a partner as the band of fiddlers and drummers strikes up with a lively jig.

I've never seen a ballroom as beautiful. Three enormous chandeliers dominate the ceiling, illuminating the joyous guests reeling across the polished floor below. I watch as the twirling dancers gleefully switch partners: their grasping hands entwine amidst the laughter and loud music. A variety of tartans are proudly displayed on sashes, cummerbunds and dress ribbons in the name of honour and heritage, but each pales into insignificance below the swathes of emerald-and-navy tartan hanging from the decorative plaster cornices. 'Dust collectors', as Dottie calls them, but if only they could talk; I'm sure they've witnessed many happy gatherings in years gone by for the Campbell clan.

'Did you have a good Christmas?' asks Isaac, appearing at my elbow as I admire the joviality upon the dance floor.

I turn to focus on the attractive figure dressed in a dark tuxedo. Boy, he looks suave! It's a far cry from his daily lumberjack shirt. Suddenly I'm wishing to re-enact our mistletoe moment for those who missed it. What was the term he used for me? 'Scrub up well'. Touché.

'I did. A quiet one, but still. How are you?' I ask, eager to hear any snippet of his holiday.

'So-so. A few days with family is relaxing and fun, but cabin fever soon sets in. I'm eager to get back to a daily routine, to be honest. And you?'

'Pretty much the same, with dutiful visits, roast dinners and endless Christmas puddings. But I'm determined to start the year off well.'

'And long may it continue.' His gaze is stuck fast on mine; I don't need clarification. As I suspected, yet didn't dare to hope, the Christmas bauble was more than a mere gift – more of a symbol. I'd spent the holiday reigning in my imagination; kidding myself that Isaac had done the rounds that morning, delivering beautiful gifts to all his friends.

We stand admiring the gallivanting couples, as Dottie and Mungo twirl by in a blur of tartan and smiles.

'Amazing what folk can do, once they've sampled the fruit punch!' I add, not wishing to suggest inebriation but admiring their energy.

'They'll pay for it in the morning, with aching backs and hips,' jests Isaac, smiling at the approaching waiter, redirecting his route to retrieve two flutes from the silver tray. 'Thank you,' he says, before offering me one and adding, 'Cheers, to us.' His fingers brush mine in the brief exchange.

I feel a tiny shock like a spark struck against a flint over dry kindling.

'To us,' I murmur, as he clinks the side of my glass before taking a sip.

His smouldering gaze holds mine throughout. A flash of warmth bursts through my innards, causing me to blush intensely. This is lovely; neither one of us feels the need or social pressure to keep talking. We're simply enjoying each other's presence like we do in the forge. Contentedly working on our own projects, knowing the other is about, grabbing coffee orders and cajoling each other along. We definitely work as a team ... but what about as a couple?

'Nessie, there you are!' calls Verity, waving and approaching around the edge of the dance floor.

Our moment is broken. I'd love to have the nerve to usher her away, to preserve this moment alone with Isaac, but I wouldn't be rude to my friend.

'I'm here,' I say, darting an apologetic glance over the rim of my glass.

Isaac sighs and shakes his head. Where's the mistletoe when you need it?

'You need to come with me, Jemima needs your help.'

'Really?'

'Hurry, she's waiting.' She grabs my hand and begins dragging me away. 'Bye, Isaac.'

'Sorry,' I mouth, leaving Isaac's side.

'Thanks a bunch, Verity. That was just getting interesting,' I moan, as we cut through the crowd, disposing of my empty glass on the nearest table.

'Shush with your complaining. Every man needs a few obstacles to make him realise what he's missing and act accordingly,' says Verity, giving me a knowing look. 'You'll thank me later.'

'Is that your ploy with our Magnus?' I quip. 'You've attended several of my family gatherings in the past week, yet he's nowhere to be seen tonight.'

'All in good time. He opted to stay with his parents to see in the new year, given the recent upset, but he's joining us very soon.'

She leads me out of the ballroom into the tiled hallway where Jemima is organising a gathering of pipers, in full tartan regalia.

'What's going on?'

'Jemima wants to surprise Ned with a procession,' explains Verity, positioning me behind the pipers.

I pull a face; I don't understand.

'The haggis!' exclaims Verity.

I should have guessed.

'She wants you to carry the coal.'

'Cheers, very symbolic. Surely, my pink hair and gender make me the wrong choice to be the "first foot" nipping around the Lerwick estate,' I mumble, as Verity shoves a basket of coal into my clutches. 'Mind my new dress! It won't be lucky for me if I'm covered in coal dust!'

'It makes a nice change from your dungarees. Anyway, stop with your moaning; as if Isaac would care about coal dust! Isla's presenting the haggis, I'm carrying the whisky drams, so please, just play your part. Jemima wants guests to receive a piece of coal to take home as good luck for the new year,' she urges, then pushes me towards the formation of pipers, each with their silent bagpipes under their arms. I want to explain this isn't the 'first footing' tradition – or even her true heritage. Though I daren't, given that Verity is as tense as Jemima appears to be, busy biting her nails. Amazing how everyone wants Highland blood running through their veins come Hogmanay.

'What are we waiting for?' I ask, clutching my heavy basket.

'Isla. She's coming up from the kitchen; she'll walk between us but slightly ahead.'

'Who's addressing the haggis, then?' I ask, pretty certain I couldn't.

'Apparently, it's Ned's party trick. He can recite Burns' poem off by heart, so Jemima's hoping he takes his cue on seeing the procession.'

'It'll be a tumbleweed moment if he doesn't.'

'Jemima's primed Mungo, just in case. Look sharp, here comes Isla.'

I turn to see Isla cautiously enter from the kitchen, under the weight of a huge silver platter, carrying the largest decorated haggis I've seen for a long time.

'Boy, no expense spared here,' I whisper to Verity, who shakes her head.

Isla joins us, slotting into the formation between us.

'How's Isaac?' Isla bleats at me.

The very mention of his name releases a cloud of butterflies in my stomach.

I shrug, aiming for nonchalant, but know I've failed on seeing her expression.

'Don't come that with me, Nessie. You guys look dead cute together.'

My mouth drops open; if only she knew of the tentative attraction growing on either side.

'He was hardly offended by your mistletoe kiss, was he? He couldn't wipe the smile from his face!'

'I missed it,' complains Verity.

I blush to my core. 'Oi, forgive me, but I lost myself for a moment there, thanks very much. He was simply being chivalrous – he could easily have made a formal complaint about my actions.'

'Complain? Pull the other one! The guy has more sense than that. He won't be wasting time in the new year,' chuckles Verity.

'I won't, either,' says Isla. 'I had a lovely meeting with Ned and Jemima the other day in which I proposed a few new ideas . . . and they agreed!'

'And?' I ask, knowing I also have news following a brief post-Christmas meeting.

'Out with it!' shrieks Verity, breaking our straight line to hear the details.

'I suggested a mobile bakery delivering fresh bread and cakes around Shetland. Basically, like The Veggie Rack from the allotment plots, but with my gran's bakes on wheels.'

'A mobile bread bin?' I jest, knowing that such a concept is much needed in desolate rural areas where communities are sparse.

'Exactly, though an artisan bread bin,' quips Isla, adjusting her hold on the haggis platter. 'Secondly, given that Lachlan's cruel actions forced me to type each of Gran's recipes for my own printed copy, Jemima reckons I'd be on to a winner by getting them published as a complete cookery book. Gran would have loved sharing her traditional bakes with a wider audience.'

'Sounds ideal,' says Verity, glancing at me and giving me an encouraging look.

'Do you know?' I ask, sensing a message conveyed in her expression.

'Maybe.'

Isla looks confused, so I spill the beans. 'The Campbells have commissioned me to create a sculpture park leading from the driveway. They're going to provide a picnic area and shrubbery landscaping a short distance away, enhancing the beauty of the unused land. I can't wait. Along with the commissions from Lerwick Town Hall, I'm buzzing. I've designed new railings that mimic rustic vines, with coastal flora entwined – they're beautiful.'

'And the weathervane?' asks Verity.

'I have a funny feeling it might look like old Jutt in the paddock next to your cottage.'

'Imagine that, my pony Jutt looking out across Lerwick.' Isla begins to jig in excitement.

'Oi, watch that bloody haggis!' I say, spying Jemima's growing tension as she stands before the ballroom's double doors. 'And you, Verity? I can't imagine that you haven't had a mini-meeting with the big bosses. Or did the family reunion rule that out?'

'They've all flown back, safe and sound, including Francis; I'll miss cooking dinner for him. Workwise, I'll continue to knit one and purl one at The Yarn Barn, not much change there, but they have asked if I would like to join a special home-grown venture. Next spring, Magnus and faithful Floss have agreed to establish and tend a new flock of sheep on pastures behind the manor. The Campbells have asked if I'd be interested in creating a new brand of Lerwick Manor yarn from the flock . . . hand-dyed, of course.'

'Of course. Because your "fifty shades of sheep shite" yarn sold very well,' I say, letting out a belly laugh and nearly dropping my coal basket.

'He told you! Oh my God! Just wait till he gets here. Magnus promised me he wouldn't say a word.'

Isla looks baffled.

'I'll tell you later, Isla. Nothing's ever a secret in our family, that's the first rule of joining it, isn't it, Isla?' I say, giving Verity a wink, before asking, 'Where is Magnus anyway?'

'You're joining our family?' asks Isla excitedly.

Bang on cue, a heavy, hearty hammering starts upon the aged wooden door, making the three of us jump.

'Talk of the devil and he shall appear!' declares Verity proudly, settling into our line-up position beside Isla.

Jemima scurries to the great entrance and drags the door wide, revealing Magnus in all his tartan finery: emerald kilt, sporran and ghillie brogues.

'He still scrubs up well, Verity. A possible glimpse of your wedding photos, eh?'

'Oi!' snaps Verity, before a wee smile adorns her face.

'Ahhhhh,' sighs Isla. We both turn to see her dreamy face. 'He's acting as our "first foot" with his dark curls to bring good luck for the new year.'

Magnus gives Jemima a peck on the cheek before striding over to our position.

'Evening, ladies, happy new year. Excuse me,' he says to me and Isla, before planting a smacker of a kiss squarely on Verity's mouth, much to her astonishment. Then he walks to the front of the pipers. 'Let's get this started.'

The pipers begin their distinct wail. I can only imagine the startled expressions in the ballroom on hearing the noise. Magnus thumps noisily upon the double doors, which Jemima flings wide, and we stride forward as the guests stand back to honour our unexpected haggis accompanied by our dark-haired 'first foot', Magnus.

Ned's face is a picture; Jemima sidles up alongside him, planting a kiss on his cheek. Do they make the perfect couple or what?

The pipers march in line before separating, allowing Isla and her haggis to lap the room displaying the platter to every guest before it's placed on a table before Ned. I follow suit, handing pieces of coal into outstretched hands; Verity follows, offering the drams of whisky. Magnus empties the contents of his shoulder bag – offering salt, shortbread and black bun fruitcake – on to the haggis table.

Thankfully, Ned eagerly steps forward to make the traditional formal address, complete with a hand-held microphone and a ceremonial sword. Jemima really does think of everything.

I seek out Melissa, who's proudly rubbing her bump, standing alongside her husband, Hamish, making sure they have an extra-large piece of coal to mark their recent baby news. Levi is busy taxiing partygoers around Lerwick, so I hand Kaspar two pieces and ask him to pass one on via the allotments.

I spy Isaac watching from the sidelines beside an enthralled Mungo and Dottie. On handing him a piece of coal, his wry smile confirms everything I need to know. Despite being last minute, my participation in this traditional performance was vital. It's not just the coals that are burning brightly in the forge: partnership and futures could definitely be glowing. As for love and romance, they might be red hot too.

Acknowledgements

Thank you to my editor, Kate Byrne, and everyone at Headline Publishing Group for believing in my imagination and giving me the opportunity to become part of your team.

To David Headley and the crew at DHH Literary Agency – thank you for your continued support. I couldn't ask for a more experienced or dedicated team to champion my career.

Thank you to my fellow authors/friends within the Romantic Novelists' Association – you continue to support and encourage me every step of the way.

A heartfelt thank you to the Shetlanders for providing such a warm welcome whilst I holidayed in Lerwick, Shetland – who would have thought that this little girl's dream of visiting the top of the weather map would result in another story!

A huge thank you to Andrea Jeromson, Lerwick registrar in Shetland, for confirming the requirements necessary for a wedding at the Town Hall. You were generous with your time, ensuring I could write my wedding scene with confidence.

Thank you to my family and closest friends, for always loving and supporting my adventures – wherever they take me.

And finally, thank you to my wonderful readers. You continue to thrill me each day with your fabulous reviews and supportive emails. I'm truly humbled that you invest precious time from your busy lives in reading my books. Without you guys, my characters, stories and happy-ever-afters would simply be daydreams.

from
Shetland,
with love at
Christmas

Bonus Material

Verity's Special Care Baby Blanket Pattern

Materials

175g of DK wool and size 4mm needles

Instructions

Cast on 2 stitches.

Row 1: K1, then knit and increase by one stitch into the second stitch.

Next rows: K1, knit and increase into the second stitch then knit to the end.

Repeat the above 'Next rows' until a side measures 58cm*.

K1, then K2tog, knit to the end of the row.

Continue decreasing until casting off one stitch.

Note: This is the perfect blanket size for use in Special Care Baby Units. Please ensure there are no holes and sew in loose ends securely, preventing damage to tiny fingers or toes.

* or desired size for a full-term bairn, though additional wool will be required.

Ned's Honey Cake Recipe

Ingredients

170g honey
140g butter
85g light muscovado sugar
2 tbsp water
200g self-raising flour, sieved

2 eggs, beaten
For the icing (optional)
50g icing sugar
1 tbsp honey
A little water

Method

Preheat the oven to 180°C/Fan 160°/Gas 4. Grease and line an 18cm baking tin.

Add the honey, butter, sugar and water to a pan. Heat and stir gently until combined. Remove from the heat and allow to cool slightly before adding the warm mixture to the sieved flour and beaten eggs. Mix thoroughly. Add a little extra water, if needed, to combine smoothly.

Spoon into the prepared cake tin and bake for approximately 45 minutes. Test with a clean knife or skewer inserted into the centre; the cake needs to be springy when touched. Leave to cool on a wire tray.

Icing can be added, if required. Mix the icing sugar and honey well, adding a little water to give a runny consistency, and drizzle liberally over the cooled honey cake.

Isla's Shetland Bannock Recipe

Makes 12 bannocks

Ingredients
550g self-raising flour
½ tsp bicarbonate of soda
½ tsp salt

275g buttermilk
275g whole milk

Method
Mix the dry ingredients together and then slowly add both liquids to resemble a very thick batter. Turn out on to a wide pile of flour, and sprinkle some more on top. Pat down gently until the bannock mix is more dough-like in texture, and about 2cm thick.

Take a quarter of the dough and shape on a floured surface into a circle. Cut into equal quarters. Put aside for cooking, before repeating the last instruction three more times.

Cooking: traditionally done using a hot griddle over an open fire, but a hot frying pan does the job just as well. Cook over a medium heat. You won't need oil or fats, simply place the bannock on to the hot surface to cook through on each side. Turn when they look well risen, allowing as long as 5 minutes on each side. Reduce the heat if they are going too dark.

Serve warm, torn in two, with plenty of butter.

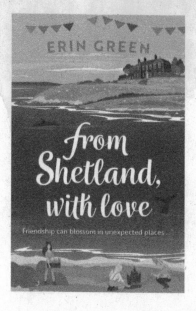

New Beginnings at Rose Cottage

Don't miss this perfect feel-good read
of friendship and fresh starts from Erin Green,
guaranteed to make you smile!

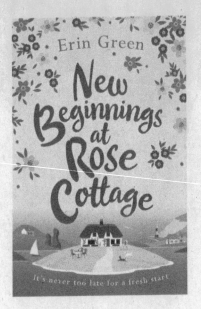

Available now from

REVIEW

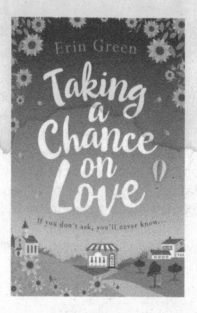

Bookends

When one book ends, another begins...

Bookends is a vibrant new reading community to help you ensure you're never without a good book.

You'll find exclusive previews of the brilliant new books from your favourite authors as well as exciting debuts and past classics. Read our blog, check out our recommendations for your reading group, enter great competitions and much more!

Visit our website to see which great books we're recommending this month.

Join the Bookends community:
www.welcometobookends.co.uk

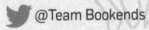 @Team Bookends @WelcomeToBookends